To: Drake Butler, please enjoy!

THE GOD OF WAR

When I Rode with N.B. Forrest

The Letters of Henry Wylie

By

Robert S. Chambers

Robert S. Chambers
"Keep the 'SKEER' on!"
april 22, 2004

King Phillip Publishing
Cleveland, Ohio

King Phillip Publishing
7616 Big Creek Parkway
Cleveland, Ohio 44130

ISBN 1-889332-30-5

Published as part of
The Journal of Confederate History Series
by
Southern Heritage Press
4035 Emerald Drive
Murfreesboro, Tennessee 37130

First Printing January 1997
Second Printing September 1997
Third Printing August 1998
Fourth Printing December 1999
Fifth Printing March 2001
Sixth Printing November 2001
Seventh Printing September 2003

Printed in Tennessee, U.S.A.

Cover painting courtesy of the artist,
John Duillo

Dedication

To all those who read this manuscript and gave me ideas and input – and they were many. To my three children for their understanding, support, and patience. But mostly to my wife Linda – as always – for everything. Many thanks to all.

Robert S. Chambers was born in 1954 and has been a student of the Civil War for three decades. A former high-school teacher, he has been a park manager for the Cleveland Metroparks for more than 20 years. He lives with his wife and three children in Middleburg Heights, Ohio. This is his first novel.

TENNESSEE AND SURROUNDING STATES

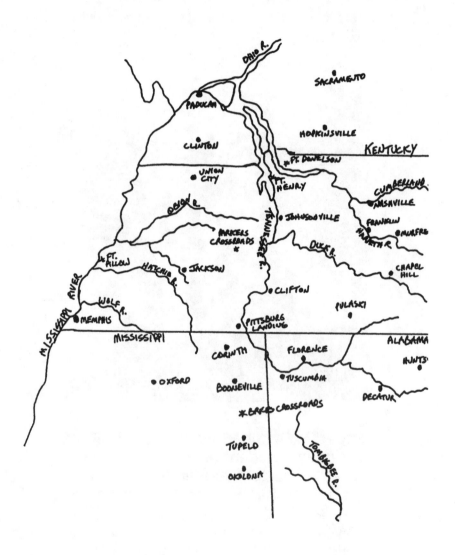

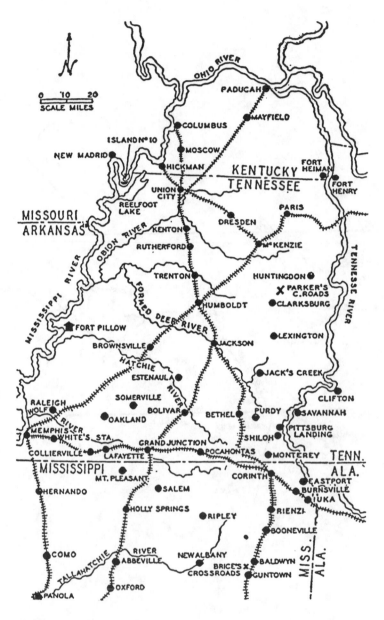

WEST TENNESSEE, KENTUCKY AND NORTHERN MISSISSIPPI

MIDDLE TENNESSEE AND NORTHERN ALABAMA

NATHAN BEDFORD FORREST

Introduction

To the Reader:

This book contains great historical accuracy, but before you embark upon *The God of War*, allow me to remind you that it is historical fiction, and naturally many readers want to know just what is fictional and what is factual within the text.

Briefly, Henry Wylie is a fictitious character and therefore his personal history, relations, and episodes and dialogue specific to him are fiction. However, everything else he reports upon is historically accurate. The dates, locations, weather-citings, statistics on troop numbers and names of officers, topography, and anything that describes action involving Forrest's soldiers are as accurately depicted as the author could make them, within the context of one man's (Wylie's) observation.

And of course, Nathan Bedford Forrest was most definitely real. Everything in this book concerning him is factual (at least as far as the author's extensive research could reveal). Only Forrest's direct discourse with Wylie is fiction, and the author has elaborated upon some of the many factual anecdotes involving Forrest. But mostly, when you read something about the incredible Forrest that is just too unbelievable to believe...believe it.

In the back of this book the author has included an "Afterword" which provides a brief chapter-by-chapter explanation of what is fact and what is fiction within. For those readers who would like to read an excellent Forrest biography, including much more extensively detailed battlefield tactics and strategy, I would recommend any of the following:

> *The Campaigns of Lieutenant General N.B. Forrest and of Forrest's Cavalry* by Thomas Jordan and J.P. Pryor
> *That Devil Forrest* by John Allan Wyeth (Louisiana State University Press)
> *First With the Most* by Robert Selph Henry (Mallard Press)
> *Nathan Bedford Forrest* by Jack Hurst (Vintage Civil War Library)

This writer is much indebted to these biographies and their authors.

TABLE OF CONTENTS

Page

HENRY WYLIE

Preface

On January 19, 1986, Paul Henry Wylie Jr. died in Knoxville, Tennessee at the age of 87. He had Parkinson's Disease. He had emphysema. His wife had died thirty years before him, and all four of his children preceded him in death. He seemed to have left little behind besides the small bungalow on Whittle Springs Road in which he had lived for over half a century. Little of intrinsic value was found inside the house — well-worn furniture, semi-modern appliances, a silver place-setting from a bygone wedding. In the dusty attic, however, a treasure chest was discovered. It took the shape of a battered tin box. In the tin box were 65 carefully preserved letters, each individually wrapped in cellophane. Every one of these letters was written by Henry Wylie, the grandfather of Paul Henry Wylie Jr., to Henry's wife, his dear Elizabeth.

Why are these 65 letters a treasure? Because they chronicle in a most descriptive and fascinating manner the four years Henry Wylie spent serving as a Confederate cavalry officer. And not just any Confederate cavalry. Wylie served four tumultuous years in the cavalry of Lt. Gen. Nathan Bedford Forrest — the Wizard of the Saddle. The incredible thrill and horror of battle; the day-to-day life of a Civil War soldier; amazing, amusing, and revealing anecdotes; the suffering and doubts of warfare; and the personal eye-witness accounts of one who was intimately associated with the legendary Bedford Forrest are all wonderfully described in the 65 letters of the simple farm boy from Memphis.

Henry Wylie was born September 3, 1837 on a small farm on the southern outskirts of Memphis. Schooled very well at home by

1

his mother, he spent his childhood and formative years helping his father (and a single slave, Sam) work the farm. In May, 1859 he married his Sunday-school sweetheart Elizabeth Parker, and on April 6, 1860 they celebrated the birth of their first child, Mary.

During the summer of '59 Henry took a job as pressman for the *Memphis Daily Appeal*, and he and Elizabeth bought a small house in town. Still Henry managed to work long hours on the family farm.

Then in 1861 their lives took a sudden change, as did the lives of virtually everyone in the country. The War Between the States erupted, Tennessee was no longer part of the United States, and Henry Wylie joined a local Memphis regiment of cavalry — Company C of the Forrest Rangers. It was then, on October 3, 1861, that Corporal Henry Wylie inked the first of his 65 letters. And from that day forward, and until he was discharged in May, 1865, whenever he had a moment off the saddle, Henry dutifully wrote a letter to Dear Elizabeth.

And what letters they were. In spite of the limited education, phonetic and dialectical spelling, and absence of literary polish, Henry Wylie graphically described in writing everything he experienced, observed, or felt. Reading the letters, one is thrown into the turbulence of the times, feels the excitement and terror, and gets to observe up close a truly colorful and unique soldier — Gen. Nathan Bedford Forrest, whom Henry clearly revered above all others he met during the war.

If these 65 letters are so rare, how came they to be unpublished for over 130 years? The main reason is Henry Wylie himself. After the war Wylie worked for the *Memphis Commercial Appeal* as typesetter, but under the tutelage of *Appeal* editor Matthew C. Gallaway (whom Wylie had known well during the war), Wylie became a reporter and evolved into one of the outstanding journalists of his age. Certainly within the 65 letters were the seeds of greatness.

Gallaway, John Markbright, and others who knew of the existence of the letters urged their publication, but Wylie steadfastly refused, claiming they were too personal. (The reader, however, will find little intimacy by today's immodest standards.) And when his dear Elizabeth died in 1885, his refusal to publicly display his private letters was adamant.

Surely a fascinating biography of Wylie's post-war years could be written. His almost clairvoyant ability to be at the site of breaking news events was uncanny. He was in Deadwood Gulch in August of 1876 when James "Wild Bill" Hickock was gunned down by Jack McCall. He was visiting Martinique in the spring of 1902 when Mount Pelee erupted, destroying St. Pierre. He was in attendance when Jake Kilrain failed to step from his corner for the 77th round on July 27, 1889, leaving John L. Sullivan unofficial heavyweight champion. He broke the story when on May 1, 1900 he reported the nearby wreck of Locomotive 382 and the death of its engineer, Casey Jones.

Ironically and sadly, the most renown for Henry Wylie came immediately after his death, when he became inadvertently involved in the most sensational story of the age. In the stuff fiction is made of, at age 74 he was sent to England by the *Saturday Evening Post* to report on the maiden voyage of the luxury liner *Titanic*. He perished April 15, 1912 with 1500 other passengers, but survivors' accounts of his courageous actions during the panic are certainly reminiscent of the fearless cavalry officer who many years before had faced death so many times.

After Wylie's death the letters passed into the care of his daughter, Mary Wylie Stackhouse, and it is she we must thank for their careful preservation. Again those who knew of the letters urged their publication, if for no other reason than to help redeem the besmirched reputation of Nathan Bedford Forrest. But Mary Wylie Stackhouse demurred for the sake of her father's wishes.

Upon Mary's death in 1937 a legal skirmish ensued between the Stackhouse and Wylie descendants over possession of the letters. The court awarded them to the oldest surviving member of the Wylie family, Paul Henry Wylie Jr., grandson of Henry, son of Paul, and nephew of Mary. And thus they came to rest for almost fifty years in the battered tin box in the dusty attic of the small bungalow on Whittle Springs Road in Knoxville, Tennessee.

And now, after another decade of legal haggling and 130 years after the last was written, the letters have passed through the hands of the editor and to the eyes of any interested reader. The term "editor" is used but loosely, for the letters themselves required remarkably little editing. In spite of the dim light cast by a fading campfire, or the numbness of near-frozen fingers, or the clumsiness of repeatedly dipping a pen into an ink bottle, the letters were surprisingly easy to read. The handwriting is neat and firm, the aged ink still quite legible. The most difficulty in deciphering was when both sides of a page were written on (no doubt when paper was scarce) or when writing was crammed sideways in the columns. Twenty-two of the letters were written in pencil, and they were much more faded. The editor changed little of the text – a comma added or deleted, a dash inserted here or there, and very occasionally when an obvious word was omitted, it was added to keep the continuity of the lines. But the inconsistent and dialectical spelling, the fragments and run-on sentences, the verb tense and agreement errors were all left just as they were penned by Henry Wylie, and first read by Elizabeth. The division of the letters into chapters was done by the editor to make reading easier.

In conclusion, it must be added that upon first reading the letters, the editor believed they were strictly a meritorious tribute to the most remarkable soldier of the Civil War – Nathan Bedford Forrest. And indeed they are a rich legacy of that man, written by a gallant, observant, and wholly-admiring subordinate. All the incredible successes achieved by Gen. Forrest are explicitly detailed here – the escape from Donelson, the fighting at Shiloh, the wildly exciting and successful raids into Tennessee, the stunning victories at Brentwood and Brices Crossroads, the tragedy at Ft. Pillow, the running down of Abel Streight, the escape from Nashville. All here and much more. The book was named, as Henry Wylie himself suggested, for this colorful warrior. But on a second, third, and many successive readings, the editor realized that another remarkable hero emerged. A hero perhaps greater in some ways than the great Forrest himself. Enjoy.

Robert S. Chambers

Chapter 1

October 3, 1861 through December 30, 1861

October 3, 1861
Columbus, Ky.

Dear Elizabeth,

I can not beleve it is only been three weeks since that last farewell kiss, so many things been happenin. I am sorry I been remiss bout writin sooner, but I aint had a moment up to now.

I will try to be a good newspaper man (though reportin really aint my line) and not omit anything that would be of intrest to you.

You remember how back in late August Charley May was goin round recruitin hisself a company of horse men and talkin bout a "second revolution" and "states rights" and defendin our women folk and children from invaders, well he not only got me to his side but sined up bout ninty of us, all from Memphis. I know a good many of the boys in this group for a long time, and I am sure you would recognize some too like the Turner boys – Ned and Mark, Al Devoss you probly know from church, the same as Lewis Hyam, Buck Wayland, and Johnny Marsh. You know Mr. Treach the butcher, his boys Jeff and Jesse is in this bunch too. And a whole lot of the young guys you seen round town for years.

Well, we are all here and Charley May will soon get three stripes on his collar and become Capt. May, and we all are to be Company C of the Forrest Rangers – Forrest bein the man who

7

gatherd eight such companys together to become a regiment. I beleve we got 650 to 700 men here now.

You may know Mr. Nathan Bedford Forrest, as he and his brothers run a big slave trading post right on Adams St. in Memphis. He musta made alot of money in the bisness cause he is payin for a goodly bit of this whole outfit. Bridles and halters, rifles, pistols, saddles and even some sabers is comin from his pocket, so I hear. He even purchased some horses for the boys who aint got a mount.

Of course, many of the boys is like me who brung there own belongings. And I do not mind tellin you, Lizzie, I aint half so homesick as I might be just havin old Maybelle here with me, along with my own saddle and blanket, tack, and my trusty shotgun. And for sure, I cherish the Colt revolver Pa give me before I rode off.

We was issued our uniforms last week. Wish Mary could see her daddy in his fine coat and riding pants – they kinda yellowish gray in color, made of cotton of course, fit good and feel quite comfitable. Some of the boys got knee high riding boots.

My mess mates – them being the five boys I cook meals with – is fine and hardy lads, and one – Billy Tupper – loves cookin and is always stirrin a pot of broth or clankin pans over a fire. Tups, as we call him, has a few specialtys, one bein a rabbit stew thats outa this world. The foods darn good so far and plenty of it, often some fresh beef or bacon, sometimes chicken, fresh corn bread, sometimes potatos.

"Come and get it, men" shouts Tups at meal time, and we all gather round the fire, sittin on logs or stumps, Tups with a apron tied round his back, and evryone talkin back and forth bout the days events. Camp life, I must admit, is appealin most the time, but like evry thing else it got its down side too.

I gotta go now, Lizzie, Tups is russlin up some grub right now by the fire. Write me soon please.

Your loving husband,
Henry

October 20, 1861
Dover, TN

Dear Elizabeth,

So good recevin the letters from you and Ma. Gives me comfort knowin you all is goin on with life back home same as always. Hope the cows get over there milk fever.

I am not sure if I tole you last time or not, but we had our election of officers awhile back — took a good part of the day — and guess who along with a few other boys was elected corporal? Yes indeed, yours truly. I do not rightly know why the boys chose me unless it be I am a little older then most (manys not yet twenty years old) and they know I got some schoolin. I dont rightly know what a corporal does yet but reckon I will find out. Anyway I left you a couple months ago plain old Henry Wylie, printer man for the *Memphis Daily Appeal*, and now I am Corporal Henry Wylie, Company C of the Forrest Rangers.

Charley May was elected captain of the company, he bein the one who formed us, and Lorry Tate was made 1st leutenant, Mark Ingram 2nd Lt, and John Vanderleer is sargent. Poor Capt. May, since all the boys has knowd him for a long time, they all go cryin to him — sort of a second hand father to us all — bout evrything from a jammed rifle to a lost canteen.

For instance, yesterday I seen Lester Downs of our company go up to Capt. May and say, "Captain, I need to get me a new canteen."

"What's wrong with your old canteen, private?"

"It got stole," says Lester, "Johnny Marsh took it."

"Now, Lester, why would Johnny Marsh steal your canteen?"

"Cause his got burnt up," says Lester.

"Now how the h___ did Johnny Marsh burn up his canteen?"

"Well," says Lester, "he was warmin his ass by the fire, and..."

"Okay" says Capt. May, "I dont want to hear the rest. Go see Corp. Wylie for a new canteen."

Thats the kind a thing Charley May gets to deal with dayly — its like havin a hunderd kids some times. But Capt. May, who is probly fifty or so, is a strict but patient man and can deal with most anything. After all, he been boss at the stockyards to many of these lads, and knows how to give orders and get things done.

The whole regiment elected officers as well, and in no suprise at all, Mr. Nathan Bedford Forrest was elected Lt. Colonel, and Capt. David C. Kelley (formerly a man of the cloth in Huntsville, Ala.) of Company F was elected major. The new adjutant (who assists Col. Forrest in all things) is C.A. Schuyler, J.P. Strange is sargent major, and Dr. Van Wick is the surgen.

I am sure used to camp life now as is most the boys, although I catch some younger lads cryin alone sometimes. Most the time we spend practicin with our arms, learnin the bugle calls and doin drills. They teach us how to dismount quick, tether the horses and advance on foot at double time. We learnt diffrent kinds of manuvers to diffrent bugle calls, and how to control our mounts in a fight. Some times we gather all the horses right near the battery of artilery and let the gun boys blast away to give them practice with the guns and the horses used to the thundrous noise.

When we aint drillin or tendin the horses a lot of the boys is playin cards. Seems evryone brought cards or dice. Some of the men hold cock fights, and you best beleve some heavy bettin goes on. The men sing, have foot races, chase greased pigs, create games, some read books (the Bible is pretty common round here), and of course most evryone writes home and loves gettin letters more then anything. One thing is absolutely forbidden here and that is horse racin — Col. Forrest dont allow the animals used that way.

Oh no, time for after dark drills — write soon.

Your loving husband,
Corporal Henry Wylie
Co. C.

P.S.

Give Mary a real big hug for me.

Nov. 22, 1861
Hopkinsville, Ky.

Dear Elizabeth,

We been on the move a good bit since last I wrote and I got some news to catch you up on. I know in my heart you been writin to me, but gettin letters from home is most difficult seein how we aint in the same place twict.

Early last month when our regiment, the Forrest Rangers, was just formed, we made the long ride from Memphis to Columbus, Kentucky at a slow pace. We was gatherin up new companys, learnin formations, huntin for food and just takin our jolly good time. There was little direction and our 700 members looked more like a peaceful caravan of nomads wanderin cross-country then a cavalry regiment.

But a month of hard drill, instruction and organization has changed all that. We look and act alot sharper, more like a real military unit, and our rugged trek from Columbus to here in Hopkinsville, Kentucky was a whole lot quicker. There was no men wanderin off on there own this time, no stoppin durin daylight to eat or rest. We are startin to look and act like soldiers now.

We are gettin tough, too. While we are on the move we dont take time for fancy meals, and Tups just whips up simple grub he can fix quick. We sleep under the stars most nights, and pull up the gumcloths when it rains. And though the men still complane bout this, that or the other, no one got time to listen.

I guess you could say I been in my first action with the enemy. Last week Maj. Kelley picked a number of companys, mine included, to go on a scoutin detale along the Ohio River. A day and half ride through dense forest brung us to the banks of the river, and in a short while we come acrost a yankee steam transport anchord to the south shore. Maj. Kelley sent Sgt. Thompson of Company A and about a dozen boys up ahead quite a ways to make a fuss — they built campfires and we could hear them choppin trees and shoutin orders way back where we was hidin in the brush. Sure nough, a small group of men carryin rifles got off the yankee boat and went along the bank in the direction of Thompson and his men. Soon as that group of men (maybe a dozen or so) got out of sight, Maj. Kelley and half of Company B crept down and borded the boat. They found it was bein held only by a couple of nigras left on bord. At a signal the rest of us come down, waded through the water (I was over my boots in mud) and went about unloadin all kinds of army supplys off the boat. Blankets by the score, tents, haversacks and varius useful things we unloaded and then disappeard back into the wood line without thirty minutes goin by. Back at camp we met Sgt. Thompson and the boys and we all laughed and felt proud that we outsmarted the yanks in such a fashon and without a shot fired.

That evning a little row broke out as Johnny Marsh, lookin proud, pulls out a fancy ivory-handle pistol he took from the boat.

"Ya," says Johnny, admirin the shiny side-arm, "some yankee officer sure gonna miss this beauty."

"Thats stealin, what you did," says Tups, who was pretty sensitive bout that kind of thing since the canteen incident.

"It aint stealin, Tupper," Marsh snaps back, "its goods captured from the enemy. Same as them blankets and hardtack."

"But you took it just for yourself, not for no one else," says Tups.

"You dont like it Tupper, you can go to the chaplin."

I had to step in and break it up fore it got outa hand.

12

Next morning Maj. Kelley got orders by messenger from Col. Forrest to head southward in good haste to meet up with the rest of the regiment at a location on the Cumberland called Canton Landing. The horses bein fresh and well fed, we made good time and was at the site by sundown and met up with the rest of our men.

Almost as soon as we joind up we seen a yankee gunboat steamin up the river (I later was to find out the boat was the Conestoga). We was all unhorsed and crouchin in the timber and behind logs, the boat well within sight, when Col. Forrest orderd Lt. Sullivan to open up his four-pounder gun and see what damage he could do. Sullivan and crew got off two rounds but before a third could be fired (the first two misdirected) the gunboat opend up a barrage of shot and missils that set the ground shakin. It was the loudest, most constant boomin I ever witnessed, and though I coverd my ears the echo still caused my head to ache. For more then two hours we withstood this bombardment and I daresay not one man failed to stand his ground. No one got serius hurt, but a number of boys was hit on the head and back by fallen limbs. In fact I seen a limb with a goodly size squirrels nest get blowd off and come crashin down on Sgt. Vanderleers head. He wasnt hurt much and lucky for him the squirrel wasnt home at the time. Then the yankee gunboat drifted away in the dark. That was our first encounter with the enemy.

We rode back to Hopkinsville and I am thankful for a few days to groom Maybelle, who has held out good so far. I can tell you this, Col. Forrest will not tolerate a unfit horse. You best take better care of your mount then of yourself or you will have the devil to pay.

I will continue this already too long letter soon as posable.

November 25, 1861
Hopkinsville, Ky.

If you wonder, Lizzie, why I continue this long letter insted of postin it and startin another, the reason is cause sometimes it is as hard sendin a letter off as it is recevin one, and as no letters been posted out for more then a week, I gotta just keep writin and waitin for delivery. Also, dear one, I know I do not need to remind you of this, but please take the trouble to ride out to the farm and show Ma and Pa these letters, as I am sure they would be intrested in my doins, but I aint got time or paper to write them and you too.

I feel that we may be encounterin the enemy more fully in the near future cause night fore last Col. Forrest got all the men gatherd together and made a speech. This bein the first time he adressed the regiment all together. He was settin on horseback and we drawd in close, and as I was up front I could hear him clear and inspect him full.

He is a tall man, a good two inches over six foot I should say, with a lean and powerful build. He has rough red hands, and as he often works bout camp with no coat on and his sleeves rold up, you can see his arms is like those of many a farm boy, muscular and with vains showin plain.

I would say the colonel is in about his 40th year, but he is as agile as any youth in this camp. His hair is wavy and iron gray, usully combed back but often under his broad-brim cloth hat. He has a thick mustash and heavy chin whiskers, these both black in color, and his teeth is strait and very white. I think, Lizzie, you would declare him a handsom man, but his dark eyes and skin, with those high cheek bones and set jaw give him a fearsom look, and I can honestly say I never looked upon a human face so filled with determenation and fiercness. And it aint just a impression either, as he has a sharp temper and we all seen him lash out at some one or other with such abrupness that we all shrink back, and most the boys fear him more then the enemy at such times.

14

The colonel spoke to us for a short time, says we was "fightin for honor and homeland," that we was to "welcome the people of Kentucky to our side," and we would "have a heap of fun and kill some yankees." He says he beleves in always attackin the enemy and was confident "a little bulge" against the enemy would turn them rearward and once in flight, we would be "keepin the skeer on."

He spoke soft, like a man of bisness, but his voice carryd in the still night air. And when he got done speakin I felt confident and brave, as I am sure the others did too.

Today was a plesant day, sun shinin and a cool nip in the air. Sgt. Vanderleer and I rounded up a squad of men to go into the countryside and russle up some cattle, hogs, maybe some horses and even goats and chickens all for future use. They call this "requesitioning." It did make for a enjoyable day. And good old Johnny Marsh didnt disappoint me, he come ridin back to camp with 24 chickens − yes and I counted evry one − 24 chickens tied to his saddle. I guess his sticky-finger problem can work to our advantage some times. (Tups now calls Marsh "Hooks.")

Its now time to smother the fires and get under our gumcloths. It gets cold enough at nights to keep the mosquitas away. With all my love to you and a big hug for Mary.

Your loving husband,
Henry

Later

I just herd some terible news. Col. Forrest and a small squad was on reconasance near the town of Marion last evenin, and a sniper from inside a house fired a single shot at the men and hit Dr. Van Wick square in the heart. That is the first death in the regiment. Doc Van Wick was ridin at the side of Col. Forrest, I hear. Coulda killed the colonel just as easy. The sniper escaped out the back door. I think anyone who would kill in that fashon is a damn coward.

December 25, 1861
Hopkinsville, Ky.

Dear Elizabeth,

I do not need to tell you how much I miss you on this special day. I would give most anything to be settin by the fireplace with you next to me and Mary in my lap, with Ma and Pa makin the trek in for supper later. But this cannot be, as I have commited myself to this purpose and give my whole heart to it. I did receve the best Christmas gift I could get though, when yesterday the curier brung three letters from you and two from Ma. Makes me so glad to know you are all bearin up well. I read each letter three times over.

You best beleve I did apply for a five day furlow, as did most of the men, but bein how we are off in all directions scoutin and gatherin supplys, they was all denied. One of my dutys as corporal is to help the fellas in my squad with the papers we need to fill out, includin the furlow forms. One lad, Will Davis, got turnd down like all of us, but as he was real homesick he applyed again. He got denied again. Then he come to me and pert near begged me to submit yet again a request for furlow. I tole him it probly do no good. Well, next day he come to me with a sad face and the returnd form. On the paper in writin so bad I know it come direct from Col. Forrest was wrote, "I have tole you twict goddamit no!" I shook my head and smiled, so did Will.

It must be gainsaid, Lizzie, that Col. Forrest is a most profane and forward man. He give orders in a way as to not allow debate. His orders is commands that best be carryed out direct. "Now hurry up and move them damn horses and make haste about it!" "Wield to the right and be goddamn smart about it!" He speaks with much force, and you can but follow his command.

And dont fool yourself into thinkin it be just his speech that is forcfull. Sgt. Brady of Company A was settin by the fire next to me one night and tellin me how he knowd Col. Forrest for many a year back in DeSoto County in Mississippi. Sgt. Brady tole me the colonel was a young man in the livestock and livry trade with Jonathan Forrest, his uncle. One day bout fifteen year ago, right in the public square in Hernando, Brady says three rough men name the Matlock brothers and there overseer started a scuffle bout some bisness concern with the older Forrest. One Matlock pulled a gun and killed the old uncle. But, fore he could do the same to the nephew, young Forrest shot dead the Matlock insted, then shot and damn near kill the second Matlock, leapt from his horse and attacked the third Matlock with a bowie knife, and only spared the overseer cause he was beggin on bended knees for mercy. No sir, the colonel is not a man to be crost.

To be fair to the colonel, Lizzie, I must say though he is a profane man of action, he is no vulgar ruffian. To show you what I mean, let me explane that there is in my squad one very loud mouth foul tongue fella named Hoot Evers. Most the boys get along fine and try to be helpful, but old Hoot is always cussin and startin rows and complanin bout things we all just tolerate. One day Hoot was cussin up a storm bout hisself bein too goddamn cold at night and how new blankets should be give to us, and carryin on using vulgaritys I would be too shame faced to repeat to you. Sure nough the colonel come up behind him hearin all this foul mouth swearin, and grab Hoot by the shoulder and swing him round with great violance and holler in the face of Hoot that them kind of vulgaritys will not be tolerated in this camp. "You understand me, boy?" Even Hoot, who I daresay would not back down from a grizzly, was struck dum with fear and could only get out "Yes sir." For the best part of three days Hoot was splittin firewood and served lookout duty evry night for a week. I might add however, a new load of blankets was handed out a week or so later.

I must close for now. I know this letter is very long but I take great comfort in writin to you as it makes me feel that I am near you in spirit, if not in person. You are not to worry bout me on these cold days and nights. The whole regiment is fixed in tents with good wood floors we made, warm beds and plenty of food.

The colonel has his wife in camp with him and always has his son, Private Will Forrest, near his side. War is not all bad you see, just bein from home. With all my love and give Mary a Christmas kiss for me.

Your loving husband,
Henry

P.S.

Just bout all the boys, myself included, has finaly receved sabers from the goverment. It hangs on my left side and you best beleve that after the first few saber charge drills there was plenty of injurys to both men and horses.

December 30, 1861
Sacramento, Ky.

My Dear Elizabeth,

As long as I live, I wont forget the date of Saturday, December 28, 1861, on that date we fully encountered the enemy and I found out what war is.

I shall try to recall evry moment that should intrest you and those I love back home, but first let me asure you that I am fit and unhurt.

Early on that cold day, the boys of my company and sevral others, plus a group of Kentucky boys under Capt. Merriwether was joind by Maj. Kelley and his three companys and bout forty new recrutes under Capt. Starnes. Col. Forrest was leadin all of us, maybe 250 in number, on a reconasance toward Rumsey, Ky., when a scout up ahead reported a large passel of mounted men in blue, perhaps 200 of them, headin toward Sacramento. Col. Forrest had us kick up our horses in pursute.

After bout a hour hard ride and just outside the town of Sacramento, we seen the yankee horse men up ahead, and Col. Forrest grabbed a rifle and fired at them. The blue troopers quick

18

spred in to line of battle on either side of the highway and commenced firin at us at bout 200 yards.

Col. Forrest had us draw back a couple hunderd yards when he seen how strung out our batalion was after the long ride. Me and Maybelle kept up pretty good though. We was hidin behind trees and logs and a fence rail, and Col. Forrest orderd the boys who was carryin Maynard rifles or other long range guns to dismount and return fire on the enemy who was startin to creep forward, probly thinkin we was in retreat.

Col. Forrest then orderd Capt. Starnes to take his men still mounted round the brush on the left side of the field and circle behind the enemy, and as the colonel says, "Hit them hard on the end." Then he called up Maj. Kelley and orderd him to procede in the same fashon round the right side of the enemy.

Lizzie, I was settin on Maybelle within ten paces of the colonel this whole time and never seen his face so intense before now. He kept gazin back as the rest of our boys on the slower mounts was stedy drawin up to our position. Our sharpshooters was returnin fire as quick as they could while the rest of us stayed mounted and back outa sight. All of a sudden the men of Starnes and Kelley started firin on the left and right flank of the enemy and Col. Forrest quick draw his saber in his left hand and screamed over all the comotion "Charge, boys, charge!"

Col. Forrest shot from the line as if fired from a cannon, and all us mounted men was inspired by his fury and courage, and we all charge without a semblence of order but with drawd pistols and sabers into the face of the enemy.

With Col. Forrest way out front madly swingin his saber and standin high in the stirups, and bein a good head and sholders taller then any man on that field, he was screamin "Charge men, charge!" in a very piercin voice much unlike his usual tone. Bein fired upon from left and right and forcfully attacked from the front, the entire union line broke into a retreat as fast as hoofs could take them.

Then a long pursute in full gallup commenced right through the town of Sacramento. The disorganized men in blue bein chased by us pistol firin disorganized men in gray. Townsfolk run in all directions. For sevral miles this mad pursute led and our ranks was thinnin as many of our tired horses pulled up lame and fell back. Suddenly a cluster of blue horse men reined up to regroup and faced our advancin ranks and we crashed right into them.

I cannot beleve, Lizzie, that I was ever able to such violence. I remember slashin and lungin at any thing that moved, friend or foe alike, as the dust from rampagin horses was kicked up. The terible noise of panicked horses, crashin steel, and constant screamin made my head whirl. A young man in blue with saber held high slammed it down at my skull but some how I got my saber raised in time and his blow glance off my handgard. I slashed back and honest to God, Lizzie, I do not know if I struck the man or not, but he was unhorsed and lay still on the ground. It was a horrible mess to be in.

But I could not stop fightin or turn back cause I could see the whole while Col. Forrest, still raised high off the saddle, his face flushed a deep red, his eyes on fire, his teeth grit in hatred, slashin with savage violence at the enemy. Never have I seen such strength and fury. Four of the enemy surrounded him as I tryed to come to his side. But in a instant he shed blows from all directions, lunged forward and killed a young captain, swang behind him gashin another in the neck, and when a private shot a bullit through his coller, Col. Forrest killed him with a pistol shot to the temple. Another yankee charged his terifyed horse direct into the colonels horse, the blue soldier fallin hard to the ground. The man tryed to raise his pistol, but Col. Forrest slammed his saber broadside on his wrist and the man yelled "I surrender, I surrender!" Even as sudden Col. Forrest was throwd far from his horse as the near mad beast plunge into two riderless horses, and I was just able to grab the reins and return the horse to the colonel in the midst of the fray.

Lizzie, if I live to be a hunderd I wont forget the look of the colonels face − all the rage of a wild beast, the most fierce and frightful human countenence I ever seen. Even Mars hisself, if confronted by that man, would surrender or been vanquished.

All this action took place in very few minutes and when the union men rode off in disorder, we found many a wounded man in blue left behind. I am sorry to say Capt. Merriwether, who bravely led his Kentucky boys in the fight, lay dead of a gunshot wound to the brain. And my heart sank in sadness when I rold over the lifeless body of private Will Terry of my own company, stabbed to the heart. He was a brave man.

I hope I aint unduly worryin you, Lizzie, by all this killin and fightin and I plead that you thank the good lord for sparin my life.

My uniform is tore in sevral places and very dirty, and Maybelle got a pretty messy cut to her ear, but we both is fine and proud of defendin our rights and country. As God has protected me on the battlefield, so may he gard you in my absince. With my love to you and Ma and Pa and specialy my little Mary, I truly am

Your loving husband,

Henry

Chapter 2

February 6, 1862 through February 26, 1862

Feb. 6, 1862
Clarksville, TN

Dear Elizabeth,

If I have not writ sooner it is cause we have done nothing the past month of an excitin nature, and also I been short of writin paper and only now aquired some. Enclosed you will find 18 dollars as we finaly receved pay (though they is still months behind) and I kept but two dollars to purchise paper and ink.

Something most suprisin and good happend to your adorin husband and I will relate the whole story in due order.

I just stated we done nothing of a exitin nature these past weeks and that is true if you compare it to the exitements of Sacramento. But we been busy with scoutin detales, food foragin and other dutys. And of course, we been tendin to the horses and gettin them fit again, as in Col. Forrests camp a sore back horse is a felony.

Last week as I was curry combin Maybelle, I seen Hoot Evers (him with the foul mouth and temper to match) kickin his horse hard in the hind quarters. The horse must not been standin still for him and this drove Hoot to more blows, which of course made the poor beast more restless. Hoot was cussin him and kickin and kickin till his spur screws was gougin the raw flesh. Then he

23

picked up a heavy stick and swat the confused animal which bucked and kicked in its fury.

"Hoot Evers" says I runnin over, "quit abusin that beast this instant! Thats a order!"

Let me tell you Lizzie, the two stripes on my coat sleeve mean very little to most the men in this outfit.

"Go to h___, Wylie, you son of a b___!" he hollers, and comes at me swingin that big stick.

I just ducked in time to receve a glancin blow off my shoulder and bein crouched down and all, I lunged into him and tackle him to the ground.

There we was tusslin on the ground while a little crowd gatherd and I managed to land a few blows to his nose and lip, which bled nice. The fight was broke up as Hoot and me was pulled apart by some officers, includin Lt. Markbright of the escort, even as the boys was all tellin how it started and that I was clear in the right. But Lt. Markbright says "Old Bedford aint gonna like this."

Within the hour I seen old Hoot go to the colonels tent in answer to a summons and honest I do not know what was said, but I do know that for the next three, four days Evers was curry combin and groomin all the officers horses. Then sure enough, young Will Forrest come to me and says the colonel wants to see me. I beleve as I marched up to that tent my heart was poundin worse then in the midst of the scrap at Sacramento.

"At ease, corporal," says the colonel in a soft and easy way, "What is your name?"

"Wylie, sir, Corporal Henry Wylie, Company C," I could feel the sweat rollin in beads down my neck.

"Where you from, Wylie?"

"Memphis, sir."

"I understand you orderd a man to stop beatin a horse and a fight started, is that so?"

"Yes, sir."

24

"Thats very fine, corporal, these men must obey all orders from any officer without question, and no man in this regiment will ever abuse a horse."

Could this quiet man, speakin in a soft, low tone, really be the selfsame man of uncontroled rage I personaly seen overpower four stout men in hand to hand combat? Then the colonel looked hard at me and caught me off gard by sayin, "Tell me, Wylie, wasnt it you I seen at Sacramento fightin so gallantly, and in the midst of the fray grab and return my horse to me?"

"Yes sir, that was me."

Then lookin me in the eyes he says slow, "I can appreciate a brave fightin man, Wylie, and I want you to join my escort."

"Me, sir?" I tryed not to look too disbelevin.

"Yes Wylie, you will join the escort if you so desire."

"I do sir, very much sir."

"Okay then, I will make the arrangments. Now you are dismised, sargent."

"Thank you sir, but its corporal sir."

"You turnin down a promotion, Wylie?"

"No sir, no sir!" And I left the tent.

You must know Lizzie, the escort of Col. Forrest is a company of men, probly fifty in number and mostly officers, that the colonel uses for special missions and such, and keeps close to him when confrontin the enemy seems likely. Some times they carry his orders direct to officers spred wide, and he expects them to start the "bulge" in time of attack. I will have my dutys as sargent of Company C, which I am glad for, cause I want to be with the boys, but when out in the field with the enemy I join the ranks of Lt. Markbright, Capt. Starnes, and the colonels brothers William and Jeffrey as men of proven grit that he can depend on at all times.

Must close for now, Lizzie, I just hear tell we got orders to move outa Kentucky and back to Tennessee to a fort on the Cumberland called Donelson. With all my love,

Your proud husband,
Sgt. Henry Wylie

Feb. 19, 1862
Nashville, Tenn.

Dearest Elizabeth,

I must tell you these last two weeks has surly been the saddest and most miserble that I had yet since joinin up almost six months ago. So much happend since last I writ to you, and I will tell all now that my hands is thawd.

Back in early Febuary Gen. Clarke orderd Col. Forrest to lead his regiment to Ft. Donelson on the Cumberland, just a mile from Dover. At that time the weather was fair and all us Tennessee boys was glad in our hearts to be back in our home state.

Ft. Donelson is a flat area, clear of trees and brush with tall earth walls enclosin the fifteen or so acre compound. It sets high above the Cumberland and its heavy guns protect that river from enemy invasion. Another fort of similar size, Ft. Henry, sets bout ten miles from Donelson due west and gards the Tennessee River from the enemy, but by the first week of Febuary it already got shelled by union gunboats into rubble and was abandon. Now with 20,000 yankees landed nearby, protectin Donelson become much more important to us.

We got to the fort on Febuary 11. Gen. Pillow, in command of the fort, put Colonel Forrest in charge of all the mounted men, givin us a nice group of over 1300. Col. Forrest was orderd to take a squad on reconasance to the west and locate the enemy movin in from Ft. Henry. We went no more then four miles fore spottin a detachment of union cavalry. Without hesitatin Col. Forrest put us in battle position and hollerd "Charge men, charge!"

and we attacked headlong in the face of the blue horse men. The area was wooded heavy and very brushy, and we was all broke up and in disorder. But with pistols flarin and us screamin like injuns, the yankees broke and fled. We persude as best we could leavin more then a few of there boys under our hoofs, when Col. Forrest had the bugler sound "halt and fall back" on his horn. The colonel seen a large body of union infantry up ahead and did not want us fightin impossible odds.

I was comin to realize that when Col. Forrest attacked with uncontroled vigor, he was a man posessed by the demon of war, but was in fact not out of control but always very alert to evry thing goin on round him on the entire battle field. He had no military trainin, but insisted that fifteen minutes "of bulge" against the enemy was far better then three days of tactics. But I learnt he never let his command be needlessly exposed to danger. We regrouped and headed back to the fort.

Once back inside the confines of the fort we could relax a bit. The vast open area with high earthen walls formed a horseshoe off the steep bluffs of the Cumberland, and at the end farther from us was barracks, storage buildings, and a arsenal, and artilary was spred all along the fort walls. Us and our horses took up just a small area on the east end of the massive enclosure, and we could see thousands of infantry boys goin bout there busness throughout the fort. Musta been 14,000 of our boys in the vicinity.

There was lots of activity goin on outside the fort as well, as miles of earthworks formed a irregular line of outer defenses and the constant sound of gunfire echoed back to us inside the fort.

Some of the boys was settin round a low fire that evning with me and Sgt. Vanderleer. "Seems no matter how much drill and formation practice we have, our lines just fall apart when we confront the enemy," says Vanderleer.

"Ya" says Ned Turner, "looks more like a free-for-all then a orderly attack."

"Some times it cant be helped" says I, "when the terrane is rugged and your racin through the midst of a forest you cant keep your lines strait or even keep your eye on the man next to you." Beleve me, Lizzie, this is true.

We bedded down under the stars that night, and though the breeze was cool, sleep come easy.

For the next two days Col. Forrest and Maj. Kelley led varius squads on scoutin details and had sevral short but severe encounters with the enemy. On the 13th of Febuary, I was settin atop a brushy hill on the advance skirmish line when Col. Forrest rode up close and stared hard with his naked eye (I never yet seen the colonel use field glasses) at the enemy line up ahead. He says, "Look there Wylie, see him?" and points out what he thinks is a enemy marksman settin in a tree a goodly ways off. The colonel grabs a Maynard rifle from a man near at hand, takes aim and fires, and sure as can be, we seen a man fall head first from out the tree.

Next day Friday, Feb. 14th, the weather took a nasty turn on us and the rain and wind become a blizard of sleet and snow, and tempatures kept fallin fast till all the ponds and creeks turnd icy on top. It was the most bitter cold I ever felt, and we all huddled close behind the embankments of Ft. Donelson. At this time union gunboats steamin up the Cumberland let loose a barrage of artilary that filled the air with thunder. The shells exploded storage buildings, smashed wagons, destroyd redouts and recked evry big gun in the fort but one, which returnd fire with good aim. Durin this bombardment, I seen Col. Forrest turn to Maj. Kelley and shout, "Parson! For Gods sake, pray! Nothin but God Almighty can save this fort."

The shellin from the river boats finaly stopped, but the cold got worse and worse. Cause the weather of late been unusualy fair, many of the boys dumped extra blankets and over coats along the road to lighten there loads. Now many of them, stationed in freezin rifle pits spred out round the fort, was gettin frostbit and agonizin in pain.

28

The union army, probly numbrin more then 20,000 men, was spred all along the fringe suroundin Ft. Donelson. With our troops suffrin mightily, enemy gunboats settin ready in the water, a army nearly twict the size of ours ready to attack, the fort was in great danger. Late at night on the 14th while we huddled up in froze blankets, a counsil of war was held. The three generals in the fort — Pillow, Floyd and Buckner — and Col. Forrest decided that next morning the whole command would try to pound a opening through the union right side to make a route of escape.

Lizzie, you must pardon me, but fatigue is overtaken me and I must rest a while fore goin on. I must also get Maybelle to the farier for some "equipment repair." After all, she done more then eighty miles these last three days. I will continue later.

Feb. 20, 1862
Nashville, Tenn.

Dear Elizabeth,

Last night was the best night sleep I got in over a week, and though I still feel very tired, I am better off then many of the boys who is suffrin badly from measles and ague. The bitter cold of last week has left many with swollen fingers and feet and one can hardly sleep at night for all the coughin in camp.

As I last stated, on Friday night of Febuary 14, the generals Pillow, Floyd and Buckner met with Col. Forrest and they reckoned the only way to save the command was by crashin a hole in the suroundin yankee line.

At 4:00 a.m. on the 15th we was all stirred up and ready for battle. I feel most the men was just as glad to be shifted into action as the night was so bitter none could capture sleep anyways. The entire command was put in battle formation, and Col. Forrest and our cavalry was to lead the attack on the union right flank. Just before sunrise, with a wind that cut through all your clothes and chilled strait to your bones, our cavalry swung in a great arc round the federals and at 6:00 a.m. a brisk cannon volly from our gun boys started the battle.

We had to get close to the enemy lines cause many the boys, me included, was firin squirrel rifles and shotguns with short range. As soon as the first round of artilery was fired, Col. Forrest bared his long saber, secured the two pistols in his belt, let loose a blood curdlin "Charge!" and bolted from the line with the cape flyin behind his coat.

Without hesitation evry man amongst us spurred the horses and 1300 screamin horse men desended on the enemy. In a moment we was amongst the yankees who barely got time to turn and fire at us. The fightin was close and severe and I throwd my ungainly shotgun down and relyed on my pistol and saber. Men in blue, (I learnt was a Illinois regiment) bein attacked from front and rear, put up a bold and obstinent fight, but fell back gradual or surenderd with empty cartrage boxes. As the Illinois boys was startin to break, Col. Forrest galoped at full speed to his superior, Col. Bushrod Johnson, and begged him to make a full advance by the entire line. But Johnson, ignorin the advice of the upstart colonel, would not order such without consultin Gen. Pillow and a rare opportunity was lost.

On a slight incline some ways behind the union line was a battery of six guns blastin canister in the face of our men. Col. Forrest, this time actin without orders, led those of us still on horseback on a mad charge to capture the guns. They was heavily protected by union infantry, but the colonel led us on a wild charge into them with great violence. I soon emptyed my pistol, some shots I must say at point blank range, while bullits screamed past my ears and bayonets slashed from all directions.

I managed somehow to hold in the saddle while Maybelle was in a perfect frenzy, kickin and rearin and boltin out of control. Col. Forrest, standin high in the stirrups, was firin shot after shot from one pistol then the other and then slashin with his saber. I seen Lt. Jeffrey Forrests mount killed by a artilery blast and the colonels hard fightin young brother was throwd to the ground. The colonels horse was bleedin bad too from many wounds and finaly colapsed dead, but the colonel quick grab a riderless mount and resumed his fearsom attack. After a bloody while the blue foot soldiers run off, leavin there six guns, and Col. Forrest orderd a number of men to haul them behind our lines.

He then pointed to another set a cannons doin great damage to our lines and orderd us to attack and capture them too. I just had time to reload my pistol before joinin our men in his mad persute. These two guns however, was settin behind a tangled mass a undergrowth and briers so thick as to be almost unpassable, and the men on foot moved just as fast as us on horseback who had to hack and slash a path through it. The deafinin clamor, Lizzie, of boomin cannons, trees crashed to splinters, billows of black smoke, men screamin in pain and terror, and the never endin blasts of thousands a muskets bein fired at once was something one can never forget.

As we neared the guns I seen Col. Forrests horse receve the full effect of a cannon ball in its hind quarters, blastin the poor beast to bloody fragments while the colonel was throwd hard on his face. The fightin was bitter acrost the whole front and Col. Forrest, now on foot, soon receved word from Gen. Pillow that all troops was to retreat behind the intrenchments of Ft. Donelson. The attempt to break through the union lines was over. It failed. It was now past two and I swear to the lord I was so involved with the fightin that I beleved one hour, not eight, coulda past. After all this bloodshed, we was pullin back, all 14,000 of us – infantry and cavalry – our goal denyed.

As we slowly backed up through the ground we fought so gallant to win, my heart reached a new depth of sadness when I found the body of Charley May, our gray haird captain of Company C who such a short time ago gatherd us Memphis boys to his side with dreams of glory. This is what glory is, a mangled corpse left as a monument to our cause. I sickend at the sight.

Once the entire command was pulled back inside the fort and all fightin stopped, Gen. Pillow orderd Col. Forrest to take his cavalry and scour the battlefield gatherin any articles of war, specially rifles. So back on the battlefield we went, most of us on foot, and it was now after the intense exitement of sustaned fightin that bitter cold and fatigue caught up to us.

As I stumble along froze earth in the fadin light, bitter cold achin my hands and feet, I look up at the desolation of war all round me. I seen many a young man, clad in both blue and gray, scatterd on the ground. Some with vacant eyes starin right at me. Dead horses, shatterd trees, recked wagons evrywhere. On the other side of a brushy knoll I come upon Johnny Marsh, bendin low over one dead soldier, then movin to another, then another.

At first I though he was checkin to see if they was alive or not, but then I realize he is riflin the bodys and stuffin things in his pockets.

"Johnny Marsh, you stop that now!" I yell, runnin up to him.

"I aint doin no harm," he shouts, suprized to see me, but stuffin a gold watch in his pocket, "they dont need this stuff no more."

"Get your hands outa them soldiers pockets," I order, "and help us gather military goods like your suppose to."

"Yes sir," he snarls with a big salute, and runs off.

We did recover close on 4,000 small arms, plus many cartriges and loaded back packs, and many of us helped the ambulence men remove some of the thousand injurd men, so many cryin for help. It was bitter work, Lizzie. Once I tripped and fell down, it was all I could do to make myself stand up and keep workin.

But our adventures on this horrable day still was not over. After hours a duty on the battlefield we limped exausted to the confines of Ft. Donelson once more, and set by the fires. Most the men in spite the brutel tempatures fell readily asleep. But in the midst of the night, 1:00 a.m. of Sunday Febuary 16, me and the rest of the officers in the escort was woke up by a irate Col. Forrest who said he just got back from a counsel-of-war with generals Pillow, Floyd and Buckner. He says they was fixin to surender the fort and the entire command at sunrise to the union army. The generals said the fort was surounded by twict the size army of us, and the men was fatigued and unable to cross a frigid river without great illness and loss. And cause amunition was low and yankee gunboats stood ready to attack, that further fightin or attempt at escape was a lost cause. Col. Forrest spat in disgust "I did not come here with the purpose of surenderin my army," and when the generals asked what he would do, he said "If my cavalry will follow me, I will cut my way out if doin so saves but one man."

Back with us he explained this whole bisness and sent two trusty men (with the aid of a local boy from Dover) to quick scout out the flooded Clarksville road and the crossin at Lick Creek. In a short while these men, Adam Johnson and Bob Martin, come back filthy and half froze but reported to Col. Forrest that the road was ungarded and pasable, but the ford icy and three foot deep.

That was all the colonel needed to know. He got us officers to quick stir the boys outa there well earnd sleep, pack up with two days rations of salt bacon and corn bread, roll our blankets and saddle the horses. Less then a hour later our whole survivin regiment of 1100 horse men, includin the ailin Jeffrey Forrest, filed out of that fort of doom. Without seein so many as one yankee, we past Dover and come to Lick Creek, the black icy waters flowin a hunderd yards wide. Col. Forrest out front as always, hesitated but a moment and slow waded his horse through the current, crackin the thin crust of ice as he went. Up the frosty bank on the far side he halted and seen to evry one of his men crossin. I was close to the front and as I enterd the stream I lifted my feet from the stirrups. The water just reached my saddle skirt. In but two minutes I was on the other side and I confess, Lizzie, a serge of warmth when Col. Forrest nodded at me and said, "Keep up the fine work, Sargent Wylie."

The whole regiment was acrost inside a hour and I will never forget the sight of steam risin heavy from the wet but heated horses. We was a ghostly parade. Col. Forrest would not permit rest, perhaps in fear we might freeze and form so many statues. The cold was so bad, my numb fingers inside froze gauntlets could not let loose the reins, and my knees seem so froze in the bent position I might never get them strait again.

We rode 25 mile that Sunday afternoon. After a brief rest we got to Nashville early next day. We are exausted, many sickly, but thanks to "Old Bedford" we are alive and not bein transported to northern prison camps like the 12,000 poor souls we left behind in Donelson.

Thats been my adventures, Lizzie, the past few weeks and they was chock-full of sadness and misery. Capt. May dead on the battlefield along with 400 others of our brethern and many more bein sent to army hospitals. And our Confederacy been shook bad with the capture of 12,000 of her finest soldiers. Now the yankees are free to patrol gunboats and transport armys up and down the Tennessee and Cumberland Rivers at will.

The good news, of course, and please join me on my knees in thankfulness to the good lord, is that I am still alive and survived another battle, still have my friend Maybelle here with me, and though I am god-awful fatigued I am ready for more action. I will write again and hope so much your letters find me here in Nashville. As always,

Your loving husband,
Henry

P.S.

Must purchase more paper and ink here in Nashville.

Febuary 26, 1862
Nashville, Tenn.

Dear Elizabeth,

I been here in Nashville for the best part of a week and I feel so much better and fit. I dont beleve I tole you that in the battle for the cannons outside Ft. Donelson I did receve a bullit wound in my left arm. It felt like a hot iron layed on the skin, but since I was fightin for my life at the time I payed it no nevermind. The blood soaked my sleeve and then froze hard, and evry time I moved that arm the froze coat scraped the wound. I soon rapped it fresh and after the long ride here to Nashville Dr. Cowan, our surgon, tended it and just tole me now the arm will not need amputated. In fact it is recoverin nice, as is my strength, and if I was afeard to tell you before, I know I can tell you all this now without concernin you overly. Col. Forrest hisself stopped by a couple times to inquire the condition of my health, as he done for many of the boys round camp. This is all part of war, Lizzie.

Couple days ago Col. Forrest sent Maj. Kelley and most of our regiment on to Murfreesboro where the army is gatherin together. The rest of us, mainly the colonels escort and a company or two, was kept here to move the huge stocks of comisary and quartermaster stores southward by rail and wagon. We feel the yankees will soon invade Nashville in force, and we dont want to leave no supplys for them when they come.

You aint seen nothin, Lizzie, like the panic we arrived to in this town. The folks of Nashville musta thought this war was for other people in far off places. They got no fortafications or batterys for protection, and now of a sudden Donelson falls and the yankees is steamin up the Cumberland to take the city. Panic followd. Hunderds of people crammed on the trains to Chattanooga. They was stacked on top the rail cars. Evry citizen was tryin to leave town as quick as they could. The city leaders all skedaddled and the state goverment closed up. Even the young ladys attendin the Nashville Academy was sent home for good. The newspaper closed shop, evry bank and bisness locked the doors, and citizens is beggin for help and protection.

The city managers, before runnin away, tole the people they could help thereselves to any food and supplys held in the big warehouses. Gen. Sidney Johnston, in overall command of this area, orderd Col. Forrest to save as much as posable for army use and send it south.

Yesterday Col. Forrest has the rest of us at the warehouses loadin wagons, but we kept gettin pesterd by a angry mob who was tryin to take as much of the goods as posable. It got to a point we could not even load the wagons for all the people linin up with carts and wheelbarows, many just grabbin things and stuffin there pockets. They was grabbin clothing, blankets, cases of bacon, anything they could reach. I bumpted into a angry man in a sweaty shirt pushin a cart with a barrel of flour and case of bacon on it. "Get back here with that" I shout at him, "you cant run off with that."

"The hell I cant" snaps he, "I got as much right to this stuff as you do."

"No you aint" says I, runnin beside him, "it belongs to the goverment."

"There aint no goverment buster, they all took off at the first sine of trouble."

"No" says I, "the Confederate goverment, and its for army use." The man was gettin away from me.

He looks back over his shoulder and shouts, "Then let Jeff Davis come and get it," and he disappeard in the mob. Finaly after none of us could control these looters, Col. Forrest orderd us all to mount and charge with drawd sabers in the midst of the mob. You best beleve they scatterd, but not one soul was hurt.

Later as we was loadin wagons — we loaded hunderds of them with meat alone — the crowd started amassin again. Then a big stout Irishman, who I spect was worse for drink, grabbed Col. Forrest by the coller and yells in the colonels face that he got as much right to this stuff as any body else. Col. Forrest quick drawd his pistol and whacked the man hard upside the head with it. This calm the clamor for a while. A hour later when another group a rowdy, cussin men started pushin for the warehouses again, Col. Forrest had us pump a heavy blast of ice cold, dirty river water into them usin the steam-power fire engine. When the mob seen there leaders nocked on the street wallowin in the icy mud, many laughed at the sight and all gave up any further atempt at takin the supplys.

We got most all the stores loaded out finaly, includin many wagons of amunition and rifles. I was most thankful when the colonel hisself presented me with a spankin new Sharps carbine of my own. He said he seen me rasslin with the old shotgun and said, "A good trooper, sargent, needs a good firearm." "Thank you, sir," says I. He turnd to go but paused and says, "I know this here is a good rifle and I seen you, Wylie, hold your mount in the midst of the fray for them cannons at Donelson, and I know sir, you are a good trooper." I do not remember bein so honored since the day you took my hand in marrage.

We are all packin up now. Almost evry one got issude decent blankets, uniforms and half-tents, which is good cause many the boys left all there stuff behind in our quick getaway from Donelson. Tomorrow its off to Murfreesboro and probly new adventures. Till you hear next from me, I am as always,

Your loving husband,
Henry

Later

Great news, Lizzie! Lt. Barker just tole me there is a good chance the whole regiment will be furlowd for a fortnight once we leave Murfreesboro. If this be true, I am the happyest soldier in the army.

Chapter 3

March 19, 1862 through June 30, 1862

March 19, 1862
Burnsville, Miss.

Dear Elizabeth,

Here I set by the campfire feelin sad and lonely, knowin that just one week ago I was with you and Mary. She sure growd alot and I know she disrememberd me, but that didnt last long. Them two weeks at home was the fastest I ever spent, and I like to remember evry hour of each day I was there and what I was doin. That memory makes me feel joyful inside, but also sad. I aint the only fella feelin this way, the Turner boys I rode back to camp with is feelin blue now also, and Mark is playin "Lorena" on his mouth harp, which always brings tears to our eyes. Though each one of us charish the memory of our furlow, evry single mothers son of us return to camp on time and ready for action. Many the boys brung back new recrutes to fill our ranks.

Which brings me to the point bout your brothers, Lizzie. I know they is anxous to sine up, but dont dare let them run off and join a infantry company. They would regret that mighty. I aint had a chance to mention the boys yet to Col. Forrest, but Maj. Kelley says he dont see no reason why a 16 and 17 year old can not join up. After all, the colonels son Willie hisself is but 15 or 16. I spect fore long the brothers Bobby and John Parker will be ridin

39

with Col. Forrest too, specialy if your father can provide them with horses. Tell them not to do nothin till they hear from me.

Some of the boys at the Daily Appeal showd a intrest in sinin up too, and I tole Mr. Ray not to bother holdin my job for me, seein how this aint goin to be no short war. I also tole him he better start lookin for more hires as I feel most evry man tween 15 and 50 is goin to be in this war some time or other.

Please tell Ma and Pa how I enjoyd bein with them so much, and tell Pa I urge him very strong to keep puttin up the fence row we started in the deep ravine in the far west wood lot and stash as many of the horses and livestock as he can down there, as it is most out of sight. I know from experiance these armys, north and south, is foragin heavy and will strip a farmer bare of all he got.

Once back in camp, Col. Forrest seen to it that each man is outfitted right, and many exchanged there squirrel guns for good carbines. The colonel takes very good care of his men and in return expects blind obediance to all his orders. As always, the horses too get all they need – new shoes, saddle blankets, what have you.

Our regiment has growd in size as the colonels young brother Jesse raised a company, as did Adjutant Schuyler, both men now captains. Col. Forrest is now joind by his brothers William, Jeffrey and Jesse, and of course son Will is always near by. We been drillin daily, servin outpost and picket duty, and gettin back in fightin shape.

I hear tell from Maj. Rambaut that we will soon be movin out to join the rest of Gen. Johnstons army in Corinth Mississippi, as the enemy is said to be amassin in large numbers near there.

How I miss you two dear ones and am as always,

Your loving husband,
Henry

April 9, 1862
Corinth, Miss.

Dear Elizabeth,

Since last I wrote to you, we was engaged in the most fearsom blood-lettin encounter with the enemy any one could beleve. I never in my life thought it posable to see so many brave men killed and wounded as I seen this past week. But let me ease your mind now – I am healthy and unhurt exeptin a sore shoulder after Maybelle throwd me off her back when a cannon ball exploded near us. But I will tell you all in order.

Back round the first of this month our regiment was orderd north to join the whole western army under Gen. Sidney Johnston. We was to confront a large union army headin south under there general named U.S. Grant, who was the same who chased us outa Donelson. Our mounted unit, close on a thousand men, took up position on the far right of Johnstons army. By April 2 we got in close to where the enemy army was amassed at a small town on the Tennessee River called Pittsburg Landing. That night we bedded down in a quiet churchyard next to a small wood chapel called Shiloh.

That evning we set round a low fire, Billy Tupper, Hoot Evers and me. "What do you think, Henry" asks Tups, "I hear the yanks is bringin a good 50,000 men here soon."

"It aint always how many men you got" I says, "but how good there used."

"Ya, who cares how many yankees come our way" shouts Hoot, "we can whip the hell outa them no matter how bad outnumberd we are." His face was all over honey, which he brung back from home in a jar, and leafs and twigs and other stuff was stuck to his fingers and hands. As he talked he flicked his fingers and rubbed his hands to rid the stuff but more clung to him, and he was lookin like a man who been tarred and featherd. Tups and me got a good laugh anyhow.

41

Next few days we spent scoutin round the area and Col. Forrest reported back to Gen. Johnston that we seen the enemy debarkin from transport ships in heavy numbers. By Saturday evning, bein April 5, we was close enough to the union lines to exchange a few shots with them and that night we could hear the quiet and sad music of the union bands driftin through the cool night air.

Orders was passed through camp that next morning, at the crack of dawn, we would attack the yankees. You best beleve the boys was uneasy that night. A stedy rain was pourin down too, and it was none too comfitable neither. In the wee hours of the night one of our men on picket duty, Pvt. Yancy Wetmore, stirred the whole camp up cause he herd the enemy advancin toward us "clear as a bell I herd them," claimed Yancy, "clomp clomp clomp of horse hoofs." You never seen men move so fast to grab firearms, pull on boots and saddle horses. Soon we all herd the clomp clomp clomp comin toward us down the road – then they emerged in our front – just couldnt beleve our eyes as a single confused artilery horse, draggin his broken tether behind, advanced. A hunderd carbines was aimed at his head. That was the enemy that spooked Wetmore so bad. Poor Yancy wont live down the time he give in to jumpy nerves.

Sure nough just as the sun cracked the horizon a barage of artilery fire broke from our lines and the infantry boys was set in motion. We could hear the echo of the rebel yell. We was still off on the flank and Col. Forrest had orders to protect the end of our line from the enemy. As I peerd acrost the distance, watchin our embattled army advance through the once peacefull churchyard, I wonderd to myself what God must think of the way we honored his sabbath, the day bein Sunday.

Bitter fightin raged acrost the fields and through the dense woods. From our position we could see the union ranks fallin back in great numbers, but only after desprate fightin. Seemed all organization was lost – no units complete on either side or doin fancy parade ground manuvers, it was more a giant free-for-all with small groups a men fightin against other small groups.

By 11:00 am, after the fight been goin on for many hours, we was still way far from the action. Col. Forrest rode back and forth, back and forth acrost our line. I could see he was anxous. Never a man to be kept from battle, he turnd to us and says "Boys, you hear them muskets and artilery? It means that our friends is fallin by the hunderds at the hand of the enemy, and here we sit gardin a damn creek! What say you to goin and helpin them?" We let out a healthy roar and the Colonel spured his horse into a gallup and we all followd, headin strait for the sound of battle.

We soon arrived at a sceen of intense fightin. Gen. Cheatham and a brigade of our boys was engaged at very close quarters with a stout union force at a sunken road. The "hornets nest" they now call it. Never have I witnesed such slauter, and Lizzie, never hope to again. They been at each other for five hours and I seen body after body piled on top of each other, sometimes four deep, limbs dismemberd and boys with blackend faces and eyes starin blank. The screams from evry where could be herd high above the constant rumble of gunfire. As I moved toward the front line I seen the bodies of two men, one in gray and one in blue, each with a bayonet thrust in the others heart. As they layed there in death side by side, a stedy stream of blood from each rold down the embankment and formed a single pool of red.

Col. Forrest rallyed us and pointed to a battery of cannons that was firin on us from a hillside sevral hunderd yards ahead. He orderd us to take them guns. The bugle sounded and as before, the colonel bared his saber and bolted strait ahead in the face of the artilery. We followd close at his heels and as we drawd near a blast of canister and explodin shells killed a number of our boys, unhorsed sevral more. Even Maybelle come to a dead stop throwin me right over her head. I landed on my left shoulder in a boggy meadow, and though it was jammed hard and hurt like hell, I remounted Maybelle and tryed to catch up. But the meadow got very swampy just shy of the guns and the horses was all bogged down. Boys on foot pressed the charge on and the union gunners quick drawd back there pieces.

Col. Forrest led us back to the hornets nest and we was just in time to help suround the gallent union division there. They finaly had no choice but to surender there exausted command, many of which was fightin for hours with no amunition left. More then 2000 prisners was marched off.

Col. Forrest moved us up the line further where he orderd us to dismount, evry 4th man holdin the horses in the rear, and we joind our brothers in the infantry in fightin. I crouched behind a old stump for a goodly time firin shot after shot at the slowly retreatin enemy. The barrel of my new Sharps carbine got so hot you couldnt touch it, and I never knowd if I was hittin any thing or not. I felt many thuds as bullits struck the stump I was leanin against. With my shoulder achin bad, I was right glad to find such a good spot. Fore long the light faded and a general cease fire was orderd, but only after we drove the entire enemy force to the very cliffs of the Tennessee at Pittsburg Landing. Though the enemy had at least 50 cannons circled by the bluffs for protection, Col. Forrest was stompin and hollerin that our army should press the attack now, even in darkness and drive the enemy into the river. But the commandin officers would not listen to him and the days fightin was over.

Lizzie, my hand hurts from writin almost as much as my shoulder, so I must continue this letter tomorow.

April 10, 1862
Corinth, Miss.

Dear Elizabeth,

I see Capt. Cooper is collectin mail, so I better hurry and finish this letter so you can get it in a timely fashon.

After the first days fightin was over we bedded down in a wooded ravine, but we was close enough to the battlefield that I could hear the pitiful crys for help, the moanin of thousands of wounded men layin untended acrost the field. To make matters worse a cold rain fell stedy and continude well into the next day. There was not much sleep with these conditions in spite our exaustion, and besides that Col. Forrest had a number of us, me included, out scoutin the river area till after 2:00 am. All night we watched as thousands of fresh soldiers in blue landed on the banks. I knowd tomorow was goin to be trouble.

As I stumble back toward camp on a night dark as pich, I become a little separated from the others. I werent scared for I knowd I could find my way back, but I was a little concernd I might bump head-to-head with a enemy scoutin party. I soon come upon a open field that seen plenty of action this day. In the darkness I could just make out forms, motionless forms, scatterd thick upon the plain. I suspected what them many heaps was, but the foul reek of the gentle breeze made it certain — they was dead bodys, decayin flesh of many a poor boy lost in battle this day. But it wasnt the lifeless remains that set my evry nerve on edge, it was the other forms — alive, movin, crouchin over the dead soldiers. At first I thought they was men, like Johnny Marsh, pickin over the bodys for valubles. I layed low, watchin, and seen this was not so. The creatures were makin noise, grunts and bass growls, then I realized the truth — they was hogs, packs of hogs tearin the flesh and eatin the inards of those poor lifeless souls. The site disgust me so bad I almost fired my pistol at them, but I knowd that would do nothin but create trouble. So I hurryed back to camp.

Just after five next morning the yankees commenced to fight again and from the first shot we was simply overpowerd by there reinforcments. The blue tide slowly swept onward pushin our tired army backward over ground still thick with yesterdays wounded. Col. Forrest again had us fight dismounted and though our army fought stout, we could not stop the blue tide. Finaly by 2:00 in the afternoon, after many thousands a deaths and injurys, Gen. Beauregard (now in command after the death of Gen. Johnston) orderd a retreat. Col. Forrest was tole to have his cavalry close in behind to protect the rear of the army.

There was no panic, we faced the enemy, but we was indeed in retreat. Heaps of bleedin, cripled boys was hauld off on litters as we pulled back slow a good three mile. A endless caravan of wagons, as far as the eye could see, carried these poor souls to Corinth, where evry church, school, house and barn was made a hospital. It was a pitiful sight. Toward evening the yankees ceased the persute and the fightin died down.

But we was not done yet. Next morning, Tuesday, April 8, the army still shuffled along to Corinth and us cavalry still protected the rear. All the while I seen Col. Forrest glare back as a section of union infantry, followd by there cavalry, was ever creepin closer. Finaly, as if he could take this no longer, the colonel orderd us to halt, form a line a battle and get ready to attack. We was only bout 350 in number and the enemy looked to be a brigade of sevral thousand. The colonel gave no never mind to this, for I seen his blood was up and his face took on that angry red look as in battle.

The field tween us and the approachin enemy was once woods but looked recently cleard for nary a tree stood but the ground was strewd with fallen timber and brush piles. At a signal the bugle sounded and Col. Forrest burst from the line high in the saddle and screamin "Charge, charge." We was soon with him and attacked in good order, the boys lettin go hoarse screams and swingin sabers and firin pistols.

The advanced union infantry was took by suprise at this sudden fury, never fired a shot but let go there rifles and fled. They slammed into there own cavalry comin up behind, and as we come on hard, the blue horsemen whipped there horses round and scrambled to retreat. Men in blue stood and surenderd, but Col. Forrest slashed right by them screamin at us to "keep the skeer on."

This was all very exitin and my heart beat hard. I hardly had control of my senses, but of a sudden we reined up at once as we seen up ahead a solid line of blue infantry regrouped and aimin muskets right at us. They musta been a thousand, holdin stedy. We all knowd this meant death and it was time to fall back to our lines. All of us that is, but Col. Forrest.

I have seen nothin like it, Lizzie, as that furius man raced way out ahead by hisself and was soon circled round by a hunderd men in blue. They was screamin "Kill him, kill the damn rebel, nock him off his horse" and they jabbed bayonets at him and badly wounded his horse. The colonel was thrashin all round with his saber and his horse was kickin and rearin and fightin for room. A soldier thrust his rifle in the colonels side and pulled the trigger. The force of the blast nocked Col. Forrest just bout out of the saddle and we all knowd our fearless leader was captured and probly dead. But then with a surge of strength the colonel righted hisself in the saddle, reached down with his left hand and plucked a blue soldier by the coller and flung him up onto his saddle, holdin the man tight to his back. The bleedin horse swung round, the colonel with pistol now drawd, fired rapid shots clearin a path strait ahead and spurd the horse to a gallup back toward our line. With hunderds of the enemy behind him, rifles fixed at his back, the colonel held on to the stund soldier till a goodly ways off then dropped this human shield to the ground. It was a sight never to be forgot. We cheerd our throats raw when he reached our lines.

Once back to safety, the pain from the gun shot got intense and the surgons probin for the bullit found it lodged hard against the colonels spine. They said they could not operate and the wound probly fatal. In terible pain the colonel managed to ride a new mount (the poor creature that carryed him to safety soon fell dead) all the way to Corinth where he was sent home to Memphis with a 60 day leave of absence to try and heal.

Those are my experiances of the past week Lizzie, and now I am here with my survivin comrads thankin the dear Lord he seen fit to keep us alive and prayin to Him that our wounded brothers can heal up good and that Col. Forrest can live and some day ride again. I will miss him. Have Mary pray for her father and beleve me to be as always

Your loving husband,
Henry

May 7, 1862
Corinth, Miss.

Dear Elizabeth,

Here we been settin for almost a month. We been spendin time drillin new troops, gatherin up livestock, mendin wounds, and gettin the horses back in fit condition. Best thing that happend to me this past month is recevin four of your letters and two from Ma. Cannot tell you how good it makes me feel to read and read again the news from home. I am glad all goes well with you and I sure am happy Mary is on the mend after her spill — now she know not to try goin down the celler stairs without holdin her mamas hand. I also beg of you Lizzie, to listen to your mother and father and move into there house with them. These is rough times and a person must depend on her family for help. Also, dont let your brothers do something stupid like run off and join some infantry unit. I hear-tell Col. Forrest, now in Memphis to recover, is roundin up some fresh troopers and I urge strong that Bobby and John sine up with us. At least I could keep my eye on them a little.

Something hard to imagin happend this week and I will explane it to you best I can. I beleve I tole you in my last letter that Col. Forrest was sent home to Memphis to recover from a serius gun shot wound that left a yankee minie ball stuck in his spine. The field doctors, if you must call them such, was fraid to operate and suppose the wound fatal. So the colonel was sent off in a ambulence to Memphis with a two month leave of absence to try and heal up.

Well, it did not take long for things to go bad here. Our regiment is still with Gen. Beauregards army, and as usual the boys on foot regard us on horseback pretty lowly. They think we got it too easy, gatherin glory and admirin glances from the girls while they do the fightin. If they seen us at Sacramento, Donelson, and Pittsburg Landing they know better. But we soon found out we was not recevin our fair share of goverment supplys. Many of our boys is barefoot and some in rags that once was a butternut uniform. It is hard gettin amunition for our rifles as so many men is carryin diffrent kinds of guns. And up to this time we always seen to feedin ourselvs, but now foods given to us from the general comisary and I can tell you its not plentiful and tastes bad to boot. This want for vittles and supplys is not necesary as the warehouses in Corinth is stuffed with food, clothing and amunition, and the infantry boys get all of evrything they need or want.

This situation gone on for sevral weeks and some how or other word musta got back to Col. Forrest in Memphis that his regiment was not bein treated right. Sure nough, Lizzie, at the end of April and only three weeks after his scrap with death, the colonel come ridin back into camp strait as a ramrod. The boys let out a holler when they seen Old Bedford back in the saddle amongst us. And beleve me, he soon set things aright. Bein a sucessful man of bisness he knowd you got to keep your customers happy, so with his usual energy he took over the comisary and quartermaster for our regiment. Soon evry man-jack here got the things he most need, whether it be boots, gauntlets, spurs, ridin gear, amunition, and the colonel seen to it that we supply ourselvs with the food we need. Spirit was soon restord here.

But I could see the colonel was not recoverd and was yet bad in pain. When he mount his horse or bend over to pick some thing up, he would reach for his back and wince in pain. Bout a week after he come back to camp a small group of us was out on patrol and we waded the horses acrost a small creek and then jumped a log on the opposit bank. When the colonel jumped his horse over the log the bullit lodged in his spine musta shifted, for he was paralized with pain. He could just barly move one mussle without screamin in torment.

Lucky we was pretty close to camp and the colonel managed to stay on his mount though I thought for a while we was gonna have to carry him back on a litter. Dr. Cowan was brung direct to the colonels tent and said he would have to operate right then and there or Col. Forrest would surely die. We cut the jacket and shirt from his back as he lay there face down on his bunk. Dr. Cowan got his kit and right away pulled out his scalpel and made a cut over the colonels spine. The colonel took no anistetic and would never touch a drop of alcahol. We was bracin him by the wrist and ankles to keep him from squirmin as Doc Cowan spred the cut apart. He probed with his doctor tools into the wound and said he felt the ball against the colonels backbone. Col. Forrest was grittin his teeth so hard I thought sure they would crack. Then Dr. Cowan says "Ah" and with a little tug he pull a flattend bullit from betwixt the bones of the spine. He worked quite a while on the wound, but at last says, "Let him rest." I was glad the brutel doins was over and the colonel lay still as if in a deep sleep.

He was sent home to Memphis again to see if he could get hisself back in good condition. I hope this amazin man can survive this ordeal. I gave my best wishes to him as his ambulence pulled away, and I thought to myself just what manner of man is this here? This man I seen strole bout camp talkin soft and kind to all his men, checkin on the sick and wounded, even treatin the many nigras bout camp in a humane and man to man way. Then I see him flare up at something or other he dont approve of, nock a man to the ground with his fist and cause all round him to hide from his anger. Will not allow a horse be mistreated and works hisself to the bone providin for all our wants. Then in the midst a battle he becomes a red demon, expectin blind obediance to all commands, and orders officers to shoot any man who wont fight – at Shiloh Church I personly seen him shoot one of our soldiers in the back whilst runnin away from battle. I seen him rise high in his saddle and slash with such violant hatred he dismemberd four of the enemy with his saber and gun down as many more. The anger and fury of the man is frightnin to look upon for all, but much more so for the enemy. Four horses been killed from under him and many times he been throwd to the ground. He faced sure death when surounded at the fallen timbers, receved a severe wound but yet got strength to yank a man to his saddle and fight his way out. After the fightin at Donelson I counted myself fifteen bullit holes through his uniform. So I ask again what manner of man is this? Did the Almighty create him special, send us a warrior from Mt. Olympus to lead us in battle? Is he of mortel man? Some times I wonder, Lizzie.

Anyway the colonels now in Memphis, so get your brothers to join up if he does any recrutin. Please take the best care of your self and Mary, and remember me to be as always

Your loving husband,
Henry

June 30, 1862
Chattanooga, Tenn.

Dear Elizabeth,

I am sorry I been tardy in writin to you but as we been in the saddle the best part of three weeks I just now got time to set and write. Though after 350 mile on Maybelle from Corinth to Chattanooga, standin is a bit more comfitable.

As you may remember the colonel was sent home to Memphis early in May to heal his wounded back where Doc Cowan dug the yankee slug out. In spite such a bad injury, Old Bedford was down for only a couple weeks and soon come ridin back into camp bringin a passel of new recrutes from Memphis with him. As you well know two of them recrutes was your brothers Bobby and John. It was sure nice for me to see them two familier faces full a smiles come ridin in to camp. I seen right off that little Bobby and William Forrest, the colonels 16 year old son, was becomin fast friends. Young Pvt. Forrest is a good boy, very polite, quiet and helpful bout camp, and calls me sir regular, though I aint sure if its for the stripes I got or my age. Any how, William took Bobby and John all through the camp, showd them what they need to know bout requesitionin supplys and amunition, learnt them some basic drills and in evry way bein a good friend to them. I was glad to see the names John Parker and Robert Parker added to my roster of Company C and they is fittin in nice. The horses your father packed them off with is fine lookin animals too and a lot of us enjoyd the tarts your mother sent.

Col. Forrest was just gettin settled back into camp life there in Corinth when he receve some new orders from Gen. Beauregard that stun us all. Our regiment of cavalry was bein turnd over to Col. Kelley who was to head off to central Mississippi with the rest of the western army while Col. Forrest was to ride east to Chattanooga and take command of varius regiments of horsemen and form them into a brigade. This new brigade will be servin with the army of Gen. Braxton Bragg.

This was sad news indeed. This fine battle tested regiment spilt blood for Old Bedford through the fightin from Sacramento, the bold midnight escape from Donelson, and the blood bath at Pittsburg Landing. These same boys that Col. Forrest grab from behind plows and desks ten months ago was now bein seperated from there leader. This is the nature of war. All the boys was bad hurt however, as we all know it was the colonels strength and daring that made us strong and daring. His dash and courage made us men dashing and couragous too. He made each one of us feel better bout ourselvs. The colonel hisself was upset and not at all keen to the idea, but bein a good soldier he knowd he must do what he was orderd, cause it was for the good of the Confederacy. I personly beleve the generals on top was doin this cause they knowd

Col. Forrests old regiment was now a fine fightin unit and they want him to train the next one in the same way.

The colonel, now made actin brigadier general, had to leave his now famous regiment behind, but he was permited to take a portion of his escort company with him. Course, he would keep young William at his side and at once took his brothers Jeffrey, Jesse and Bill, plus Doc Cowan and Lt. Markbright. But just after supper one night the colonel (no, I should say the general) was strollin through camp, seen me washin my pans, walks over and says, "Sgt. Wylie, you are plannin to stay with my escort, am I right?" Lizzie, I had no notion what ever to that moment that he was fixin on keepin me with him. "If you want me sir, I would be honored," says I. "Well good Wylie, I think we can have some more fun killin yankees once we whip this new command into fightin shape, what say you to that?" "Yes sir, I am sure we can, sir." And that was that.

I was full a pride in myself knowin the general hisself wanted me to acompany him to his new command but when I realize this ment leavin all the fellas I knowd so good and so long, I hurt inside. I was thinkin how I might never see these boys, many I growd up with, again. Ned and Mark Turner, Jeff and Jesse Treach (Jeff recevin a severe wound at Pittsburg Landing), Buck Wayland and the others I been livin with for the best part of a year. And then there was your brothers. I promised you I would look out after them two youngsters and I was settin to leave them after they was but a few weeks in camp.

I was havin serius second thoughts bout leavin Company C, but somehow the thought of fightin without Gen. Forrest seemed imposable too. Then the matter was resolved for me when your brother Bobby come runnin up to me next day with young William Forrest, both grinnin from ear to ear.

"Hey Henry, I mean Sgt. Wylie, did you hear the news?" ask Bobby.

"What news you talkin bout?"

William burst out, "My father, I mean Gen. Forrest, says that Bobby can join the escort and come with us to Chattanooga!"

"Honest to God? Now why would the general take this raw soldier when he can select so few?"

"He knows I am gonna be a good soldier, thats why he wants me," says your brother, a little edgy.

"Its mother, thats why," says William, "any time she is in camp she pesters father bout me not havin someone my own age to be with. She dont worry bout me fightin or nothin, but she worrys bout who my friends are."

"And Mrs. Forrest says she dont want me seperated from my brother so she press the general into lettin John come along too. Aint that great Henry, Sgt. Wylie, me and John in the escort too?"

"Well that is grand," I says, "and thank you mostly, Willie, for takin these young rascals under your wing like you done. There sister and parents be right glad to know theys still with me."

So on June 11 we said our last farewell to our friends and comrads of the old regiment, and of Company C specialy, and mounted our horses and started the long ride to Chattanooga while they stay in Corinth. The weather was mostly perfect, some rain but warm most days, and our little party of thirty or so made good time along dirt roads and pathways through the dense woods. Not once did we encounter the enemy. Young William Forrest and your brother Bobby twict along the way shot a buck that provided us with fresh meat. It was a most plesant few weeks fore we come ridin here into Chattanooga. Now we gotta get aquainted with a whole new set a officers and men who will have the honor to ride with Gen. Nathan Bedford Forrest.

Now your caught up on all the news, please pass it along to your mother and father and as always Ma and Pa. Hopin that all is well with you and Mary, remember me to be

Your loving husband,
Henry

Chapter 4

July 16, 1862 through November 6, 1862

July 16, 1862
McMinnville, Tenn.

Dear Elizabeth,

Been more then two weeks since I writ to you and since then we was involved in a grand scrap, and I can tell you now the name Gen. Nathan Bedford Forrest is bein ballyhooed far and wide acrost the south. But fore I get too caught up in a report, let me tell you what you want to hear most, and that is that the good Lord has kindly protected me and your brothers from harms way, but I can asure you the boys now know what fightin means.

As you may recall from my last letter Gen. Forrest and us in his escort rode from Corinth to Chattanooga cause the general been orderd to command a new brigade and whip them into fightin shape. Joinin this new brigade was a regiment a tough Texas cattle ranchers and cowpokes under Col. Wharton. These boys been ridin horses and firin guns since they was shorter then there rifles. Then two regiments from Georgia under Col. Morrison and Col. Lawton join this brigade. After a couple tough weeks drillin and gettin to know each other, Gen. Forrest was ready to move out. "Besides," says the general, "the best trainin scheme is active duty against the enemy."

So on July 9 our new command left Chattanooga, headin northwest. After ridin forty miles we held over in Woodbury, where we was joind by a couple hunderd mounted boys from Kentucky and Tennessee lookin for some yankees to fight. This brung our force to round 1400 men. The folk in Woodbury was right glad to have the southern cavalry back in there town and they treat us all to a exellent dinner, plus dozens of cakes and pies, mostly apple and blackberry.

While we was havin this fun the general sent scouts out ahead who come back reportin a nice concentration of union soldiers twenty mile ahead holdin the town a Murfreesboro. Thats all Gen. Forrest need to know. He said we was goin to capture that command and rid middle Tennessee of that yankee invader. By noon of July 12 we moved out toward Murfreesboro.

Aw shucks Lizzie, I just been orderd to take a squad on outpost duty – a man can get no rest round here. Will continue later.

July 17, 1862
McMinnville, Tenn.

Dear Elizabeth,

You shoulda seen your brother Bobby and Willie Forrest chasin this chicken all round camp this morning. Had all the boys laughin, even fellas injurd in the fight, though it pain them to laugh.

But to pick up where I left off yesterday, Gen. Forrest soon move us to the outskirts of Murfreesboro just after midnight of July 13, that Sunday bein his 41st birthday. Our scouts did a reconasance and reported back to the general that the enemy was spred out in three seperate camps. One group of Michigan infantry was stationd just a little east of Murfreesboro. A regiment of Minnesota soldiers was camped a mile and a half west of town. And the last passel was in the town of Murfreesboro itself.

Our scouts captured bout fifteen enemy pickets who was took completly by suprize and without a struggle. From them we learnt

56

the position of the yankees and that they numberd bout 1500 in all. In command was a Gen. Crittenden, and he was headquartered at the inn in the center of town. Most the yankees holdin the town was holed up in the courthouse. Some womenfolk tole Gen. Forrest the jail in town was chock full of citizens from Murfreesboro that the enemy claim was southern simpethizers. Our scouts learnt that a few captured Confederate soldiers was bein held in the same jail as spys and would be executed this very day.

Gen. Forrest quick made his plan. He would send Col. Wharton and his Texans stampedin into the enemy camp east of town, the Georgia boys was to engage the enemy west of town, and Gen. Forrest would hisself lead the rest on the attack in town. Those stayin with the general and attackin the town would divide into three small groups – one to capture the yankee general at the inn, another to free the prisners from the jail, and the other to engage the enemy holed up in the courthouse.

At 4:30 that Sunday morning just as the sun was startin to make a light along the skyline, the three-prong attack comenced. I know there was shock and panic in the enemy camps all round Murfreesboro when the general unleashed us screamin horsemen on them. Whartons Texans burst into the yankee camp jumpin there horses right over the tent strings and the Michigan boys scrambled in all directions. They was tough fellas though, them yankees, and most managed to get behind a cedar fence or loaded wagons and return fire. The Texans dismounted and a fire fight ensude for hours and was pretty much a bloody stalemate. At the same time the Georgians attack the Minnesota boys west of town, and after some heavy loss the yankees pulled back to a small hill good for defense and the fightin turn nip and tuck there too for all morning.

Gen. Forrest led the charge on the town center with the escort and a couple companys from Tennessee and Kentucky. The Kentucky boys was directed to the inn by Maj. Smith and they swarm inside so fast little resistance was made and they soon had the yankee general and his staff as prisners. The courthouse was surounded but a brisk fire was returnd and more then a few of our boys was unhorsed. The enemy fired down at our men from evry window and vent and Maj. Davis stationed sharpshooters in trees, behind fences and inside houses to return fire.

In the midst of this excitment Sgt. Roth and a number of men grab big logs layin nearby and use them as batterin-rams to nock in the courthouse doors. Sure nough, the front and rear doors give way and in rush one brave man after another, each so caught up in the frenzy they give no thought to bein killed. Hand to hand fightin ensude, but as the men poured in stedy and our sharpshooters was pickin off the ones inside, the yankees ventualy surender therselves and the courthouse.

My duty at this time was leadin a squad of men to the jail to free the captives. It was defended pretty light and we dismounted, spred out and comenced a stedy fire into the office area and soon a white banner was stuck out the window. As bout a dozen yankees come crawlin out with there hands raised, little did we know that one particlar villan lit a stack a newspaper on fire and shoved the flamin mass under some loose floorbords. He was tryin to burn the men in the jail alive. Soon smoke and flames rose from the windows and desprate screams herd from the men in the locked cells. Breakin through the steel doors was very hard and we was overcome with smoke while workin. Finaly after bangin with crowbars and steel pipes was we able to force the locks and free the terifyed prisners. We all flung ourselvs on the dirt outside coughin hard and with black faces. God alive Lizzie, those men freed was most thankful to us.

Gen. Forrest was ridin tween all the sites of battle that morning and I could see his blood was up. Red faced and savage, barkin out orders that you best obey. Once a group of frightend ladys from the town come out of there houses and approch the fray at the courthouse. Gen. Forrest stopped them cold and in a most patient and kindly way says, "Ladys, you must return to your homes at once for it is very dangrous here. But dont fret, we will provide for your safty." And they left.

As my squad lined up yankee prisners we captured at the jail, Gen. Forrest rode up to Capt. Richardson, who was one of them held captive as a Confederate spy. General says to Richardson, "Captain, I understand you was treated inhumane while in jail. Can you show me which ones of these prisners was responsable?"

"Only one," says the captain, "and that was the man who started the fire and tryed to burn us up."

"Can you point that man out?"

"Yes sir, General," says Richardson, "its that man there, name Crowther."

"Okay Captain, thats all." Gen. Forrest stared hard at the man named as if fixin his face in his mind.

I must mention Lizzie, that a few hours later when I was readin the roll-call of prisners, when I holler "Crowther" there came no reply of "Here." I shouted again "Crowther" and again no reply. Gen. Forrest was near me and says in a quiet tone, "Pass on Wylie, pass on. Its all right."

After all these doins, it was gettin near noontime now, the general took his escort company and a squad of Kentucky boys on a mad dash round the far east side a town and circled behind the hard-fightin Michigan boys who still battled with our Texans (Col. Wharton been shot early in the affair). Gen. Forrest spred us thin and orderd a charge into there rear. We suprized them bad, and bein fired on now from front and rear caused a hunderd men to surender on the spot. Cept one nigra camp-follower. While the others was layin down there rifles, he raised his and fire from only thirty feet directly at Gen. Forrest. The shot nock the hat clean off the generals head. Too bad for the nigra, for Old Bedford swung round and shot the man through the heart dead.

With us in the rear firin as fast as we could load, the Texans pushed hard on the exausted northern men. Finaly Gen. Forrest called a halt and sent in a truce flag to Col. Parkhurst, the yankee commander. With the shootin stopped, the general wrote a surender demand and sent me and Lt. Markbright to deliver it. Me and Markbright rode through the enemy line, and you best beleve I was prayin hard that none of them yankees had a itchy finger on his trigger. I took a look at the note and it read:

Col: I must demand a unconditional surender of your force as prisners of war or I will have evry man put to the sword. You are aware of the overpowering force I have at my command and this demand is made to prevent the efusion of blood.
I am Colonel, very respectfuly, your obedient servent,
N.B. Forrest
Brigadier General of Cavalry, C.S. Army

Col. Parkhurst talked with his officers and I hear one say quiet, "They must have 3,000 men." While they confered, Gen. Forrest sent groups a men marchin to varius open areas where they was clear in sight, givin the impresion we had alot more men then we really did. What with his men very tired and alot of casultys already, plus the threat of no quarter should the fight continue, Col. Parkhurst sent his surender note to Gen. Forrest.

Now we got a whole lot a prisners to deal with, but Old Bedford was not satisfyed yet. Again he left behind only enough men to corral the captured men and load up supplys, then dash off to the west a town where the Georgia boys was still fightin the yankees on the ridge. Same as before, Gen. Forrest led us round the rear of the yankee line and charged hard. They been shootin all day and was low on amunition and tuckerd out, and when suprized by our rear asault, they was done in. Again a truce flag was sent over, and the general sent me and Markbright with the same message to the union colonel in charge. His name was Col. Lester and he ask if he could consult with his commander, Gen. Crittenden. When informed that Gen. Crittenden was a prisner of

60

war, he seen it was useless to continue fightin and he surenderd. This time we took 400 more prisners.

In all we held the entire brigade (bout 1200 men) as prisners, plus the killed and wounded. We took all of there muskets and pistols, and more then fifty wagons full a salt pork, bacon, sugar, coffee, loads a amunition and supplys of all sorts. But what made this birthday best for the general was them three 6-pound brass smoothbore guns and the 10-pounder Parrott. This become the first artilery in our outfit. Any guns we captured fore this, like at Donelson, was soon took from us by the army. But now we got our own along with six caisons of amunition, now we just need some one or other who knows how to use the things.

This day of victory was concluded by us tearin up rail lines and burnin bridges over nearby Stones River. As we rode southeast to McMinnville, satisfyed that Woodbury and Murfreesboro was now free of yankee invaders, we found tryin to control so many prisners (they was as many as us) and movin so many captured wagons to be pert-near imposable. So Gen. Forrest, never at a loss, promise all the prisners (cept officers) he would parole them if they would drive the captured wagons to McMinnville. The yankee boys was plenty glad for that opertunity, as they would much rather be paroled and sit out the war at home till officialy exchanged then become prisners of war and sent to a camp some wheres. Thats what we did and arrived two days later safe and sound in McMinnville, where our hunderd wounded men was put in the hospital here.

Thats our adventures of the last few weeks Lizzie, and you must confess it was a proud moment for us all, and your brothers done there duty as brave troopers. I know your writin to me but no mail curier could ever keep up with Old Bedford. I hope some day

Mary can understand our cause and be proud of her fathers part in it. With all my thoughts, I am

Your loving husband,
Henry

Near Sparta, Tenn.
Aug. 14, 1862

Dearest Elizabeth,

If I have not writ for quite some time it is cause we been stedy on the move for almost a month. Even now I got but a few moments to write as we are makin to move out very soon. We stop at no location more then a few hours, eat a little food, catch a few hours sleep, let the horses graze, then we are off. It seems, you see, when we captured the whole brigade at Murfreesboro and the commandin general too, we caused a major panic amongst the northern army and now there terifyed Old Bedford will strike again at seven diffrent places at one time and there sparin no men to hunt us down.

The Confederate army of the west, that retreated last spring from Pittsburg Landing to Corinth, is now on rail headin to Chattanooga where Gen. Bragg intends to invade Kentucky and bring that state back to the Confederacy. Our job, so Gen. Forrest says, is to badger the union army under Buell and cause him so many problems he cant take time to concentrate against Braggs army.

And we are doin our share. After leavin McMinnville July 18, we drove into Lebanon where the jubalant townspeople fixed us roast pork, ham, chicken and sent us off with rations to last a while (to go along with the 50,000 rations we captured at Murfreesboro). Course Gen. Forrest dont like carryin extra stores on wagons cause he says the whole brigade cant go no faster then the slowest wagon. He is right bout that.

We left Lebanon and rode hard toward Nashville, all the while cuttin telegraph wires, tearin up railroad track, and torchin bridges over Mill Creek. One railroad bridge was garded by maybe 90 yankees behind a strong stockade, but Gen. Forrest quick fire our captured artilery at them, blew the stockade to a shambles, and cause the surender of the garison. We then lit the bridge which colapsed a hour later with a beautiful thundery noise.

Next day we rode to the rail depot at Antioch, had us a lively encounter with the yankees holdin the station, and after recevin some artilery they raised the white flag and we made off with as much goverment supplys as we could carry and sent the rest up in smoke. All prisners paroled cause we cant tend to them.

By late July we gone back through Murfreesboro, now bein held again by a large union force, head down to Manchester, then over to McMinnville, all the while burnin bridges and trestlework, cuttin telegraph wires, burnin depots, and gettin in vigerous spats with the enemy and then quick disapearin in the forests. We was doin our job, as the yankees spred there army in search of us at all these locations and always gettin there a bit too late.

I learnt quick that Gen. Forrest was just as clever at avoidin a fight as he was agresive to get in one. We played a grand game of hide-and-seek against a huge army and they quick found out that no foot soldiers could catch up to our men on horseback. After goin so many places and so many miles old Maybelle got footsore, so I grabbed me a fine quarterhorse we captured at Murfreesboro and tote Maybelle along till she got her strength back. I call my new mount Buster.

Thats what we are up to now and fixin to move soon again. Your brothers Bobby and John is doin good, seem to be enjoyin therselves immensly, and there fine horses is fit and strong. One evenin last week Bobby and young Will Forrest took off on there own to do some foragin and was gone for quite some time and the general sent out a party lookin for them. When the boys come marchin back in camp way after dark the general give them both a good scoldin. We got no letters for a long time and postin any is not easy, but I hope this letter finds its way to you and Mary, and you both are well. Till next time I am

Your loving husband,
Henry

October 2, 1862
Murfreesboro, Tenn.

Dear Elizabeth,

Here we finaly come to rest a spell in Murfreesboro after runnin the federals on a wild goose chase that lasted almost two months and coverd over 1000 miles. These past five days we run more then 165 miles almost nonstop. Takin time to write and postin a letter been most dificult and recevin one darn near imposable. We done nothin but run and fight, the men is tired, and the horses plum wore out. Along the way we musta destroyd three dozen bridges, downed miles a telegraph wire, twisted railroad track all over middle Tennessee, captured lots a prisners and tons of army stores, and simply made life miserble for the union army. You could tell they was annoyd by the number a troops they sent out after us.

Near the end of August for instance, not far from Altamont, Gen. Forrest receve word from the scouts that our position was bein closed in on from all sides by union brigades. So the general, Capt. Hollester and me spur our horses to a mountain top overlookin the Sequatchie Valley and could see with our naked eye union colums convergin on us from Winchester, Manchester, and McMinnville. The situation seemed desprate as we would not stand a chance fightin such overwhelmin numbers. But the general led our brigade down a hidden cove into a dry creek bed under high banks where we just rest in silence as the marchin hords of blue soldiers past us by.

On Sept. 3 we finaly joind the western army of Gen. Braxton Bragg as he moved on the state a Kentucky. Our orders was to gard the left flank as the army procede northward, and badger the flanks and rear of the union army of Gen. Buell. The campane for Kentucky was on, and we was doin all we could to delay the federals advance, and for a couple weeks we was in continuos tussles with the enemy. We fought our way into Kentucky, meetin the yankees in places like Tyree Springs and Franklin, where Gen. Forrest got his shoulder crushed when his horse was shot and rold over on top of him. On Sept. 17 we was joind by the infantry circlin round Mumfordville where after a day of brisk fightin the garison of 4000 yankees was surenderd.

But we was not destind to play a part in the great battle for the state a Kentucky, for even as we rode through Bardstown and was aproachin Louisville, Gen. Forrest (nursin his sore shoulder) was orderd to meet Gen. Bragg at army headquarters. There he was tole that his whole brigade, which fought and rode so galant all summer long for him, was bein turnd over to Gen. Joseph Wheeler. Gen. Forrest was tole to return to middle Tennessee and raise for hisself a new brigade of cavalry and procede to operate against the enemy in Tennessee any way he saw fit. So for the second time Gen. Forrest was losin the men he made battle worthy through vigerous engagment with the enemy. The feelin bein, I spect, that Old Bedford can raise and train anyone or other into first class soldiers. Still it dont seem fair — but we all know there aint nothin fair bout war.

The good news, I reckon, is that the general was rejoind by four companys of our old regiment, boys who fought with us at Sacramento, Donelson, and Shiloh Church, and of course that loyal group of fighters called his escort company goes with him.

So now I find myself in Murfreesboro again, your brothers Bobby and John right here next to me shufflin some cards. Nice to relax some. Theres even a poker game that goes on nights in Gen. Forrests tent. You wont catch me in no high stakes gamblin

65

though. New men is comin in camp from all parts of Tennessee and points south, and the general is comencin daily drill and field formation routine again, and us in the escort is teachin them the right way to soldier and how best to serve the man newspapers is callin "The Wizard of the Saddle."

Hope this letter finds you and Mary well. Have not herd from you all summer and gosh I get homesick at times. Perhaps now a letter can reach me. With love to Ma and Pa and best regards to your family, remember me as always

Your loving husband,
Henry

November 6, 1862
LaVergne, Tenn.

Dear Elizabeth,

I just got done readin all the letters I receve from you and Ma for the third time. We was positiond outside Murfreesboro long enough for the mail to catch up to us and just bout evrybody got letters and some packages. (I never seen sadder faces then on them poor souls who got nothin from home.) Tell Ma the socks she nit me is specialy handy as the nights is gettin cool and my old socks is more holes then wool. I am sorry to read the yankees took Memphis and hear tell that Gen. Grant (him of Donelson and Shiloh Church fame) is headquarterin right there on Main St. and fixin his sights on Vicksburg. I feel you was wise to leave town and stay by your parents home, and now Mary can ride grampapas back any old time.

I beleve I writ in my last letter that Gen. Forrest, his escort and four of our old companys under Capt. Bacot was sent back to middle Tennessee to round up a new brigade of cavalry and turn them into the kinda fightin unit Old Bedford likes. We spent the entire month of October in that pursute and now have a fine brigade of maybe 2000 men broke into four regiments. We had little trouble recrutin as Gen. Forrests reputation as the hardest fightin soldier out west got men flockin to his command.

Our four new regiments is the 4th Tennessee cavalry under Col. James Starnes (he been here since we was formed way over a year ago), the 8th and 9th Tennessee cavalry under Cols. George Dibrell and J.B. Biffle, and the 4th Alabama cavalry under Col. Russell. These is fine men all lookin forward to whipin the yankees, but there the most sorry lot for weapons you ever seen. Gen. Forrest been doin all he can to get decent arms for these men and he been pressin our brigade quartermaster, Maj. Severson, and our chief comisary Maj. Rambaut for all they can get. Yet each request to Richmond for short arms and sabers for cavalry come back stamped "imposable." Just how we are supposed to fight the war usin shotguns and squirrel rifles I dont know. Most the men in Dibrells regiment is usin 1812 flintlocks and most a them is missin the flint! I think Gen. Forrests resined to outfit this unit like he done his other commands, and thats takin them from the enemy in battle.

We also got in our brigade a fine battery of 6-pounder iron guns and a couple 12-pounder bronze howitzers under the command of Captain S.L. Freeman. One evenin last week I set down by the campfire next to a very youthful lutenant who introduced hisself as John Morton, just sent here by Gen. Bragg to command our artilery. This young fella (cant be twenty years old) reported with his orders to Gen. Forrest, and when Old Bedford seen this kid been asined to take charge of his artilery I guess he blowd his temper as he does some time. Morton said the general hollerd, "What the hell is Bragg doin. I dont need no tallow-face boy to deploy my artilery, I got a fine comander in Capt. Freeman." I herd the general was fixin to send Morton back to Gen. Bragg till his brother William Forrest convince him to let the lad have a chance. I explained to the sad-face lutenant that some times Old Bedford acts first and thinks things out second. Just from talkin to young John Morton I found this lad was in charge of the batterys at Ft. Donelson, been a yankee prisner, receve sevral wounds and is a veteran soldier now. I feel he will be a valuble member of this brigade and a ready friend to me.

Funny thing happend a while back. Know how I mention some of us receve packages from home, well a fella name Lester Marks from Co. B of the Alabama regiment got a box sent by his wife all the way from Huntsville, and in this box rapped tight as can be was three apple pies. Can you imagin them makin it all this way fresh and not crushed at all? Alot of the boys crowded round Lester tellin him to cut the pies up for all them. No shouts Lester, these here pies was made by his wife special for him and evry one else just stay back. That night he ate a whole pie by hisself and garded the others like a old miser. Later his belly starts achin so bad you could hear old Lester groanin all over camp, and he keep crawlin out his tent and run to the sinks. This went on for a goodly while and one time when he got back he bumped right into the head of a big old black bear settin in his tent eatin his pies. Well, Lester screamed and run one way and the bear run the other, the whole camp stirrin and Capt. Hayes yell at Lester he probly woke up the yanks in Nashville. The moral is he shoulda shared them pies.

As you no dout read in the papers Gen. Bragg lost his battle for the state of Kentucky at Perryville and his army is slow movin back into Tennessee bein followd by the federal army. There is a large unit of the blue army holdin Nashville at present, and two days ago Gen. Forrest decide it was time to test the ability of his new brigade under fire of the enemy. So on Nov. 4 Gen. Forrest spred the four regiments out, each approachin Nashville by diffrent roads from the south. Next morning fore dawn, each unit fired on enemy pickets and drove them to there outer fortifications near Dogtown, and the 4th Alabama boys under Col. Russell was engaged heavy and took some casultys. Capt. Freeman set his line of artilery and the gun boys hammerd at Nashvilles inner defenses. The Nashville garison had maybe 8000 yankees there and they was spredin out and movin into battle lines while we move in amongst

68

the trees and hedges gettin as close to there brestworks as posable. After four hours of firin, Gen. Forrest had the Tennessee regiments of Starnes and Dibrell pull back westward, where they met the enemy on the Franklin pike and made a good showin there. The general withdrawd slow all his command back to LaVergne. I do not know if there was some grand desine behind this demenstration against Nashville, but I feel Gen. Forrest was just assurin hisself that his officers and men was ready to fight and could obey his orders. We will see what the future brings.

Thats all I got for now and beleve me, it was a relefe hearin from you. Know that I am safe, as is Bobby and John, my love to all and a big kiss for Mary. I am as always

Your loving husband,
Henry

Chapter 5

December 25, 1862 through February 6, 1863

Dec. 25, 1862
Union City, Tenn.

Dearest Elizabeth (and Mary too),

Though I cannot be with thee on this most holy of all days, please know that my heart and soul is amongst you this moment, sharin the fixins and enjoyin the blesedness of this time. This is the second Christmas I am away from you and the lonliness in my heart is more painful at times then any gunshot wound the enemy can inflict. Know that if the Good Lord will it, I will be home with you some day.

In truth I aint had time for reverys as we been givin the yankees the most god-awful devil of a time the past ten days. Old Grant is sendin half his army of 100,000 men in search of us.

It started back on Dec. 10 when Gen. Bragg call Gen. Forrest to headquarters and tole him his next asinement was to take our command to west Tennessee (that whole area tween the Tennessee and Mississippi Rivers) and do evrything posable to make life misrable for them yankees who is spred acrost the whole region and fixin to take Vicksburg. Old Bedford complaned bad bout the shoddy firearms most the men got, but Gen. Bragg pay him no never mind and says there aint nothin he can do to remedy that.

On Dec. 13 Gen. Forrest led us to Clifton on the east bank of the Tennessee and had a crew a workmen make up a couple small flat-boats to haul our army of 2100 mounted men acrost the icy river. The Tennessee is one big river, make no mistake there, at least three-quarters mile wide and at that point a good four to six feet deep. We all packed up as many provisions as we could carry and on Dec. 15 we started loadin the flat-boats, only 25 or so horses and men at a time. We all took turns on the poles as the boats crost the river, and any time we seen a union gunboat crusin the water we would duck behind a small island near the east bank. I was ridin Maybelle at the time but my other horse Buster was along too, helpin to pull some of our seven guns, seein how big and powerful he is. It was slow goin, took the best part of two whole days, but Gen. Forrest thought it worth the while not makin the horses swim such a great distence in such cold water. He knowd we need them fit and healthy once on the enemys side of the river.

As soon as we was on the west side we sank the flat-boats near the bank so as we could bring them back up when it come time to ferry back over again. Gen. Forrest sent our group of scouts out on reconasance. This group a forty clever and hardy men is the eyes and ears of the brigade and led by Capt. Bill Forrest, who is maybe the only man on earth more fearless then the general hisself. These scouts is called "independents" cause they aint really part of our oficial brigade, but a little army unto therselves. The general knowd the yankees would be after us in great numbers and he wanted us to make a quick strike, do as much damage as posable in a short time, and hurry back acrost the river fore gettin trapped on the enemys side.

We spent a cold night in the rain on Dec. 17, and I was thinkin of home while there under my gum cloth — we dont carry tents when on the move. Couldnt even build no fires, it was so wet. Next morning after hearin from the scouts, Gen. Forrest ment busness and sent Col. Russells 4th Alabama to attack the union position at Beech Creek just outside Lexington and round up as many prisners and supplys as posable. At the same time he sent Col. Dibrells 8th Tennessee to confront the yankee garison holdin the railroad above Jackson. Gen. Forrest led the rest of us in a demonstration aganst the large force of federals occupyin Jackson itself and keep those troops tied up while Russell and Dibrell did there work.

Shortly after sunrise Gen. Forrest spred us all round the south side a Jackson and at a signal we stormed the outer defenses with a violent, screamin rush and you best beleve we woke up them yankee boys. There pickets hardly returnd fire as they scramble back toward the city and the main fortifications. Then we dismounted and took cover, me behind a handy boulder just big enough for one crouchin man to hide, and we engaged in a stedy fire fight for sevral hours.

This was plenty a time for Col. Russell and his regiment to vigerously attack the small garison at Beech Creek. They had some trouble crossin the creek under yankee fire as the yankees pulled the planking off the footbridge. Even while the enemy was firin down on them those hardy Alabama boys tore down a nearby fence and layed the bords acrost the stringers. Now they could charge over and up the hill, chasin the federals back to Lexington. This mad rush led up a slope where the yankees was firin two cannons as quick as they could load, and a squad a men made it there business to take them guns. The first man to the guns was Sgt. Kelly, a friend a mine and as brave a man as ever served, and he took a full blast a canister direct in the face – for him the war and fightin is over. The guns was soon took and when the enemy found they could not outrun the men on horseback they throwd down there guns and was captured. A goodly number of the fleein yanks did manage to run back to the defenses of Jackson, but Col. Russell and the Alabama boys round up 147 prisners, includin there commander, Col. Ingersoll, as well as 70 horses we need bad, a goodly amount of muskets to replace them old flintlocks, and best of all two 3-inch Rodman guns with amunition. The Alabama boys who number only bout 500, charged so furocius that the yankee colonel Ingersoll claim his Illinois boys musta been attacked by 5000 horsemen!

While we was holdin the major union force inside the defenses at Jackson, and Col. Russells boys was capturin prisners and guns at Beech Hill, Col. Dibrell and his Tennessee regiment quick over-run the garison holdin the railroad above Jackson. Over 100 yankees was took prisner, there fine Springfield rifles captured, along with there tents and supplys, and the railroad tracks was heated over bonfires and twisted beyond use.

We regrouped late at night on Dec. 19 at Spring Creek where we hid low in the ravine and could build some fires. We lost five men killed and a couple dozen more was hit by enemy fire durin the fight and Doc Cowen tend to them as best he could. We was all tired and dirty but right proud of our days work. Many the officers, me included, was writin out parole forms fast as we could so as to releve ourselvs of all the prisners. Most them yankee boys I delt with was just as plesant and polite as can be, and I was glad so many was captured and so few killed. I even seen the captured commander Col. Ingersoll engaged in a game a poker with Cols. Dibrell, Biffle, and Starnes, and there was quite some laughter comin from that tent – I guess even though theys the enemy, they can still be friends too.

Next morning, Dec. 20, Gen. Forrest had the brigade up early and was passin out the rifles we captured to those who need them most. I seen the general hisself strap on a fine new saber and had one of the boys sharpen it with a whetstone to a razors edge (against army regulations). Again the scouts, led by that daring man Bill Forrest, reported enemy movement to the general and he devised another three-prong attack to confound them. He orderd Col. Starnes and the 4th Tennessee to attack the govt. depot at Humbolt, orderd Col. Dibrell and the 8th Tennessee to take the garison at Forked Deer Creek and destroy the bridge, while the general would hisself lead the escort and Col. Biffles 9th Tennessee against the large body of union troops and supplys in Trenton. Col. Russell and the Alabama boys was orderd to protect the rear of our advancin colums as Gen. Forrest knowd yankees from all over was pursuin us.

Col. Starnes regiment sneaked up on the garison at Humboldt, no loud shoutin this time, and captured the whole shebang without firin a shot. They took 200 prisners, four caisons loaded with amunition and the horses, 500 rifles and all kinds of supplys. After they was loaded down they torched the depot and burned up the rest of the govt. stores.

Col. Dibrells regiment did not do so well takin Forked Deer Creek. They met heavy fire from the large garison there and after a two-hour brawl he pulled the boys back with few casultys but the bridge there still in tack.

At 3:00 in the afternoon Gen. Forrest, Col. Biffle and the rest of us surounded the south and west of Trenton and charged hard, screamin like wild Injuns. The yankee boys was spred out in all the buildings and warehouses bout town, firin on us from evry window and door. They unhorsed a number of us, includin Jake O'Reilly (the mess mate of your brother John) who took a bullit in the neck and was garglin blood as he died. It was a sorrowful sight. We quick pulled back to the outskirts of town, dismounted, and returnd fire on the buildings. Gen. Forrest called up Lt. John Morton to deploy his guns, includin our new captured Rodmans, and he started such a deadly poundin that bricks and mortar and lumber exploded from the buildings with each shot. In a half hour white flags was stuck out of all the hidin places. Yankees come streamin out of evrywhere with there hands raised. In all, we took 700 prisners (I started takin names and writin paroles before they all was surenderd), 20,000 rounds of artilery and hunderds of cases of small arms amunition. We carted off thousands of rations but had to destroy thousands more as well as burnin 600 bales of cotton, 200 barrels of pork, and hunderds of hogsheads full of tobacco that we just couldnt manage to carry off.

We was almost overburdend as we reunited that evenin outside Trenton. We spent hours parolin prisners, countin and handin out new muskets, packin provisions and tryin to get organized. Quite a haul in two days time.

Of course, Old Bedford wasnt satisfyed, nor would he set still even one day knowin we was bein chased from all directions. Next day, Dec. 21, we set out in the crisp mornin chill in a north direction, followin the railroad tracks through Rutherford to Kenton and Union City. All the while we was tearin up railroad track, burnin trestles, destroyin culverts, torchin depots, and engagin the enemy where ever we found him. At Union City we surounded the garison in three minutes and Gen. Forrest sent in his highly feared "unconditional surender or no quarter" letter, and they soon raise the white flag and surenderd there men and supplys.

From Union City on Dec. 22 we marched in to Kentucky and took the town a Moscow, reekin as much havoc as posable to the yankees. I must say Lizzie, in all these towns we was greeted by the citizens as conquerin heroes come to liberate them from the enemy. But the general would not let us stay long enough to enjoy any of there favors, and kept us on the move.

75

After takin Moscow, Ky. our far-spred scouts come back reportin that whole divisions of union troops was on the move after us. We musta been makin quite a stir for the yankee high command. Gen. Forrest decided we best start makin our way back southeast again as we traveled a good 120 miles since crossin the Tennessee River.

So here we are, on Christmas day, outside Union City again. We been fightin hard, workin hard, and ridin hard but got lots to eat, the horses got grain, plenty a warm blankets and some of the boys is imbibin in some captured spirits. Maybe I will trust myself to a toast in your honor. Afterward I best get some rest cause we still have to make our way to the Tennessee and get acrost. Your brothers is fine, dont seem near as homesick as myself, and remember me on this special day to be

Your loving husband,
Henry

January 2, 1863
Mount Pleasant, Tenn.

Dearest Elizabeth,

After two weeks of furius fightin, ridin and exitement, we are back on the east side of the Tennesee River and able to rest. I am very sore in my left shoulder and neck but otherwise healthy but I do have some sad news to tell you. I cannot spend much time writin this acount cause Mr. Matthew Gallaway, our mail courier, is leavin for town shortly. Mr. Gallaway is a civilian reporter for the Memphis Avalanche, who often rides with Gen. Forrest and reports our doings.

My last letter of Christmas Day tole how we was stormin through West Tennessee attackin the enemy, capturin stores, twistin railroad track, and generly makin life a misery for the yankees. After reachin as far as Moscow, Ky., Gen. Forrest decided we best make haste back southeast to our crossin point on the Tennessee.

On the day after Christmas the freezin rains started pourin, makin us cold and misrable, and on Dec. 28 we had to cross the swollen Obion River, and the only means to do so was a rickety old bridge that needed lots a repair. No one much felt up to the work, but Gen. Forrest hisself grabbed a axe and starts choppin trees with vigor. His example give us new energy and fore long we got the old bridge shored up and Old Bedford got up on the seat and drove the first of our many captured wagons over the bridge. It was rough goin, and though he made it fine, sevral others manage to slide off the edge and get mired in the swamps. Then there was nothin else to do but hitch up 25 men to a wagon and at least 50 to a gun and pull them through the muck by main force. We throwd logs and chunks into the deep mud holes, and even some times flour sacks and cases of coffee just to get the rigs over. We was tired, wet and filthy, but we got all men, horses, caisons, guns and storage wagons acrost.

By Dec. 30 we was past McLemoresville and headin toward Lexington, Tenn, only forty mile from the Tennessee River, when Capt. Bill Forrest and the scouts reported a large body a union troops just in advance of our position, and sevral others closin on our rear. Gen. Forrest quick decides we must attack and defete the enemy in our front cause if we tryed to evade them, they would no dout catch up to us durin the slow river crossin and destroy us while in transport.

Early on the morning of Dec. 31 a light snow fallin in our faces, Gen. Forrest deploys our guns on a slope and spred us in a battle line where two roads met called Parkers Crossroads. He dismounted most of Dibrells men who was to make a charge up the center on foot, while Starnes and Russels regiments was to stay mounted and sweep round the right and left sides of the compact union brigade, and as Old Bedford was wont to say, "Hit em hard on the end."

At 9:00 the bugle sounded and the feared "rebel yell" was sounded in each our throats. The charge was on – this is the fifteen minutes of "bulge" that Gen. Forrest lived for – and as so often happens the most advanced men in blue instently pulled back in fear for there life. Our line kept pushin forward, men runnin from tree to tree, from stump to stump, slowly movin the federals back though at times we was only fifty feet seperated. This slow drive last for hours as the union men fell back to better defenses. At one time Col. Napier of Dibrells regiment advanced his squad of Tennessee boys dangerous close to the enemy lines and they was fired upon by well hid federals and cut down horible like a sythe through grass, evry man in the squad dead on the field or writhin in pain. Col. Napiers body had ten bullit holes.

Many yankees holed up in a strong position behind a thick cedar fence and seemed well protected while firin on us, but the big guns of Capt. Freeman and Lt. John Morton was fired so accurit that shot after shot smash into the fence blastin wood fragments like missles in all directions. Finaly the regiments of Starnes and Russell got into the action, and this sudden onslaut from all directions was too much for the enemy, and soon flags of truce was raised and Gen. Forrest was preparin to send in his fearsom "Surrender or else" message.

And then something happend to us, Lizzie, that never happend before and pray to God never happens again. Completly unbenownst by us, another enemy brigade come stormin upon us from directly in our rear, squeezin us betwixt two enemy forces both equal or bigger then ours, and firin like mad.

I do not think there is another officer on either side who wouldnt surender his whole command at that time. Certain capture or useless loss of life seem the only answers. But Gen. Forrest, seein that Cols. Starnes and Russell very wisely resumed there attack on the forward enemy, screams orders for evry one else to gallup there horses tween the enemy lines down the highroad toward Lexington. But the general seen that the enemys in our rear would be upon us too quick for the men and guns to get out. So he gathers us in his escort all together and led us hisself in a wild charge into the faces of the quick arrivin federals, with the purpose of stallin them long enough to let our army escape. Though I was mad in exitment, I seen waves a blue soldiers rushin on foot right at us. They was only a hunderd yards off and Gen. Forrest, his face dark red and eyes crazed with a demons fury, charged into there midst slashin with incredable violance his giant saber.

And then it happend, as I spurred Maybelle and raised my saber to meet the enemy, a bullit slam direct into her left eye and she crashed to the ground. I musta been sensless for a moment as the horible clamor of shots and screams went silent. Then in a instant the noise resumed, I shaked my confused head, and layin flat on my face looked back at the huge lifeless form a Maybelle, her limbs and ears twitchin in her death spasm. I had no time for pity though, as bullits was whizzin by my ear, kickin up dust all round me, and thuddin into Maybelles body. On my hands and knees I scrambled for my carbine, whirled round on one knee and fired a shot into the enemy line. Our fearless attack halted there advance and lookin left I seen most of our brigade escapin down the road.

Now the men of the escort pulled back, still firin pistols, and spurred there horses down to the open road. I was still dazed in the head, but thought to start runnin and did, but of a sudden the commandin voice of Gen. Forrest at my side says, "Wylie get up here!" As I looked up, my shoulder was grasped by a strong hand and I was lifted with little effort behind his saddle. He spurred his giant mount and with me holdin on for dear life we run through the closin gap of blue soldiers, while bullits and shouts was fired at us from both directions. But we raced to safety.

What happend at Parkers Crossroads was a shame, and the dismounted men of Dibrells regiment was mostly captured as there horses fled in panic with the suprize attack, and three of our guns was took. But that 1500 of us should escape to safety, as well as most our artilery and a lot of the wagons, is truly amazin. Gen. Forrest is a man who dont accept surender and now I owe him personly for my freedom and probly my life.

The next day we raced 36 miles to the place of our Tennessee River crossin, only stoppin once to feed men and horses and tend to the injurd. I was lucky to receve only some bruses and am fortunate that Capt. Freeman give me my other horse Buster, who was helpin pull artilery. Buster is a fine quarterhorse who obeys me real good, but I will never forget my poor Maybelle who always made me feel the farmhouse of my youth was over the next hill. I will surely miss her.

A company led by Maj. Jeffrey Forrest got to the Tennessee in advance of the rest of us, and hauled up the sunk flat boats and even made a few smaller rafts to haul men acrost. Our brigade arrived soon after and by dark we was loadin up the boats. Gen. Forrest sent the guns over first, orderin they be set up for protection on the east bank. This time the horses was made to swim acrost, as men on the boats pulled the reluctent animals by the reins. The crossin took only ten hours, and after a brief rest we rode here to Mount Pleasant to regroup and rest.

In spite of what happend at Parkers Crossroads, the two weeks we spent raidin West Tennessee was a huge success. We rode over 300 miles, mostly on roads made unpasable by rain. We engaged the enemy evry day and three times fought pitched battles. We captured and paroled more then 1500 prisners as well as four colonels. We took five guns (though we lost three of them at Parkers) and a dozen caisons loaded with amunition, and best of all armed our entire brigade with fine Springfield rifles to replace the shotguns and flintlocks. Along the way we destroyd 80 miles of railroad — many times makin a huge fire of piled ties and layin the rails over it till they bend and twist beyond repare. We burnd evry bridge we come to, destroyd trestles and culverts, cut miles of telegraph wire, torched depots, and sent tons and tons of yankee supplys up in smoke. Plus we caused Grant to brake up his army in pursute of us. It was truly a hard-earn but satisfyin acomplishment.

I see Mr. Gallaway collectin letters so I best post this. I hope letters from home can find us here too. With a hello from your brothers, and a big kiss for Mary, remember me to be

Your loving husband,
Henry

Jan. 23, 1863
Columbia, Tenn.

Dear Elizabeth,

So nice to receve your letters and those of Ma too. It was a comfort readin that you, Mary and your parents made the long buggy ride in the cold to the farm for Christmas. I am releved to know that squad a yankees was kindly to you and left you all to procede on your journy. Tell Pa to keep what geese he got left hid as much as posable, or I can asure you the yankees will clean evry critter from the pond if they get there. Roast goose and all the fixins sounds good to me, but I am sure that you all felt a bit sad and lonsome seein how your marryed sisters is so far off in St. Louis and New Orleans and your brothers here servin with me. But the cosy fire and little Mary runnin round must have cheerd the place up. When you was preparin for bed in my old room, the room that seen me grow from a infant to a boy to a man, had you but looked under the bed you mighta seen in the slats the old wood sword I made as a youth and carryed at my side on many adventures – slayin dragons and vanquishin pirates. I little thought I would be doin it for real.

We been here in Columbia the best part of a month, healin wounds and restin man and beast. My shoulder and neck is a lot less stiff after my fall from poor Maybelle and I am quite in good health, though a lot of the men cough and many got the runs. Cant hardly sleep at night for all the coughin.

This war is a strange thing. Us tryin to kill all the yankees and them tryin to kill all us. Last week I went on a little scoutin foray as we herd there was yankees not far off. We was just six – me and your two brothers, Bobbys friend Willie Forrest, my mess mate Lt. John Markbright, and my friend Lt. John Morton, the young artilery man who is provin to Gen. Forrest how expert he is with the big guns. We rode for hours along windin paths and gravel roads, in dense woods and acrost wide meadows. I must admit to losin my direction many a time, but Markbright always knowd where we was at – he got a kinda sixth sense when it come to directions.

It was cold and crisp out, the horses breath steamin in smoky puffs from there nostrels as we walk, but the sun was bright and the sky without a single cloud, and we was very comfitable under our caped overcoats.

We was ridin in a colum of two, me and Markbright jawin quiet side by side, followd by Morton and your brother John (them two get along nice) and behind by a little distence was Bobby and Willie. We could hear them two a laughin and carryin on like school boys, and so often me or Markbright would hush them up as we was scoutin for yankees and not on a picnic.

As we rode along, Morton says, "You know Henry, Old Bedford is one smart soldier, but I dont think he is real familier with artilery use yet."

"Hows that" asks me.

"Well, you know a few weeks back at Parkers Crossroads" says Morton, "the general had us spred our guns on the slope and start firin at the enemy lines. Well the enemy was returnin fire and tryin hard to take out our battery."

"Yeah, what of it" I ask him.

"Well, Pvt. Douglass was runnin the limber and amunition chest behind the line out of range, as is ordinary proceedur" says Morton, "when Gen. Forrest all red in a rage come flyin up to Douglass, whip him on his back with the broadside of his saber, and hollers in Douglass face — Turn those damn horses round and get back where you belong or by God I will kill you! Douglass says to him he aint runnin away, just haulin the amunition outa enemy range, and the general yells back at him — No you aint, I know how to fight and you cant run off with our amunition chest."

"Ill be damned" says I. "What happend?"

"Well" says Morton, "Douglass tole me all this later, and after we was safe acrost the river I took my artilery manual to Gen. Forrest and showd him how it was nesesary for the horses to move off outa range, and I offerd to give him a exibition drill so he could see the reasons for it."

"And then?" asks Markbright.

"He was much intrested" says Morton, "and took my manual and I seen him readin it many times the next week or so. And Douglass come to me some time later and says the general apoligized to him personal for givin him what for durin the heat a battle."

As this conversation was goin on we rounded a sharp curve on the road and we suddenly come face to face with another small band of eight horsemen, and they was all in blue. We all put our hands on our pistols and they done just the same, but no one yet drawd them out.

"Howdy do fellas," says a older man with two stripes on each side of his shoulder strap, "awful nice day aint it?"

"Yes indeed, Captain" replys Markbright.

Evry man in this little group was very tense and still squeezin there pistols, some now half drawd.

"We dont want to make a lot a noise and disturb the peace on this beutiful day, do we boys?" says the yankee captain.

82

"Not us" says Markbright glancin back at us, "we wont start nothin if you dont."

I notice three or four of the yankees instently let go there weapons and relax there spines. Then the horses walk forward and we was all intermixed and side by side.

"Thems some fancy rifles" says your brother John to a young yankee soldier.

"Its a Henry repeatin carbine" says the youth, unslingin the gun and showin it to John.

Then next you know we was all comparin firearms, showin our sabers, checkin each others canteens, ridin boots, saddles and evry other thing. There was a good bit a laughin and some gentle ribbin, and the captain offerd a cigar to us, and Markbright trade one of his cigars for one of the captains.

"What outfit you boys from?" asks the captain.

"Come on Captain, you aint goin to get nothin from us" says Morton, and we all had a good laugh at that.

Willie and Bobby was conversin with a lad in blue who says he was a drummer and fourteen years old. I think they was suprized to find that the enemy could be even younger then therselvs. For maybe fifteen or twenty minutes we exchange plesantrys and hardtack, then the captain says they must head back fore dark comes, and us too, so we swing our horses round and head in oppisit directions. And we was all thinkin the same thing. If we should meet these nice fellas again, it will be with us tryin to kill them and them tryin to kill us. As I say Lizzie, this is a strange war.

I know Mary must be growin fast and how I miss bein able to see her in her new frock. I pray to the lord at night some times Lizzie, that one of them yankee bullits dont find me fore I see Mary in her new frock. With all my love,

Your loving husband,
Henry

Feb. 6, 1863
Columbia, Tenn.

Dear Elizabeth,

Here I set by a cracklin fire, close as I can till my front side gets so hot I got to turn round. Soon then my hands start gettin too numb to write as it is bitter cold out here and no place to hide. I cant hardly see my own writin on the paper as the fire provides the only light for me, but I will do my best.

We are here in Columbia where we spent most the month of January, but we did have some action. Gen. Forrest was gone some place earlier this week, and his commandin officer Gen. Joe Wheeler, who is the head of all cavalry out west, orderd us to pack up quick and head north with the mission of disruptin union gunboats on the Cumberland River not far from old Ft. Donelson. We hardly got time to pack amunition and rations fore we set out. We was joind shortly by Col. Wharton and his brigade.

Couple days later Old Bedford catches up to us, and as he always does, made a close personal inspection. He hisself checks out damn near evrything – the horses shoes, the condition of our arms, the artilery and our rations. I could see in his fiery blue eyes that he was not happy that most men took off with only bout twenty rounds of amunition and I hear him cussin bout the big guns not havin full caisons. We would never took off in this sorry condition if he been there.

Couple days later we got to the outskerts of Dover where the yankees was holed up behind strong fortifications. Gen. Wheeler orders Gen. Forrest with our regiment to circle round the right of the union line, and Col. Wharton to take his regiment round the left of the fortifications and prepare for asault. Lt. John Markbright and me was near Gen. Forrest and he look at us and says "This aint right boys. I protested this attack but got no where. We will do our duty and fight like men but this asault aint right." It was clear he didnt like the way we was situated for battle.

The charge on the yankee stronghold was not a united effort like it was suposed to be, but was piece meal like. Gen. Forrest seen what he thought was a weak spot in the enemy line, and had us burst from the woods and charge the east outskerts of Dover. We was met by very heavy fire from the union boys hid good in

84

redouts and behind breastworks. Many of us was unhorsed in a few minutes, includin Gen. Forrest whose horse was shot dead. The general lay still under the fallen horse, and we all thought our leader been killed and many a man retreated in fear to the woods. But soon Gen. Forrest untangled hisself from the beast and calls a halt to the charge and we run off to the woods, the general still on foot.

After regroupin and lettin our artilery take a turn, the general orderd bout 200 men to dismount and get into formation for another asault. Us officers was to remain mounted. Again the bugle sounded and the men poured forth at the yankee line screamin murder. The fire was very hot but we kept pushin closer to the enemy. They was firin double-canister from there cannons and I seen one of our boys take the full effect of a double shot square in the chest. I swear his whole body burst into a thousand tiny fragments.

We was takin a bloody lickin no dout, and just as Gen. Forrest orderd us to withdraw, for the second time today his horse takes a hit and fell dead on top of him. Maj. Anderson and me rush to pull him out from under the huge beast and we could see he was shook pretty bad. But under his own strength he mounted a riderless horse and rode off after our retreatin army. The firin slowed down, and as I started to remount Buster I noticed something shiny by the generals dead horse. I reached down and pick up a gold locket that musta belonged to the general though I never seen it before. Inside the locket was a ivory siloett of a woman. I shoved it in my pocket, got on Buster and spurd back to safety. Our whole force then moved back southward.

This day was a disaster. We gaind nothing and lost almost 200 boys dead or captured. As we sat round the fires in the freezin night air, depresed and wore out, I felt the locket in my shirt. I set out right then to find Gen. Forrest who was restin at a nearby farmhouse.

I was guided to the little cabin and met at the door by a couple officers who let me by when I tole them I had to see Gen. Forrest. I nocked on the door and sure nough Gen. Forrest hisself, lookin very tired, opens it and says real quiet "Sgt. Wylie, what brings you here?"

Holdin the locket up I says "I found this on the field by your dead horse, sir."

He put his hand to his neck as if just realizin the locket was gone, and says "My God, I wouldnt lose that for anything." He took it from my hand, opend it and stared at it, his eyes soft. "My mother. The siloett is my mother, Wylie. Thank you so much. Come in here, sargent, warm yourself by the fire."

I thanked him and followd him into a back room. He limped very bad on one leg and held his left shoulder up unatural. "Hurt bad in the fall, General?"

"Just shook up, Wylie. Twict, you know, today."

He come to the back room where a nice fire was blazin in the fireplace, and I was more then a bit unnerved when I find the only other men in the room was Gen. Wheeler and Col. Wharton. Gen. Forrest introduced me to both and I was suprized how small and young Gen. Joe Wheeler was. He could be but 25 or 26 years old, no more than 5'4", already climbed high in the service and known far and wide as a most bold and inteligent leader.

"Sit down and warm yourself Wylie," says Gen. Forrest, who showd sines of pain as he layed down slow on his back and place his boots up on the harth.

Gen. Wheeler looked to be writin a report of the days battle and says out loud "It seemed to be a uncoordenated, poorly timed attack."

Gen. Forrest snaps his head at his commandin officer and says "Gen. Wheeler, I advised against this attack and said all a subordinate officer could say against it, and nothin you can now say or do will bring back my brave men layin dead, or them wounded and freezin round that fort tonight. You can have my sword if you demand it, but there is one thing I do want you to put in that report to Gen. Bragg — tell him that I will be in my coffin before I will fight again under your command."

I sat like a statue there, froze, wonderin what this young general would say to such a tongue lashin by his inferior officer. "No, Gen. Forrest," he says quiet, "I can not take your saber, and I regret exeedingly your determenation. As commandin officer I take all the blame and responsability for this failure."

There was silence in the room and soon I notice Gen. Forrest was asleep there on the floor. I excused myself quiet and returnd to camp.

So here we are Lizzie, regroupin again and waitin for our next asinement. Got to go as my hands are freezin and most good men are turnd in. Give Mary my love and remember me to be,

Your loving husband,
Henry

Chapter 6

March 7, 1863 through May 5, 1863

March 7, 1863
Spring Hill, Tenn.

Dear Elizabeth,

Hope you and Mary are holdin up well, as I myself am alive and healthy. I aint got much time to write but I want to inform you of my where-abouts since I aint wrote in a month.

After our disaster at Dover where we was licked darn good, we was all fixin for a chance to redeem our pride. Gen. Forrest had us drillin extra hard each day and we was outfited good. All through Febuary we was playin hide and seek with the yankees, who was gatherd round Nashville after there bloody stalemate with Braggs army at Murfreesboro.

Gen. Forrest and our brigade of 1500 men was asined temporary to the large cavalry division of Gen. Earl Van Dorn (we no longer serve under Gen. Wheeler). Van Dorn was on the track of a large passel of yankee infantry.

Finaly on March 4 we closed in on a yankee division holed up at Thompsons Station, and that night the two camps was so close I could see the shapes of yankee soldiers settin round there campfires.

Next morning Gen. Van Dorn spred his division wide and thin formin a half circle round the little town, and our brigade was on the far right of the line. Bout 10:00 in the morning the firin started along the whole line and was returnd prompt by the union forces crouchin behind a long stone wall. Gen. Forrest seen none of our forces was makin progress, so he orders Capt. Freeman to haul his four heavy guns up a hillside far to the right and way in advance of the rest of us. When them big guns started blastin the enemy line on the left flank, many of the yankees was blowd to bits and many fell back in confusion.

While this was goin on I seen something I could never imagen. Off on the left of our position, a Arkansas regiment was havin a very rough go against a stubbern bunch of men in blue. One side would charge, get hurld back, then the other would try with the same results. I seen the color-bearer of the Arkansas regiment get shot down, try to stand and raise his banner, and get hit again. The flag was layin on the ground when of a sudden a young girl in a dress, probly in her teens, runs from a house just back aways and grabs the banner and runs toward the enemy line wavin the flag for the men to rally round. The men was crowdin to the flag when I had to leave that spot and join a charge on our front. I never found out what become of that brave lass.

Gen. Forrest had moved our brigade far on the enemys flank and pert near in there rear when he spurd his favrite mount Roderick and led us in one of his fearsom charges. We smashed through a stand of cedar trees and right into the enemy. As we was a good thousand men strong and the yanks was took by suprize, most of them throwd down there guns and surenderd. The whole union line saw how hopeless more fightin was as we raced through there ranks, and we captured a good 1200 of them plus all there officers. It was a total victory. But unfortunatly Capt. Montgomery Little, the man who the general had recrute, organize and lead his escort, was killed on the battlefield. He was the right arm of the general and kinda like a father to the rest of us. Gone now forever.

Your brother Bobby tole me somthing of intrest after the fight was over. As we engaged the enemy durin that last mad dash, Gen. Forrest out front as always, was gettin shot at from all sides and his horse Roderick was hit sevral times and bleedin in many places and growin weak. The general jumps from his horse, grabs the mount of his son Willie, and tells him and Bobby to ride to the rear leadin Roderick back to safety. (I think the general had more in mind here then savin his favrite horse by sendin those young boys to the rear.) Anyways, Willie and Bobby haul Roderick off behind the range of fire and procede to remove his saddle and bridle. Roderick, who I often seen followin the general bout camp just like a pet dog, never wore a halter, never needed to. As soon as the gear was off him, even though bleedin bad, the horse prick up his ears at the sound of battle still ragin in the distence. He broke loose from the boys and tore away acrost the fields, jumpin fences and logs strait for his master. With the boys in pursute the horse run through the battlefield and just seen his master when another bullit smashes through his head and the loyal beast drop dead on the field.

This victory at Thompsons Station redemed our reputation as the best fighters in the Confederacy. Even the boys in the infantry, who always look on cavalry as dandys who get the glory without doin the fightin, respect Forrests mounted men. Now we are roamin loose again and ready to find more yankees, so I best finish and give this letter to Mr. Gallaway to post. I hope the good Lord finds my two angels well, and remember me to be,

Your loving husband,
Henry

March 8, 1863
Spring Hill, Tenn.

Dear Lizzie,

I just got to add a little to the letter from last night as I got some good news. After I got done writin you I set by the fire for a while with my friend and tent-mate Lt. John Markbright. I already tole you, but the Markbrights is Memphis folks too, and his pa is a lawyer and John was practicin to be a lawyer fore the war broke out and he sined up. He is marryed and got two little ones so we got a lot in common and spend a good deal a time talkin just bout evrything – horses, guns, our family, religion, whatever come to mind.

Anyways, we was settin there jawin when Gen. Forrest hisself come walkin up from the darkness, pulls up a stump and sets down.

"You know boys," says the general in the slow, quiet way he talks when he aint near a battlefield. "Now that Capt. Little is gone I will need you two to step forward and take his place."

"How so General?" we ask.

"Well, Markbright, your father done some law work for my bisness back home, and I know your good with letters too. And just like at Murfreesboro, when you boys was near at hand to take my surender message to the enemy, I will be needin you for that kinda detail from now on. And Wylie, I want you to keep bein the brave soldier you are, leadin the escort and showin the courage the rest of the men need to see. I need you two, and the rest of my officers, to be the leaders of the escort and brigade."

"We certenly will try General, to serve you right."

"Thank you Markbright, you are now a captain of the escort, and Wylie, you are second lutenant."

"Thank you sir, I wont let you down."

And that was that. Aint that a honor for the general to single us out special? I can see him needin Markbright bad, he got a gift with words and a fearless fighter. But me, I just follow orders and do my best.

Well, thought you might be intrested to hear that I am changin my sargents stripes for a collar stripe. Think your brothers will call me "sir" now? I miss you and Mary, and I am,

Your loving husband,
Lt. Henry Wylie

April 12, 1863
Spring Hill, Tenn.

Dear Elizabeth,

How are you all doin back home? I hope this letter finds you healthy and safe, and that your not suffrin from the shortages of food and other stuff that many of the south is suffrin. Please give Mary a big kiss for me and explane to her as best you can why her daddy was not there for her on her 3rd birthday. I was with her in spirit that day and I get very sad thinkin of her growin day by day and me unable to share in the fun. That is what war means — lonliness, hardship, suffrin.

We been chasin, dodgin and rasslin the enemy for the last month or so in the area strechin forty miles from Columbia to Nashville. After the big fight at Murfreesboro (back in January) Gen. Braggs army marched to Tullahoma and is still there, while the big union army they fought is still spred round Nashville. Now Gen. Forrest and our brigade is free to roam independent in the area twixt them. We are always lookin for enemy supplys to capture, or bustin there telegraph lines and disruptin rail trafic.

On the morning of March 25th Gen. Forrest led our brigade to the town of Brentwood where our scouts reported bout 500 yankees gardin the govt. stores, and another 300 garisoned at the railroad bridge over the Harpeth a mile away. We had to make our way to Brentwood careful as it is twixt the towns of Franklin to the south and Nashville to the north where large union forces was camped.

Gen. Forrest orderd Col. Starnes to take his Tennessee regiment round the east a town while the general led the rest of us round to the west. Fore the yankees could even deploy we was surroundin the garison there and Gen. Forrest put all our guns in plain site to be seen. From the yankee point of view in town we musta look like a division of 10,000 men, which of course is just what Old Bedford wants the enemy to think, even though we was less than a thousand.

Then Gen. Forrest calls me and Markbright to his side and says "Capt. Markbright, take in a flag of truce and tell them I have them completly surounded, and if they dont surender I will blow the hell out of them in five minutes and wont take one of them alive if I have to sacrafice my men in stormin there stockade."

Beleve it or not I had great dificulty findin a white hankerchief. The boys had blue ones, red ones, spotted ones, but no one carrys a plain white one as if posession of such was a sine of cowardace. I did find one at last (one of the nigra teamsters had it) and put it on the end of my saber.

Markbright and me then aproached the enemy redouts and stockades, many of those men in blue not lookin kindly at us, and was met by a yankee major. He led us to a Colonel Bloodgood who treated us polite and asks quiet, "Do you realy have so many men?"

"Indeed we do sir," says Markbright "and strongly urge you do as Gen. Forrest sugests to prevent needless efusion of blood."

They surenderd, the whole garison of 500 men without firin a shot. The prisners was quick rounded up, stores and equipment loaded on captured wagons, and the whole outfit herded on the Hillsborough Pike headin south.

As soon as this was done Gen. Forrest had us spur our horses toward the garison holdin the railroad bridge and depot over the Harpeth. As this was a small, compact stockade we had it surounded inside of fifteen minutes, and Gen. Forrest had Capt. Freeman fire a shot from one of his guns as a warning, and again called on me and Markbright to deliver his message under a flag of truce.

"Damn, General" says I, "I lost my hankerchief."

"Use your shirt Wylie," says the general, a grin on his face.

So sure nough I pull off the linen shirt I wear under my uniform, and though it was none too clean, I hung it on my saber and we rode toward the enemys stockade. Again a meeting took place and after only a few questions as to our strength the command surenderd.

In a matter of hours we captured 800 men and all there arms and amunition as well as sixteen wagons loaded with food and supplys, a number a mules and horses, plus a whole lot a camp stores – tents, blankets, pots and pans. But we almost lost it all as the fightin wasnt done yet.

As this train of wagons, prisners and men was headin in a long line down the pike, the rest of our colum was suprise attacked in the rear by a goodly force of union cavalry and the slowest and least hardy of our men stampeded in panic. and fear. This caused mass confusion as one squad after another was caught up in the frenzy and it seem we was bout to be over run.

But when Gen. Forrest in front of the colum herd what was happenin in the rear, he took the escort and a few companys of scrappy souls and raced back. We soon come upon a mass of our own men ridin hard up the pike, screamin they was bout to be routed. Gen. Forrest grabs a double barrel shotgun, levels and fires direct into the faces of the men runnin out a control. Sevral was knocked off there horse, and the rest stop dead in there tracks. With this Gen. Forrest yells "Charge boys, charge" and led all of us in a mad dash strait at the enemy. The pursuin yankees, wavin sabers and shoutin, took a look at us chargin the opposit way right at them, turnd and fled as fast as hoofs could carry them. We did not want to chase them far anyways, as we had to tend to the many prisners and move the wagons. But Brentwood was another big victory for our hard-fightin brigade.

We rode back into Spring Hill and now we been goin off scoutin and foragin for food. Hope them yankees holdin Memphis aint causin you and your folks no trouble, for some of them people can be down right mean.

We found this out a couple days ago when we made a expedition against the large union force at Franklin. The town is defended heavy by maybe 10,000 blue soldiers and us havin only a thousand or so wanted to give them a little scare. Gen. Forrest spred us out round the town pretty good, kept us on horseback for a quick getaway, and orderd us to commence firin. We suprized them nice and drove there pickets back and had the whole camp of yankees buzzin like a overturnd beehive. The fight was on.

Capt. Freeman was bout ready to unleash his six guns when he was attacked on the flank without warning by a group of enemy horsemen. In minutes the yankees swept through the battery capturin all our guns and bout fifty of our artilery men. Word got back to the front in a hurry bout this sorry state, and Col. Starnes got a company or two of Tennessee boys to race back and reverse that situation. When the yankee troopers seen all them rebels roarin at them, they dropped all our cannons they just captured and tryed only to hurry there prisners behind the yankee lines. The mounted enemy drawd there pistols and says they would shoot any prisner not movin double-quick to the yankee side.

As we was tole later, poor Capt. Freeman, bein older and less fit then the other men, fell behind some. A mean-spirited yankee hollerd at him to go faster, and when Capt. Freeman protested he could go no faster, he was shot down in cold blood.

A short while later when Gen. Forrest arrived on the scene, I seen him neel by the side of Capt. Freeman, grasp his lifeless hand, tears rollin down his cheeks and say "Brave man, none braver." That is the most moved I ever seen the general and could read by the look in his eye that if we ever meet the union 4th Cavalry again, they best beware. And Capt. Freeman was truly a brave man. When all the rest the artilery commanders set there guns way behind the lines, old Capt. Freeman would rush them to the very front, just as far as his commandin general would let him. We will all surely miss him. Now my friend John Morton, who Old Bedford once called a schoolboy and tryed to send back, has been made commander of our batterys and will try to fill the big brogans left by Capt. Freeman.

Here we are in Spring Hill, just a few miles away from Chapel Hill where Nathan Bedford Forrest was born 41 years ago, and I can tell you this beutiful country of rolling hills, wide farms and pastures, numerus rivers and creeks, can have no better defender then her native son.

Give my best regards to your folks, Ma and Pa and especialy Mary, and remember me to be,

Your loving husband,
Henry

May 4, 1863
Rome, Ga.

Dear Elizabeth,

I am finaly able to write you. I must tell you that the last ten days been the most intense since I been in the service. I am just woke up after ten hours sleep, which is more I think then I got the whole week combind. I am fine and unhurt (so is your brothers) exept in the area where a man meets the saddle, which is so sore I might not walk normal for days.

On April 23 Gen. Forrest was orderd by Gen. Bragg to take his brigade (we was bout 1200 strong then) from Spring Hill, head south and cross the Tennessee River into north Alabama, cause there was reported a goodly body of mounted and well-equiped union men cuttin a swath on a raid acrost north Alabama headin toward Georgia. We knowd ourselvs how much destruction a raidin party can do, so we was off fast and on April 26 the whole brigade was ferryed acrost the Tennessee to Alabama. Next day we rode hard eastward, through Tower Creek to Courtland and almost to Tuscumbia. It been rainin pretty stedy for days and the dusty roads turnd to mud and the goin was tough. The roads was narrow and hilly, people pretty sparse in this country, and some times we would be in dense pine forests but would come upon large fields of

96

sand and scrubby brush. But we stayed in the saddle all day and most the night, goin at least 90 miles in a day and a half. We hardly took one hour outa ten to stop and rest, unsaddle our sore-back horses and feed them what shelled corn we could carry. A man couldnt hardly releve hisself fore he was orderd back in the saddle. I can not tell you Lizzie, how lucky I am to be mounted on my powerful quarterhorse Buster, who dont never seem to tire and require very little water or forage to keep movin. I think he might be part camel. As we rode hour after hour our colum streched out sevral miles as the slower horses and less fit men fell behind. But the escort company pretty much was always in the lead.

On April 28 we had a brisk encounter with union infantry who we swept aside, and learnt from captured yankees that we was on the track of the union raidin party. We learnt they was 2000 strong, mounted on mules for better endurence, and led by a Col. Abel Streight. There mission was to ride to Rome, Ga., destroyin all our govt. supplys and arsenels along the way. Our scouts, led by the untirin Bill Forrest, reported we was but sixteen miles behind the rear of Streights colum.

That Tuesday evenin of the 28th we prepard for the chase of our life. As he always do fore a time of crisis, Gen. Forrest hisself inspected each man and horse for soundness. The portable forges was fired up and the farriers shod any horse that needed it. Amunition was past round and checked for quality. Rifles and side arms was cleaned and readyed. Rations for three days was cooked and saddle bags stuffed with shelled corn for the horses. Supplys and gear of evry sort was gone over, with Gen. Forrest hisself watchin evry move all the time makin what ever plans he might need. As always he payed special atention to the big guns for he liked them best. Many a time the general would sit and talk amongst the artilery boys, askin questions and inspectin the guns. Finaly when all the preperations met his aproval, at 1:00 AM of April 29th Gen. Forrest shouts "Lets move on up," and the whole brigade in spite the pich dark rode out in haste.

What a ride it was. We rode all night long and did not stop for rest or food till 11:00 next day, and that was for but a hour. Then back in the saddle, my legs and back achin like evry one else, and though it was stedy drizzlin and the roads sloppy, we kept up a goodly pace. By late in the afternoon I seen men sleepin as they set in the saddle, and more then a few fell right off there horse. Many the mounts was throwin shoes and comin up lame. A couple times I seen horses just wander off in there own direction as the rider was so asleep he payed no nevermind. One fellas horse drifted off to the woods and nocks him clean off on a low hangin branch. Another mans horse just decide to lay down from exaustion, and no amount of pullin or proddin could get it up. Long bout supper time the general calls a halt again for only a hour or so, just long enough to take the saddles off the tired brutes and grab a quick bite to eat. I just let Buster graze a bit on the scrubby brush while I layed flat on a rock, the small of my back achin worse then I ever rememberd. As I layed there like evry one else, more tired and sore then any time in my life, I look over and seen your brother Bobby standin high on a big rock tossin a apple back and forth to Willie Forrest who was standin on another big rock a ways off, tryin not to pull each other off the rock with there throws. I thought where on earth do them kids get there energy. We was soon stirred up and back in the saddle, spurrin the horses due eastward.

After trekin another five or six hours and night time all round us, Gen. Forrest finaly calls halt just fore midnight. We been in the saddle for the past 23 hours, stoppin only twict for a brief spell. Us on good horses musta coverd more then 70 miles, but the brigade was now spred over many a mile as both man and horse been tested to the fullest, and a goodly portion was way behind. Though it was still rainin off and on, that didnt keep no one awake. Evry one just pulled there rain gear over there head and fell asleep. Bill Forrest and some of his remarkable scouts was even further ahead of our lead companys, and reported to Gen. Forrest that we almost caught up to Abel Streight and his hard ridin cavalry. They was makin camp just four miles ahead at the base of Sand Mountain. I could see Gen. Forrest was well pleased, and he says to us "Get some sleep boys, tomorow we do some fightin."

Fore dawn of April 30 we was back in the saddle in hot pursute of the yankee raiders. We climbed the narrow, rocky road up Sand Mountain, on either side sandy ridges and thin woods of scrawny pines and sage brush. The general again sends Bill Forrest and the scouts up ahead to keep the enemy in sight.

As we was aproachin the summit of Sand Mountain at a place called Days Gap, Capt. Bill Forrest and his scouts, the bravest men I know, creep up closer and closer to the rear of the union colum and decide to attack. As they charged hard into the rear gard they rode right into a union ambush and found therselves bein shot at from three sides. The first volly outright killed sevral of those fearless men, sevral more was nocked from there horses, and Bill Forrest hisself took a nasty shot in the thigh bone. Fore a second round could be fired they retreated quick to our position.

Gen. Forrest got real angerd when he hears of the trap his scouts fell into, and I think he was much moved when he seen the serius nature of his brothers wound. He quick orderd all of us who kept up the pace to spur our horses up ahead and get into battle formation. As most horses was wore down only us of the escort company and a goodly part of Dibrells Tennessee boys was up front to line up for battle. A couple of Mortons guns under Lt. Wills Gould soon join us. As we was formin up our ranks, the whole enemy brigade burst right at us with pistols, carbines and sevral big guns flarin. We was outnumberd by alot and caught off gard, so we fell back in some confusion. As we fell back to form a new line, I seen the artilery boys strugglin to move there guns, but got over run by dozens a yankees who captured the cannons.

I never in my life seen Gen. Forrest in such a rage. When we come scurryin back it made him very angry, but when he seen the guns get captured he lit into poor Lt. Wills Gould like a mad man. Screamin profanitys at Gould and evry other man near at hand till I thought for sure the veins in his neck would burst. He was tearin up and down the line like a crazed demon, slashin with his saber, ready to dismember any one, friend or foe, that crost his path. "Form battle line, goddamn evry one of you, double quick, we gonna get them guns back." At times like this he seem to not recognize people he knowd well. He orderd evry man to dismount and tie there horse off to a bush or sapling "no goddamn horse holders this time," he hollers, "evry man will fight. We will retake those guns if evry man dies in the attempt. If you dont succede you wont need your damn horses anyway."

Men on the slower horses was stedy comin up and fallin in line, and now the sides was at least a little more even. I was neelin behind a small ridge waitin for the order to charge, when my buddy Markbright comes crawlin over to me. "Here Henry" he says, pullin a small piece of ham from his coat pocket, "better eat this now I reckon, cause the way the old mans rantin bout gettin them guns back, we may not be eatin any time soon – if ever." As my mouth was bone dry and my canteen low I refused, "thanks anyways, and just stay outa his way." We both smiled.

When the bugle sounded charge, we all rush forward ready to receve the enemy fire, but this time nothin happend. The yankees, happy to win this scrap and carry off our guns, already skedadled eastward.

Gen. Forrest, calmed down some now, got us back mounted and again in hot pursute of the enemy. It was late morning now and we kept up the pace in spite of bein bone-tired and hungry, and sevral times we just avoided fallin into ambushes the enemy set like they did to our scouts.

We kept pushin, pushin, pushin. Not stoppin all day for food nor water, sand kickin up in the face, wind burn the skin, and bones achin from neck to toes. But Gen. Forrest knowd if we was hurtin like this, the enemy was too and the men and beasts with the most grit and guts would win the day.

We rode deep into the night time, the only light provided by a near full moon. We left Sand Mountain behind us and was climbin a goodly size hill called Hag Mountain when we run smack into the yankee force who stopped runnin and drawd up in line of battle. Finaly, after ridin day and night to catch them, we come face to face with the enemy. We was outnumberd again, as our line was streched way back and the enemy was pretty much bunched together, but Old Bedford would not stand for a retreat here and placed each man who come up in formation. "Shoot evrything blue" he screams, "and keep the skeer on." It bein so dark I couldnt make out the color of no uniforms and the only way I knowd where to shoot was by the muzzle flashes of the union rifles. A stedy fire fight ensude, and it was quite a sight seein all them bursts a fire in the darkness. Durin the hours of fightin Gen. Forrest thrice got his horse shot from under him, and still he was fearless in keepin up the attack. When Biffles regiment finaly caught up, Gen. Forrest sends it quick on a march round the enemys right side, and when they got in position and joind the fight, the yankee troopers seen enough. They remounted, pulled back, and resumed there mad race even in the night time, toward Rome, Georgia.

When the yankees pulled out they left our captured guns behind and this pleased Gen. Forrest so well he called a halt for the rest of the night and give us a few hours to water and feed the horses, and for us to get some grub and catch a little rest. I never ever was so completly bone-weary. I hardly had strength to unsaddle Buster. We chased Abel Streight and his men over forty miles that day, and over a hunderd the last two. We was just plum tuckerd out and many the boys never caught up as there mounts failed them at varius stages of the chase.

My bones still ache Lizzie, and even now I feel heavy tiredness come over me. I must rest for now but will continue our story some time tomorow I hope.

May 5, 1863
Rome, Ga.

Lizzie, I feel much refreshed after a good night of sleep and this afternoon the fine people of Rome showd there gratitude to us as saviors of there city by puttin on the grandest picnic you ever will see. They served us ham, bacon, chicken, yams, sweet corn, collard greens and all manner of dessert. It was the best meal we got in weeks and Gen. Forrest seen to it that our many yankee prisners got some nourishin food too.

Anyways, to continue my story, even though we was in the saddle for 44 of 48 hours and fightin for almost 18 non-stop hours, the general allowd us only a few hours sleep that night of May 1, and fore dawn we resumed our trackin of the federals. We chased them through the town of Blountsville, where the wily Abel Streight set up another of his ambushes, again our scouts most in the advance took a lickin.

I seen a incident that almost made me laugh. Just outa Blountsville, while we was ridin hard and engagin the rear of Abel Streights colum, one a Bill Forrests scouts come ridin hard up to the general, pulls up quick in a cloud a dust, and says real anxius "General, I just found out there is another force of union cavalry bigger then Streights party, on a road just north of us!"

"Did you see these yankees yourself?" asks the general.

"No sir, but a citizen of Bountsville tole me he seen such a force."

Gen. Forrest got red as a beet, shouts "You damn fool, the countrysides full a yankee simpathizers." And quick as a wink Old Bedford jumps off his horse, grabs the scout by the neck with both his hands, pulls the man from his horse and starts bangin the mans head up against a tree hollerin in his face "Now damn you, if you ever come to me again with a pack a lies you wont get off so easy!" Gen. Forrest is a most quick-temper and violant man. It was a bit comical, but you dont dare laugh.

On and on we raced all day, many a time pullin in line a battle, havin a quick skirmish with the rear of the yankee colum and then racin onward. They was runnin and we was chasin. Finaly round 5:00 in the afternoon we come to the Black Warrior River, a swift flowin and deep mountain stream. The yankees somehow got acrost and we would follow. As we climb down the rocky west bank, the general was tellin evry one "carry your powder up high boys," and though the water come up to my knees, my amunition and scant rations stayed dry. When came time to get the big guns acrost, Gen. Forrest had Mortons men tie long ropes to the muzzle, then a team of eight horses on the far side would pull each cannon acrost, the guns goin completly under water fore emergin on the east bank. The caisons was unpacked and each load was carried over on the shoulder of a man crossin. Once we was all on the east side of the Black Warrior, Gen. Forrest sends Col. Biffles regiment on ahead to keep on the yankees tale while the rest of us was allowd to dismount, take off saddles, grab a bite to eat (though rations and forage was scarce) and take a few hours rest. After this rest the general got us all mounted again, and for the third time in a row we rode all night long.

Now I come to a most intrestin occurance. By morning on May 2nd our most advanced units, mainly the escort company and Gen. Forrest hisself, caught up to Col. Biffles tuckerd out Tennessee boys, and the general tole them to take a well earnd rest and we would press the pursute on. We was closin in on the yankees again, though most of our brigade was strung out way behind us, when we come acrost a major obstacal. We got to a very deep, dangrous to cross stream called Black Creek. We was still on the main road tween Blountsville and Gadshen, and to get acrost this trechrous creek was but one rickety bridge for many a mile. By the time we got to the bridge, the yankees was already acrost, piled a tangle a fence posts on it and lit it afire. The bridge was destroyd, and I am sure the enemy thought they captured some breathin space.

The general looked concernd as he eyed the blazin bridge. We must cross, but how? Just off a short ways was a small farmhouse, not much more then a cottage, surounded by barren fields. We seen a young girl maybe 15 or 16, bendin over a small garden. "Come with me" says the general to me and sevral other of the fellas near at hand, and he spurred his horse toward the lass.

"Pardon me miss," says the general in his soft voice and raisin his wide-brim hat, "do you know of any other crossin on that stream beside that bridge?"

"There is a spot just up stream a bit" says the young girl in the sweetest little voice, "where the cows cross when the waters low."

"Can you show me this place, cause we got to catch them yankees?"

"Yes I will" she answers "if you can saddle me a horse."

"We aint got time for that miss," says the general, "just get behind me on the saddle and direct us there."

The general reaches down, gentle and very easy lifts the lass up on the back of his saddle and starts off when the girls mother come runnin out the cabin.

"Emma Sanson," she says in a severe voice, "what on earth are you doin?"

"Dont fret madam," says the general introducin hisself, "I will have her back directly, safe and sound."

103

What a sight, that dainty girl settin side-saddle with her puffy skirt blowin in the breeze, clingin with both hands to the broad shoulders of Gen. Forrest. After goin just a couple hunderd yards young Emma points and says "Just over the bank there, we could see it better if we got down." So the general jumps off his horse liftin the young lady down, and though we was hid from the oppisite bank by heavy brush, a squad a yankees on the other side was takin shots at us. We was crawlin on hands and knees, Emma out front with bullits whizzin right by, and the general says "I am glad to have you as a pilot, young lady, but I am not goin to make brestworks of you." The general climbs out front, seen what he wanted, and we all beat a hasty retreat back to the farm house.

By this time much of our brigade caught up though in truth we was down to maybe 600 men with good mounts outa more then a thousand who started out. A few shots of canister from Mortons guns scared off any yankees on the oppisit bank, and fore long our whole command was wadin acrost the "lost ford" of Emma Sanson. The general asks her for a lock of her hair and left a note thankin that young lady for her help and bravry, and I am sure he wont soon forget that fetchin lass. Again the caisons was unloaded and the cannons pulled acrost with ropes, but we was all confident the yankees was much suprized and greatly dishearted when they seen us in close pursute again.

We chased the union raiders as fast as our poor horses could run, keepin a stedy fire on the rear of there colum, and we could tell by the increasin number of yankee stragglers they was tired too. In fact the story from the ones we captured was the men was even more exausted then us, and there mules seemed worse off then our horses. We overtook numerus fallen mules and dozens of enemy horsemen layin asleep like dead men, scatterd along the road. Gen. Forrest seen our boys too fallin from the saddle in sleep, so he calls a halt after dark to let us rest the night. That was our first nights sleep outa four, and from April 29 to May 2 we chased the yankee raiders more then 140 miles and almost never stopped fightin with some portion of there command.

Short time after I bedded down that night of May 2, your two brothers and Willie Forrest and another half dozen of our escort company come ridin in. I was releved the boys caught up and though they was sore and tired like evry one else, they was still in good spirits and those fine horses your father sent them off with was still holdin up well.

But I was not to get a good nights sleep after all. Only a couple hours after droppin off I was shook awake by Markbright and joind forty others of the escort and Gen. Forrest, who says "Boys, the enemy knows his only chance is to get to Rome and burn the bridge over the Oostenaula and buy therselves a few days time fore we can get acrost." He said we must "devil them all night" and keep up such a fire they will think the whole brigade is on there tail. "You wont have no trouble keepin on them as there goin slow now," he says, and promised he would catch up to us with the rest of our men by mid morning. He said he would be much suprized if they kept ridin. So us forty saddled up to resume the chase.

Again we was ridin hard and in the dark of night we could just make out shapes of yankee horsemen darker yet against the background. We rode and fired, reloaded on horseback (some thing evry good cavalry man can do) and by sun up of May 3rd we could tell they couldnt go much further. Up ahead they was tryin to organize in some type a battle formation, but with so many stragglers and exausted men it werent too orderly. We reined up ourselvs and chose some good hidin places to fire from, and though we was only forty in number, our shootin was takin a toll.

By 9:00 that morning, just as the yankees was makin this last stand, we turnd round and seen Gen. Forrest and the rest of the brigade comin quick up the road. The general give us a big salute, spred his men wide in all directions so as to form a semi-circle round the enemy position, and then rode up to me and Markbright.

"Markbright, draw me up a surrender note" says the general, "tell them I want imediate surrender, there outnumberd bad, and that they will be treated as prisners of war — officers to retain there side-arms and personal property."

He turns to me and says "Wylie, pull off your shirt again and wave it as a sine a truce. Just hope they honor it."

A few minutes later Markbright and me rode the few hunderd yards seperatin us from our quarry. We was amongst the very men we been chasin and fightin for five strait days and over 150 miles of mountainous, rugged terain. Evry man we seen was layin on there face, guns ready, but almost evry one sound asleep. There was no fight left in them, they was simply wore out complete.

Col. Abel Streight met with Gen. Forrest to discuss the situation, and all the while the general would issue orders bout bringin up this regiment, or backin off that regiment or holdin so many guns in reserve. Dont forget Lizzie, he is one fine poker player. It ends with Col. Streight surenderin his whole command, bout 1500 men right there and another two or three hunderd other stragglers we gatherd up. Col. Streights face was struck dumb when he seen our measly five hunderd men roundin up all his 1500.

Next day, that bein yesterday, we led the captured yankee raiders into Rome, Ga., there original destanation, and after seein that the prisners was fed good and rested, the general had them sent south to prisner of war camps. The people a Rome welcomed us with great celebration and treated Gen. Forrest like a national hero, which of course he is. Runnin the entire brigade of yankee raiders into the ground will probly live in history as one of the great chases of all time.

I must turn in now Lizzie, hope you enjoyd hearin of our latest exploit. I dont know what is next for us, but I hear we will probly be movin out tomorow. Best wishes to all my loved ones, and remember me as always,

Your loving husband,
Henry

Chapter 7

June 16, 1863 through October 7, 1863

June 16, 1863
Columbia, Tenn.

Dearest Elizabeth,

Thank you for the wonderful letter I receved yesterday. Just to read of you and Mary goin on with your life makes me so homesick. Many the men from Alabama and Mississippi got furlows the past few weeks and I am green with envy. But since the yankees is holdin Memphis and the whole region, Gen. Forrest says its too risky for us boys from West Tennessee to go home. It just aint fair. Now with the beutiful weather we been gettin I miss bein home more then ever. I would give anything for right now to be settin by the far pond on the farm, as you and me done so many times when we was courtin. Layin on our backs in the tall grass with a hot sun makin our faces feel warm, just starin up at the clouds and seein fantastic shapes float by. Remember how the many dragonflys would hover over the water and we would set hand-in-hand in silence, without a care in the world? Now you must protect our dear child, suffer hunger and privation, while I live in a soggy tent, suffer from saddle sores, and face death almost evry day. How I long to return to the peaceful days.

A terible thing occurd day fore last and I must confess I feel some what responsable for it. You remember from my last letter (and from newspapers too) how our small brigade boldly chased and fought the much larger command of Col. Abel Streight and finaly forced its surender. You may also recall how at the fierce battle at Days Gap we was suprized by a yankee charge and lost some prisners and two of our guns under young Lt. Wills Gould, and

107

how Gen. Forrest went into a rage. Well, a month later Gould gets orders for a transfer to duty some wheres else. And one evenin last week Capt. Markbright and me was settin by the campfire jawin when Wills Gould come up lookin troubled and ask to join us.

"You know Mortons away" he says (Lt. John Morton, who is in charge of all Gen. Forrests artilery) "but I feel some one should hear me out. You know I been transferd out, right?"

"We was just talkin bout it," says Markbright, "we will miss you Gould."

"It aint right, you know, it aint fair him doin this to me" says Gould and he was gettin pretty worked up. "Cause them two guns got took at Days Gap. Thats why he is sendin me off. Its like sayin I lost them guns and I am a cowerd." He slapped his fist on his thigh. "I woulda saved them but for the dead horses gettin tangled in the harness."

"Naw, Gould" says I, "no one thinks your a cowerd. Why, there aint a braver man in the unit, evry one knows that."

"Not him" he snaps, "he smacks my pride and dignity. I will not stand that from no man, not even Gen. Forrest!"

"Listen Gould, cool down" says Markbright, "you know how the old man is. He blows his top, gets furius, then a short time later he settles down and dont hold no grudges."

"He is holdin a grudge" growls Gould, "thats why he is sendin me off."

I will tell you Lizzie, Wills Gould is a proud man and truly felt his honor was trampled on by the general. I did not give this conversation much thought till yesterday when young Wills Gould went to have a talk with Gen. Forrest at headquarters in the Masonic Building in Columbia. Gould confronted the general in his office, said the transfer was a intolerable injustice and spoke with great anger till General Forrest tole him he would not revoke the transfer and orderd him outa the room. Gould then reaches under his linen duster and pulls out a pistol which he fires at point-blank range, hittin the general in the left side. The general, always dangrous as a wounded tiger, grabs Goulds gun hand so as to keep him from firin again, then pulls out his pocket knife with his left hand and opens a big blade with his teeth and slashes Gould a wicked gash in the abdomin. Gould breaks away and staggers out to the street, just makin his way to a tailor shop where he falls on a low bench, holdin his bad bleedin side. The general also limps out the room and a local doctor was called to examin his wound. Cause it was a gut shot the doctor tole Gen. Forrest it was probly fatal. This sent the general in one of his fearsom rages, screamin "No damned man shall kill me and live!" Without gettin no treatment he lunges out the building, yanks two pistols from a saddled horse in front, and went off huntin for Gould.

A crowd was gatherd at the tailor shop and it scatterd fast as the general come staggerin up firin shots from both hands. Poor Gould hears the general comin, rolls off the bench leavin a big pool a blood under it, and stumbles out the back door. The general chased him best he could, and by the time he catches up to Gould, the man is layin on his back in some tall prarie grass, blood gurglin from his mouth. By this time other officers come and settle the general down, and all could see clear nough that the doctors could do naught for Lt. Gould.

Doc Cowan examind Gen. Forrest and found the ball from Goulds pistol pierced the generals side, but hit no vital organ and come to rest up against his pelvis bone. He tole Gen. Forrest he could operate to get the slug out, but the general tole him no, "Its nothin but a damned little pistol ball, let it alone" and orderd him to attend to Lt. Gould and make him as comfitable as posable. I know the general well and could tell he was sorry for the whole ugly epasode. But regret could not save Gould. He died a short time later, but the general is gettin better.

I wish now Lizzie, I talked more on that night with Wills Gould and maybe prevent this from happenin. I feel pretty low Lizzie, and wish more then ever I could be with you and Mary. But till I can be with you again, remember me to be,

Your loving husband,
Henry

July 10, 1863
Kingston, Tenn.

Dear Elizabeth,

Hope this letter finds you both healthy and content, though the early part of this month finds our poor country neither. It is painful for me to think of the grand Mississippi closed to our people and under yankee control. The fall of Vicksburg to that man Grant and his union hord has rend our nation in half. This so vexes Gen. Forrest that I herd him rantin bout how he could make the old Miss unsafe for all yankee gunboats if he only got the chance. And then, of course the loss sufferd by Lee and his grand army of Northern Virginia in Gettysburg has stole the heart and soul of our people in the east.

And here in Tennessee, after holdin there lines for months after the great clash near Murfreesboro on the Stones River back in early January, Gens. Bragg and Rosecrans are startin to move there armys again. In fact ever since Gen. Forrest recoverd from the bullit wound from Wills Gould, we pretty much been gardin the rear and flank of Gen. Braggs army the last month as it drifts slow toward Chattanooga.

The treks been slow and we got rain for almost two strait weeks awhile back, and I cant hardly describe the discomfit of always wearin wet clothes, sloggin in soaked shoes and socks, the ugly sores from chafin wet leather saddles and ridin boots. Nights is particlarly uncomfitable as you hate layin in mud but cant hardly find no place dry. One fella, Les Atkinson got so tired a sleepin on rain-soaked ground, tryed sleepin in the crux of a tree. You can probly guess what happend all right. Soon as he falls to sleep, outa the tree he come and pert near broke his wrist. Doc Cowan just scrach his head when treatin old Les.

As we been gardin the rear, we have encounterd the enemy advance units on sevral ocasions. At one time we got in a nice skirmish with a squad a yanks. After a brisk fight, the general calls me and Capt. Markbright over to him. "Boys, I think I seen a flag a truce wavin up ahead. Prepare a statement Markbright, and Lt. Wylie get your shirt on your saber and lets go talk to these people bout surenderin."

Gen. Forrest, Markbright, Major Rambaut and me rode a ways behind union lines and in amongst a small group a yankees with rifles aimin right at us. A gray haird yankee captain with a thick mustash says "Hey General Forrest, that aint no truce flag you seen us flyin, thats a signal flag. You best hi-tale outa here." Gen. Forrest, heedin the kindly advice, takes off his hat and bows low to the captain, and we swung our beasts round and spurred them outa there. I guess even in war some soldiers can still be gentlmen.

Unfortunatly durin another rear gard action which has been mostly light on the blood lettin, I seen the gallant Col. Starnes take a gun shot to the face that rip his lower jaw almost clean off. It was a horible sight seein the mangled face of that brave man who led his Tennessee regiment to so much glory.

But I have learnt Lizzie, there aint really no glory in war, only death and misery. The cause may be just and right but not glorius. We marched off to war young men, dreamin of the glory of war like the poets do. But now I seen war and death for real, and when men is killed in battle they dont clasp there hand to there heart nor look skyward as they fall back to the ground whisperin "mother" on there lips. Death in battle is ugly and horible. Its gettin your face blowd apart like Col. Starnes. A bullit to your throat rippin your neck in pieces, leavin you alive just long enough to feel your life blood pourin down your chest and the horible sickness come to your body. Death on the battlefield is blackend faces and bloated bodys, arms and legs tore off from the trunk and scatterd wide, disoriented men tryin to push there stomachs and guts back in to there exploded abdamen before death, glorius death, releves them of there earthly misery. I am sorry Lizzie, to scare you this way, but aint a man here that aint thought the same thoughts. It is the reality of war.

Last week we was ridin hard to catch up to the rear of Braggs colums through the town of Cowan, a husky elder woman steps from her porch as she seen the general and the escort racin by and yells at the top of her lungs right at the general "You big cowerdly rascal, why dont you turn and fight like a man insted of runnin like a cur? I wish Old Forrest was here. He would make you fight!" Rambaut and me was laughin so hard Gen. Forrest turnd bright red and says "Id rather face a whole battery then that woman."

Anyways Lizzie, Gen. Braggs holed up in Chattanooga now, the union army under Rosecrans is creepin closer, and our brigade is positiond here near the fair town of Kingston, and we are ridin reconasance, scoutin, gatherin supplys and lettin our backsides recover. Hope you and all my love ones is well, and I am,

Your loving husband,
Henry

Aug. 14, 1863
Kingston, Tenn.

Dear Elizabeth,

I must confess these last five weeks or so been the most enjoyable we spent in a long time. We been camped just outside this fair city of Kingston, the one-time capital of our state, for most this time and goin on some few excursions scoutin the enemy movement southward toward Chattanooga.

The weather been sunny and warm most evry day, and the boys all been havin great fun swimmin daily in the clear mountain streams. It sure feels refreshin to be clean again and have clothes on your back that aint caked with mud and grime. Willie Forrest and your brother Bobby found a slippry bank along the Tennessee where they lay on there back and slide a goodly ways right in to the river. They was doin this together for hours one day and musta lost track a time cause they missed evenin roll-call and the general got pretty concernd till the two lads come ridin back to camp after dark all smiles. They spent the next two days cleanin the fish the boys was catchin in the river.

Toward the end of July I was out on a little reconasance with a squad of twenty men spottin sines of enemy movement and rasslin up a little grub. We was cuttin a path through the dense woods of a mountain side and your other brother John right ahead of me brush by a tree limb and let it swing back and bushwack me in the face. It damn near unhorsed me, which of course got a laugh from the boys, but I got a nasty poke in the eye from it. It felt like a bee sting, but I just rubbed it out and kept goin. Later that night my eye got all red and swelled up and very painful, and I pert near lost sight in it. Next day when we got back to camp I went to see Doc

Cowan. He examen my eye, took out a medicine book and read a little, and says "Come back in a few hours, Wylie, I should have some thing then." So back I come a few hours later, my eye stingin like hell and swelled shut, and Dr. Cowan took a jar of white pasty stuff, said he just made it up, and rub it all over my eye. "What is it?" I asks. "Just a mix a tree sap, alcahol, quinine and a few plant parts" says Doc Cowan, "now go lay still till tomorow." Sure nough Lizzie, by afternoon the next day the swellin was way down, the pain gone and I could start seein again from it. That Doc Cowan is a clever man.

Last week our brigade was out scoutin and run up against a goodly size unit of yankee infantry. Gen. Forrest did not want us too heavy engaged as we was outnumberd bad, but had the men hold the enemy up long enough for Jeffrey Forrest and us from the escort to swing behind the yanks position and nab us a whole herd a beef cattle they was trailin behind them. You shoulda saw us russlin up them cows. We was movin them pretty good, but when one run off by itself, your brother John throwd his rope round its neck and by gum that critter yanked him right out his saddle and on to his face in the dirt. He is a good and brave soldier but a pretty pitiful cowboy.

Markbright just got done roastin up a wild turkey so I better dig in while there is some left. Sounds like we might be movin in to Georgia soon. Kiss Mary for me,

Your loving husband,
Henry

Sept. 12, 1863
Ringgold, Ga.

Dear Elizabeth,

Those plesant weeks at Kingston is now gone as we been on the move again the past week or more, formin ourselvs on the right flank of Braggs army as he pulls outa Chattanooga and in to Georgia. The army is spredin out along the curvin banks of Chickamauga Creek.

The letters I receve from you was so long and full a news I feel I been home on furlow, when in fact that is imposable (as long as the yankees hold Memphis). I read with great concern of Marys illness. Praise the good Lord she is recoverin, and please continue to follow all the directions of Dr. Blanchard, as small pox is a plague on all the land. Evry company in Braggs army lost many a boy to the pox, and the ranks been depleted more by measles and disentary then enemy bullits.

After leavin Kingston, our cavalry been actin pretty much as the eyes and ears for the army of General Bragg. I would wager there aint a better group for gettin information then Capt. Bill Forrest and his forty scouts (often referd to here as "the forty thiefs"). Gen. Forrest got them highly organized and there aint no place those darin men wont go. They been knowd to put on blue uniforms and sneak right into the enemy camps, settin at the yankee campfires, jawin with the men and officers. Many a time they capture yankee pickets and get military information from them, or dressed in civilian clothes befriend yankee stragglers and worm all the secrets they can from them. Some times one will allow hisself to be captured and took to the enemy camp where he pretends to revele important information (wrong information) as to our strength and where-abouts, then escape in to the night. I dont beleve there be another man in the Confederacy with a more complete and reliable system of scouts then Gen. Forrest. It is just another part of his ability to win at war.

You know Lizzie, after our great success at places like Murfreesboro and Brentwood or after our escape from Donelson or the capture of Abel Streight, you read in the newspapers and hear people talkin bout Gen. Forrest bein "a genius." They say only a genius could do what he done without ever goin to West Point or some other military school. Now I been observin Nathan Bedford Forrest real close for two years now, and I know he does have a uncanny way of choosin the right places and right times to unleash his fury. Even though we are usualy outnumberd bad, he knows how to pick the key position and as he says, "get there first with the most men" and so win a great victory. But I can tell you or any one else the secret to his success in battle is not "genius," but his hard work and unmatched courage. Before headin into a posable engagment with the enemy, Old Bedford hisself checks out the shoes of evry horse, is there when amunition is bein passed out to

make sure its pure and dry. Its General Forrest that rides
reconasance late at night to check the lay of the land, and he places
artilery pieces just where he wants it to be. If a bridge needs made
to transport the command acrost a river, the general is swingin an
axe cuttin down trees, he is waist-deep in the water settin timbers,
and its him steerin the first wagon acrost. He personly makes sure
each man has proper food and a decent uniform, and he watches the
horses real close to make sure each one is fit for service. They call
it genius that he can get his whole brigade acrost a river in two
hours while the yankee brigade crost in ten hours. But the "genius"
is cause he hisself is rowin the transport, he hisself is tuggin the
ropes on the artilery, he hisself is watchin to make sure evry man
is doin there duty as quick as posable. He is the hardest workin
man I ever seen by far, and I dont know how he dont fall over from
exaustion. He drives evry man in his command hard but none near
so hard as hisself. If that is "genius," then I guess he got it.

As I mention earlier we been pullin back with the main army
of Gen. Bragg, gardin the right flank and rear, and yesterday we
had a crisp skirmish with the enemy at Tunnel Hill just in north
Georgia. We was dismounted and firin on some union infantry
when I seen Gen. Forrest, who was up front and still on horseback,
take a shot in the back. He winced in great pain but stayed in the
saddle, and soon the back of his uniform was all over blood. He
stedfast refused to leave the field and had Doc Cowan dress the
wound right amongst all the firin. He never left the scene a battle
but I knowd he was in great pain for he took a big swig a whiskey
– something he never done before. In a short while we remounted
and rode here to Ringgold.

Now all sines point to a major battle fixin tween these two
huge armys along the Chickamauga Creek. I hope to God there
aint a useless loss of life. Until you hear from me again, I am

Your loving husband,
Henry

Oct. 4, 1863
LaFayette, Ga.

My Dearest Elizabeth,

I am sure you know by now of the horendous battle and great Confederate victory that took place along the Chickamauga Creek back on Sept. 19 and 20. And perhaps because of the great simpathy that we always had between us, you also know that I receved a severe wound to my left leg durin that fight. Its now been two weeks since that dark moment when I beleved all my worldly hopes and dreams would wither unfulfilled, and only now am I able to hold a pen and share my experiance with you. Doc Cowan says it is still early but he is hopefull that I am on the right road to recovery and further surgery will not be nesesary. I know already that I shall never be able to run after Mary as she scats through the tall grass, nor walk at a natural pace without a heavy limp and persistant pain, but these are small prices to pay when so many thousands of my brethren have left all but there imortal souls on the battlefield. Please forgive me if my words sound selfish and full of self-pity, for I should not speak such, but offer words of praise to the Almighty for sparin my life through this ordeal, and makin me more aware then ever of the value of life and the depth of love in my heart for you and Mary.

Lizzie, I just took a brief rest and now feel more fit to go on and detale the particlars to you and my love ones back home. By Friday, Sept. 18 our cavalry took there place on the far right flank of Gen. Braggs army, and in the afternoon we crost the Chickamauga at Reeds Bridge and made camp in a peacefull meadow where the only sounds we herd was the crickets and night owls. Next morning, Saturday the 19th, we stocked ourselvs all the amunition we could stuff in our boxes, packed in some biscuts and salt pork, and filled our canteens cause our scouts seen heavy legions of union infantry desendin on us from the LaFayette Rd. due west.

By 9:00 the thunder started. A massive line a blue-coated infantry spred before us through the dense underbrush and scatterd trees. The musketry started and we seemed caught in a deadly hailstorm. Gen. Forrest dismounted most men keepin only the officers and the escort company on horseback. The men fired like

116

mad from behind trees, rocks and fence posts, and in spite the rough and hilly terain did there best to keep some semblence of organization.

We was outnumberd bad and Gen. Forrest sent curiers back to Gen. Polk with desprate pleas for infantry suport. When none come, Gen. Forrest cursed but vow to hold this key position on the right flank of a three mile front till the last man. And I was beginin to beleve it would come to that as I witness more men bein killed and disabled then in any of our many fights. As I gallup Buster up and down the line, fillin in where ever a gap would open, I seen many of the men I knowd so well fallin for there country — Edwin Close shot down, Henry Eller shot down, Corp. Boyd and Sgt. O'Leery killed by a artilery blast. I seen Gen. Forrest lose his horse — the beutiful roan give to him as a gift from the gratefull people of Rome, blowd to bits by artilery fire. The general remounted a riderless horse. He wore his long linen duster held tight round the waist by an amunition belt which held his two Colt revolvers. On his steed, saber wavin overhead and the breeze blowin his duster back, he was screamin that all men must hold there position or die. As we surge forward slow, movin the enemy backward ever further, I seen a young private whose name I forget lose his courage amidst this violance and start creepin to the rear. Gen. Forrest ever watchful, spurs his horse to the man and draws his revolver, aimin at the cowards head. I could not hear Old Bedfords words above the clash of battle but I seen the man lift his arms and talk as if pleadin with Gen. Forrest. Then the general with disgust on his face, slams his pistol back in his belt and swings his horse back to the battlefront. The man continue to the rear.

This savage fightin lasted for hours and we was leavin many of our boys, and more of theres, behind on the field. Gen. Forrest as was his singular custom, kept movin John Mortons guns up to the very front and firin double-shot canister like giant shotguns acrost the field into the enemys face, though the irregular terain made artilery less affective. After three hours heavy fightin we pushed the enemy a good half mile back, after we finaly receved infantry suport. Even Gen. D.H. Hill, well knowd for his low regard for cavalrymen, rode to Gen. Forrest and tole him personly he never seen any cavalry fight so brave or in such good order.

117

Then the blue infantry made a bold and massed counter charge and we was forced to fall back a ways. As our artilery was up on the front line, Morton and his men done all they could to quick hitch up the big draft horses to the guns and pull them back to safety. This they done with remarkable speed, but at one gun, a nice bronze six-pounder, the draft horses was all shot down and the gun left there for the enemy to capture. But Gen. Forrest hates above all things losin a field piece. He quick orders four men from the escort company, me and Markbright included, to pull the collars and hames from the huge necks of the fallen artilery horses and hitch the traces to our saddles and pull the gun ourselvs to safety. This we done under intense enemy fire and was just wheelin the gun round when a enemy artilery shell exploded at my very side.

The explosion was so loud my eardrums musta popped, for the first sensation I had was silence. The roar a battle went numb and I thought perhaps I been killed. But that was just a instant, for the second sensation was the most intense pain anyone could ever experiance in my left leg. Some how still mounted, lookin down I seen a horable mess where my knee use to be, looked like a bloody sponge. A single round bone, my knee-cap I supose, hung off the side and I by instinct slapped it back where it use to be.

How to describe such pain? I supose if you was to lay your leg on a railroad track, then let the train very slow roll over it, you might experiance the crushin agony I felt at that time. In a moment I become very dizzy and so sick to my stomach I vomit over Busters neck. I just remember reelin in my saddle, losin all direction, and fallin off the left side. As I fell my left foot stuck in the stirup and I land on my back, my mangled left leg streched up to the stirup. Blood that filled my ridin boot splash down on me, and the pain so severe I beleve I past out.

But that pain soon brung me back to my senses, though I was now slung over Busters saddle and Markbright leadin him by the reins at a canter pace. With each bump and jossle my leg throb so bad if I coulda reached my pistol I might well blowd my brains out. Lizzie, I must rest here as my poor leg seems to throb yet as I recolect that moment.

Oct. 6, 1863
LaFayette, Ga.

My Dearest Elizabeth,

Doc Cowan just called on me and seemed satisfyed with the condition of my leg. Says my foots warm and the flesh bout the knee area seem to be healin. That is good news indeed and the pain is not so severe.

To continue where I left off – my good friend Markbright saved my life by hoystin me over my saddle and leadin Buster way behind the battle front. Its a wonder we both wasnt killed in that intense fightin. He led me to a grassy field where layed in evry direction wounded men. There musta been a hunderd ailin souls, evry one with mangled limbs, bloody clothes and agony on there faces.

Markbright and another young man, who seem to be some kinda nurse or medic, tryed liftin me down from Buster as gentle as posable, but I could not help squealin in pain. They layed me on my back in the tall grass and the young medic took from a black bag a metal divice with a strap atached to it. The strap he rap round my leg just above my blowd out knee and turnd a handle on the divice. This was a turnicut, and the man says to Markbright "This should stem the bleedin."

Markbright says "What can you do for him now?"

"He can lay here till the litter bearers carry him to a ambulence and then take him to the field hospital set up on the other side of Alexanders Bridge."

Markbright neelin by my side with one hand on my head says "listen Henry, there gonna make sure you get treatment. I must get back to the front now. God bless you."

I squeezed his hand as he pulled away but that was the only thanks I could muster at that time. The young medic stood up and says to me "I will come back shortly to remove the turnicut and put some kinda dressing on that wound." I nodded.

So there I layed perfectly still on my back as the least move of my body cause a stab a pain in my leg again. The constant roar of battle was clear to my ears but some what distant, and I was suprized to hear the clamor on a front that musta streched for miles. The sun was direct over head and shined hot in my eyes, and the blood on my uniform and round the wound dryed fast and become hard.

More and more injurd boys was brung to the open field and all round me the air was filled with groans. Men was cryin for help, pleadin for relefe or a drink a water, and from many places I hear crys of "mother, mother." The boy just to my right was a young blond-haird kid who musta got hit in the guts, as a bloody white cloth was rapped all round his abdomin. He groaned with evry breath, probly as much from fear as pain cause evry man in the army knowd almost all gut shots is fatal.

The man on my left, whose three stripes tole me he was a sargent, and his blackend powder-burnt face tole me he was a hard fighter, had no right arm below the elbow at all. He layed still and quiet, but musta sufferd great pain cause I could see and smell that he releved his bowels and bladder while layin there.

All the while I could see groups a litter-bearers, many of them black boys, carryin injurd men away to open ambulence wagons. There was a number of men, like the young fella that helped me, tendin to as many men as they could. Some how in spite of all this, I musta drifted off to sleep cause I didnt notice the medic helper come back with a roll of white linen. He was stoopin down, put his hand to my forehead, then took off the turnicut slow. He looks close at my knee and says very low "good." I reckon the blood flow musta stopped. He proceded to rap the linen round my leg, and though was very careful the pain was fierce as he went round and round. When that was done he stood up and says "They will haul you to the hospital directly."

"Think I will lose my leg?" I asks.

Without a moment a thought he says "Yes."

Sure nough a short while later my turn musta come up. Two nigras, one had to be in his fiftys, lay a strecher beside me and the younger one cradles me in his arms and lift me up on to the strecher while the older man tryed to hold my legs still. In spite of there efforts to be gentle the movment made my leg pound like hell and I had to let out a groan. "Sorry, young mister" says the old black man.

They lift and procede to carry me at a good pace toward a wagon, and the josslin of there movment made me cringe in pain.

120

The young man layed the edge of the litter on the end of the open wagon, then he jumps up inside and pulls the litter into the wagon bed. Then he lifts me off the litter and sets me on the wagon bords. Again pain and a groan.

There was another wounded man already in the ambulence and as soon as I got situated the teamster, also a nigra, tug the reins and the wagon lunge forward and starts rollin. The bumpin and bangin of that wagon rollin over ruts and holes in the road bounce me all over the floor bords. Me and the other fella was perfectly howlin in distress, and as the field hospital below Alexanders Bridge was more then two miles off, I truly did not think I would survive the transport. But finaly after what seem a ungodly long time, we pull in to a large open field with dozens of big tents set up all over.

Again Lizzie, I must stop to rest. Continue later.

Henry

October 7, 1863
LaFayette, Ga.

Dear Elizabeth,

I must be gettin a little better cause I can get myself to a settin position without a groan now. I can tell you Lizzie, these matron ladys who nurse all us sick and wounded men in this hospital here in LaFayette is amongst the kindlyest people I ever met. They work non-stop changin dressings, emptyin bed pans, givin medicine, writin letters for the boys unable to do so therselvs, and generly doin anything they can to make life better for these men. I can not say enough good things bout them all.

As I was tellin you (and my love ones back home) I some how survived the terible ambulence ride to the field hospital near Alexanders Bridge (which was sevral miles behind the battle front still ragin that Saturday of Sept. 19). When the wagon come to rest, very shortly two men come with a litter, put it next to me on the wagon bords, and try to lift me gentle on to it. As before it paind me like hell. There was a whole lot a big white tents set up all over the field and though I did not think of it at that time, I now feel them tents musta been aranged acordin to the type injury each

121

man had, cause I was placed in a tent where evry man there had a injury to the arm, leg or shoulder.

The tent I was set in was pert near pack full, and the litter bearers left me layin on a straw mat right near the tent opening. This ended up bein good luck for me as the air was very hot and stuffy, and stank terible of urine and feces. The tent musta been fifty feet long and 25 wide, and men was placed almost shoulder to shoulder along each side formin a double line of suferers. They musta been fifty men, some moanin, some cryin, others pleadin for mercy. Sevral women actin as nurses was tendin as many the boys as they could, tryin to ease there agony by givin them water or makin them some how more comfitable. Many men layed still and quiet.

At the end of the tent and just in front of me was hung a sheet, and behind this curtan was the doctor and four men actin as medical asistents. As I layed on the straw tryin hard not to move a tiny bit, I stared at the shadows behind the sheet and some times catch a glimps of the action there. A couple times I seen the doctor step from behind the curtan. He was a older man maybe in his fiftys, and he look extremly tired with sweat rollin from his brow and his gray hair all matted and uncombed. He wore what used to be a white coat or jacket, but it was evry inch coverd in blood, and once I seen him wipe a long bloody knife on his bloody coat. Sevral times I seen his shadow through the sheet rase a bottle, probly whisky, to his mouth and take a long drink.

It was easy knowin what was goin on behind the sheet though, as they spoke loud enough for me to hear, and most evry patient got the same treatment. Two of the medical asistents would come from behind the sheet carryin a strecher, walk down the middle tween the two rows of injured men, pick one out (perhaps the one who looked most desprate?), load him on the strecher and carry him back. They lift him to the table in front of the doctor and the others would usuly cut the clothes off the soldier.

The doctor then probes the wound, often causin the injurd man to scream and squirm, but he was held down by the four medicos. In evry case I seen, and as I layed there on the bloody mat I seen plenty a men go in behind that curtan, the doc says "This limb must come off." Some times the soldier would plead no or beg why. "The bone is shatterd and will never heal" was always the answer.

Then the real strugglin comence as the doctor picks up his saw and says "Ether." One of the men would hold somthing, a sponge or rag I supose, to the injurd mans face and often the soldier was makin one last atempt to get away. But they soon was layin still enough for the doctor to do his work, and of all the things I seen and herd that day, the one thing I will remember most to my dyin day is the sound of that saw grindin through bone after bone. It sound like a rasp on wood and it was that hatefull sound which turn me sick.

Each amputation took but a few minutes and I set watchin as the medicos carry each dismemberd limb to the tent door and throw it outside on a pile of arms and legs startin to look like a haystack. What a sight.

After watchin this for hours and wonderin if my turn would come or not, I hear one of the men say to the doctor "Last bottle of ether and its almost gone." "Check and see if Dr. Willard or Dr. Green have any to spare" says the doctor.

The man returns shortly and says "Doc Willard is almost out too and Dr. Green says he is now givin his patients only a little whisky before cuttin." And I for sure took notice that the last sevral men carried to the table still did a little squirmin and moanin even after the ether was put in there face. Musta been usin less and less. This did not make me feel well either.

As the day wore on and the distent sounds a battle was slackin, and still more and more men was bein brung into the tent, I begun to think I might be forgot and die right there on the straw. Then Doc Cowan walks in. He seen me and says "There you are Wylie, Gen. Forrest sent me lookin for you and I musta searched a dozen tents. So how are you boy?"

He neeld down, took off my blood-soak bandages and examend my leg. "How long you been in here Henry?"

"Dont know sir, I reckon six hours or so." He whistles soft, pats my hand, and as the two medical asistents with the strecher was comin from behind the screen Doc Cowan says to them "I am Major Cowan, a medical doctor and I want this man treated this instent."

Without a word they set me on the strecher and carried me behind the curtan. There was the exausted doctor, a tray beside him with a couple big knifes and saws, a spool a thred and sevral large needles, and a empty whisky bottle. One man was wipin the bloody table with a bloody towel, and I was layed on top.

For the first time that day my fear was greater then my pain. I reach back and says desprate, "Dr. Cowan..."

"Dont worry Henry, I will stay here if the doctor dont mind."

"Not at all" says the doctor with no expresion of voice or face. My uniform or what was left of it, was sliced off my injurd leg. My knee was a sight to see and they examind it close. "Leg got to come off" says the doctor. Doc Cowan made no response but says "Move your toes Henry." I was suprized myself to see them left side toes move. "Shake your feet Henry" and again I was able to do that, although with pain. "Rase your left leg Henry" orders Doc Cowan, and this time the pain was intense but my leg rased from the table.

"Doctor" says Doc Cowan, "this leg can be saved I think if we can spare a few extra moments. I see no deep bone injury, the knee cap of course, but mostly muscle, ligament and tissue damage."

"Perhaps Doctor" says the other, "if you care to tend this man I can step outside for air and a little rest."

"Yes indeed Doctor, you certenly deserve a brake" says Dr. Cowan.

Dr. Cowan looks at me and says "I will do all I can Henry, to save your leg." Then to the attendant, "Now give this man ether."

"We aint got much left Doc, just whats left in this rag" he says, and puts it up to my face and says "Breathe deep." I got dizzy in a instent and fell in to a light sleep. I seem to remember driftin in and outa sleep and feelin pains and pressure on my knee as if Doc Cowan was pullin and probin inside the mess.

In what seem to my mind a very short time I was lift off the table and carried outa that tent of misery and took to another tent. This musta been for recoverin soldiers cause evry man there was all rapped in neat bandages with blood spots showin through. Dr. Cowan followd me there and after I was set down on a straw bed coverd with a blanket he says "I did my best Henry. If it takes, you will keep your leg. If not and gangrene sets in, I will take it off."

Though I was in pain and felt sick in my stomach, I felt much relefe and says "Thank you Dr. Cowan, thank you for evrything."

"I hope I helped, Wylie" says he, "tomorow you will be moved to a hospital in LaFayette. I promise I will come and check whenever I can. Gen. Forrest will be glad to hear you survived."

He left the tent and I will tell you Lizzie, in less then ten minutes I musta fell in to the deepest sleep of my life. Next day, the same Sunday of Sept. 20 that our army burst through and rout the enemy all the way back to Chattanooga, I took a little food and drink and later was loaded on to another wagon and hauld with many others to this hospital in LaFayette.

I been layin here in this bed ever since but with abundent praise to the Lord above, and my endless gratatude to that great man Doc Cowan, and my many thanks to all these nurses and medical people for there kindness and help, I beleve I am goin to survive in tact and hopefully go on defendin my country and servin Gen. Forrest. I do so much want to come home and be with you and Mary forever, but I must see this thing through and return in peace. Please understand, my dear Lizzie. And till that time I am as always,

Your loving husband,
Henry

P.S.

If this long letter drags on and on, you must remember how idle I am here and how much I miss you. Writin to you is a relefe to both these.

Chapter 8

November 1, 1863 through January 31, 1864

Nov. 1, 1863
LaFayette, Ga.

Dear Elizabeth,

My God how things changed in these past three weeks. For weeks I been layin here in bed, disparin of ever bein any use to you or my country again. Feelin pain in my leg and pain in my heart without relefe. I must admit to a black depresion. Then how sudden evrything changed! When I seen you and Ma comin down the isle to my hospital bed I sure as shootin thought I was havin another a those dreams that would leave me sad and lonesom.

My goodness Lizzie, I never seen a more beutiful figure of a woman then when you walked in. When I finaly come to realize that you and Ma was with me for real, I felt such a surge a strength, such a healin power come over my body that I never felt before. You and Ma and your wonderful smilin faces did as much to heal me in five minutes as all the doctors medicine done since the time of my wound. The pain, the dispare, the sadness all melt away like rain drops on a warm stone before the word "Elizabeth" could escape my mouth. Only when I rapped my arms round the two of you was I sure you was with me for real.

How can I ever thank you both for that sacrafice. I know that goin from Memphis to LaFayette direct is a long, hot and uncomfitable trip abord bumpy trains and even rougher dusty

127

stagecoaches. But now in the midst a war, the twisted and round-bout journy in broken down trains on uneven track goin miles and miles outa the way, is a testement to your strength and resolve and yes, to your love for me too. You and Ma both are very special ladys.

I sure wish that Mary could come with you but of course your so right in sayin she could never stood the travel. But I do so miss her — been twenty months since I been home, and the way you describe her prancin bout and talkin a blue streak makes me want to be with her real bad. And please Lizzie, thank your mother and father most sincere from me for watchin our baby the whole time you was visitin me.

I am sorry you never got the chance to see your brothers, but you and Ma no sooner borded the coach on Friday when Bobby and John and Markbright come ridin in to town to check on me and some of the other men. The boys was so exited there big sis was in town that day, they pert near mounted up to chase the coach down. Markbright, not bein a wild kid like them two, orderd them to stay put.

Markbright was tellin me that after I was hit on Saturday and the big skedadle by the yankees on Sunday, Gen. Forrest was the only one in our entire army leadin troops in hot pursute of the enemy. Bragg some how just let them slip away, and acordin to Markbright Old Bedford was ragin mad bout losin this chance to really finish the yanks.

Markbright tole me at one point during there mad chase of the retreatin union army, Old Bedford was ridin out front as usual and his horse took a shot in the neck, causin a river of blood to spirt out. Well, the general dont stop or nothin, puts his finger in the bullit hole to stem the flow a blood and keeps on ridin. When they finaly come to a halt the general pulls out his finger and Markbright says the horses knees soon buckle and the poor beast falls dead on the ground.

I spect theres something else I should report to you, but this aint so amusin. A couple days after you and Ma left here Dr. Cowan come in to check on me. This fine man done this many a time over these past weeks and I know I might not be alive, much less on two legs, without him. I owe him so much. While he was examinin my knee and dressin the wound, he was tellin me of our brigades pursute of the enemy after Chickamauga, and how mad Gen. Forrest was when Bragg would not follow with the rest of the army. Gen. Forrest could not accept such a golden opertunity bein lost.

Then Doc Cowan tells me that a few weeks after the battle, Gen. Bragg took away Old Bedfords entire command and transferd it to Gen. Wheeler. This aint the first brigade Gen. Forrest rase hisself, outfited with yankee guns and supplys, and shaped into a real fightin unit, was took from him. (Markbright tole me later that all the general has left to him is McDonalds batalion with less then 140 men, John Mortons battery and 67 gun men, and of course his ever faithful escort company of 65 men).

A few nights later Gen. Forrest has Doc Cowan ride with him to camp headquarters. Dr. Cowan little knew why and says the general was quiet and surly, unlike his usual self. When they got to the headquarters tent the general struts past the sentry without salutin, and just barges right through the flap. There set Gen. Bragg, a full general and commander of the Army of Tennessee, by hisself at a writin desk. Doc Cowan says Old Bedford stomps up to Braggs very face, jabs his index finger in Braggs chest, and begins to berate him for his "cowerdly and contemptable persecution" and for robbin him "in a spirit of revenge and spite" of his first command that he equiped from the enemys of our country. Still drivin home evry point with his index finger in Braggs chest, Gen. Forrest went on bout his reputation for sucesful fightin bein second to none, and how Bragg now in a "work of spite and persecution" stole the second brigade that he rased, trained and equiped hisself. Then Gen. Forrest finished by sayin "I have stood your meaness as long as I intend to. You have played the part of a damned scoundrel, and if you were any part of a man I would slap your jaws and force you to resent it. You may as well not issue any orders to me for I will not obey them." Doc Cowan says as the general turnd to leave the tent, he looked back at the startled Bragg and finished, "and I say to you that if you ever again try to interfer with me or cross my path it will be at the peril of your life."

Then the general stomps from the tent with poor Cowan behind him, leavin the stunned Gen. Bragg in his chair.

"Now your in for it" Doc Cowan says to Gen. Forrest.

"No" says the general, "he wont say a word bout it. He will be the last man to mention it, and mark my word he will take no action in the matter."

"What will happen now?" asks the doctor.

"I will ask to be releved and transferd to a diffrent field" says Gen. Forrest "and he will not opose it."

So thats what Dr. Cowan was a witness to, and sure nough Old Bedford was right. Insted of facin a court-martial for gross insubordanation, he had a private meeting with President Davis hisself, and now the general and our brigade of only bout 300 men is asined to create as much havoc for the enemy as posable in West Tennessee – our homeland now entirely behind enemy lines.

I hear tell Gen. Forrest is bringin his little brigade right near here to Rome, Ga. in the next few days, and I now feel Lizzie that I am able to join and ride with them. Thanks to God almighty, Doc Cowan, all these kind medical people, and specialy to you and Ma for givin me back my strength and health. As you seen yourself I can now walk pretty fair, and once I bend my knee I can keep it bent and feel sure I can hold in the saddle. I am very anxous to join my comrads and can not tolerate bein in bed no more. So next you hear from me, I will be back in the saddle in the field. Till then, remember me to be, most truly,

Your loving husband,
Henry

Nov. 20, 1863
Okolona, Miss.

My Dearest Elizabeth,

Here I am back in the saddle again. Theres times when I think maybe I hastend my recovery a bit too much. Not since we run down Abel Streight have I been so darn tired, and after a few hunderd miles on Buster these past couple weeks I dont need remindin my knee was bad hurt, it lets me remember itself. Walkin aint too bad, I just kinda shuffle along strait-leg on the left side. And ridin aint bad neither, once I get my leg bent. Its the in-tween part that hurts pretty bad. But in early November, just a couple days after writin my last letter to you, Doc Cowan come and check my leg out and said he would let me leave the hospital if I so desire. I tole him I do so desire, and very much for I was plum wore out just layin there. So Markbright and Morton come ridin up next day with Buster in tow, plus a fancy new uniform and camp gear, plus my saber, Sharps carbine and pistols and I was ready to ride.

First problem I encounter was mountin Buster. No way could I get my left foot up in the stirup, so I got to mount from the right side which is awkwerd for me, but old Buster soon catch on and lean down for me. Once on, I forced my left knee to bend, tryin not to cry out loud, then on to Rome, Ga. to meet up with the rest of our small brigade. It was nice to ride into camp and see all my chums, specially them of the escort company. There was your brothers, harden soldiers now, smilin and clappin me on the back. Willie Forrest was right glad to see me, as was our unoficial leader of the escort company Lt. Nathan Boone, who looks at me and says

131

"Was you gone Wylie?" All the boys come up to me and shake my hand or ask to see my knee, and many of them showd me wounds they receved at Chickamauga and other places. Then Gen. Forrest hisself come from his tent to greet me. "Well Lt. Wylie, glad to see you back in camp. Dont you think you layed in that hospital long enough?"

"Yes indeed, sir" says I, "I am right glad to be back."

"And not a day too soon Wylie, we got a army to round up you know," says he "and I will be needin some a your fancy talk to get these absentees and deserters to ride with us."

"You think sir," I says laughin, "my knee might not be the right advertizin to perswade them to join up?"

"Dont worry Henry," he goes on "we will perswade them one way or other" while pattin his revolver.

Now we been here in Okolona a few days, and while Gen. Forrest is badgerin the goverment for arms, amunition, supplys and money to buy some of these things, we been ridin out recrutin us some young men who for one reason or other aint a soldier already.

Yesterday me and Markbright found a couple young fellas, they aint brothers but cousins, livin together on a sizable plantation with many nigra slaves workin the fields. These boys, both seventeen name Olin and Turner Richards, is intrested in joinin up but dont have to on acount the size farm the family has and the number a slaves they keep. They was askin alot a questions bout the cavalry and Gen. Forrest, and since they can provide there own mounts they seem a good choice. Markbright and me invite them back to camp for a little look-see, and in the evning we set round the fire and russle up some grub. They was curius bout my wound and one finaly asks, kinda embaressed, "Lt. Wylie how do you know you wont be, well scared, you know chicken, when you face the enemy the first time?"

"Well you dont," says I lookin in to the fire, "at our first fight back in Dec. of '61 at Sacramento, I truly did not know if I would be brave or not, but then I decided I had to face the bull."

"Face the bull sir" says Olin, "what does that mean?"

Then Lizzie, I tole them this true story that means so much to me and I dare say you hear me tell before, and I relived it many a time while layin on my back in the hospital.

I says "Boys, I growd up on a small farm outside Memphis, just Ma and Pa and myself and we growd maybe fifty acre a corn and wheat, and kept some cows and chickens and a few hogs and sheep. One of my chores since I was shorter then that rifle was muckin out the cow barn. We had a couple dozen cows there and one old ornry bull who pretty much had his way in evrything. One cold day (it mighta been in November) when I was ten years old, I was in the barn rakin out the muck. Some one musta forgot to close the pasture gate, for just as I start workin in the bulls stall I hear a angry snort and here comes that old bull runnin through the barn door and lookin hard at me. He seen me in his box and come right at me snortin loud. I was just parilized in fear, for no one ever messed with the ornry old brute, and best I could do was fall back against the wall and scream as loud as I could "Pa, Pa help!" That bull just keep on comin at me and I knowd he was fixin to do me in, you could see it in his eyes.

Right then Pa come runnin round the corner and seen the situation right quick. He grabs a shovel and starts walkin fast toward the bull, yellin all the while at the top a his voice "Get out, get outa here right now!" That old bull, not likin this interuption, swings round and stares right back at Pa. Then the angry snortin growd louder, puffs a hot breath come from his nose, he lowers his head with them great horns and starts stampin his hoofs in the ground fixin for a charge. But Pa keeps comin forward yellin as he come. My pa aint a big man, but with his fearless aproach, his determind voice and his thick hands holdin tight on that shovel, he seem to me at that moment even bigger then the bull. And it must seem that way to the old bull too, for he skedadles, side-steppin right past Pa who give him a little swat on the rump as he race out

133

the barn. Once gone, Pa turn to me and says "Its OK Henry, you can come out now."

I run to him and throwd my arms round him. "Wasnt you scared Pa, what would you done if he charge you Pa?" He thinks a moment, "I dont know" he says, "tryed to get out the way I reckon. Didnt have time to be scared."

I done a lot a thinkin that day, and learnt two lessons. One was that there comes a time when fearless action is requird of a man, a time when he must act without thinkin of no consequences. You cant take time to be scared for that may weaken your nerve. And when we lined up at Sacramento to make that first darin charge in the face of the enemy, I knowd that instent I had to face the bull, nothin else just face the bull, and I would do my duty."

"I think I understand Lutenant" says Turner Richards, "but what was the second lesson you learnt that day?"

"The second lesson my young friend, was that some times you dont need to read a story book to find a hero for yourself."

This morning Lizzie, Olin and Turner Richards come ridin in to camp on some fine lookin horses and sine up to join our new brigade. Now I supose I will be like a mother hen to them chicks too. Oh well.

I hear tell that tomorow we might move outa Okolona and ride back to our homeland in West Tennessee, probly up to Jackson, where we begin in ernest roundin up a army. Well I must get ready to bend my leg, so till next time I am as always,

Your loving husband,
Henry

Dec. 13, 1863
Jackson, Tenn.

Dear Elizabeth,

Here we are, all 450 of us in Gen. Forrests army in the middle of enemy teritory that just happens to be our homeland. I am feelin better and stronger evry day, though I do not beleve I will ever get my leg back to workin right without pain.

We been workin very hard these past few weeks recrutin men to join our ranks. Gen. Forrest, who knowd this area better then any man alive, set up "recrutin stations" in evry single county in West Tennessee. These stations often as not take the shape of small tents set up in the dense underbrush or deep woods cause the yankees patrol heavy and got there own recrutin stations set up in the towns. To find men willin to become soldiers, we fan out in to each town, passin word on the sly at evry saloon, church gatherin and place a bisness that any intrested party can find us at such and such a place at such and such a hour. We been findin, not like in years past when recrutin men, that good prospects is scarce.

With the help of our new commanders like Col. Tyree Bell, who spent his entire life in West Tennessee and got lots of political and bisness conections through out the country side, we are gatherin recrutes at a rate of 50 to 100 men a day. And of course the biggest factor helpin us bring in soldiers is the reputation and fame that spred far and wide of Gen. Forrest. The storys of our great victorys is makin him a legend through the south, and even the most reluctent men want to rally round his flag.

To be truthful Lizzie, though we are getting enough men, they aint what you call the pick of the litter. Them good ones been soldiers long since. Most of the men me and Markbright and your brothers (we usualy act as a team) sine up been in the army before, but many was 12-month enlistments who skedadled when there time was up, and a good many is just plain deserters who walk off from there commands and dont come back. For instence, Col. Richardson who join our brigade last month in Okolona, left Tennessee two months ago with 800 mounted and armed men, and by the time he got in to Mississippi the brigade shrunk down to only bout 150 men, the rest just meltin in to the country side as they march south. Just deserters and run-aways.

Its these type a men that we pull in from evry where, and I dare say our ranks is swelled to 3000 men now, most got horses but few with decent rifles. And there are, I must confess a certan number of helthy and able-body young men whose just too lazy or cowerdly to fight for there country, and we perswade them to join up usualy at the point of our saber.

Last week Markbright and me was in a barber shop outside Purdy, wearin civilian clothes of course, and talkin to a few fellas bout joinin up. Settin there was a big hulkin young fella with a loud voice and vulgar tongue, who was tellin us in no uncertan terms that he aint joinin no army, he dont give a damn bout no Gen. Forrest, cause he is makin more money doin farm labor now then ever before in his life. "Besides" says he puffin out his big chest, "I dont take kindly to no man, specialy not a blow-hard like this Nathan Bedford Forrest orderin me what to do."

"What make you think Gen. Forrest is a blow-hard?" I asks.

"Cause" says he, "these generals let them stars go to there head. All these poor bastards sayin yes-sir to them all the time makes them think there kings or some thing. Why I show them diffrent."

"Would you like to meet Gen. Forrest in person?" asks Markbright, "Henry and me will take you to him direct and you can tell him all you want."

Well, we went on talkin to this chap a long time and it end by him joinin up next day. His name is Truman Slack and he come without horse nor gun (I think he spends all his farm money in the saloon each night) and only time will tell if this loud-mouth braggert will mount to much of a soldier. He seen the general walkin through camp a few times but aint yet gone up and give him a piece of his mind. Me and Markbright is just waitin for that.

The generals workin hard tryin to get horses, rifles and pistols, food, forage, uniforms and camp supplys from the goverment for all these new recrutes, and I hear tell he spent over $20,000 of his own money outfittin us already. Besides gatherin soldiers, our boys is roundin up food still on the hoof, and we got at least a couple hunderd cows and even more hogs. Col. Richardson apointed your brothers Bobby and John as chief herders, I dont know why, but there gettin ready to move there "recrutes" southward in to Mississippi real soon.

Something you and your folks might be intrested to hear was tole me by Gen. Forrest hisself a couple weeks ago. It seems on the same day I got hit at Chickamauga, that night neither Willie Forrest or your brother Bobby was to be found in camp. Gen. Forrest, as busy as he was makin plans and scoutin the area, gets real anxous at the absense of his young son and your little brother and went out on the battlefield hisself checkin bodys for them two lads. After hours of this grisly search, he had no luck and return to camp wore out and concernd. Next morning fore the fightin was resumed, marchin in to camp comes Bobby and Willie with 25 yankee prisners held at gunpoint. The general said he did not know if he should shake there hands or tan there hides. I think he musta did some of both cause Bobby never mention this epasode to me at all. Quite a soldier that boy is becomin.

Anyway Lizzie I got to pack up for I hear were off tomorow. The general is movin this rag-tag bunch south to Mississippi to train and organize them into a real army corp, and cause Bill Forrest and the scouts report no less then five yankee commands convergin on us from evry direction. Thats the price we pay for the fear inspired by the name "Forrest" amongst the yankee high command. Yet he managed to round up a army under there very nose. Seein how maybe less then a third of these 2500 new soldiers even got a gun, I hope Old Bedford can slip us through enemy teritory without a major engagment. I will sure let you know if we ever get in to Ole Miss. Till then I am as always,

Your loving husband,
Henry

Dear Elizabeth,

How can you ever explane to our little daughter why her daddy is gone away for Christmas. For the third year in a row I spent this blessed day not with my beloved family, but amongst a group of harden men campin on the cold ground. Not like the other years, this Christmas we could make no special note of the sacred day as we was ridin hard to elude the pursuin yankee colums.

I beleve I tole you in my last letter that by mid December our recrutin of a new brigade was done, and Gen. Forrest wanted to move this hodge-podge of poorly mounted and mostly unarmed men south to Mississippi fore all the many yankee commands catch up to us.

So by Dec. 15 we left Jackson behind and Gen. Forrest broke our brigade in to three colums. Col. Richardson took bout 500 men with rifles down the east roads, Col. Wilson made his way down the west roads with a like number, while Maj. Gen. Forrest (yes, he been recently promoted to Major General) took the bulk of 2000 mostly unarmed men strait south, movin the livestock with us. Our three colums was to converge near Estenaula to cross the Hatchie River.

On Dec. 23 the three colums was fallin together as planned near the swampy banks of the rain-swelled and partly froze Hatchie. Some clever manuverin by Gen. Forrest allowd us to avoid contact with the enemy. Col. Richardsons colum did meet and tussle with the enemy but manage to escape and join us up.

By this time the yankees long since burnd all the bridges crossin the Hatchie, but them brave and resourcful scouts under Capt. Bill Forrest did russle up one old rickety ferryboat. So on Dec. 24 which was crisp and sunny, we comence sendin our 3000 men and horses, our 500 cows and hogs, our forty wagon loads a bacon and supplys acrost the muddy Hatchie.

It was slow gettin all them anxous critters on bord the flimsy boat, keepin them still for the twenty minute ride over, unloadin and headin back again. I figurd the yankees sure as heck would catch us up, and sure nough the scouts report seein bout 600 union infantry aproachin the Hatchie from the south, the side we was crossin over to.

The only troops who got acrost yet was unarmed, undrilled recrutes, and us 65 veterans of the escort company. Many a time fore this Gen. Forrest rely on his escort men to fight like a regiment of many hunderds, and so he done again. With the yankee foot soldiers arrivin after sunset to within a couple miles of our position on the south bank, the general led just us men of the escort out ahead to meet them. He payed no nevermind to us bein outnumberd ten to one. We creeped up to a quarter mile of the yankee campfires, only a cornfield seperatin us. The general spred each of us a good ten paces apart and tole evry fourth man when we got the order to charge they was to shout out orders as if linin up a company in a brigade drill. A moment later the general draws his saber and hollers "Brigade charge!" As we all spur our horses, evry fourth man was screamin orders to imagenary companys to do this or that. The rest of us was hollerin and whoopin and with the horses smashin through the dryed cornstalks we made a considerble racket. We was all emptyin our revolvers as we charge, and by God them yankees musta thought a brigade of hunderds was attackin. They quick grab up all the belongings they could muster and fell in to a disorganize rout. It was a sight to see and we spent time gatherin up some usefull supplys. Some left coffee still boilin in the kettle. Next day the scouts report them yankees near ten miles off.

Been more then three months since my injury, but I can tell you Lizzie, the exitement of that charge and the hard spurrin of Buster cause my knee to ache bad. After chasin off the enemy we rode back to help with the river crossin. The night was frosty and a stedy breeze blowd the cold river air in our face. I stayed mounted on Buster cause I feard standin on my leg, but lots of men was buildin low fires to keep warm.

Durin one trip acrost the river in the midst of the night, some of the animals on bord musta shifted, for the frail ferryboat tipped and capsize. Men, horses and a team of mules hitched to a wagon, pitched in to the dark current. It was a perilous moment and Gen. Forrest hisself and a number of men jump off the south bank and swum out to the scene. The men and horses was all able to swim to shore, and the ferryboat was righted and dragged back. I seen Gen. Forrest up to his armpits in the freezin water, cuttin the harnesses off the thrashin mules tryin to save them from drownin. All the while this exitement was goin on, Truman Slack, that strappin loud-mouth recrute I wrote you of, was stompin up and down the bank tellin evryone that he aint goin in no g-damn froze river for nothing, and no officer nor any one else could make him do it. When the general and the other heros come wadin out, the men on the shore cheered them for there effort, exept Truman Slack who called them fools for savin a bunch a dumb animals. As the general was crawlin up the muddy bank, he slip back in once and I could hear Truman Slack goin "heh, heh, heh." When Gen. Forrest finaly got out, muddy and near froze, he didnt say nothing but walks right up to Pvt. Slack, grabs him by the neck and seat of the pants, and flung him with great strength high and far out in to the river. The men stood real still, but when Old Bedford walked away we all broke out in uncontrolable laughter at the sight. Truman Slack learnt a big lesson that night.

By the afternoon of Christmas day our reunited brigade resumed our march southward. At one point our command was pressed by yankees headin east from Colliersville and west from Grand Junction. The general split our brigade in half, had even the unarmed men line up in battle formation, and attacked the yankees in both directions and drove them off. These new recrutes is learnin quick what it means to fight with "The Wizard Of The Saddle."

When we got to the Wolf River just ten miles north of the Mississippi line we found a bridge the yankees burnd but the stringers was still standin. They was chard and frail, but Gen. Forrest led the repair crews and we fortifyed the stringers, relayed the planking and drove our brigade, livestock and wagons over.

After crossin the Wolf we was pursude heavy by varius squads of yankees, had a minor skermish, and I must say I got a bit homesick as Gen. Forrest led us within nine miles of Memphis to avoid more yankee colums. On Dec. 30 we rode into Holly Springs, Mississippi and on Jan. 1, 1864 we got here in Como, where General Forrest is goin to take some time organizin his army, trainin and drillin them, and doin his best to outfit and arm them. I reckon we will be here for a while and I am hopin to receve some letters from home. Please know that my heart and soul was with you on Christmas day, as it is evry day, and remember me to be,

Your loving husband,
Henry

Jan. 31, 1864
Como, Miss.

Dear Elizabeth,

We been here in Como for a month now and this group a ragtag individules is just startin to resemble a cavalry brigade. We been drillin these greenhorns, misfits and deserters evry single day and they seem now able to act with each other as a unit. Also Gen. Forrest been talkin with his department commander Gen. Stephen Lee, and together they been able to get some decent rifles, amunition and supplys sent to us. Now dont get too exited when I tell you, but I even receved some back pay — the first cash I seen, Confederate or Federal in many months. I enclose all of it exept enough to buy a few simple comforts such as ink and paper and some tobaco for my pipe. Pert near evry man smokes a pipe or cigars, or chews. Them that chews mostly got black teeth.

I also been much fortunat for I receved a passel of letters from you and Ma, dated since before my wound on Sept. 20. I enjoyd readin them very much, and sounds like Christmas was a pretty solum ocasion, what with the shortages and all. At least Ma and Pa still got a little livestock left to provide food.

I am writin this letter in the small hut me and Markbright share — it is pretty snug for it has post and rail walls pack tight with dryed mud, and though the weather is exeptionly cold most nights we manage to stay some what warm and comfitable. Some of the boys got home made fireplaces in there huts too, but we feel they just aint use to the cold like us.

As I am settin here writin this letter Gen. Forrest hisself poke his head in our hut to ask Markbright a question bout some requesition or other. The general seen me writin this letter usin Busters saddle as a writin table and says "Seems like any time you got a spare minute Wylie, your writin to some body. Whose the lucky recever of all them letters?"

"My wife sir, I like keepin her informd of evrything I do," answers I.

"Well thats grand Wylie, very good of you to take the time for your loved one. You know," says he "I should write home more often myself, but I cant see a pen but what thinkin of a snake."

I laughed and says "Course, General, you dont need to write so much seein how Mrs. Forrest is in camp so often." Its true Lizzie, when ever we make camp for more then a few weeks, the kindly Mrs. Forrest finds her way to her husbands side.

Besides, I seen the generals writin many times and it aint much to look at. I know I aint no book-writer myself like Markbright, but its some times hard to even read the generals writin. But yet when listenin to him talk, you soon learn he got a gifted way with words. He is a born speaker and when he talks to you alone or to the whole brigade, his words are clear and strike at the heart of the matter. Once speakin to us after capturin Murfreesboro, Brentwood and Abel Streight, he said the three great victorys would "enshrine your names in history as a demonstration of your prowess." Nice words, aint they Lizzie?

Anyways, the general finaly got this corp reorganized in to something he can work with. We now got close to 3500 men total, with four small brigades of four or five regiments in each. The four brigade commanders is Brigadere General R. V. Richardson (mostly West Tennessee boys in his), Col. Tyree Bell and his five Tennessee regiments, Col. Robert (Black Bob) McCulloch with some boys from Missouri, Kentucky, Mississippi and Texas, and Col. Jeffrey Forrest, the generals youngest (and I beleve favrite) brother with all Mississippi regiments. And now second in command to Gen. Forrest is Brig. Gen. James L. Chalmers, a young (cant be but thirty or so) Virginian. He was a college man and lawyer in Holly Springs, Miss. before the war, and he seen alot of action at Pittsburg Landing and Murfreesboro. He is pretty populer with the men who serve him, they often call him "Little Un" when he aint listenin, but he is a hard drivin man with a quick temper, a lot like the general hisself. Though Gen. Forrest apointed him second in command, these two forcfull men sometimes butt heads a bit. We can but wait and see how good they can work together now.

Markbright tells me we got more drills to call tonight so I best get goin. Though they seem to be learnin how we fight, these new recrutes is still the most rowdy, wild and some times ornry group I ever delt with. Lots a times there in groups all laughin and shoutin, then sure as heck some fight brakes out and men is punchin and swingin things. They always got some game or other goin on, and I dare say more then a few decided to just walk off and not return. The general can tolerate fights, games and rowdyness, but he wont brook no runaways.

Anyways, it was very satisfying hearin from home and you and Mary are always in my thoughts and prayers. Till were together again remember me to be as always,

Your loving husband,
Henry

P.S.

I know this will please you Lizzie — Markbright received a package from home this week and in it was a spankin new strait razer, and with it I shaved off that beard you was so averse to when you seen me in the hospital. All I left was the mustash and chin-whiskers same as Markbright and Gen. Forrest got. Now when we meet again you wont be afraid to kiss me.

Chapter 9

February 19, 1864 through March 14, 1864

Feb. 19, 1864
Near West Point, Miss.

Dear Elizabeth,

I really dont have much time to· write a letter cause we been ridin hard these past ten days through this state of Mississippi. But Mr. Gallaway says he is headin back north and will post any letters he gets. So I will quick catch you up to date as we are restin the horses a spell.

I got to tend to Buster as he lost a shoe this morning when trottin through a strech of muddy roads. Nothing pulls the shoes off a horse quicker then mud, but Gen. Forrest had the smiths make a extra set a shoes for as many horses as posable, Buster included, and I carry them in my saddle bag with nails too. Sure dont want my powerful steed to come up lame now, as confrontation with the enemy seems likly soon.

The first week a Febuary the scouts started reportin to the general a huge union army of infantry settin off from Vicksburg with the most likly target bein Meridian, Mississippi where the amunition factorys is. The general reckons the yankees will move through Mississippi to Selma, Alabama to destroy the foundrys there and maybe go all the way to capture Mobile.

But we cant worry bout there infantry. What we got to cope with is the large cavalry force sent out ahead of that infantry

145

movment. One of our scouts, a absolutly fearless man name Nate Benson, mixed hisself in the ranks of the yankee cavalry for a day or two without bein discoverd, and he reports them at maybe 7000 strong, very well armed (he seen many with breech-loadin repeatin rifles) with the purpose of trackin down and destroyin the cavalry of Gen. Nathan Bedford Forrest. Benson says the union cavalry is led by a general name William Sooy Smith (thats what he says, "Sooy," aint that a odd name?) and he has bout twenty artilery pieces and is ready for action.

By Feb. 8 Gen. Forrest decided the trainin, drillin and organizin of his new corp was over and he best move out to try and head off this union cavalry. We been hoofin ever since. The weather been mostly plesant and dry, dont mind cool air if the sun is shinin. In the past week we rode from the swampy Tallahatchie bottoms of west Mississippi to the furtle praries of east Mississippi with all its big plantations.

This new corp is so far doin pretty good holdin itself together – many of these boys is facin there first campain against the enemy. While we was in camp in Como durin Jan. we was havin some problems with men just walkin out a camp and not comin back. Some complaind bout not havin warm clothes, others say they dont want no part of fightin, others want to earn money some wheres else.

But Gen. Forrest dont take kindly to deserters, and the last straw come a few weeks ago when 19 boys walked away one night and wasnt there for morning role. Oh Lizzie, the general was irate when he herd this. I herd him all the way crost camp cursin them "g-damn cowerds." He was so furius he orderd his brother Capt. Bill Forrest and a passel of his scouts to hunt them deserters down. You know a flea couldnt hide in a jungle from them fellas, and sure nough a day later the scouts come back leadin the whole bunch at gunpoint.

A court-martial was held next day, Col. Tyree Bell in charge as the deserters was from his brigade, and 17 of them was found guilty of desertion and sentanced to be executed in two days. (Two brothers was not found guilty cause they showd a letter sayin there mother was very sick and bout to die).

Next day a old barn was tore down and from the lumber them 17 men made a coffin for therselves, and then they was led to a clearing where they spent some of there last hours diggin there own graves. At this time a group of local women went to Gen. Forrest in person pleadin the lives of these men be spared. The general was hard as flint though, dismissin the sorowful ladys by sayin flat "I will have no cowerds in my command."

Next morning Friday, Feb. 12 (I wont soon forget that day) the condemed men come out with hands tied behind there backs. They was loaded on to wagons and rode out to the open field. There they was placed in a long row with each man settin on his coffin beside a open grave, while Col. Tyree Bells brigade was lined up on three sides to watch the execution. Forty men from Col. Richardsons brigade was orderd to be on the firin squad, as nary a man from the whole corp voluteerd for the service. (I beleve evry man in his heart knowd why they run off, for we all been homesick, specialy at the beginin, and these boys was just a little weaker then us).

The condemed was led by Capt. Brown in prayer for a few minutes, and when Parson Brown says "Amen" real quiet, I herd many men round me say "Amen." As a mournful drum sounded, Col. Bell took his place by the firin squad. The blindfolded men stood ramrod strait, though one poor fellow buckled to his knees and I herd a quiet whimper from his lips. Raisin his saber half way the colonel yells "Guns loaded!" "Ready" shouts Col. Bell. "Aim," raisin his saber higher. "Halt!" shouts a sudden voice from the crowd of watchin soldiers. Gen. Forrest on horseback rode from the line, orders the guns down, and rides to the quakin men. "Do you men promise to serve as faithfull soldiers of the Confederate States of America?" Of course they all plead yes, yes, yes. "Then I pardon you for your crimes" he says, and turnin so evryone could hear he shouts "but if there is any further desertions or disobediance of orders by anyone in this command, there will be no leniancy."

With this a mighty cheer went up from the ranks as the prisners was untied and the graves was filled in. Many the womenfolk in the town cryed as the news spred, and now Lizzie, a week later and a battle with the yankees drawin nigh, not one man has left the army without permision. I guess Gen. Forrest made his point.

This letter is already takin too long. I got to tend to Buster and pack three days rations fore we start movin again.

As always, I am

> Your loving husband,
> Henry

Feb. 27, 1864
Columbus, Miss.

Dear Elizabeth,

I am very thankful to the good Lord above that I can set here inside my tent restin on my bed role and write a letter to you, for I must say this past week was maybe the most frightfull since I been away. Thank God I am safe and mostly unhurt, cept for sevral cuts on my left arm and a small gash on my head that look a lot worse then it really is. Your brothers too is both alive though both receve minor injurys now bein tended. Them two boys done some mean fightin this week.

You may recall from my last letter the yankees was sendin a major infantry force from Vicksburg to Meridian where they was to join up with a fine outfit of union cavalry (bout 7000 strong) comin from Memphis. Gen. Forrest reckoned them forces was plannin to destroy the heartland of the Confederacy as they storm through to Selma and maybe on to Mobile. The only army of the south capable of gettin in there way was our little corp of new troopers.

Gen. Forrests plan was for us to cut off the union cavalry fore it could link up with the infantry at Meridian. In this he suceeded cause we hardly set out from West Point fore the scouts reported seein the yankee cavalry just a few miles off near Okolona. At once the general orderd Chalmers division north acrost the Sakatonchee River to attack the yankees when they first come into sight.

Gen. Forrest, as is his trademark in battle, sent the brigades of Bell and McCulloch northward both east and west of the main road so as to close in round the flanks of the aproachin yankee cavalry. And on Sunday Feb. 21 the enemy horsemen first come in contact with Chalmers advance troops. The sudden boom of distent cannon fire made the coffee cup in Markbrights hand stop halfway to his lips, he looks at me and says "Time for fun Henry." The thunder of artilery was pickin up and we could just make out the sound of musket fire and evry one in camp was stirrin and anxous. For most it would be there first fight with the enemy. Big loud Truman Slack was very quiet as he set checkin his gear, and as I rode past the Richards boys Olin and Turner, they look pretty serius and I says "Time to face the bull men."

Didnt take long for our little command, we was less then a thousand men here, to get mounted and form in to colum as we headed north to cross the Sakatonchee and join Chalmers men who was already busy fightin the yankee hords. As we lined up, the escort company in the lead behind Gen. Forrest, I could see the general startin to get worked up to that frightful pitch he assumes in battle. He was barkin orders in short temper, and itchin to go.

We was soon gallupin northward in a colum four men wide on a dusty road, the prarie wide and open on both sides. After just three or four miles I could see lookin back that our colum was gettin longer as the slower horses was already fallin back. All the while the sound of battle gettin louder. We rounded a bend and come upon a narrow span called Ellis Bridge, over the Sakatonchee and just beyond this the battle was ragin.

We crost the bridge and soon come upon Gen. Chalmers. Gen. Forrest rode to him quick and says in his harsh battle voice "Whats goin on at this front Chalmers?" Chalmers seem to me a little suprized at how severe the generals face and voice was, and he says "I am waitin for reports from the front, I have not been to the firing line myself." Gen. Forrest none too happy, snaps at him "Is that all you know? Then I will go there goddammit and find out for myself." And turnin toward the men just crost the bridge, "Come on boys."

Then I seen something kinda unusual happen. Just as the general turn to go we see a soldier come runnin from the battle all in a fit. I seen that look of battle panic before — his gun and hat gone, eyes wild, no saber or nothing to slow his flight from the front. Gen. Forrest right then jumps off his horse and grabs the tremblin fella by the shoulders and throws him to the ground. Then he drags the man by the coller acrost the road, broke off a tree limb right there and starts whippin the man with it. He give him a severe thrashin, the man wisely makin no resistence. Then the general pulls him to his feet and hollers in his face "Now goddamn you, go back to the front and fight. You might as well be killed there as here, for if you ever run away again you will not get off so easy." Markbright and me just look at each other and I beleve we both woulda cracked a smile as the scene was a bit comic, but we knowd we would be gettin the thrashin next.

Again the general shouts "Come on boys," and we soon found ourselvs in the midst of the fray beside the tired troops of Chalmers. I jump down from Buster and gave him over to the horse-holder. My leap down caused a shock of pain in my knee, but I run forward and crouch behind a nobby mound of grass, and comence firin my Sharps carbine. Our artilery wasnt up yet, but I counted at least six pieces they was firin at us and fortunatly they aimed most shots too high. This fray last a good hour or more, neither side movin forwards or backwards. Finaly by late morning the brigades of Bell and McCulloch come in to action on the flanks of the enemy, and soon the yankee soldiers was remounted and pullin back.

At the sight of this Gen. Forrest got us all back on the horses and in wild pursute of the fleein yankee cavalry. They was headin up the main road toward Okolona, the very highway they just tramped down earlier that day. This flight was startin to look like a rout as the yankee thousands was flyin pell-mell up the dusty road. In close pursute, we captured laggin enemy soldiers and picked up six of there artilery pieces that fell behind.

To us who been there, this wild chase was remindfull of the trackin down of Abel Streight and his command. Twict along the way the rear of the yankee colum stopped, regrouped and fired on our lead troops. On the second ocasion Gen. Forrest did not stop to regroup our spred-out colum, but kept the charge on and soon he found hisself and us handful of men in the midst of the enemy. Surounded by grimy-face yankees, I was firin my pistol at short range and here receved a bad cut to my left hand, though little realized it at the time (I beleve I was grazed by a bullit). Lizzie, I dont want to frighten you unduly, but I woulda been killed most certin here as a enemy horseman close behind raised his pistol to my head, but seein Gen. Forrest near by fired at him instead of me, blowin the generals coller off his uniform but missin his body. Gen. Forrest swung round and shot dead this man.

Many yankees surenderd here, the rest resumed there flight back toward Okolona. The chase was on again with dark desendin and the air crisp, and we rode in close pursute for another hour or more. Now there was no colum of men, just a long line of racin horsemen spred over many miles. As dark come on, Gen. Forrest and a few of us in the escort was so far ahead, the rest of our men was firin pot-shots at us, confusin us for the fleein yankees. This got real serius when Micky House got hit in the back (and later died) and even Gen. Forrest got nicked by firin from behind. With this the general call a halt for the night, hopin to regroup our corp.

We was lucky for we stopped right near the camp sight the enemy used on his way down and we was grateful to the retreatin owners for leavin us food and water, and specialy stacks a firewood as the night was downright cold.

All evning and in to the night tired boys kept ridin in to camp. Even though we was exausted we tended the horses first, then set down to eat and rest ourselvs. Markbright dressed my cut hand, and your brothers come to our fire and we talked bout the hard fight and wild ride of the day.

Next morning fore 4:00 we was up and runnin again. Some of the tired boys was moanin and groanin and many the men was on broken down horses by now, and our ranks got thin. Still we gallup northward knowin full well the yankees was there, and Gen. Forrest wanted to "keep the skeer on" and run them outa our heartland.

Couple hours after sunrise we come upon Okolona and pulled to a halt as we seen on the horizon the vast cavalry of yankees spred acrost the prarie and fixin for a fight. They musta been four or five thousand men strong at this point and we stood with Gen. Forrest, just the tireless escort company and a hunderd others who kept up. The general looked to the south, hopin to see men drawin up, when off to the east we catch sight of a body a mounted men comin on to the field. It was Col. Tyree Bell and his brigade of a thousand men. Couple days before, Bell set out on a paralel rout to releve crowdin on the narow road. He promised Gen. Forrest to join us up this very morning, Feb. 22 at Okolona. Col. Bell kept his word.

Gen. Forrest was most encouraged by this timely arival of Bells brigade. Standin high in his stirups, his face turnd a fearsom red, he put us in battle formation and yells "Charge men, charge." We kicked up our poor beasts, many frothin at the mouth, pulled our pistols and screamed with vigor in our attack. The yankees, some firin rapid fire carbines, put up a good show and emptyed many a saddle. But the fury of our attack broke a section of there line and as they started fallin back, the whole line gave way and they was racin away from us.

Again the chase was on. Not for long though, as the yankees pulled up in a hilly wooded plantation called Iveys Hill. Again they formed for battle, this time takin positions behind the stone walls of the peacful homested. They hid in the white-pillord house, the stables, the ginhouse and other outbuildings, placin there artilery and throwin wide flankers. There was a powerful lot of them too.

Our troops was slowly catchin up and regroupin, many of the men on foot for miles after there horses broke down. In any regard we was outnumberd bad. But as always Gen. Forrest was on the ofensive and sent what men he could muster round the right through a wooded section, his brother Col. Jeffrey Forrest in the lead. As soon as this flankin movment swept in to the enemy, the yanks loosed a mighty volly of artilery and rifle fire. In this first volly Col. Jeffrey Forrest receved a shot in the neck which musta cut a major artery, as blood gushed free to the ground. The young colonel, his uniform all over red, very quick expired. I was with the general as he raced to his brothers side. Even amidst the intense gun fire and clamor of battle, Gen. Forrest dismounted and kneeld by his brother, lifted his lifeless head, and whisperd most quiet "Jeffrey, Jeffrey." Tears rold down his grimy face as he clutch his little brother, seventeen years younger than hisself. The general tole me long fore this sad moment that he loved his youngest brother best and expected Jeffrey to rise the highest in life and make the Forrest family proud. All these hopes dead on the ground at the Iveys Hill plantation. The general was froze there with his eyes shut, as if denyin it was so.

His inaction was but momentary for he soon remounted, survayed the progres of the attack, gatherd as many men on horseback or on foot as he could, and tole Jacob Gaus our bugler to sound the charge. With the escort company and sevral hunderd others comin up, the general spurd his horse forward direct in the face of the union soldiers. Now I been with the general on many a headlong attack against a superior enemy, but even to me this charge seem more reckless and desprate then any other. I thought perhaps the general in his dispare was hopin to join his young brother. Never had I seen him attack with such fury and expose hisself to such danger. As we fought toward the enemy line, the generals horse was shot dead from under him. He took the horse from another man and continue his headlong attack. As we battled the enemy in front, Col. Bell and Gen. Chalmers come sweepin in from the flanks. Thus threatend from all sides, the yankees started rollin back again.

"Keep on them boys, keep on them," the general shouted, and even as he spoke his second horse was shot and tumble to the ground. Gen. Forrest was shook up but quick back on his feet.

"Here general," says I ridin over, "take Buster, I can find another."

But this was not nesesary for right then young Willie Forrest come ridin up to his father with King Phillip, the generals favrite steed in tow. The general hitch his saddle, mounted King Phillip and the chase was on again.

For many a mile we galluped in pursute of the fleein yankees as they race northward up dusty lanes. The way was litterd with discarded weapons, blankets, fallen horses and stragglin men. My mind marveled at the strength and endurance of Buster as he kept up the chase for mile after weary mile.

After hours of this flight you can beleve our corp was melted down to maybe a couple hunderd men and horses still able to keep up the pressure. Gen. Forrest astride King Phillip, maybe fifty of the escort, and a handfull of others was all thats left. And finaly in the late afternoon of this memrable Feb. 22, the rear gard of the scatterd yankees pull up to a halt, formin maybe 500 men in a line of battle for one last fight. They was a game bunch, them exausted yankees, formin three lines of troops, each line a good hunderd yards behind the other, the last bein the widest with the most men.

The general quick pull our little group together, arange us in battle formation, and tole us "Boys, put your sabers away. When they get within rifle range, aim in on one man and shoot. When they get within pistol range, aim and shoot. If they make it to our line, fire your pistols till your out of amunition, then give them the point of your saber."

I must admit it was a grand and frightenin sight when the three lines of well-spaced union cavalry spurred there mounts and begun this last charge acrost the wide open prarie. We held still and there was no tree, building or fence rail to interfear with our sight lines. When they got bout 250 yards away we opend with our rifles and a good thirty men on there most forward line fell from the saddle. When they was within 150 yards we started blazin with our side arms, most of us with a revolver in each hand. More saddles emptyed.

In a instant the rest was upon us and thus comence the most furius hand-to-hand fightin I experianced for a long time. We was like gladiators in the days of old, men on steamin, kickin horses thrashin at other men in a constant life and death struggle. Dust was kicked up heavy, men and horses screamin in the extream exitement. Men was slashed, men was shot, men got trampled, cryin out in pain, anger and violance.

Gen. Forrest was the very demon, standin high in the saddle and uncontrold rage in his evry move. I seen at least three enemy troopers layin dead on the ground round the general as he slash and stabbed.

I now remember clear (though at the time it was just another moment in the confusion of the fight) how a young man in blue raised his pistol at my head from a few feet away and pulled the trigger. The gun did not fire and for a instant fear lit his face as I plunge my saber direct through his right shoulder, his pistol fallin from his hand. So hard was my thrust, the point showed a good foot out the back of his uniform. He groaned in pain, reeld forward in the saddle but could not fall for a moment as I had trouble extractin my blade. I give a yank and the man fell to the ground. I pulled the pistol from my belt, aim down at the young mans head and from a sittin position he raised his left hand in front of his face as if this would stop or misdirect my shot. For a moment he stared in my eyes, I couldnt hear his voice amidst the clamor but his lips voice the word "please." I held stedy my aim, then put the hammer down slow, jam the pistol in my belt, drawd my saber and swung Buster off in a diffrent direction. I aint no cowerd Lizzie, and I pray that in my hour of judgment the good Lord will forgive them who broke his sacred Fifth Commandment durin this cursed war, but I could not pull the trigger on a unarmed man, though a moment before he woulda killed me cept for the hand of fate. I knowd besides that a wounded soldier is a worse detrament to his army then a dead soldier.

This deadly free-for-all did not last but a few minutes as more of our troops catched up and joind the fight. The yankees seein us reinforced either surenderd or turnd tale and run. The main body a yankees such as it was, was already miles ahead hoofin northward as fast as there tired horses could run. Gen. Forrest give us rest for sevral hours (and time to round up the prisners) then sent Col. Gholson and his less exausted men ahead to make sure Gen. William Sooy Smith and his weary, dishearted and disorderd cavalry kept high-talin all the way back to Memphis.

And they did. With the union cavalry under Gen. Smith completly foiled in there mission to join up with the yankee infantry, the entire yankee campain of destroyin the heartland of the Confederacy from Vicksburg to Meridian to Selma and maybe even Mobile just may be abandond, and our little corp of new recrutes done great service to there country and citizens. We are proud, proud we "faced the bull" and stared him down.

Now we rest here in Columbus. Dressin wounds, shoddin the horses, gatherin food, talkin bout our sucess and mournin the loss of Col. Jeffrey Forrest and forty other men who give there life for there country. The people here in Columbus sure give us a warm welcom and that reminded us of what were fightin for.

This letter gone on long enough Lizzie, but I get comfort writin to you as I feel I am with you at least in spirit. With my love to Ma and Pa, a kind hello to your folks, and a big hug for Mary, I am

Your loving husband,
Henry

March 14, 1864
Columbus, Miss.

Dear Elizabeth,

We been restin here, regroupin and healin for more then two weeks and I am feelin quite myself again. The injurys I sufferd in the sixty-mile fight we had with Gen. Sooy Smith and his yankees is healin nice, and most these men here feel kinda porky knowin they aint raw recrutes no more. The young Richards boys Olin and Turner tole me they kept up pretty good durin the chase and even come to fairly close quarters with the enemy, and neither lost there courage.

Couple weeks ago Doc Cowan checked in on my head cut and tole me a intrestin story. He says that after we drove the yankees off the Iveys Hill plantation, the general herd loud squeels of pain comin from a small shanty on the grounds. Gen. Forrest and sevral others went in this building to see what the fuss was. You never guess what they found Lizzie. They say the little hut was bein used by the yankees as a field hospital and when the yankees pulled back all the doctors skedadled too. And layin there on a operatin table was a poor yankee soldier with a amputation saw half way through his leg, and him all alone and screamin for mercy. Gen. Forrest found a bottle with a little bit of cloroform in it, splashed it on a rag and put it to the suferers face. With the man now outa his agony for a while at least, the general sent for the doctor to complete the surgery. Doc Cowan tole me the man is now recoverin in a hospital in Okolona alongside our wounded.

Last week I was settin all alone by the campfire fixin some broke straps on my saddle. Just then Gen. Forrest walks up and says "How you doin Leutenant, no serius injurys?"

"No sir," says I, "I am quite well. Sure sorry bout your brother sir, were all gonna miss the colonel."

"Yes indeed Wylie," says the general and he set down right beside me on the ground, leant back against a tree and streched his legs toward the fire as if fixin to stay a spell. "I will miss Jeffrey more then I can say, and I dont know how to tell Mother the right words. She loved him so."

Then his face growd sad and he spoke very slow and quiet as if speakin to hisself as much as me. "My mother has sufferd many hardships. My father William was a poor blacksmith, never learnt to read nor write, and traveled from town to town all over West Tennessee and north Mississippi tryin to scrach out a living. My mother, God bless her saintly soul, is a very strong woman and bore my father many children, me bein the first," he says with a sad smile, "cept my twin sister who died on her first day a life."

"When I was but a lad sixteen years old," he says "my father past on, leavin me and Mother to watch over our family. Four months after my father died the last of ten children was born, Jeffrey. From the first day I took that wee baby under my wing and raised him more like a father than a big brother. As I growd up and become prosprous in the cattle and horse sellin bisness, I tole Mother I would provide the best education money could buy for Jeffrey, and I held his small hand evry day as I walk him to and from school. My other brothers John, William, Aaron and Jesse was growin in to fine, strappin men, but Jeffrey was special — always just a kind and helpfull little boy to me. Two of my sisters died young and John join the army and got a severe wound in the Mexican War that left him on crutches with useless legs for life.

And though we all done well in bisness it was Jeffrey who carryed all my hopes for a bright future when he went off to study medicine at college. Then come this war and William and me joind up, then Aaron and Jesse got in too, and finaly against my wishes Jeffrey left school and answerd his countrys call. Just like evrything else he done in life, he give his all. There was no braver, less selfish or loyal man in the service then little Jeffrey. Now I must tell Mother." The general then set up, seem to snap outa his revery and ask "What about you Wylie, whats your family like?"

"Well General," says I "my pa is a farmer, got a little spred just outside Memphis. Been in the family for years. Gramma and Grampa lived in the house too till they past on. We got cows and other livestock, and growd enough corn and grain to feed the animals and us too. Ma and Gramma always tended a big vegtable garden."

"You got slaves Henry?" he asks.

I smiled. "Just old Sam, been on the farm since fore my pa was born. He limps round the barn now helpin out where he can, more like a friend then slave, I reckon. I dont think he would leave anyways if he was set free."

The general smiled. He probly thought havin one slave pretty meager, as he brung at least forty of his own slaves to war with him, made them all teamsters for our wagons and offerd each one freedom if they stuck it out through the war.

"You got brothers, sisters Wylie?"

"Well my folks seen hardship too General," I went on, "I was the youngest a three children, and in '40 when I was yet three years old my brother Paul and sister Mary catch the pox and both died. In fact most the kids in there school died that spring, and from that day forward my ma done her best to keep me on the farm. She wouldnt let me go to school but give me lessons each day herself. And she was strict bout it too, I can tell you. Evry morning after chores she would say "Henry, time for school" and the lessons begun. She learnt me to read and write and to cipher and made me

learn music on a old piano we had. She made me read alot —
history books, poetry, mithology, philosophy. Any time we went
in to town she brung back new books for me to read. After a few
hours the lessons was done and I would go outside and help Pa on
the farm."

"Did you ever mix with people your own age?" the general
asks, and he really seem intrested.

"Not much General," I says "I got cousins but we dont see
them much cept on ocasions. Each Sunday though, we went to
church in town and after the service I stayed for a little study. You
know it was there I met Elizabeth Parker, the girl I marryed years
later."

"Parker," says the general, "I forgot them Parker boys was
your relatives. Good soldiers."

"Yes indeed, sir."

Then just as quick as he come, he jumps to his feet and says
"Nice talkin to you Wylie, glad you are well."

"Thank you sir," and that was the end of my conversation with
General Forrest.

Anyways Lizzie, I think our period of rest here in this fine
town of Columbus is almost over. Our corp been joind by a group
a Kentucky boys under Brig. Gen. Abraham Buford, and now Gen.
Forrest divide our corp in to two divisions — one under Gen.
Chalmers and the other under Gen. Buford. I beleve Gen. Forrest
is fixin soon to lead Bufords division northward through West
Tennessee and maybe in to Kentucky to capture us some more
recrutes and as many horses as posable, seein how broke down so
many of ours is right now. And of course where ever Gen. Forrest
goes, the escort company goes too.

Till later, my dear ones, remember me to be,

Your loving husband,
Henry

Chapter *10*

April 9, 1864 through April 17, 1864

April 9, 1864
Jackson, Tenn.

Dear Elizabeth,

We been more then three weeks in the saddle. Those of us who got a horse that is. Some of Gen. Abe Bufords Kentucky boys is followin us on foot, and in truth the major goal of this ride into West Tennessee and Kentucky is to round up some horses.

Things been pretty good for us so far. We left Gen. Chalmers and his division back in north Mississippi to try there luck gatherin fresh horses and supplys there, so us bein only bout 1500 in number we can travel crost country at a goodly pace. We left Columbus on March 16 and rode strait to Jackson, a good 150 miles in only four days. I must confess Lizzie, I was suprized and hurt at the condition of our beloved West Tennessee. Seems the whole country side been layed waste — fields, farms, towns all stripped bare and the citizens just able to survive. I pray to God that you, Mary and my love ones is copin tolerable well and not suferin from dire want like so many people I seen. It made my heart sink to see this deprived state, but renews my comitment to our cause and country.

But the desprate condition of our home state is nowheres near so bad as the utter destruction done in north Mississippi by union Gen. Sherman and his army of hoodlums on there recent march to and from Meridian. I know well that war is a terible thing that brings pain and suferin to all people, but still I never seen such a sight before. They did not destroy just the railroads, depots, bridges, arms factorys and other military needs, but this army of thiefs and outlaws burnd homes, schools, shops and churches, plunderd private property and destroyed crops and farms thus deprivin civilians a means of living. I admit that many in this new corp of ours is the most rowdy bunch a varmints we had yet, but them yankees went beyond all rules of civilize warfare. I would be ashamed to be part of that army.

Our journy to West Tennessee and Kentucky been most suceful so far, and in spite the stedy spring rains turnin the roads to mud, we been makin good progres. Once we drove to Jackson, Gen. Forrest sent a brigade under Col. Duckworth to capture the garison at Union City. While we was holdin the town of Paducah, Ky, clearin out the yankees supplys and corralin many hunderd federal horses, Gen. Buford and his brigade was capturin the forts west of Paducah and at Columbus. Funny thing − at each of them yankee garisons, once our boys closed in and fired a few shots, the now famous "Surender or else" message was deliverd and sined "Maj. Gen. N.B. Forrest." In all these places the yankee commander surenderd even though Gen. Forrest was no wheres near the place. Such is the respect and fear inspired by our leader. And from these victorys we are capturin lots a prisners but more important, we gatherd up some fine horses. Many hunderds so far we drove back here to Jackson. Now the Kentucky boys can quit walkin and mount up.

I am feelin fit and healthy. We got plenty a food ourselvs, compliments of Uncle Sam. Wish I could get some of this bacon and sugar to you and Mary. No way to get it there anyhow, no trains runnin or nothing in West Tennessee, maybe a handcar. Sufferd some pretty intense pain early this week while ridin back to Jackson. Evry so often Buster wants to show me whos boss so he scrapes me up close to a tree. I usuly see it comin but this time I didnt and sure nough he squash my bad leg right upside a tree. It hurt so bad I fell from the saddle. "Henry you all right?" asks Markbright all concernd.

"Ya, I can make it," says I brushin myself off and flexin my leg. From that moment on Markbright laughed for two hours strait. Even Bobby and Willie Forrest start in on me. Oh well, what are friends for?

We been restin up a spell here in Jackson, but I hear tell from Capt. Carnes we might be makin a move on the yankees at Ft. Pillow bout 50 miles due west of here on the Mississippi River. Might be horses there for us to capture I hear. Till next time, I am as always,

Your loving husband,
Henry

P.S.

Mary, please know that your daddy loves you more then words can say, and I wanted to be with you so much for your 4th birthday. I know times is tough, but I promise we will be a family again some day if the dear Lord is willing.

April 15, 1864
Jackson, Tenn.

Dear Elizabeth,

I seen things these past two days so horible they will haunt my soul for the rest of my life. You might think seein death and bloodshed so regular these past three years would harden my heart to such sights, but I can asure you this is not so. I can also asure you that if there is not a forgivin and merciful Almighty in the heavens, a few of my own comrads will surely face hell-fires for eternity for there actions this week.

As I tole you in my last letter of only a week ago, Gen. Forrest was fixin to take the yankee garison holdin Ft. Pillow on the Mississippi, bout fifty miles due west of our position in

Jackson. He orderd the brigades of Col. Tyree Bell and Col. McCulloch, bout 1500 men all under the direct command of Gen. Chalmers, to converge near the fort. This they done in the darkness fore dawn of Tuesday April 12. Gen. Forrest and us in the escort company would join the scene a little later that morning.

I must tell you that Ft. Pillow (first bilt by the Confederate army and named for its commander Gideon Pillow, but since taken over by the yankees) is a horseshoe shape enclosure with four-foot thick earthen walls and a deep trench all round it. It is a very strong fort with six artilery pieces inside. I here draw a little map so you can better understand the situation:

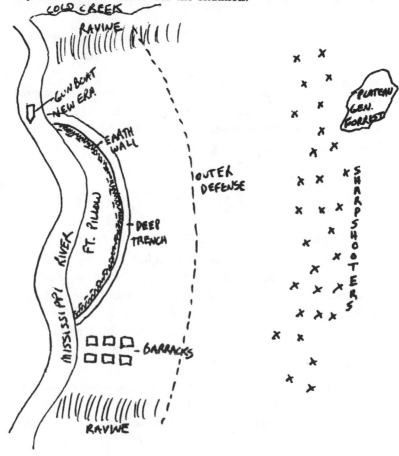

The fort sits atop the high bluffs overlookin the Mississippi. To make the position even stronger, the yankee gunboat New Era in the river could fire its big guns at us at will.

Early on April 12 Gen. Chalmers had his men charge the outer defences, and the few yankees there quick run back behind the walls of the fort. Them thick walls was bout eight foot high but the ditch all round the fort was close on six foot deep, so scalin them walls was no easy matter.

We learnt from scoutin reports that the fort was held by close-on 550 yankees. Half of these was nigra troops, the other half bein Tennessee Torys, good boys from our own state turn traiters. So when Gen. Forrest and us in the escort got to the field at 10:00 that morning, Gen. Chalmers already had his 1500 men streched out front the fort in the outer defences, firin on the yankees within.

Gen. Forrest is a very smart man, and the first thing he done was post sharpshooters behind evry tree, stump and rock suroundin the fort. These men, maybe 250 of them, firin Maynard and other long-range rifles, was hid evrywhere, but mostly on the grassy hills and nolls. From these higher areas they poured a deadly stream of fire on the defenders of the fort. I tell you Lizzie, any yankee stickin his head above the parapet was like as not to get it shot off. We was in a good position right from the get-go, and though the yankees probly thought they was safe within the walls, I could see defendin it was gonna be pert near imposable.

After placin the sharpshooters Gen. Forrest tole Chalmers he wanted the ravines both north and south of the fort occupied, and if posable the deserted barracks too. By 11:00 the orders was past along, and in rapid fashon men was organized and charge forward and took cover in the ravines. I do not beleve a single man was killed in this movment, cause very few shots was fired from the fort. Our sharpshooters had there sights on any movin object above the parapets and a yankee raised up to take aim was likely to get killed.

Just after the ravines was took Gen. Forrest call to me and Capt. Charles Anderson to join him on a reconasance of the fort. Gen. Forrest always relyed heavy on the scouts and sent out men to gather information all the time, but there aint no one he trusts as much as hisself. If posable he always makes a close personal inspection of evry battlefield, often at great risk, fore makin a decision on how to fight on it.

We no sooner climbed up a brushy hill to view inside the fort when the generals horse got shot in the neck by a stray bullit. In panic it reard up and fell over backward on top of Gen. Forrest. The beast was dead and we pulled the general from under it. As he raised back to his feet slow, he rapped his arms tight round his chest in pain and was shook up bad.

"General should I call for a strecher?" asks Anderson.

"No Anderson, we aint got time for that. Get me another horse."

"Maybe General," says I "we should walk out."

"What for, they can hit me as easy on foot as on horseback."

I could see the general was hurtin bad and in no mood for conversation. In a short while Anderson got back with another horse and we started our ride again. Within ten minutes though, this horse the general was astride took a hit in the flank, bucked outa control (the general in spite the pain held in the saddle) and Anderson had to lead it from the field and again bring another.

As Anderson come back he looks serius at the general and says "they was drawin straws General. That is, the horses was drawin lots to see who gets to serve you. Short straw had to come." The general never smiled.

After checkin the lay of the land for almost two hours Gen. Forrest calls Gen. Chalmers and Cols. Bell, McCullough and Barteau together. He tole them to move the entire line forward as close as posable to the fort, but not to make a charge at the fort itself yet. "The men are gettin low on amunition General," says Bell.

166

"Have them pull in tight to the fort and hold that position till the ordnance wagons catch up" says Gen. Forrest. "They should be outa danger up close. None of them yankees is damn fool enough to climb on top the walls to fire down at us. They cant depress the artilery that low either."

The order was past along and soon I could see our boys in small groups and single men alone, workin there way forward in short rushes, hidin behind stumps and mounds, creepin forward through the thick underbrush. In a short while with the sharpshooters still firin with deadly aim in to the fort, most of our men was within a couple hunderd feet of the wide trench at the base of the fort walls.

By 3:30 the amunition wagons was rollin up to the scene. With this Gen. Forrest sent over a flag a truce, Capt. Walter Goodman of Chalmers staff and myself doin the honors, with the message drawd up for the rankin union officer Maj. Booth:

> *Major — I demand the unconditional surender of this garison, promisin you that you shall be treated as prisners of war. My men have receved a fresh supply of amunition, and from there present position can easily asault and capture the fort. Should my demand be refused I cannot be responsable for the fate of your command.*
>
> *Respectfully,*
> *N. B. Forrest*
> *Maj-Gen Comanding*

As me and Goodman drawd close to the fort to receve there messenger, a handfull of black soldiers climb atop the walls and was shoutin curses at us and shakin there fist. In truth I could not make out all they was hollerin, I just know it was loud, mean-spirited and vulgar. A party of three white officers come from the fort, exchange salutes with us, spoke in very serius and formal tones, took the generals note and rode off. Goodman and me waited outside the fort for a reply, but rode back a ways to put some distence tween us and them people. I swear some of them nigra soldiers musta been drunk, the way they was carryin on.

A half hour past fore the union officers returnd carryin a note from there comanding officer to Gen. Forrest. We rode back behind our lines and found the general still mounted and in plain discomfiture, along with Gen. Chalmers and Cols. Bell and McCullough. Meanwhile a scout come back and reported to Gen. Forrest that a yankee transport boat loaded with union soldiers was steamin down the river and would get to Ft. Pillow in a hour or less.

"Are you sure of this information?" the general growls at the scout. "Its in violation of this truce for them to receve reinforcements at this time." I could see the general gettin very red and very angry. "Bell" he orderd, "have 200 men in each ravine move down to the shore line with orders to prevent any reinforcments from landin.".

The returnd message from Maj. Booth read:

> *Sir — I respectfully ask one hour*
> *for consultation with my officers.*
> *In the mean time no preparations*
> *to be made on either side.*
> *Very respectfully,*
> *L.F. Booth, Major Comanding*

"There stallin for time General," says Bell.

"I know that, dammit," snaps back the general. "Wylie, go back and tell him I want a clear yes or no to my demand in twenty minutes or we asault the fort."

So me and Goodman rode tween the lines again, close as they was, and repeated the generals terms to the three union officers. In less then the twenty minutes demanded, they come back with a simple note we took back to Gen. Forrest. It read:

> *General — I will not surender.*
> *L.F. Booth, Major Comanding*

"Damn him" Gen. Forrest spit, "God damn that fool to hell. He is responsable for what is to follow. We can wait no longer, prepare to storm the fort."

I knowd for sure the general was very unwell at this time for he said he would stay behind on this grassy nob 400 yards away from the fort, and observe the action. This was completly unlike him, as he never missed a chance to personly lead his men in battle.

"General" I asks, "do you want me to stay with you or may I join the charge?"

"No Wylie, I will be alright, you go off and join the men."

"Thank you General" I says, "You see sir, that tall flag above the fort — it will be down directly." I tied Buster up to a tree and run off to join the men crouchin near the walls.

Elizabeth, I must stop this large letter right here cause Capt. Thompson and me got to organize some of the captured supplys we got. I promise I will continue as soon as posable, besides I want to get this all off my chest bad. Till later, I am

Your loving husband,
Henry

April 17, 1864
Jackson, Tenn.

Dear Elizabeth,

I will add this letter to the last which I have not yet posted. In these past two days I herd things, storys the men tell in hushed tones, bout what they seen at Ft. Pillow. It was a bad bisness, and I aint sure we herd the last of this. To pick up where I left off the other day. I left Gen. Forrest on the grassy noll a quarter mile from the fort, and run up to join the men spred out in a arc round the fort. Most the men was within a couple hunderd feet of the earth walls, and as I tole you in my last letter we was all pretty safe as the yankees couldnt fire down on us without exposin therselves to the deadly fire of our sharpshooters.

We was all double checkin to make sure our pistols was loaded full. Then we waited for Jacob Gaus to sound the charge from his batterd bugle. We been orderd not to fire a shot till we got over the walls.

Then the old germans bugle sent a shrill note through the air and in a instant, more then a thousand men sprung up from behind the bushes, stumps and hills and run double quick toward the fort, evry tongue soundin the rebel yell.

As we charge, many the yankees inside the fort tryed to get shots off at us, but they was either shot down in the atempt or there hurryed shots misdirected. Within two minutes hunderds and hunderds of us was jumpin into the deep ditch circlin round the fort. I ran forward best I could and without stoppin to take a look, plunged forward into the trench and found myself in mud and water half way up my shins. Not suprizin with all the spring rains we been havin.

Once in the trench we was quite safe as none of the enemy dare climb on top the parapet to fire down on us. The whole time this was goin on, the gunboat New Era in the Mississippi was lobbin shells at us, they made alot a noise but was flyin way behind and was no factor at all in the asault.

In the trench the men did not act in panic, but keep in good order and started formin human ladders, bendin over to allow others to climb on there backs and scale the high walls above them. From the ditch bottom to the top of the walls musta been a good fourteen feet, and as men was strugglin up the sides I was prayin the yankees wouldnt start rollin short-fuse artilery shells over the parapets. This could cause us some serius problems, but in fact they did not do this.

Just as I start climbin on the back of a big private, I lost my footin (my stiff leg dont help) and fell on the seat of my pants, waist-deep in mud. The horse-face young fella looks at me settin there like a fat sow in the muck, and starts laughin. I soon was to my feet, up on his back and scrambled up the crumblin wall. On top I reach back and drug a couple other fellas on top too.

Within minutes many hunderds of us was in the fort and firin pistols at point blank range in to the enemy. Men was screamin and dyin all round me, and I seen panic in the yankees faces as they seen more and more of us pourin over the walls. I started firin my pistol quick as my finger could pull the trigger, but I didnt feel no recoil and soon realized my fall in the mud left my sidearms useless. Here I was, standin in the enemys fort amidst the desprate battle, and me with no workin weapons.

Before I could think what to do, the outnumberd and terifyed yankees turn tale and run to the back of the fort tryin to escape by climbin down the steep bluff and seekin protection from the gunboat off shore.

It was a grusome sight seein them men in blue get funneled in the narrow paths from the fort and bein shot down in the back by hunderds of our frenzyed men. At that moment amidst this blood-bath I was thankfull to God above for lettin my guns jam up and not forcin me to resist the temptation to shoot men runnin away.

Lizzie, I seen (and will never forget the sight) groups of black soldiers throw down there rifles, fall on there knees and raise there hands to the sky, beggin "I surender, dont shoot, I give up," and see my own comrads jerkin there guns in a upward motion and yellin "stand up, stand up." Soon as them nigras stood up they was shot down in cold blood like rabid dogs.

I yelled "Halt! Stop firin" and when a specialy mean southern soldier shot another unarmed black man in the face, I ran over, put my useless pistol to his head and screamed "I tole you, goddammit, stop firin." That wild-eye man looks right at me and says "You goddamn nigger lover" and runs off with the others in pursute of fleein yankees.

Over the bluffs the enemy poured in a rush, many still carryin there rifles and some times firin back up at our men chasin them down toward the river. Once down to the riverbank they turn and run southward like a pack of scared deer lookin for safety. They went barely a few dozen yards fore they run smack in to the 200 men Gen. Forrest earlier sent down to the river bank to stop reinforcments from landin.

Point blank rifle fire mangled the terifyed yankee soldiers. Many again fall to there knees beggin for mercy, and again may God have mercy on our souls, some was shot down (I will not say murderd) by hatefull Confederate soldiers who thought it not a terible sin to kill a unarmed black man or Tennessee yankee.

I was still in the fort above, starin helpless at this horrid work goin on below. Many yankee soldiers dove in the river hopin to swim for there lives, but they become easy targets and patches of red floated down the river from all the blood spilled.

This tragic scene took only fifteen minutes or so, and then I thought of something important. I seen a man I know, a quiet young Tennessee private name John Carr runnin by me. "Carr," I yelled, "hurry climb that parapet and cut that damn union flag off that flagpole. On the double."

"Yes sir," and this he done. Within a few minutes Gen. Forrest come stormin on horseback in to the fort and rode to me direct.

"Wylie, whats the situation here?"

I tole him quick how the yankees fled out the back almost as soon as we crashed in to the fort. I also tole him I seen some of our men outa control and on a rampage. He could see for hisself the ungodly number of dead yankees scatterd all over the fort, and most the baracks, tents and storage bildings was already set ablaze

172

by angry southern soldiers. "War means fightin," he says serius in answer to my look, "and fightin means killin."

I could see in Gen. Forrests face anger and physical pain. "Start organizin these men as prisners of war Wylie," he shouts as he swung his horse toward the rear of the fort. There was still many yankees both white and black bein held at gunpoint by our men, and I got them in to groups and started recordin names, regiments and companys.

There was still some shootin goin on below the fort, but with Gen. Forrest now on the scene order was restord quick. More prisners was brung in from below the bluffs and as they was lined up and recorded, I counted only bout 200 of them in all. That dont leave many prisners of a garison numberin almost 550. As I limped round the fort helpin move prisners out, I could not help but greve at the loss a life. Bodys of dead yankees was scattered evrywhere, some in piles on top each other, many with hideus wounds to the head or face, and bodys lay in unatural twisted positions. And in many, specialy the nigra soldiers, there lifeless eyes yet had a trace of that terror I seen in there faces as they pleaded for there life. I know to many a southerner the black man is less then human, a animal resource God provides to get our work done, and killin one is no more a sin then shootin a ox or mule. But so help me God Lizzie, all I seen when lookin in them frightend eyes as they begged for mercy was desprate men terifyed to die.

Within a few hours we got the prisners sorted, burial partys out diggin graves for more then 200 dead bodys, and the wounded was loaded on the transport ships under a flag a truce. We buryed our dead, counted only fourteen, and loaded our eighty or so wounded on to wagons. By darkness we found our horses and rode back toward Jackson and away from that place of death.

The capture of Ft. Pillow and takin the garison was another great and total victory for our corp, yet I did not feel the pride I felt after so many of our other suceses. The sights I seen there left me depressed, even ashamed, and I truly feel that if Old Bedford did not get hurt and led the charge hisself as he most often done, things might a been diffrent. I knowd all along many of these men we recruted just four months ago was not the best boys the south had to offer – the pick of the litter was long since servin there country or in graves. These are wild reckless boys held under control by Gen. Forrests strong hand, and something like this was bound to happen.

Next day Wed, April 13 the general sent a squad of men back to the fort to make sure no wounded was left, to gather up the captured rifles and six guns, and clear out any useful supplys and food. Anything left that could burn was set ablaze.

Lizzie, I now relate something I find dificult to put in words. One of the men sent back on the clean-up detale was Capt. John Markbright, my mess mate and friend. That evning as we was eatin our supper I could see in his face and by the way he picked at his food that something was on his mind.

"Whats the matter, John?" I asks.

He choked up and says "Henry, I seen something today I cant bare thinkin of." He looked all round and spoke in low tones. "You know" he says "how some of our boys set fire to the baracks and cabins durin the attack?"

"Yes, go on" I says.

"Well today as we was goin through the ruins we found that those cabins wasnt all empty."

"What do you mean they wasnt all empty?" I asks, "you mean like there was still people, yankees in them when they was set on fire?"

"Yes Henry, but..." he seem not able to get the words out, "that aint all. We found three or four bodys chard but not completely burnd, and they was" again he was stutterin, "they was nailed to the floor bords so they couldnt get out."

"Nailed?" I asks in disbelief.

"Thats right. Hands and feet tied and nails through there cartrage belts and clothes holdin them fast to the floor."

174

"Cant beleve any of us, not even the worst, would do something like that. What should we do bout it?" I asks.

"Well" says he, "couple of us seen this, and Major Anderson says he would report it to Gen. Forrest. Aint likely, though, anything will come of it."

Lizzie, I dont want to unduly sadden you by this letter, but I want you to understand what we been goin through. Please know that if you start readin reports in the newspapers bout the "massacker" or "blood bath" at Ft. Pillow, please know that only a few in our army is so terible. The great number of us is tryin to win this war and protect our homeland and freedom, but not cold-blooded heartless killers. Why must this cruel war continue?

I am sorry Lizzie, if I cause you pain. Know that I and your two brothers is alive and well and fought like honorble Confederate soldiers. I miss you so much. I hope Mary does not think bad of her father, and I am as always,

Your loving husband,
Henry

Chapter 11

May 15, 1864 through June 13, 1864

May 15, 1864
Tupelo, Miss.

Dear Elizabeth,

I know its been nearly a month since I last wrote to you and Mary, and this long absince been for two reasons. One, it has took that long for me to recover my spirits since we stormed Ft. Pillow. The bad effect that bisness done to our reputation as soldiers left me depresed, and only now am I ready for more action. Second, after my long and heart-felt letter to you about Ft. Pillow, I run out of paper and pert near out of ink, and only now got a chance to buy some here in Tupelo.

We been here almost ten days now, and though its been rainin a good bit and I never get a chance to dry out complete, it is nice to be back in a land where the farms aint all burnd down and corn is still growin — after all this part of north Mississippi is knowd as the "granary of the south," and it sure looks like it.

Today May 15 is a Sunday, and Gen. Forrest kindly suspended all military dutys as far as posable so that any soldier who wants to attend services of thanksgiving and intersesion by the chaplins can do so. I must say attendence seems pretty good to me.

As you may remember, after our asault on Ft. Pillow we pulled back to Jackson and stayed there a good two weeks mostly conscriptin any male still capable of ridin a horse. I led a squad out capturin deserters. Theres many of them out there, and they mostly turn to stealin to stay alive. Once captured there headed back to there regiments, usuly at the end of a gun.

While we was in Jackson your little brother Bobby and his bosom pal Willie Forrest went on one of there scoutin detales they like doin so much. These often result in search partys goin out after them two rascals, but so far they always seem to find there way back.

On this one trek, so Bobby tole me afterwards, they went a long way from camp — not for any paticlar or useful purpose, but just to wonder off as youthfull men do. Seems they was miles from camp when Bobbys horse Daniel step on a sharp rock or something and injured the frog of its right fore-hoof. It come up lame and Bobby had to dismount and lead him on foot. As they was miles off and darkness startin to fall, they was gettin a little worried the general might send some one lookin for them again, and they knowd this was bad.

"Come on" says Willie, "lets get you another horse."

They come upon a small shabby farmhouse with fields yieldin but a poorly crop, but behind the fence stood a small but healthy-lookin Morgan, black as pitch.

As the boys aproach the little homested they seen a woman bendin over workin in her garden with a hoe. She was a stout, buxam woman with a weatherd face and nobby hands.

"Good evning mam" says Willie as they draw up to her," we are Privates Will Forrest and Bobby Parker, and we want to requisition the use of your horse, as ours here is broke down."

"O you do, do you?" she says standin up with arms on her hips, starin at them two dusty boys, "well you shant have her, dammit."

"The southern army needs here though" pleads Willie.

"Damn the southern army" she answers, "first they took my old man and I aint seen hide nor hair of him for two years, then they took my two boys, and one a them is gone now for ever. I aint givin them no more."

Before Willie could further his case she went on, "They left me and my three girls to run this farm, which dont grow enough to keep a family fed, and then them damn soldiers in blue come and run off with most of the chickens and geese, then them damn soldiers in gray come and run off with the rest of my livestock, and alls I got left is that horse to get us to town. So you cant have her."

They pretty much was standin there as if bein scolded by a school marm when Willie desided he had enough and the time come to get tough.

"Im sorry, mam" he says "but I hereby requesition that horse for use by the cavalry of the Confederate States of America."

"Well you can hereby get off my land and I mean right now. Dolly, Lily, Mary come out here now."

Three girls come on to the saggin front porch to witness what the shoutin was for. Two the girls, Bobby tole me was well growd lasses clearly takin after there stout mother, while the third was yet quite young.

But Willie was not to be denied and says "Come on Bobby," and was fixin to open the gate where the horse stood. At that the three girls come runnin out and grab the boys in a most unlady-like way and start rasslin with them in the corral. The little girl was kickin Willie in the shins again and again, and Bobby says one gal was tuggin like mad on his hair. This ungainly hand-to-hand combat lasted but a few moments as it stopped abrupt with the firin of a shotgun. It was the mother, standin on the porch and levelin the shotgun direct at the boys.

"Now get off my land, you damn horse thiefs and dont ever set foot here again."

Without another word the boys gatherd up there hats, there horses and there pride and stride off the farm. They come limpin back to camp way after dark, but lucky for them the general was else where engaged.

After Bobby related this story to me next day, I tole him thats one of the few engagments involvin a Forrest that the southern army had to turn tale and run. Lucky for Bobby too, that Daniel recoverd pretty quick from his injury.

Anyways, round the first of May we got orders to move south to Mississippi, as the yankees was reported sendin another large division to run Old Bedford and his cavalry down. We herd this line before from Abel Streight and Sooy Smith.

So the first week of May we spent movin south pullin our captured guns and wagon loads of supplys with us, mostly with slow movin oxes drove by our nigra teamsters.

We had one brief skirmish with the enemy on our way here but aint seen hide nor hair of them since. I am glad of this as I did not have much fightin spirit of late anyways. I do feel alot better now though.

I hear we may be movin up to Middle Tennessee again in the next few weeks to cut the supply line feedin the massive army of union Gen. Sherman as it crushes in on Atlanta, Georgia. Till you hear from me again, I am

Your loving husband,
Henry

June 9, 1864
Booneville, Miss.

Dear Elizabeth,

Rain, rain and more rain. There is a stream runnin where our tent use to be. The camp site is muck, the roads is quagmires, and evrybody and evrything is soggy. But here we set, me and Markbright under our drippin dog tent, both writin letters home fore our engagment with the enemy tomorow.

And all indications point to such. On the first of June our 3300 men on horseback set out from Tupelo with ten days rations and a hunderd rounds of amunition for each man, plus a wagon train and John Mortons four baterys of twenty guns. Our purpose was to enter Middle Tennessee and cut the supply lines that feed and arm Gen. Shermans army as it pushes on toward Atlanta. But we no sooner got as far as Russelville in Alabama when Gen. Forrest receved a urgent order from his commander Gen. Stephen Lee, to return to north Mississippi as quick as posable to counter a diffrent enemy threat. Gen. Lee reports the yankees sent out a army of 3300 cavalry, 4800 infantry, 400 artilerist and 22 guns (plus hunderds a wagons) all under Gen. Sam Sturgis, to run Old Bedford and our little corp in to the ground. Our scouts tracked them down and says them yanks was marchin in north Mississippi right through the heart of the souths best farmin plantations. Them yanks must be stopped fore they destroy the whole region like they done on there march to Meridian.

So back we race to north Mississippi. Gen. Forrest split his command into smaller units so as to cover all roads round us. Aint seen the enemy yet, but sines of him is evrywhere, and the general is fixin to cut off the movment of Gen. Sturgis and his big army at a small crossroads on Brices farm, bout 18 miles south of us here in Booneville.

I must admit to a bad feelin bout takin on such a big force, over 8000 men, with our small scatterd corp. Right now we have less then 800 men (the escort and Col. Lyons 700 men). But yesterday Gen. Forrest was sendin out curiers with urgent messages to Gen. Buford, Col. Bell and Col. Rucker, with men spred from Rienzi to Baldwyn, to converge on the morrow at Brices Crossroads.

Today we was orderd to fix rations, secure amunition, and get the horses ready for a hard ride at first light tomorow. Evryone was feelin pretty anxous bout now, and me and Markbright strode over to discuss the upcomin exitement with your brother John and his friend Capt. John Morton. John Morton, the 21-year old "pasty face" boy Old Bedford almost sent away less then two years ago, was put in overall command of our four baterys a guns. Thats how much the general respects this young mans courage and ability to handle artilery. I dont know if you know this or not Lizzie, but Morton finaly talked John in to leavin the escort company to join his artilery unit. Your brother likes workin the big guns alot, and shows promise in that field.

Anyways the four of us was talkin bout tomorow when Gen. Forrest come by checkin the readyness of evrything, as was his wont to do. "Morton" says the general, "I know the roads is all mud and the goin is tough, but I want them guns at the Brice farm early tomorow morning."

"How do you know the enemy will be at the crossroads tomorow, General?" asks Markbright.

"Cause the scouts seen Gen. Sturgis and his army movin east past Stubbs farm this morning."

"General" says Morton, "you can be sure the guns will be there, and we sure gonna need them cause I hear the yankees is bringin over 8000 men this time."

"Ya" says I, "with the cavalry carryin Colts repeatin rifles and breech-loadin carbines."

The general sensed our caution and says "Boys I know they greatly outnumber the troops we have at hand, but the road there takin is narrow and muddy and they will make slow progres. The country round is all dense woods and the underbrush is so heavy that when we strike them they wont know how few men we have. Besides," he goes on "there cavalry will be way out front of the infantry and we can attack and whip them way before the foot soldiers can draw up. While we rip in to there cavalry, they will send curiers back to the infantry to hurry them along, and its goin to be hot as hell tomorow, real humid, and by the time there infantry runs the five or six miles to reach the battlefield they will be so damn tired we will ride right over them. So dont you worry boys, we will put the skeer on them and keep it on."

Lizzie, I learnt long ago that when Gen. Forrest leads one of his famous all-out asaults, a mad and reckless charge against superior numbers, it is neither mad nor reckless. It is a well thought risk he feels confident makin. He knows what we can do, he knows what the enemy can do, and he makes his plans from this. And the remarkable results so far back him up. He aint called "the wizard of the saddle" for nothin.

But you never know what can happen to any individual durin a battle. The rains still pourin but I must tend to last minute dutys. Hope I will write to you again after the battle. Remember my love for you and Mary is forever, and I am as always,

Your loving husband,
Henry

June 13, 1864
Tupelo, Miss.

Dear Elizabeth,

I tole you in my last letter of just a few days ago how Gen. Forrest was fixin to gather his spred-out troops and converge at the crossroads on the Brice farm, half way tween Tupelo and Booneville. There he was fixin to engage the large union force of Gen. Sturgis and as Gen. Forrest says, "whip them to hell."

It was just past 4:00 on the morning of June 10 that we was woke up, stowd our gear, mounted our horses and headed out southward on the Guntown Road. Even at that early hour I knowd the general was right when he said it would be hotter then hell this day. With nary a cloud in the sky, the sun rose hot and direct with nothin but our slouch hats to shield the rays from our necks. We rode at a brisk pace, there bein just 800 of us from the escort company and Col. Lyons brigade, and the general didnt alow no one to stop for nothin, so I ate a little corn bread and sip water from my canteen as I rode. Markbright ridin next to me says "Know what I miss most not bein at home Henry?"

"What" says I, "your dog?"

"No" says he, "not ever eatin proper at a table. You know, havin a nice plate, maybe a napkin and fork, diffrent food fixed nice and smells good. Thats what I miss."

The roads was narrow and very muddy in long streches, seein how it been rainin for days. The countryside was gently rollin hills heavy coverd with brush. We crost any number a steep ravines in dense woods and it was all I could do to keep from bein ate alive by insects.

After 8:00 we come upon a cleard area maybe six acres in size, with a small house, barn and sevral outbildings on it. This was the Brice farm. Even though we just come 18 miles over rough muddy roads, the general give us no time to relax, the scouts spotted yanks comin up ahead. We dismounted, tetherd the horses and took up fightin positions behind a long fence row just along the woodline of the Brice farm. We then made our position stronger by pilin brush and logs up under the fence rails. These makeshift brestworks saved many a life durin battles in the past.

Sure nough in less then a hour we could see the yankee cavalry ridin up to the crossroads. No sine of the infantry, but there was a powerful lot of them troopers, at least 3000 and they halted maybe 400 yards away along the oppisit woodline. There they dismounted and took up a fightin formation also behind a long split rail fence. So here we was, on a hot summer morning, 800 of us layin on our bellys with our rifles in fixed position, starin acrost the open farm land at a large passel a yankees, also layin on there bellys fixin there rifles at us.

With us outnumberd so bad, the best thing to do was lay low, right? Wrong. The general feard the yankees might make a frontal asault on us, find out how few we got, and run us off the field. Col. Rucker was but two miles off and bringin up 700 Kentucky boys, so Gen. Forrest has us make a little show a force to confuse the yankees. This aint a all-out attack but what we call a "feint" or "pure bluff" as Markbright says.

At the sound of the bugles we rush out from behind our fences and rush forward a couple hunderd feet screamin and firin at the enemy lines a ways off. As we was in a completly open field, we made likely targets and we throwd ourselvs down and fired from the ground. The feint worked as the yankees stayed in the woods on the other side, content to shoot at us from there.

Of a sudden though, they opend up there artilery on us, firin canister like giant shotguns, rippin up the earth all round us. Sevral the boys was hit and Col. Lyon orderd us back to the protection of our brestworks and woods. But we held out just long enough for Col. Ruckers brigade to arive and Gen. Forrest soon had them all spred out in battle formation. Now with odds closer, 3000 yanks to half that number for us, the general was ready to begin the attack for real.

Gen. Forrest rode up and down the line encouragin evry single man of his command. "Once the bugle sounds, dont stop chargin boys, keep runnin and draw your pistols at close range." As he spoke more men was arrivin at the scene. To a curier Gen. Forrest says "Tell Bell to move up fast and fetch all he can. And where the hell is Morton?"

The tired curier says "Capt. Morton is draggin his guns up through the mud as fast as horse flesh can pull, sir."

"Good, we got to whip these men fore there infantry comes up" says the general, "now come on boys, follow me."

The bugle sounded and from behind the long line of fence near on 2000 of us jump up and rush forward. We was screamin bloody murder and so unafraid was these stout southern men that each company seem to try to race ahead of the others to be the first to engage the enemy.

From the oppisit side the yankee guns started crackin with puffs a smoke fillin the field. Still on we rush, all on foot cept Gen. Forrest who raced forward on horseback, his coat tied to the

185

pommel of his saddle and his shirt sleevs rolled as high up his arms as posable. He still rode along the line screamin encouragment as we moved forward, "Keep goin boys, the safest place for us is behind there brestworks, now forward, forward." Or if part of the line would falter or halt, I could hear him cussin and usin the Lords name in vain quite freely, "goddamit get movin, keep pace or by god I will shoot you myself. Forward, goddamit, forward." He was a insparation and a tyrant. The unstopable god of war urgin his soldiers toward the enemy with words of strength or the point of his saber.

I tryed so hard to keep pace with the others, runnin as fast as my stiff left leg would move. I never will forget that race acrost the open field. Thousands of the enemy firin there rapid fire rifles at us, loosin canister in our faces, men fallin and screamin all round me. Sweat in my eyes stung and made evrything blurry, and my mouth aint been so dry since layin wounded in the field at Chickamauga almost nine months ago. Markbright run next to me, his rifle held in both hands acrost his body, and he would look back and holler "Come on Henry, come on, we are almost there."

As we drawd closer the yankees burst from the woods in a counter charge, and I could see through my stingin eyes angry screamin men with fixed bayonets runnin right toward us. All along the open field men was engaged in mortal hand-to-hand combat. A rifle once fired become a club. Markbright, twenty yards ahead of me, was set upon by two men clubbin him over the head and shoulders. Markbright fell to the ground and as one man raise his rifle to slam the butt end home, I raised my Colt revolver and sent a bullit through him. The other man seen me aim at him and he turn and fled into the midst of the battle.

"John" I says pantin up to him, "how bad are you. Tell me you aint hurt bad."

I helped him up to his feet and blood was flowin from a deep gash over his ear.

"Go on Henry, I aint bad, I just need to rest a spell."

I tore the sleeve from his shirt and tied it round his head as a bandage to help stop the blood. "Now go on back, let the medics have a look." He walked slow back toward our line.

This whole scene took but a minute and good thing, for the fightin all round was severe. Restin on my good knee, I held my pistol at arms length, took aim and shot evrything blue I saw come near me. Twict I shot men who was aimin rifles at me. When I emptyed my first revolver I pulled the other out, stood up and started chasin the yankees who was now givin ground back toward the protection of the woods. Heavy fightin was takin place all along the line – in the open field, over the brestworks, in and amongst the Brice farmhouse and buildings. This fierce fight gone on for almost a hour but I could feel the yankees givin ground and losin there fightin edge. First in small groups and then finaly the whole enemy line fell in to retreat. By 12:30 that day Gen. Forrest had got what he wanted, the yankee cavalry was now beat at all points.

But even as the fightin slacked off we could see the first regiments of union infantry arivin at the field. We dug in behind scrub oak and black jack, behind fence rails and tree stumps, layin low in the thick brush and trees suroundin the Brice fields. A unstedy calm fell upon the battlefield as union reinforcments moved up in all directions.

But Gen. Forrest got done the first part of his plan. The union cavalry was now pullin off the field a battle, exausted and whipped, before the infantry could arive after there long force march in the blazin sunshine. And even as the yankee foot soldiers was now comin on to the field, John Mortons artilery finaly come up followd shortly by Col. Bell and Gen. Bufords brigades. At last we was at full strength.

It was durin this calm before the storm that I realize how terible was the heat. My mouth was so dry my lips was stuck together and my tongue pasted to the roof of my mouth. I was layin low under a little scrub oak when I seen a fella movin toward me keepin as much outa sight as posable. It was Turner Richards, the young boy I recruted near Okolona back in November. He had slung over his neck bout ten canteens. Crouchin low he says to me "Want me to fill your canteen, Lt. Wylie?"

"Sure do" says I, handin him my wood canteen which was long since empty and he disapeard over a little mound. Bout ten minuts later he come crouchin back over the hill, the full canteens weighin his neck down.

"Here you go Lutenent," he says, "I filled them at the creek just beyond the hill." He hands me back a canteen. I snached it from his hands and drunk a swig of the best darn water I ever tasted.

"Thanks Richards" says I wipin my mouth, "I owe you one this time." I took another long drink of that delicius water and notice the cork was missin, so I found a stick, jam it in the openin and broke it off. Then I pulled this plug out and took another swig. The canteen was empty again.

We was still waitin, layin low in the opresive afternoon heat as both armys deployd reinforcments along the line. Soon Capt. Jackson of the escort come sneakin up close. "Henry come with me" he says, and I followd him back behind our lines. There the escort company been gatherd together and remounted, and Gen. Forrest tole us he wanted us near at hand to plug any holes once the fight got started again. It was just past 2:00 now, our line streched in a big arc all along the woodline and through the Brice fields, facin a much larger army of union infantry who aint fired a shot yet that day. The tired and whipped union cavalry was tryin to regroup behind them. I learnt then that Gen. Forrest sent almost three hours ago a regiment under Col. Barteau on a wide flank march behind the enemy, and they should soon be in position. Thats what Gen. Forrest was waitin on.

Finaly, at a order from the general, Jacob Gaus sent a shrill note of charge from his bugle, and our attack on the union infantry was on. All acrost our long, curved front them men of Bell and

Rucker, Lyon and Buford race forward screamin like demons. Seein our bold charge, the very center of the union line burst forward in a counter charge firin a volly direct into the faces of our men. Many a man was cut down by this savage gunfire and for a moment the center of our line seem to halt, the men fallin to a prone position. The ends of our chargin line still moved forward at a goodly pace firin all the while but the center fell behind.

Gen. Forrest seen the men in front falter, dismounted and order us of his escort to tie the horses and follow him to the hard fought center of the field. With the general hisself runnin hell-bent before us, our little group a 65 of the fightenest men in the world rush forward to the thickest part of the fray. With Old Bedford shoutin encouragment to each man on the line, our center stood up and moved forward again. The yankees started to fall back slow but fightin evry inch. "Use your pistols" the general yelled, and we soon found the infantrys rifles with bayonets was no match for our revolvin pistols. Rifles is deadly at long range but unless theys repeatin rifles, and lucky for us these wasnt, once fired they need a half minute to reload, and at very close quarters like we was at, our blazin six shooters give us the advantige in fire power.

John Morton got his big guns positiond a hunderd yards behind our advancin line, and that young man and his skilled canoneers commenced to pour a deadly acurate fire in to the enemy artilery. It seem evry blast was findin its target, and the enemy started pullin there guns further back outa the line a fire. Bang, bang, bang, a constant thunder from our guns explodin on the enemy, and long after the fight was over I seen your brother John, his face and body blacker then old Sams back on the farm. John learnt quick that firin them guns is a hot, dirty and dangerus bisness.

On and on went the desprate charge. Men strugglin through the thorny black jack and thick undergrowth comin upon a unseen enemy and shot dead at close range. Rifles was swung like clubs and men fought like crazed and wild beasts. The general run along the line praisin men for there courage, then in the same breath cussin and flashin his fierce eyes at others who needed proddin.

At this moment Col. Barteaus regiment, that spent the last hours cuttin a trail flankin the enemy position, sounded the bugle and charged fiercly in to the rear of the yankees. Hunderds of screamin wariors stampedin on horseback sent the enemy reelin as they didnt know which way to turn. At this crisis, Gen. Forrest orderd Morton to pull four of his guns up from behind and place them right out front of our line. Pullin these guns up to the very face of the enemy was risky and unusual. But we come to expect the risky and unusual from Gen. Forrest. When he orderd Morton to fire double-shot canister at point blank range into the enemy, the yankees panicked and started runnin in any direction away from us.

After two hours of most intense battle it seem the whole yankee line disolved at once. Exausted from the tense fightin, confused by the rear attack of Barteau, and panicked by Mortons close-up artilery fire, the union retreat was soon a complete rout.

Disorganized, terified men throwd down there arms and run. The union cavalry in back turnd tale and spurred away as fast as hoofs could fly. Dazed soldiers cut loose artilery horses, mounted them, and rode bareback away. The enemys huge train of wagons was tryin desprate to get turnd about, but got caught in the scramble. Animals bolted, wagons overturnd, and utter confusion ensude.

Gen. Forrest got the escort men mounted quick and orderd us to "keep the skeer on," while officers started to regroup companys and regiments to help in the pursute. It was past 5:00 but there was lots a daylight left as we chase down the enemy army. I was right glad to see my friend Markbright, head bandaged nice by Doc Cowan, strong enough to join the pursute.

I never seen such a panic-struck mass in my life. The road was jammed with wagons, artilery stuck in mud, horses with broke legs, and hunderds and hunderds of exausted frightend troops surenderin by the score and beggin for water. I seen sevral yankee soldiers so drove by thirst they grab a sponge bucket from a stuck cannon and drunk the filthy black water from it.

The chase was on. Us able to keep out front kept up a stedy pistol fire on the enemy who used any road or path to escape. Some of our men was busy corralin prisners, collectin wagons filled with good rations of bacon and hardtack, and pullin stuck artilery outa the mire. This was a rout worse then Abel Streight, worse then Sooy Smith. The yankees left evrything behind and thought of nothin but runnin to safty or surenderin. Gen. Forrest was right in his perdiction – he whipped the yankee cavalry first, then beat the infantry second.

Over the next day and a half we chased them yankees as best we could for over ninty miles all the way back to Colliersville, Tenn. The defete was complete. When it was all said and done we counted 600 yankees killed or wounded, and we round up more then 1600 prisners. Most the rest was scatterd hither and yon over the countryside. We captured sixteen good pieces of artilery plus 1000 rounds of amunition to go with them. We spent days gatherin up 200 wagons pack full with exellent rations, plus maybe 1000 horses and mules, and a vast supply a harness, quartermaster, medical supplys and thousands a rifles and amunition to go with it. It was a great honor to be involved in anything so sucesful. I am sure Lizzie, the victory at Brices Crossroads will live in our Confederate states history for many years.

I am sorry to keep you readin so long, but I want you to know the things I experiance, for I feel we are makin history evry day. I do love you and Mary, hope this letter finds you well, and remember me to be,

Your loving husband,
Henry

Chapter 12

June 27, 1864 through August 24, 1864

June 27, 1864
Tupelo, Miss.

Dear Elizabeth,

Been here in Tupelo for sevral weeks now bakin in the hot sun but otherwise feel healthy and eatin good from the captured rations of crisp hardtack and lean bacon. Sure beats cornbread evry day. The boys is still crowin over the fight at Brices farm. Here the union sent a huge well-equiped force of infantry and cavalry to hunt down and destroy Gen. Forrest and his command. It ended with half the yankees gettin killed or captured, and losin all there guns, wagons, horses and evrything else. And again, north Mississippi, where the grain still grows, is saved from the union vandals.

I must admit to feelin shame faced, eatin these good vittles while my love ones back home may be suffrin. I aint got a letter from you or Ma for a long time, which is frustratin cause I know you both been writin to me. It greves me not knowin how Mary my love is, or if you and your folks is suffrin from shortages. I wonder often if Pa and old Sams keepin the farm runnin, if the crops is allowd to grow or if the livestock survives. I experianced lots a pain and depravation durin this war but maybe nothin so bad as you folks back home. Your the real heros of this war.

Some times while layin on my bedroll at night, starin up at the stars, my mind wonders to happyer times. I think lots bout the

193

times we was courtin, quiet rides in the trap after Sunday meetin time. You always looked so beutiful in your fine dress, so polite and kind. I held the reins with one hand, you with the other. The quiet talks, I soon found you was just as smart as pretty. Remember when the dark clouds of a sudden come rollin in and we got caught in the gullywasher. And my lord, when your fine white frock got soaked to your skin, I knowd right then and there your the wife for me. Such fun times, peacfull times. Think we will ever enjoy them again?

Your brothers is here with me and the whole command is gettin prepard for more action. The wounded (we got almost 400 men wounded from the fight) is spred out in hospitals round the area. Some already rejoind there companys, but I must admit, just bout evry company is a lot smaller then it use to be. Many only got forty or so men when they use to carry a hunderd. Of course the forges is out and blacksmiths is measurin for shoes, and evry day you hear the clang, clang, clang of hammers on anvils. Buster is fit and in good shape and I was lucky to get a complete set a shoes and nails for him made up that I carry in the saddlebag. The horse gear — harness, saddles, stirups, and the others is bein repared if need be, and many a boy is sowin up holes in there uniforms. Most our clothes is a mass of patches. We all got holes in evry garment and gettin new ones is just bout imposable. We coulda all got a good set of clothes from the dead yankees who was dressed up in new uniforms, but Gen. Forrest wont alow nobody in our army to wear yankee-blue. I seen more then a few fellas goin shoeless too.

Your brother John says workin the guns for Capt. Morton was quite a thrill, specialy when Old Bedford order them guns rold up by hand to the very firin line. Them poor artilery boys was left standin in the wide open, no fence or stump to hide behind, nor rifle nor pistol to defend therself. John was mostly runnin the powder charges from the caison to the gun barrel, but when sevral of the boys was wounded he also was rammin home the charge and shells. He says after the fight was over, Gen. Forrest rode up to Morton and says "Well John, I think your guns won the battle for us."

Morton, proud as a peacock says "General, I am glad you think so much of our work, but you scared me pretty bad when you pushed me up so close to there infantry and left me without pertection. I was afeard they might take my guns."

The general laughed and says "Well artilerys made to be captured, and I wanted to see them take yours." And he rode off.

Your brother Bobby tole me something of intrest too later on. He says the day after the big battle while we was still chasin Gen. Sturgis and his command hell bent back to Colliersville, Bobby and Willie was ridin near the general when they notice he was sound asleep on his horse. It seem fatigue even overtook that tireless man, and his head tilt to one side and his eyes closed. The boys was scared to wake him up, and no one else got the nerve to do so neither, yet they worried he might fall and get hurt. While they was fussin over the situation, King Phillip (the generals horse) fell asleep itself and veerd slow on wobbly legs off the road and strait into a tree. The general unfortunatly sprung forward hittin his head direct in the tree and fell unconsius for a goodly time. When he come to, the general asks "Why the hell didnt you wake me?"

The boys both say hello to there big sister and there mother and father as well. The good Lord has seen fit again to protect us in this last battle and I can only pray he will shed his graces on us longer. Beleve me that I miss you and Mary something awful and I am as always,

Your loving husband,
Henry

July 17, 1864
Okolona, Miss.

Dear Elizabeth,

How can I find the right words to bring comfort to you and your folks when the news I must report is so terible and full of sorrow. The almighty Lord who seen fit to protect us through so much violance, rased his hand and pulled to his side one of our beloved own. It is my sad duty to report that your young and good brother John has been killed in our recent battle at Harrisburg, Miss. I will say in all honesty he died a heros death, as a brave soldier boldly doin his duty. He stood facin the enemy, workin the big Rodman cannon he loved so much, killed with six other men of his battery by enemy artilery fire after wheelin the gun to the very battle front. He is gone now, so young, never havin the chance to experiance so many of lifes plesures. But also he is spared from further suffrin and pain that all mortals must endure, and now rests in heaven with our Father and his soul shall be forever young.

I am most bitter bout the loss of some one so brave and honest as John cause I feel our engagment with the enemy July 14 at Harrisburg was a mistake and should not been faught under the cercumstances. We learnt from scoutin reports the yankees was sendin another army under a diffrent comander out to destroy Gen. Forrest and our army. Them yankees dont seem to learn no lessons. We chased the armys of Abel Streight and Sooy Smith clean out of our teritory. They may be runnin yet. And just last month we destroyd Sam Sturgis and his invaders at Brices Crossroads. And this time they was sendin a diffrent general with a great huge force out to get us.

With over 14,000 men in this new invadin army, we could do nothin but watch as they marched from Memphis to LaGrange, then seen them come south into Mississippi through Ripley, New Albany and Pontotac. As they come they destroyd most evrything in there path — not things like factorys that help our army mind you, but burnin houses and farms, churches and schools. They seem godless

vandals out to punish our people, not just our soldiers. That aint
the souths way of fightin a war, and Gen. Forrest felt we had to put
a stop to this.

On Wed. July 13 the yankee hords pullin many pieces of
artilery rode in from Pontotac and took up a good defensive
position atop a slope right near the old city of Harrisburg. The
union commander Gen. Andrew Smith chose his spot well for
bringin on a fight, as his battle line run north and south along the
crest of the low ridge. This hilltop formed the center of a open
field and beyond the open field was a deep woods. The yankees
was spred over a mile and a half wide facin due west, the direction
we must come in from. Heres a simple map showin the lay of the
land.

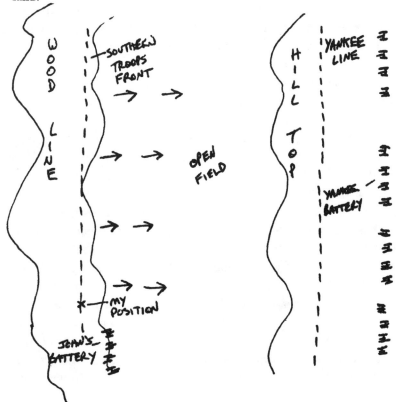

The woodline was a good half mile in places from the hilltop, and any where along our line we would have to charge acrost five hunderd yards of open field in plain view of the enemy. As I could see them yankees makin brestworks of logs and fences on top the hill, to me a charge acrost that field seem unwise. It seem unwise to Gen. Forrest too. Starin hard acrost the plain, I herd him say quiet to hisself rather then me, "Too damn many." We knowd Gen. Stephen Lee would be joinin us fore tomorow morning, bringin our strength to maybe 6000, yet less then half the enemy number. Still the general prepard us for battle, not wantin to be took off gard. But all stayed quiet that day.

The evning of July 13 was hot, and though we was spred out along the woodline in battle formation we had a chance to rest. It felt good to strech my leg out, as we been ridin hard for five days. Its been intolerble hot and we aint seen a drop a rain for weeks now, and findin places to fill your canteens gettin tougher. The roads is powder dry and the risin clouds of dust make lookin ahead tough, and evry inch of your body is thick with dirt. In your eyes and ears, up your nose and thick on the lips and teeth. It aint been much fun.

After dusk I seen Gen. Forrest throw his coat on the ground and lay on it for a spell. Of a sudden he jumps up, still in his shirt sleevs and hollers over "Wylie, you and Donelson mount up and come with me."

He decided it was time for a night reconasance so me, Lt. Sam Donelson of the escort, and Gen. Forrest mounted our horses and took off in to the darkness. The general always wanted a personal inspection of the enemy position and often took some frightfull risks in doin so, just like at Ft. Pillow.

We rode nearly a hour and was clearly in the rear of the enemy lines, as we come acrost lots a wagons with yankee teamsters unloadin supplys and tendin the horses. As it was blacker then pitch out, our uniforms was hid from view and no one payed no never-mind to us three horsemen ridin slow through the camp.

The general musta seen enough for he turnd round and headed away from the wagons. But we didnt get far when two union soldiers on picket duty seen us and says "Stop, who goes there?"

Gen. Forrest in a bold manner rides direct to within five feet of them boys and says in a angry voice "What do you mean by haltin your comandin officer?" He motioned to Sam and me to follow along, me grippin my pistol, and we rode past the two sentrys at a slow pace, them not sayin a word. I could hear some mumblin as we rode a goodly ways off, then from behind in a demandin voice we hear "Halt right now! Come back here and identify yourself!"

With this we all spur our mounts and took off fast as hoofs could fly, and a instent later a hail a bullits was whizzin by our ears. Once we rode safe back to our camp Donelson and me could smile and brethe again, but Gen. Forrest was serius and troubled. Then turnin to me he says "There position is too strong. Theys too damn many and dug in good. We cant take it no matter how bold the attack, cept with great loss a life. But one thing for sure Wylie, the enemy cant remain long where he is. And when he comes out I will turn loose my command and attack him day and night. He wont cook a meal or have a nights sleep — we will wear his army to a frazzle before he gets out of the country." The general knowd we was masters of cross-country chases.

But it was not to be his decision on whether or not this asault would be made. Later that night Gen. Stephen Lee arived with his troops. He was Gen. Forrests comandin officer and it was his decision to make. And though Gen. Forrest urged strong against a head-on attack, Gen. Lee orderd the charge to be made next morning.

The sun broke hot as usual in a cloudless sky, and by 7:00 we was all prepard to make the reckless charge. The yankees, crouchin low behind there brestworks, was ready too. There they set, close on 15,000 of them on top the hill ready to blast to pieces any one who dared cross the plowd field.

The asault went wrong from the start. I was on the far right of our line, and before we herd any bugle call, the boys in the center burst forth in a small group. It seem the whole attack lost any order and was made piecmeal by this group or that group. As always, we was game troopers and marched bold at double quick up the slope to the very face of the yankees. But with each step the ranks was thinner and thinner. Wave after wave of desprate young men rushed on the enemy, each man fightin brave but with no orgenization. It was a useless asault. We stood no chance crossin such a open field against such a strong position. The men was cut down like a giant scythe through hay. The yankee artilery blastin holes in our uneven lines with canister and grapeshot. More then a few of our boys run back to the woods, there asaults faild. Some fell to there face on the cracked and parched earth, overtook by sunstroke and thirst.

It was then, after a hour of this deadly fightin that Mortons guns was rolled by hand up closer to the enemy. Fore they got many shots off, they become the target of the well-placed enemy guns, and a deadly barage of shot and shell pourd in upon them. And young John Parker, the smilin kid who always had time to help any body in need, was mortaly wounded by a explodin shell. So many of them brave artilery boys was killed and so many guns disabled that they was drawd back to the woods in short order, but too late for the young men layin lifeless on the field.

Finaly we was pulled back to the woods where we quick throwd logs and fence rails together to make some protection. Here we stayed for the rest of the day. We lost more then 200 men killed in that short time and over 1100 wounded, includin Cols. Russell, Barteau, Wilson, Newsom, Wisham, and Maj. Parham. So many officers was lost I think Gen. Forrest will find it dificult replacin so many of his leaders from the ranks. The bodys of the dead, includin John, was carryed by wagon train here to Okolona and gave a proper military burial. Beleve me Lizzie, Bobby and me greved for you and your folks as the last shovel a dirt was throwd on top the grave.

The yankees musta been satisfyed with this one battle, for they pull out that evning of the 14th and started headin back north again. In spite the heavy loss, next day Gen. Forrest had us ride hard on the retreatin enemy, attackin there flanks and rear where ever posable. Durin a minor charge on the enemy rear that day, Gen. Forrest out front as usual took a shot to his right foot that cause him severe pain. He fell from his horse and quick was carted off in a ambulence to find Doc Cowan. Word spred fast through the ranks that Gen. Forrest been killed and a deep depression fell upon us all. Word of this got back to Gen. Forrest and a hour later in spite terific pain he come ridin King Phillip at a gallup past our whole line to asure each man our leader was still alive. With evry pace a mighty cheer rose up from the men.

We persude the enemy for a day and a half but he fled strait back to Memphis. So here we come back to Okolona to bury our fallen brethren and regroup for the next action. I hear-tell Gen. Forrest had some heated words with Gen. Lee about the conduct of the battle, with the result Gen. Lee rode off with a small group of men leavin Gen. Forrest in command of the rest. My heart pains me mighty that anyone so kind and fun-lovin as your brother now lays buryed forever in a dusty field. War is a terible thing. Why cant we be left alone to live in peace? How many other kind and fun-lovin young men will lay forever in forgoten graves fore it all ends? I cant think too deep on it for it pains me so. Express my regrets to your mother and father and remember me to be,

Your loving husband,
Henry

Aug. 17, 1864
Oxford, Miss.

Dear Elizabeth,

We aint seen a whole lot of action since that misrable time at Harrisburg that cost you and the family so dear. Yet for us the living, life must go on in spite the sorrow.

For the past sevral weeks we been playin a game a hide-and-seek with the yankees. Us hidin, them seekin. Gen. Smith this time brung a mounted army of over 20,000 men in search of us, while we got less then 5000, what with the severe loss at Harrisburg. Just a couple days ago the yankees was here in Oxford, and soon as they pull out we come ridin in. You best beleve the good people of Oxford was right glad to wake up one morning to find the enemy gone and us back.

Gen. Forrest got back in the saddle this past week but still lets his injurd foot hang loose from the stirup. For a while he was ridin round camp in a buggy, his hurt foot restin out strait over the dashbord. I beleve these past weeks been rough on the general for he looks exessive thin, dont have much color to his skin, his hair is now all gray cept his chin whiskers which is still mostly black, and seems to be so burdend in his mind he dont take much time any more jawin with the men.

The rest of us aint in a mood for much fun neither, as it been rainin on and off for weeks. Usualy this time a year is so dry here the silk wilts off the corn stalks, but this August is diffrent. I dont care how good you set up your oil-cloth tent, there aint no way to stay dry, as the ground is soaked through. I seen Markbright the other day get so mad tryin to make a fire outa soggy sticks he just throwd evrything down and stomp off toward the woods, then I seen his feet prompt slip out from under him landin him square on his behind. I couldnt help but laugh out loud. What a look he give me.

The rain is gettin some people down but not all. The other day I herd a whoopin and hollerin from the other side of camp and found a group a boys tryin to liven things up with a horse race. We all knowd horse racin is not allowd by the general, but sure nough there they was, spurrin there horses round four hogsheads they set wide apart for a track. A large group a men gatherd there, all shoutin for the horse they bet on. I thought it pretty amusin myself till I seen that one of them dare-devil riders was your brother Bobby and one of the others was Willie Forrest, the generals son. If he gets hisself in trouble, I thought to myself, there aint nothing I can do this time. The course they set up for the race went right by the generals tent to boot. Amidst all the clamor and exitement I seen Gen. Forrest limp out from his tent, stand quiet with arms folded acrost his chest, and watch the procedings. He didnt seem much upset and even made a few comments and smiled to people near him. After the race was over he hobbled back in his tent.

Couple hours later I strold to Bobby and Willies camp site and ask them what ever come over them to do somthing they know the general dont permit.

"The boys was gettin bored Henry" says Bobby, and Willie adds "and I was tired a people braggin how fast there horses was. It was fun dont you think?"

Just then Maj. Charles Anderson of the generals staff come walkin up, says hello to me, and then says, "I want to talk to them two, Pvts. Parker and Forrest."

"Yes Major" they both says at once, standin up.

"Gen. Forrest wants me to pass on his orders that you two is responsable for removin all manure from the east corral this evning, and he says if you dont finish by dark to set up torches so you can work all night long."

Willie and Bobby was no longer smilin. "The east corral sir?" says Bobby in a disbelevin voice, "theres more then 1000 horses there."

"Yes sir," says Maj. Anderson "it is a big task. Better get crackin. And by the way" he adds "the general says if this duty is not completed in good time, severe punishment for disobeyin orders will follow."

"By the way Major," says I "the other fellas in the horse race, will they be recevin a special duty also?"

"Yes Lt. Wylie" says Anderson with a smile, "now that you mention it, the other three sportsmen been asined to pluck the 400 chickens now in the pen. This duty is to be done in a timely fashon also."

After the major walked off the boys just stood there. Finaly Willie says to hisself "So thats what we get for one little horse race – shovelin sh__ and pluckin chickens." I had to laugh.

Well Lizzie, I got to go now. Markbright and me was just informed we got to help check out the brigades of Neely and Bell and sort out the sick men and lame horses. The general wants bout 2000 healthy men on sound beasts who can ride hard on these muddy roads. I know the general been very concernd bout this huge enemy after us, and he knows darn well we cannot get into any kind a fight with them and survive. So what he is ponderin to fix them yanks I dont know. I only know that 20,000 union men is very close to us here in Oxford and that Gen. Forrest is fixin to take his escort and 2000 of our best men and horses on a hard-ridin mission tomorow.

I must close for now, but if the good Lord choose that I may write to you again, you best beleve I will tell you all we do. With all my love to you and a big kiss for Mary, remember me to be,

Your loving husband,
Henry

Aug. 24, 1864
Grenada, Miss.

Dear Elizabeth,

These past days been amongst the most exiting I can remember in a long time. As I tole you in my last letter (which I still got with me in my saddle bag) Gen. Forrest was fixin a plan to unsettle the yankees and the big army they sent out to hunt us down with. A out-right fight was out of the question seein how bad outnumberd we was. As we chose men and mounts for this duty I little dreamed what that scheme was. And now you and me both know — it was his bold and darin raid on the city of Memphis itself. I am sure you read in the papers all bout it but I will detale it to you.

After pickin bout 2000 of the most fit men and beasts, late night of Aug. 18 Gen. Forrest moved us out for a unknowd purpose in a north-west direction. Before leavin Gen. Forrest left orders for Gen. Chalmers to take the remainin healthy men of our army (less then 3000 in all) and make a loud demenstration against the huge union army outside Oxford. "Make such a ruckus" the general tole Chalmers "them union troopers will think there bein set upon by a mighty hord — tie them up for at least two days if you can."

All that night and in to the wee hours of Friday Aug. 19 we pushed along through a drivin rain, the trails knee-deep in mud in places, acrost swelled creeks, and up and down slipry hillsides and vallys. The horses slid down soggy paths, sevral lost there footin complete causin horse and rider to tumble outa control. Many horses lost shoes or come up lame, so that by sunrise of the 19th Gen. Forrest had to send almost 500 unfit men and horses back to Oxford. Shows what a sorry state our beasts are in.

Durin the morning of the 19th, low and behold the sun broke from the clouds and we rode in sunshine the rest of the day. By noon we pull up to rest the horses a spell and grab some nurishment ourselvs. Markbright give me a "pork supper" — cold pieces of salt bacon tween some cornbread. Didnt taste much good, but it filled me up.

Then Gen. Forrest gatherd the men in tight and tole us his plan. "Boys" he says, "we are makin a little call on our homes. We are ridin to Memphis." This caused quite a stir as many of us was from Memphis or nearby.

"Quiet now and listen" he went on, "the scouts report three yankee generals is headquarterd in Memphis, and I mean to fetch all three." Again the fellas start chatterin with exitement.

"You know the yankees been holdin our city for two years, usin it as a center for there bisness and commerce, keepin there army there. Well I think its high time we go in and stir up a hornets nest a trouble for them." The men was shoutin there aproval.

"Now listen boys, this raid requires speed and silence. As we aproach the city you got to hush up – no rebel yell, no gunfire, nothin to alert the enemy troops holdin the city. And this is how we are goin to work it..."

He explane to us then how Capt. Bill Forrest and his scouts would take down the union pickets without firin no shots, then procede in haste to the Gayoso House Hotel and capture Gen. Hurlbut. At the same time Lt. Col. Jesse Forrest would lead a small group to Union St. and capture Gen. Washburn, who was stayin at the Williams house. Another group would head down Beale St. and capture Gen. Buckland at his residence. The rest of us, the biggest part includin the escort, would stay with Gen. Forrest in the area south of the city to engage the enemy soldiers there, givin the others time to carry out there missions.

Upon hearin this the boys spirits rose sky high. I never seen the command look more like it was out for a holiday. There was so much jokin and laughin that Gen. Forrest kept warnin us to keep quiet. That would shush the boys for a short time, then the exitement would pick up again. What with the sun shinin and spirits so high, we made good progres that day and by nightfall we neard Senatobia, a good fifty miles from where we started one day ago. But we got another fifty to go with some major chalenges.

The first problem we faced that Saturday morning of Aug. 20 was how to cross Hickahala Creek that was bank-deep in racin rain water. The scouts found one small flatboat that haul maybe four men and horses at a time. It would take all day crossin that way.

"We aint got time for that" Old Bedford says, "Chalmers wont be able to keep the enemy tied down for that long."

The general aint a man to be denyed. He quick turnd us cavalry men in to bridge-buildin engeneers, and all the boys was eager to pitch in and help. The creek is bout sixty feet wide and maybe six deep. Gen. Forrest got the axes out and had two tall trees on each bank chopped down and feld acrost the creek. These trees was stripped of all limbs and become stringers for a bridge. Next he orderd hunderds of feet a grape vines cut, twisted together to form strong cables, and these rapped round the feld trees and tied to the stumps. Then the flatboat was anchord in the middle of the creek under the trees to keep the very center from saggin down in the water while men and horses crost over. Last, groups was sent out to tear the floor from evry ginhouse and cabin in the area. These we carryed back over our shoulders and was layed acrost the cabled stringers for planking.

The few supply wagons we brung with us was unloaded, so as to lessen the weight when crossin our swayin, saggin bridge. Gen. Forrest hisself carryed the first arm full of unshuck corn acrost the span, limpin bad on his injurd foot. The whole task of bridge buildin didnt take much more then a hour, and fore another hour was up all 1500 of us was acrost, the two cannons bein rolled over by hand.

A short while later we come upon the Coldwater River, this one also a brisk current up to the top of its flooded banks. This river was a bigger chalenge yet, as its twict the distence acrost as the Hickahala. This time Gen. Forrest didnt have to give so many instructions, as the boys set upon the task of bridgin this river like they was experts in that field. Me and Markbright led two groups of men in gatherin planks from the cabins and barns in the area. By the time we gatherd a goodly amount the bridge was almost complete. In less then three hours we was crossin the Coldwater.

By sundown we got to the fair city of Hernando, where Gen. Forrest spent much of his youth. Here we unsaddled the tired horses and fixed us some grub. Old Buster was in fine fettle and I dont beleve I been able yet to wear down that faithfull beast. I just dont think you can top a quarterhorse for endurence.

Our rest was but a short one and even as darkness fell upon us, Gen. Forrest had us back in the saddle and movin north toward Memphis. In spite the blackness of a cloudy night most evryone knowd our way on these familier roads, and just after three in the morning of Sunday Aug. 21 we drawd up on the southern outskerts of Memphis.

"Gosh Henry" whisperd Markbright as we closed ranks to receve final instructions, "I would do anything to stop in at the house. What a suprize for Ginny and the kids."

"You and me both, John" I says and I can promise you Lizzie, I never in my life wanted anything so much as to race off and stop by your folks home. I got a lump in my throat as we rode acrost the old stone bridge on the main road. Many wonderful evnings you and me spent talkin and laughin while settin on the stone parapets. All those quiet talks flood over me then and I almost spurd Buster up the "Osborne Path" that leads direct to the Parker house. I coulda rode it blindfolded, so familier is evry bolder and tree. I was home for the first time in over two years, I was home. I swear to God Lizzie, as I stood upon the old stone bridge I could hear Marys voice callin me, callin "Daddy." In five minutes I could be at your house, I was five minutes away from throwin my arms round you and squeezin you tight to me. Five minutes from holdin my daughter in my arms. Could I sneak off and not be seen or missed? I knowd I could, but then I look in the faces of all my friends and comrads and I knowd they wanted to ride off and visit there love ones just like me. But if we all rode off on our own, who would be left to carry out our plans? I realized then I could not do what I would give my very soul to do.

Well, we receved our final instructions and again was orderd to be swift and absolutly quiet. The signal to move out was made and we all set out to do our part. The boys out front, mostly those

208

reckless scouts under Capt. Bill Forrest, was so overcome by the exitement of ridin into there home town, they just spurd the horses and started whoopin and hollerin, firin pistols, and makin a terible ruckus. There was no controlin them. What happend after that you are probly more familier with then me. I know the newspapers was just full of the bold raid on Memphis.

You know how Bill Forrest and his scouts raced through town and went direct to the Gayoso House Hotel. He sure didnt bother hitchin his horse to the post, but clammerd right up the steps and burst in the lobby still on horseback, scarin the wits outa the night clerk. Capt. Forrest demanded to know what room Gen. Hurlbut was stayin in, only to find out the yankee general did not stay at the hotel that night. Though he missed grabbin the general, Capt. Bill and his men did manage to round up a goodly number of prisners, almost all of them officers and most still in there night clothes.

The others didnt have no luck either. Col. Jesse Forrest and his band raced down Union St. but because of all the comotion, Gen. Washburn was woke from his sleep and just manage to escape out the back door and get to the safety of Fort Pickering north of town. But they did capture Gen. Washburns uniform which was still layed out in the generals bedroom.

The same with the group sent to capture Gen. Buckland. That general herd all the exitement and escaped to the fort. But a large amount, maybe 400 union soldiers and officers was took, rounded up and sent marchin south.

By this time a whole lot a union soldiers was organized and startin to fire back on us. A young and dashing yankee officer (I later found out he was Col. Starr) who was not panicked by the sight of so many screamin Confederates, was leadin the counter charge. Col. Starr shouted orders and swung his saber, and rallyed the yankee soldiers to him. He reminded me of Gen. Forrest the way he took command and made men obey.

Meanwhile Gen. Forrest, us men of the escort and Col. Bells brigade was in a lively spat with some union infantry south a town.

We manage to chase them off and take bout 100 good horses. When the general looked back toward town and seen the streets fillin with enemy soldiers and artilery, he orderd old Gaus to sound "recall" on the bugle and our boys started racin south in little groups of two or three. In fifteen minutes most the boys was pulled outa Memphis and headin back toward Hernando.

What with the hunderds of prisners and captured horses, goin out was slower then when we come in, and Gen. Forrest and the escort stayed back to protect the rear of our army. Even as we crost back over the stone bridge, the yankees led by that same Col. Starr was closin in on our rear. In his usual fashon Gen. Forrest turnd his escort company to face the yankees and orderd us to charge direct at them.

This we did with Gen. Forrest out front standin high in his stirups swingin his saber like a mighty battle ax. Leadin the yankee charge was the gallent Col. Starr and like two gladiaters in ancient Rome, Gen. Forrest and Col. Starr met face to face in mortal combat. It did not last long. Col. Starr lunge forward with his saber and Gen. Forrest parryed the blow with such force it almost nock the colonel from his saddle and fore he could regain his balence, Gen. Forrest thrust the point of his saber deep in the chest of his oponent. Col. Starr fell to the ground.

After this the yankee pursute slacked off. By early afternoon all firin stopped and Gen. Forrest sent Maj. Anderson back with a flag a truce and a note to Gen. Washburn askin for a prisner exchange as we lost a couple dozen boys ourselvs. Gen. Washburn sent back a note statin he didnt have the authority to grant a prisner exchange. So Gen. Forrest sends Anderson back with the request of uniforms and food for the hunderds of captured yankees, many bare foot and in night clothes. As a added touch Gen. Forrest also sent back with his complements Gen. Washburns captured uniform. A short while later the uniforms and provisions arived. But we found as we always done, that movin the slow walkin herd of prisners was more a burden on us then them, so Gen. Forrest issued each one a parole. (A parole means each man sines a promise not to return to active duty till officialy exchanged by the goverments. This was a promise most men was most willin to abide.)

Next day Monday, Aug. 22 on our way south again we receve word from Chalmers that Gen. Smith and his mighty army was pullin back from Oxford and headin toward Memphis double quick. This made Gen. Forrest smile as he seen how good his plan worked. Although we could not capture the yankee generals, our little raid through Memphis musta shook up the yankee command headquarterd there enough to recall Gen. Smith and his 20,000 man army and leave north Mississippi and its harvest alone.

Best of all, though I did not get to see you in person, bein in our home town and seein all the things that mean home and family to me has revived my spirits. Please know that I love you and miss you and that all wakin thoughts is of you and Mary. My love to all, and remember me to be,

Your loving husband,
Henry

Chapter 13

September 15, 1864 through October 21, 1864

Sept. 15, 1864
Verona, Miss.

My Dearest Elizabeth,

We been settin here in this hot forsaken place almost two weeks now drillin, shooin the horses, gatherin supplys and makin ready to move out again. But theres good news — I got lots a mail that been piled up at the post depot fore Mr. Gallaway or some other curier could pick it up. I got a nice passel a letters from you and Ma. It was the most I got at one time and I spent the better part of a whole day readin and then readin again evry word.

The parts I like most is them about Mary. I can not beleve my little baby is able to do the things you tell of. She was just able to walk when I left home, now you say she runs down the back walk and climbs up on the tree swing herself. I find it most intrestin that she can talk so good with you and I regret very bad I missed all these years of her youth.

I was most sorowfull to hear of the passin away of your aunt Liddy and will never forget her kindness and help at the time of Marys birth. I do not know if we could got on without her calm experiance. I am right glad your father is still able to work at the shop and bring home real gold pieces, and I would never beleve how prosperus Memphis is right now if I did not see some of it myself on our brief visit there. I did not realize our city was such a center of comerce now — of course it is yankee comerce. The shops looked full a goods if only you have the money to buy them. I guess havin yankees hold Memphis aint all bad.

We been pretty fortunate ourselvs havin plenty a food most the time, and the goverment just sent us 1000 new Enfield short rifles and amunition to replace many of the old, unreliable ones many still carry. It would be a great help if all of us carry the same rifle, as supplyin so many diffrent guns with amunition is very dificult, and I often got to scrounge for shells to fit my Sharps carbine.

I am pretty fit and healthy now and my hand is a lot better. I dont know if I tole you or not, but I got a deep cut acrost the back of my left hand while we was buildin the bridge over the Coldwater River last month. While I was helpin to pull planks from a cabin floor, Bob Shipps let go a half-naild plank that slam with force back to the floor and over my hand. I beleve some bones was broke too. I guess not evry injury in war time is heroic.

Couple days ago I herd alot a noise from near Gen. Forrests tent so I walked over to see whats the comotion. There was Gen. Forrest holdin up on display a spankin new full dress uniform of Confederate gray. It was a gift he said, just receved from the yankee Gen. Washburn who you might recall got his uniform took by Jesse Forrest on our Memphis raid. Gen. Forrest returnd that uniform under flag a truce, and now that enemy general was returnin the favor. The fancy new uniform was of the finest cotton sowed in Memphis by Gen. Forrests own tailer (Reed on Beale Street — same as your father goes to). I guess in this war you can respect the enemy even if your still trying to kill him.

I beleve we are fixin to move out soon cause I seen Gen. Forrest workin on a plan the last few days. You can easy tell when the general is schemin cause he will walk at a brisk pace for hours on end in a circle round his tent, his head down, hands behind his back, trudgin the same circle over and over so many times a trench forms deep enough to hold water after a rain.

When he is in this deep consentration you best stay away, far away. If you should aproach him while he is thinkin hard, the general will ignore you or give a snarl. But a couple days ago me and Markbright seen something that beat all.

First I must tell you bout the sutlers. I dont know if I tole you before who they are, but these men follow behind the army in coverd wagons and sell goods. These sutlers pass through prosprous towns buyin things soldiers want most but cant get very easy. Things like socks, pipes, books, apples and fruit, paper and ink, razers, needles and thread, sissors, mouth harps, combs, pocket knifes and many other usefull things. Of course the sutler buys at one price and sells at a higher one. They follow the main armys in herds but pretty seldom follow us as we dont usualy stay in one place long enough for them to do much bisness.

But seein how we been here for sevral weeks a few of them wagons been settin right near our camp. These sutlers is never very populer fellas, as most the men look upon them as cowerdly misers who should be in a uniform but is insted gettin rich by takin advantage of the poor soldiers.

There is one such sutler who I know only as Lewis, who I have myself bought paper and ink from (at thrice the cost in town). This rascal I must admit to be in particlar arogant and greedy. Well, couple days ago I herd angry voices comin from the wagon of this man Lewis. It seem that one soldier, a rough fella name Jake Masters, bought sevral items from the sutler Lewis, but then walk off with a small fryin pan without payin for it. Masters shouted at Lewis that he bought enough stuff from him at a outragous cost that he should get the pan free. Short of shootin him dead, there was no stoppin Jake from walkin off with the pan.

Lewis got madder then I ever thought posable, and he went stormin strait to the tent of Gen. Forrest to plead his case. Well, there was the general pacin round his tent, hands behind his back, consentratin heavy. This fella Lewis come up beside the general, matchin him step for step, sayin he demands his atention, must get

215

justace, wont stand this thevery. Gen. Forrest seem not to see or even hear this man, so the sutler Lewis steps direct into the rut the general was marchin in so as to be unavoidable. With this Gen. Forrest not even lookin up, struck the man a vicius blow to the chin, sprawlin Lewis out cold on his back. And Lizzie, I swear as God is my judge, the general kept up his pacin and his thinkin and each time round stepped over the body of Lewis as if he wasnt there at all. It was truly a sight to see. After a good while the sutler come to, crawled away, and I aint seen his wagon round camp since.

I must go now Lizzie. It was so nice to read your letters and the ones from Ma too, and I think of you all back home all the time. With all my love, I am,

Your loving husband,
Henry

Oct. 10, 1864
Corinth, Miss.

Dear Elizabeth,

I finaly got time to set myself down and write to you. We spent more then two weeks hell-bent in the saddle on another of our famous raids deep in to enemy teritory. As we done sevral times the past few years, we crost the mighty Tennessee River and rode in to Middle Tennessee with the purpose of cuttin telegraph lines, tearin up railroad track, destroyin bridges and trestles, and doin what ever harm to the enemys war effort we could. In this I must admit, we been very sucesful. Besides killin or woundin maybe 1000 yankees, we captured and sent south sevral thousand more. We took away more then 800 horses so that evry man who didnt have one at the start or rode a lame one, got hisself a fine horse to care for. We gatherd hunderds of beef on the hoof, captured dozens of wagons loaded with evrything from amunition to saddles to medical supplys all stamped "U.S." I do beleve evry one of us come back with nice new blankets, shoes, half-tents, saddles and tack, and most evrybody got a new rifle. It was a most sucesful spree.

We started our raid on Sept. 20 and crost the Tennessee on horseback at Colberts Shoal. Though the river was low, the water was still tween the horses knees and belly. We picked our way in a colum of two, along the twistin rocky underwater path almost two mile wide from bank to bank. More then a few horses lost there step, plungin horse and rider in to the dark waters, but all in all it sure beat crossin by slow flatboats.

A day later we rode in a long line through the fair city of Florence, Alabama. What a sight to behold − Gen. Forrest out front mounted on King Phillip, followd by his escort company and then Bufords division and the brigades of Cols. Rucker and Kelley. The streets was lined with cheerin citizens overjoyed to welcom the deep souths greatest hero. The general looked strong and god-like as he waved and smiled at the crowd, many of them runnin out with cakes and special treats for the men. It was one of the proudest moments of my life.

Upon leavin Florence we marched to Athens, Ala. where the yankees held a strong earthen fort. Gen. Forrest soon had us on all sides and orderd John Morton to arange his guns close and start firin. So good is those gun boys it seem evry shell explode in the fort bustin up something important. After a hour of this thunderin Gen. Forrest sent in a flag a truce (Markbright and Anderson doin the honors) tellin the yankee comander we got 8000 men suroundin the fort (course we got less then half that many) and if he dont surender we will storm the position and wont be responsable for the bloodshed. They surenderd − all 575 of them.

From there Gen. Forrest set his sights on the railroad that runs from Athens to Nashville and is a main line of yankee supplys. As we worked our way northward along the tracks, we captured blockhouse after blockhouse, rounded up a thousand yankees gardin them, destroyd the trestles the blockhouses was suposed to protect, and built great bonfires that twisted the rails beyond repare.

Sevral garisons did put up a fight. Gen. Forrest was glad enough to oblige, but we did suffer some casultys. In one spot Col. Jesse Forrest, the generals gallent young brother, receved a severe gunshot to the thigh, and him and other wounded men was hauld back south in ambulences.

We captured sevral locomotives pullin cars loaded with goods behind, and each man was issued five days more rations (mostly yankee hardtack and dryed fruit) plus all the coffee and sugar each man could carry. I mean real coffee and real sugar! Boots, hats, oil-cloths, overcoats, evrything to make us comfitable was doled out. This made us eager to keep goin. What other riches would the yankees supply us with?

By Sept. 25 we come upon a deep ravine called Sulphur Spring, and acrost this vally was a giant wooden railroad trestle spannin a good 300 feet and maybe 80 foot high. It was garded by a strong blockhouse and a well-equiped earthen fort near by. We soon was deployd all round it and as is his wont, Gen. Forrest sent in his "surender or else" message. "Certainly not!" was the yankee reply, so the general got Mortons guns spred on all four sides and for the next two hours pummeld the fort with 800 shells. A white flag rose from the fort then. As we cleard out prisners and supplys from behind the tatterd walls, I looked with pity and disgust at the many mangled corpses of union soldiers sacraficed for no purpose. They should know by now to surender when Gen. Nathan Bedford Forrest demands so. The crash of that flamin trestle as it crumbled to the vally floor is something I wont soon forget.

We kept workin our way up the rail line, reekin so much havoc it will take the yankees months to make all the repares. As we aproached the town of Pulaski my heart was gladdend by the sight of many school boys and girls settin atop the split rail fences wavin and smilin as the soldiers past by. Made me feel more like we was at peace then at war.

Pulaski is bein held by a huge yankee garison, and though Gen. Forrest had us spred into attack formation round the fort there, he had no real intention of gettin us in a fight where we was so bad outnumberd. Insted he waited till after dark and had us light as many small campfires as we posably could to give the anxous yankees huddled up behind the walls the idea we was in the majority. Then we remounted real quiet and rode off in to the night. The generals new plan was to ride crost country, off any main roads, due east bout fifty miles till we come upon the other major rail line used by the yankees for carryin supplys to Shermans army. This would be the Nashville to Chattanooga line, and we spent sevral days (Sept. 26-27) ridin hard through the steep, wooded country, passin over narow roads made muddy by the recent rains and much rutted up by us tramplin through it.

One evning after we stopped and set up camp for the night, I was settin by the campfire enjoyin my coffee with Markbright and the artilery man John Morton. Morton, settin on a stump says "You hear what happend today?"

"Nothin particlar" says Markbright, "what?"

"Do you know Capt. Andrew McGregor who directs one of my batterys?"

Both me and Markbright know McGregor. He is a older chap, maybe close to forty with a wife and a passel a kids, who speaks with a Scotch accent so thick you wonder some times what language he speaks.

"You know then" says Morton "that he is a decent enough fella, but he dont take no guff from no one. Makes him a good squad leader."

"He tole me one time" says I "he worked twelve hours a day on the railroads since he come to this country as a lad." And he looks it too. He is one of these men whos short and burly, with shoulders so thick he looks like he might tear the seams of his shirt sleevs each time he moves a mussle. "What about him?" I asks.

Morton says "Remember fore dawn this morning when we was crossin Wildwood Creek and the mud was thick as tar? With us pullin the rear with our guns, we hit a long strech churnd to a quagmire by your horses. Some of the guns sunk so deep they needed twenty horses just to pull them through. Well, the last squad was McGregors and one of his caisons sunk higher then the axels. Most evryone else was pulled way ahead leavin old Andrew and his boys to cope alone. I guess they tryed evrything to free it up. Hookin teams to it, usin trees for levers and diggin out the mud, layin down logs, and they all was mud from head to boot. Well just when they was gettin short temperd, here come Gen. Forrest ridin back to check on the tale end of the command. He seen the buryed caison and bellows "Who has charge here?"

"I have, sir" speaks up McGregor.

"Then why the hell dont you do something for Christ sake" shouts the general, "the whole goddamn army is gettin outa sight and your back here with your asses stuck in mud."

Well old McGregor, wore out and filthy, had enough and shouts back "What do you think we been tryin to do here? And I wont be cursed at by any one, not even Gen. Forrest! I will, by God, blow us all to kingdom come!"

"And with that" Morton went on, "McGregor snach up a lighted torch, throwd back the lid on one of the caisons amunition chests, and rams the torch in."

"What on earth happend then?" asks Markbright.

"Well" says Morton startin to laugh, "Gen. Forrest spurd his horse outa there just as hard and fast as posable, even lost his hat he moved so quick. Then he come racin up to me and the others shoutin "What infernal lunatic is that just out of the asylum down there? The damn fool come near blowin hisself and me and evryone else up with a whole caison full a powder!" Well we all couldnt hold it in no longer and burst out laughin. "Whats so goddam funny bout that lunatic?" demands Old Bedford. "General" says we, "Capt. McGregor unloaded that caison a half hour ago to lighten the load."

I can tell you Lizzie, Markbright and me laughed good and hearty. "What did Old Bedford say to that?"

"He just scrach his head, mumbles 'well I never seen the like,' and burst out laughin."

When we finaly rode crost country and hit the Nashville to Chattanooga rail line, the scouts come back reportin troops of yankees comin in on us from all directions. Bill Forrest reported to the general heavy consentrations of union troops at Tullahoma and many other points along the railroad. What with our casultys from battle and breakdowns to the horses from our long haul, Gen. Forrest decided we oughta git while we could.

Goin due south of course would be our quickest rout to safety, but Gen. Forrest wouldnt hear of that. No sir, he led us on a merry chase up through Spring Hill past Columbia, round Mt. Pleasant and Lawrenceburg. All the while we was capturin blockhouses, destroyin rail lines, burnin trestles and even gatherd a herd a beef cattle. I only wished your brother John was here to join the round-up.

Finaly on Oct. 2 we got back to Florence, Alabama. We had to get acrost the Tennessee River again, and the recent rains got it sweld much higher then when we rode our horses over. There would be no ridin over the Colbert Shoals this time. Gen. Bufords division arived on the banks first and they made, found or stole a little armada of flatboats and skiffs to start ferryin our men and horses, couple hunderd cattle, Mortons guns and caisons, and what supply wagons we still had with us.

It was a slow and unstedy process. What with the river runnin high and swift, heavy winds turnin the surface choppy, many a flatboat rocked and heaved, and if you wasnt rowin in a skiff you better be bailin water out.

This task went on for three full days and nights. By Oct. 6, with a good 1000 men still on the north side, the enemy started comin up on our rear. Gen. Forrest had Mortons guns sent over early and positiond on the south bank so they could fire over our heads and hit the aproachin yankees. This seemed to chase them off as we had no further trouble from pursuin yankees.

Me and Markbright and just bout evry man of the generals escort become sailors and transported the boats back and forth, back and forth for 72 hours strait crost the mile-wide strech of river. Gen. Forrest hisself made dozens of trips, each time helpin load and unload wagons, holdin horses, and pullin on the poles and oars. I was exausted, yet seein that major general workin so hard, his face sweaty and his hands grimy and bleedin, his uniform in tatters, the sight of this remarkable man renewed my strength with each passin hour. I wasnt the only one, most evry officer and enlisted man found reserved strength by watchin our leader.

But I could see fatige cachin up to him as the days went by. Most evrybody was acrost by now, and me and Dan Jackson and Gen. Forrest was polin a flatboat back to the north side to pick up any body still not over yet. We landed, it bein dark and damp out, and sure nough come acrost four young fellas jabberin away amongst therselvs while layin on the ground with there heads restin on stumps. They seem not to have a care in the world as we come upon them. I could see plain that Gen. Forrest was pretty annoyd at there casuel atitude and he says "I thought I would catch a few damn fools loafin back here in the cane as if nothin was goin on."

Once they seen who was adressin them they was on there feet quick, dustin off there uniforms and tryin to look sharp. One fella, with scragly hair stickin out from under his floppy cap and one bar on his coller says "General we was checkin this area out makin sure we left nothin behind."

"Well lutenant" says the general "if you dont want to get left all winter on this side you better come along with me. The last boat is goin over right away."

"Yes sir" says he salutin, and after the general turnd his back to leave, them young fellas turn to one another and start laughin quiet.

We grabbed any crates left in the area and loaded them on the flatboat. The general lost his footin while stowin a burlap bag of husked corn on the raft and slipped part way into the water. Dan Jackson just snached his arm in time to save him from a complete dunkin. Gen. Forrest was in no good mood.

We started pushin our poles and the raft drifted out slow in the choppy black waters. As we was pushin I notice the lutenant with the scragly hair arangin the cargo a little. Then he stopped, put his foot up on one of the crates, pull out a pipe from his pocket and filled it slow with tobacco. Then he proceded to smoke in a lazy fashon. After a moment Gen. Forrest sees him and says, "Lutenant why dont you take hold of a oar or pole and help get this boat acrost?"

The young man removed the pipe from his lips and says quiet "I dont think a officer should be called upon to do that kind a work as long as theres private soldiers enough to perform that duty."

Well Old Bedford was hot as the kitchen stove. Still holdin the pole in the water with one hand, he sprung over a coil a rope and smacks the lutenant in the face with his other hand. The man flew head first over the side and disapeard in the murky waters. He popped up a moment later, his floppy hat now gone, and grabs hold the pole Gen. Forrest was holdin out to him. The general hauld him abord like a big fish.

"Now goddamn you" shouted the general, "grab hold of a pole and get to work! If I nock you off this boat again by God I will let you drownd." I can tell you true Lizzie, I never seen a man pole a flatboat any harder then that fella for the rest of the crossin.

By Oct. 8 we all was back on the Alabama side of the river, back on our horses and headin toward Corinth. I beleve we had a most succesful two weeks. We captured thousands of prisners, killed and wounded a good many too, took some losses ourselvs,

223

capture lots of supplys, and put a hunderd miles of enemy rail outa service for months. Yet I hear old Sherman has took Atlanta already and dont need the rail lines for supply no more. I dont know Lizzie, with Grants army pushin ever closer to Richmond and that man Sherman invadin the heart of Dixie, how much longer our people can hold out. Surely the soldiers I ride with have no quit in them, Gen. Forrest wont allow it. But can the citizens of these Confederate states survive the hardships we face, and who is to replace our fallen brethren in battle? I dont know what the future holds for our people. I dont know how we can defeat the unions ever-growin armys. All I know for sure is that this last long ride in wet weather left me very chapped and sore right where the rider meets the saddle.

Other then that I am feelin well and have not gave up on our cause. We have too much to fight for. You will hear from me later. Till then I am as always,

Your loving husband,
Henry

P.S.

Think Mary will ever understand what all this fightin and hardship is about?

Oct. 21, 1864
Jackson, Tenn.

Dear Elizabeth,

I do beleve that fate is some how keepin you and me apart. I come so close to seein you a while back when we made our raid on Memphis, but at the last moment I could not turn my back on my comrads and duty. This time we was stopped by the worst luck and a deadly occurance.

Once we got to Corinth after our long and succesful raid in Middle Tennessee, the horses was in such sorry shape that Gen. Forrest furlowd any lad who lived in north Mississippi or West

Tennessee who could bring back some horses. Sure nough, your brother Bobby popped up that his pa still had some good horse flesh, as did Mickey Spillner, Ross Ewalt and Richard Marks, all these boys from Shelby County. Seein how these was all young privates, I seen a promisin opurtunity so I says "General, you want I should go with these boys so as to keep them outa trouble, and maybe I can russle up a few horses from my neighbors?"

"Okay Wylie," says the general "you boys got a good eighty miles ride and I want you back in ten days. Stay off the main roads and if a pack a yankees get on you, forget the ride home and meet us in Jackson. Understood?"

"Yes sir!" says I, and my head was light as a feather. "Russle up three days grub boys, forty rounds of amunition, cause we are ridin home at dawn!"

Next morning (Oct. 16) we was off fore sunrise. What a perfect day it was too. Cool but sunny, only a fleecy cloud in the sky. For the boys it was like a holiday. And for me too. We laughed and talked quiet as we winded our way through a zig-zag narow path in the woods that folowd along pretty close to the rail line linkin Corinth to Memphis.

Ross Ewalt been three years in a Tennessee regiment in Col. Tyree Bells brigade. He is only 21 now and maybe the funnyest caracter I ever met. He can imitate Col. Bell so good you would think Old Ty was ridin with you. Then he makes his face get so red you swear his head will pop, and says thats Old Bedford durin a fight. We was havin a jolly good time, and brother Bobby tole the story bout him and Willie Forrest tryin to "requesition" the old ladys horse. Richard Marks is also 21 and rode for a year with John Hunt Morgan and tole us sevral storys bout the darin raids he been on with that famous soldier who got killed last month. I ask Richard what was the biggest diffrence tween John Hunt Morgan and Nathan Bedford Forrest, and he says "Gen. Morgan was a brave man and darin fighter, but he loves to meet the ladys, atend weddings and such, look good in fancy uniforms, while Gen.

225

Forrest is all bisness, just bisness." You might recall Mickey Spillner — his folks farm just a few miles from our farm, and he has a older sister our age, Marcy. Mickey is a shy kid, dont add much to the conversation but listens good and laughs quiet to hisself at all the storys and jokes. Says his father (50 years of age) was took in to the service a while back, leavin his mother, three sisters and a couple slaves to keep the farm runnin.

"Think your family be suprized when you ride in Mick?" I asks.

"Cant wait to see the look on Mothers face when I walk in the door, hope she dont imbarass me by all the huggin and kissin and tears" says he.

"Thats okay" says I, "mothers is allowd to do that." And to be truthfull I was startin to feel jitery in my stomack at the thought of you seein me walk in the door.

The first night we was almost to Saulsbury and by the second night we made a little campsite away from the rails near Grand Junction. We was makin pretty good time, maybe sixty miles in them two days, and was streched out by our low fire late that night. We just got done eatin stew and was finishin a pot a coffee. I was fixin to bed down. The horses was tetherd in a little grassy area bout thirty yards behind us. It was late, probly past midnight and darker then pitch as there was just a sliver of moon and some clouds overhead.

The fire was burnin out and cast a faint orange light on us as we set close together. Bobby and me was streched all the way out, our boots toward the fire and our heads restin on our saddles. Mickey, Ross and Richard was settin round the fire pit talkin low, gettin ready to strech out and go to sleep too.

Of a sudden from no where, and evrywhere too, shots rang out through the darkness. I could see the gunpowder flashes as shot after shot exploded. In a matter of seconds Mickey Spillner and Richard Marks was screamin in panic.

226

"Oh god I hurt, I hurt" screams Mickey, "help me please, help me." I could see by the fadin light of our flame that he got a wicked wound to the neck. Marks was hit in the left shoulder and in pain.

This volly a shots last but a few seconds and in a instant me, Bobby and Ross scrambled behind trees, our pistols in hand, and returnin the fire as best we could. I just fired into the blackness where I thought the shots mighta came from.

"Mickey, Richard can you get out from the light?" I call to them. Richard crawld slow away from the fire to the darkness, but little Mickey just layed on his back whisperin "help me, oh god help me," and I could see blood oozin from his neck.

There was no way to help. To go into the light was to be shot and killed. So we just layed on the ground behind seprate trees but near each other, not havin no idea who was shootin at us, how many they was or why.

I herd a little crack to my right in the darkness, like a twig breakin gentle by some one movin but tryin not to make noise. Without thinkin I aimed there and fired four shots. No more noise. I reloaded in the dark, and boy that aint easy. Another quiet shufle noise strait ahead and this time Bobby and Richard fired a volly a shots. Who ever was out there, and I didnt beleve they was too many in number, was now as trapped as we was.

Of a sudden a voice rings out, "We wont kill you if you give us your horses and rations."

It wasnt hard for me to figure this out. A few armed men demandin food and horses was no dout a group of deserters tryin to get away as quick as posable.

I tole Bobby, Ross and Richard what I knowd to be true and also what I thought to be true. "These is deserters, yankees, probly three or four at most, desprate for food and needin horses to get some distence from there regiments. Probly low on amunition since they aint fired since the first volly."

I was sure they seen our fire, probly herd our horses, spred out a little and hoped to kill us all with that first volly. To the boys I whisperd "Fire at evry sound you hear but dont speak out." Again a little crunch to our left and this time all four of us fire into the darkness. I knowd now they was just as scared as us.

"What do we do Henry?" asks Bobby.

"Hold out a while" says I, "then I guess we gotta make a break for the horses."

"What about Spillner?" says Ewalt.

The fire light was almost died out now and Mickey layed on his back, his limp hands to his bloody throat, no longer makin a sound or move.

"We cant help Mickey now" says I. I thought to myself while layin on the ground in the blackness of a fine night, Mickey wont have to be imbarased by his mother throwin her arms round him, huggin him and cryin in joy.

Again from strait ahead (due east) in the blackness a deep voice hollerd "Give us your horses and we let you be." Again we fired strait ahead and this time the unseen enemy fired back at us. None of us was hit. Again silence.

Then a sound come to my ears even further ahead – the low rumble of many horses. And soon I seen flickers of light, like torches bein carryed, comin from that direction. This I figure is a squad of yankees on outpost duty. Bein very hard to judge a distence in that thick blackness, I should say maybe a hunderd yards ahead I herd a diffrent, loud voice ring out "Put down your guns or we will kill evry one of you. Now who goes there?" This question from one of the mounted men (there musta been two dozen men on horseback comin to the scene) and directed to our unseen enemy.

I herd some quiet voices, then the loud voice demands "What regiment you from – now speak up!" Again some mumblin, then the loud voice "I think your a long way from your regiments. Just what the hell you firin at?"

But fore I could hear a answer to this, I says real quiet "Now boys, quick, to the horses. We gotta get outa here or them yankees will capture us sure as hell."

I jump to my feet, my legs stiff from layin all tense for so long, and made for the horses as quick as I could. The others, Richard Marks too, come right behind. We each grab a horse by the bridle, couldnt tell one from another, and though none was saddled we mounted quick and race them bare-back toward the railroad tracks. In the darkness there was no way to follow the path we come in on, but I knowd the rail line forked at Grand Junction and heads strait to Jackson, where Gen. Forrest orderd us to go if we met with trouble. So there we was – gallupin as best we could, holdin tight with our knees, up the stony edge of the railroad line. And I herd no horsemen chasin us.

Oh damn Lizzie, how I hated to leave the body of Mickey Spillner behind. Such a good boy, and kind. And once we was clear of any pursute, I had time to think of that young man and the tears flowd open down my cheeks.

So that was our adventure of last week. We got to Jackson a couple days later and met up with our army. Gen. Forrest was none too happy when I tole him of the ambush, the death of Pvt. Spillner, the loss of our saddles and all the rest. But he was intrested to hear that the yankee pickets was spred as far as Grand Junction.

And besides all this sorry bisness, I lost another chance to be home with you and Mary. I beleve now that God does not want me reunited with my love ones till this miserble war is over. Now I hear we will soon be ridin north toward Kentucky – Old Bedford wants to break up yankee trafic on the Tennessee River. Sounds like more adventures. Till next time I am as always,

Your loving husband,
Henry

Chapter 14

November 18, 1864 through December 30, 1864

Nov. 18, 1864
Florence, Alabama

Dear Elizabeth,

Finaly got time to write you after spendin the last seven days trudgin through bottomless mud and risin creeks. With rain fallin daily we slopped along rivers of mud (formerly called roads) from Johnsonville (pert near the Kentucky border) to here in Florence, a good 125 miles. The big guns got stuck so bad in muck some times eight oxes couldnt pull them out.

But let me tell you first why we rode from Jackson all the way north to Johnsonville, and I think you will be suprized at what your husband done.

When we joind back up with out army after our pitiful atempt to ride home and get horses (related in my last letter) that cost Mickey Spillner his life, our army of 3000 mounted men started north through rough country. Gen. Forrest had the notion to disrupt union boats on the Tennessee which was carryin supplys to there armys in Georgia. Also scouts reported massive stores of union supplys at the river-side town a Johnsonville and Gen. Forrest fix his eyes on takin or destroyin that site.

We left Jackson on the 24th of Oct. and what with dry roads and fair weather we made it all the way to Paris Landing on the Tennessee just below Ft. Henry, by the 28th. As we crost the Big

Sandy River on a wide bridge, one of the pack mules took a misstep and plunge over the side in to the river. I seen him bob up once then sunk under the water for good.

Paris Landing is on the west bank of the Tennessee and I could see right away why Gen. Forrest picked this site for his plans. The banks from Paris Landing to Johnsonville is heavy with trees (good for hidin your guns) and high, makin easy targets of the many yankee gunboats, barges and transports we could see floatin on the river.

We soon started the dificult task of placin all the big guns John Morton had. What with Mortons thirty or more field guns, plus a couple big 20-pound rifled Parrots spred along the bank for five miles, we was goin to make it rough for any yankee ships to get by. There was no roads or even paths to roll the guns along. We made our own paths, and hackin our way through the woods as quiet as posable werent easy work. Some times the woods was so thick the horses couldnt turn about, so we rold the guns by hand. I could see that this was goin to be Morton and the artilery boys fight, as the rest of us couldnt do much but cut trails and bring amunition to the guns.

We worked the best part of two days on this task and we was all gettin anxous to start firin on the yankee boats. Them yankees been usin the Tennessee River for there own purpose long enough. Well finaly on the evning of Oct. 29 our patiance payed off as Gen. Forrest give the go-ahead to fire on a yankee steamer chuggin upstream. The boys at the guns near Paris Landing let the ship, the Mazeppa, pass by without a sound. They was smart enough to let her get well within our trap before firin. She was probly haulin more yankee supplys to the yard at Johnsonville, but she wouldnt make it this time. Once she saild a mile upstream from Paris Landing, the gunboys started firin. Morton and his men cant be beat, and almost evry shot hit something on the boat. In a few minutes she seem out of control and steamed hard to the east bank acrost the river, where the captain and crew jumped ashore and run to safety.

It seemed a waste for that nice ship, probly loaded with all kinds a good things, to lay abandond on the other side of the river. Gen. Forrest asked for and got a volunteer to go acrost the river and try and bring the Mazeppa back to us. Capt. Frank Gracey, of Chalmers division, is a rough and strong man who been wounded many times in battle. He volunteerd to cross the river which was cold and wide.

I aint seen nothin like it before. Capt. Gracey, naked as a jaybird, layin prone on a plank and a pistol on a string tied round his neck in case a few yankee sailors was still on board the boat. In the fadin light you could barely see him paddlin with his arms acrost the river. Didnt take him long neither. Then you could just make out his white body slither over the side of the dark ship way over yonder. In a short while he lowerd a skiff from the Mazeppa to the water. Then he tied the end of a long coil a rope to the bow of the big ship and started rowin the skiff back to the west bank. As he cut through the water, the rope uncoild. Once on the bank, a bunch a guys manned the rope and pulled the Mazeppa acrost the river to our side.

And boy did it pay off. That yankee ship was loaded with gouds. Shoes (maybe nine thousand pair), blankets, warm winter clothes, and casks of meat, hardtack and vegtables. It was better then a picnick. We unloaded all we could and left the ship tetherd to the west bank.

Next day we had lots of fun as many yankee boats steamed in to our trap. The gun boys kept up a stedy fire all up and down the bank, and sevral yankee gunboats loaded with high power cannons fired back. We sent .most scurryin for cover and a few was disabled and abandond by the yankee sailors.

We was able to pull two of the boats, the Undine and the Venus, to our bank. They wasnt damaged too serius, so Gen.

Forrest had the wise idea to repare them and man them with crews of our own.

"Come on Henry, lets get on them boats" urge Markbright, "it sure beats rollin them damn guns through the underbrush."

"I never been on a boat in my life" says I.

"Oh dont worry, we can teach you evrything" answers Markbright.

Gen. Forrest looked pretty doutful at us two when we volunteerd for the naval service, but shook his head and called us "horse marines."

Us and bout twenty other fellas was put under the charge of Col. Dawson, who was to skipper the Venus. Capt. Gracey was put in charge of the gunboat Undine, which still was loaded with eight 24-pounder brass howitzers ready for use. As "Comodore" Dawson borded his new boat, he turnd to Gen. Forrest and says "General, I will go with these boats where ever you order, but I tell you now I know very little bout managin gunboats. You must promise me that if I lose the fleet you wont give me a cursin when I wade ashore and come back on foot."

Gen. Forrest laughed, said he wouldnt "haul you over the coals" if he come home wet, but did warn Dawson and Gracey to stay within the range of our baterys, and if they run in to real trouble to make for the west bank, get the men off safe and burn the ships.

Next day our little navy done some drillin. Me and Markbright was orderd to the engine room. Our duty there was to feed lumps a coal to the iron furnace that heated the huge boilers. What a miserble job that was. Stripped to the waist, shovelin for dear life, I never felt such intense heat. I felt my skin must burn off any moment. Let go the shovel for a moment to wipe the sweat off your face, and the shovel handle was too hot to touch again.

"This is great Markbright" I holler, "fine job for cavalry officers to be doin."

234

Only good thing was he looked as miserble as me. I could see his forlorn look when he turn his face to the orange glow of the furnace. Fortunatly we worked the fuel detale in shifts, and I did enjoy walkin round the deck or helpin man the guns.

I am afraid we wasnt much for sailors as we barely got steam enough to fight the gentle current, and manuverin round in a circle was the most awkward thing you ever seen. Yet we managed to float a few times up and down the river.

But of a sudden the fun was over. Yankee gunboats, four at least, was steamin downstream right at us and firin there broadsides at our guns on the west bank, and then at us. To try and out-run these ships was useless cause we was so slow I thought maybe we had the anchor out. The boys on the Undine was firin there guns as best they could, but soon found it was far diffrent firin big guns from a unstedy boat then from a fix point on the ground.

Our navy was no match for real sailors. Each shot ripped through our decks. The smoke stack was shot off and without good draft the fires in our furnace quit roarin, and insted belch smoke back out and sent the engine room boys gaspin for air. When enemy shots crashed into our ship, us workin below decks had to stuff cotton in our ears for the noise and begged for mercy. I gaind alot of respect for sailors this day and felt I owed Markbright a punch in the nose.

For a time I truly felt we would be sunk and I would be trapped below decks and drown in the Tennessee River. Then I feard the boiler would get hit and blow up, leavin us all scalded to death. I was not enjoyin my navy experiance. Soon the Undine steamed unstedy to the west bank and Capt. Gracey and crew jumped out after lightin a line of gunpowder that led to the magazine. It musta went out cause the ship did not explode. But us on the Venus couldnt get to the west bank, a yankee gunboat cut us off, and Col. Dawson limped our boat to the east bank where he started yellin "Abandon ship, abandon ship." Thinkin on it now, it was pretty comical seein all us jump over the gunnel and get stuck knee deep in the muddy bank.

We did our best crawlin up the slimy bank and hid amongst the canebrakes till dark come. Layin there amidst a million misquitos and coverd with mud, prayin the yanks dont capture us, I give Markbright a good piece of my mind. We looked round for logs and planks and after dark we rode them back acrost the river. Not bein a real good swimmer I did not enjoy this epasode either.

Durin the whole of this adventure Gen. Forrest already been movin men and artilery bout twenty miles down river to a bluff acrost from the port of Johnsonville. By the time us men in Old Bedfords navy finaly got dryed out, new clothes and remounted, we got to Johnsonville on Nov. 3 and evrything was ready for the attack to begin.

I could observe alot of yankee activity goin on acrost the water, but the general had his guns so well hid I do not beleve the enemy suspected for a moment we was ready to let loose our fire. Then the command to fire was made, and in a instent the smoke and thunder of three dozen guns filled the air. After a few vollys Morton and his comanders was cuttin the time fuses so perfect that each shot exploded on target. Soon we seen small blazes startin to spred all along the wharf. Even Gen. Forrest took a turn firin the guns. Each shot smashed into the boats along the riverside or through the warehouses. Mountains of piled goods become roarin bonfires. The enemy seemed to have trouble raisin there guns high enough to hit us on the high bluff, and by nightfall a ragin fire was spred all along the opasite bank. The amount of yankee goods lost must be in the millions.

By this time Gen. Forrest got orders to bring his army back to Florence, Alabama and link up with Gen. John Bell Hood and the Army of Tennessee. Next morning Nov. 4, we no sooner broke camp when the heavens opend and rain pourd down.

That week we spent headin south was one of the most miserble I can remember. Evry creek become a ragin torent. The roads was bottomless rivers of muck. There was no way at all of gettin dry even for a moment, and sleepin was downright imposable. All the horses lost shoes sucked off by the mud, and the blacksmiths was forced to pull the steel bands off the wagon wheels and beat them in to horse shoes. Of course buildin a fire at all was pert near imposable, and though we had plenty a meat captured from the yankees, you couldnt cook it hardly. We had to "borow" oxes from nearby farms to pull the guns through the slimy muck as even the big draft horses was losin strength cause there was no dry forage. Markbright complaned bitter bout how chapped his legs and behind was, but I wasnt too simpathetic seein how he almost got me killed abord that boat.

Finaly struggled our way here to Florence where we met up with our comrads in the Army of Tennessee. This is the first time since Chickamauga we joind up with the main army. We been roamin independent for the whole of this year. Gen. John Bell Hood now commands this army and he made Gen. Forrest head of all his cavalry. Wonder if Old Bedford can get along with Gen. Hood better then he could with Gens. Bragg or Wheeler.

Anyway Lizzie, time to recoup our strength and get the horses fit. More action is quick in comin. Till then I am,

Your loving husband,
Henry

P.S.

Just seen Gen. John Bell Hood up close — I am suprized how young he is and also how tall. I felt simpathy for this brave man as he set astride his horse — strapped to the saddle for he lost a leg in battle, and also a arm that hangs limp and useless. Some of the boys in his army call him "old wood-head" — why I dont know, and of course, not to his face.

Dec. 2, 1864
Near Nashville, Tenn.

Dear Elizabeth,

   I can take but a few moments to recount the terible tragedy of Nov. 30 at Franklin. That is where Gen. John Bell Hood in useless fashon sacraficed the noble lives of thousands of gallent men and officers in the Army of Tennessee. These same men who fought so brave in Georgia against the army of that devil William Sherman, marched with high spirits to take back there home states of Tennessee and Kentucky from the enemy. So the 30,000 man army of Tennessee chased a equal size union force clear acrost the state of Tennessee, and finaly caught them on Nov. 30.

   With Gen. Forrest in charge of all the cavalry, we pushed the yankees ever northward till they finaly took there position behind the solid brestworks outside Franklin. With the union line anchord firm tween two rivers, the only aproach to there fortifications was over two miles of open field with nary a tree, hill or rock for a man to hide behind.

   And yet it was this frontal asault, a reckless charge in to the face of the enemy muskets and cannons, that Gen. Hood orderd a hour before sundown last Thursday (Nov. 30). I herd with my own ears Gen. Forrest pleadin to Gen. Hood, his frosty breath risin in puffs from his lips, "Give me one strong division of infantry with my cavalry and within two hours time I can flank the federals from there works."

   But Gen. Hood could not be moved. The charge would comence at once, even before our own artilery could catch up after the hard days march. So up and down the line the signal was made, the bugles blared and the drums sounded, and the entire line of battle moved toward the enemy. With the battle flags of each corp, division, brigade and regiment flutterin in the chilly air, the souths bravest sons marched forward as stedy as on the parade ground.

Our cavalry coverd the right and left flank and we did not receve the full effect of the yankee fire power. It was the boys in the center, exposed evry step of the way to witherin artilery fire and constant musket shots, that got hit the hardest. And yet they come on, stedy and unwaverin, as the cold sun sunk behind the horizen. Some few did make it to the yankee trenches where hand-to-hand fightin ensude. But all was for nought. It was two hours of useless sacrafice. The enemy held there position and our boys who survived raced back to where they started, leavin the field a sea of bloody corpses.

I tell you Lizzie, it was a horible sight. And it should never occurd anyways, cause we got the yankees trapped dead to rights the day before at Spring Hill. The union army got streched way out as it marched up the pike twixt Columbia and Spring Hill, and our army was positiond for flank attacks all along the line. But with bad comunication, confused orders and poor leadership this rare oppertunity was lost. Some how the enemy was let go and they made it all the way to Franklin, where Gen. Hood tryed to redeme his chance and at a great loss.

This whole march since leavin Florence been a disaster. We left on Nov. 18 with good spirit and high hope to recapture our homeland, but was met from the get-go with bitter winds, freezin rain, drivin snow and hail. On rout our cavalry did meet with succes at Henryville where we out-flanked a sizable union cavalry, but to my deep regret Col. Dawson was killed in the fight. Col. Dawson, you may remember, was the "comodore" of the steam boat I served on last month. That was a better time then.

Maybe the only good thing on this sorry march happend one night when Gen. Forrest was leadin the cavalry, me and Maj. Strange ridin alongside him. In the darkness we herd a voice call out "halt there." Gen. Forrest rode right up to the man. It was a yankee officer with a squad of men, his pistol out and almost touchin Gen. Forrests overcoat. I herd the hammer of his pistol click back, so I lunged forward just hittin his arm hard enough to misdirect the bullit. In seconds the whole escort thunderd up and the squad of yankees surenderd on the spot. When the exitement calm down and we resumed our march, Gen. Forrest rode up next to me for a moment and says quiet "thanks Wylie." I smiled and give a little salute off the bill of my hat.

This is all I got time for Lizzie. I wish I got more happyer news. This morning while the infantry is tryin to dig almost 2,000 graves in the froze ground, us of the cavalry rode off in pursute of the federals who left Franklin and is headin to Nashville. We been stedy engagin there rear gard and Gen. Forrest dont let them have a moments rest — us either. Till next time, I am

Your loving husband,
Henry

Dec. 30, 1864
Corinth, Miss.

Dearest Elizabeth,

How can I explane to you the undescribable misery of the past three weeks. Pain and suffrin can only be felt, not tole about. I last wrote you of the useless waste of life at the battle of Franklin, and I am sure by now you herd or read how Gen. Hood led the rest of the once proud Army of Tennessee to almost complete destruction at Nashville on Dec. 15 - 16. For the one and only time in this long, sorry war a Confederate army was routed by the enemy and fled in panicked retreat. Half the army was captured, 13,000 Confederate soldiers. Thousands more deserted, 70 cannons lost and yet beleve me or not, it coulda been worse, much worse. The only reason the other half of the Army of Tennessee survived the hunderd mile retreat from Nashville to Iuka, Miss. is because of one man — Nathan Bedford Forrest.

And Gen. Forrest and our cavalry wasnt even at Nashville durin the sad fight. We was at Murfreesboro, sent there on a mission by Gen. Hood the week before. Said there was a union force there he wanted took, so he orders Gen. Forrest to take his cavalry and a brigade of infantry there to engage the enemy. By Dec. 7 we was positioned outside Murfreesboro along Stones River, on the very ground a major battle took place two years before. (I seen gastly reminders of that struggle when I stumbled over white bones stickin up from the graves washed shallow by two years of rain).

At Murfreesboro Gen. Forrest readyed for battle by placin our infantry behind brestworks facin the well-hid enemy. He split our cavalry in two and sent us round each flank. Just before the battle commenced, the general rode up and down the line of crouchin foot soldiers tellin them "Men, all I want you to do is hold the enemy back for fifteen minutes, which will give me enough time to gain there rear with my cavalry, and we will capture evry last one of them."

A moment later the drums sounded from the enemy side and out sprung thousands of blue soldiers. Direct at our infantry they charged over broken terain with lots of trees, brush and ridges for cover. Our cavalry just started to move out on there flanks when the unexpected happend. After firin a volly at the enemy, our whole line of infantry neelin behind fences, brestworks and boulders, of a sudden give way. For some unknowd reason there courage falterd and our whole line broke to the rear in uncontrold panic. These same boys who fought so brave against Shermans army in Georgia, just lost there nerve here and rush rearward.

Gen. Forrest looked stund when he seen our men runnin, then his face turnd crimsen and veins stood out on his neck and forhead. "What the hell is this?" he shouts, and then to us of the cavalry "come on boys, we gotta stop this!"

The general was wild with fury and dashed in amongst the terifyed men. "Stop, goddamn you, rally to your colors," he was screamin, and with drawd saber he slashed and swatted at those near him. His giant war horse King Phillip, filled with the rage of his master, bucked high on his rear legs as the general did what

241

ever he could to stop the rout. I seen a color-barer runnin wild toward the general, who orderd the man to stop and wave his banner. But the man payed no notice and kept runnin. This inraged the general even more and he drawd his pistol and shot the man in the back. With this Gen. Forrest leaped off King Phillip, snached up the fallen colors and waved the banner high in the air.

Some of the men stopped and rallyed to the general, while many kept runnin. Usin the flag staff as a lance Gen. Forrest clubbed and hacked at any soldier in his reach who was still runnin away, and I beleve they was more terifyed of him then the yankees. He remounted King Phillip and still wavin the banner, screamed to re-form the lines. By this time the escort and much of the cavalry got the union onslaut pretty well halted. Finaly the boys in the infantry started to regroup and formed a defensive line. We held our ground till darkness come when the yankees fell back and withdrawd for good.

The next sevral days we spent foragin for food (we russled up 300 cattle and 200 hogs), destroyd enemy rail lines and two blockhouses (we took 400 prisners). And then the weather got real nasty, with freezin rain and blowin storms. The infantry men marched in ragged shoes over sharp froze roads, and the horses could barely pick there way along the icy trails. Evry man was soaked by wet snow or cold rains. On Dec. 16 Gen. Forrest receved a message tellin him of the pitiful defeat of our army at Nashville. Gen. Hood sent a urgent order for Gen. Forrest to bring up his force quick as posable to cover the retreat of the Army of Tennessee.

So with our little brigade of foot-sore infantry, our ever-faithfull cavalry, our 400 prisners and hundreds of cattle and hogs, our wagon train and ambulences of sick and wounded, we set off in the worst conditions to intersept our retreatin army and become there rear-gard.

After marchin three days over roads made unpassable by froze ruts and icy hills, we caught up with the remainder of Hoods army.

I never seen men so forlorn and hopeless. There bitter loss at Nashville, just two weeks after there defeat at Franklin, left them without spirit or pride, limpin along ragged, barefoot and bloody. Many was in shirtsleevs with bundled rags tied round there feet. Most was without rifles, packs or food, these been throwd down durin the skedadle. I seen no fight, no desire, no honor left in there faces. I only seen shame, defeat and misery.

They lost pert near half there army at Nashville, 13,000 men, and the rest of this sorry mass of spent manhood was in grave danger itself of bein overtook by the pursuin yankees and captured in total. Gen. Hood seemed dazed, not able to deal with the disaster, and thats when Gen. Forrest took over.

I can asure you Gen. Forrest was not defeated or hopeless and had plenty of fight left in him. As soon as we joind the Army of Tennessee on Dec. 20, Gen. Forrest orgenized his cavalry and the best men of the infantry in to a rear-gard ready to give what-for to any yankee units comin too close.

Next day as the army limped through a V-shape ravine where the road to Bainbridge run tween some high hills, Gen. Forrest held back the rear-gard and set up Mortons guns for a little ambush.

Peerin down the hillside I could see a large force of union cavalry aproachin the ravine. They rode fine horses, wore warm and clean uniforms all the same color, had neat packs and the best carbines, saddle bags stuffed with food. And next to me on the hilltop was Gen. Forrest. His gray uniform was tatterd and unfittin of a major general, his powerful steed was thin and its ribs stood out. As he stared in the distence the generals face was lined deep, his back ramrod-strait, his sword of many a battle drawd in his hand. He was tall and fierse, a noble warior set to pounce on the enemy. Set there rigid and poised, he looked to me like a statue carved from the hilltop granet, the ingravin underneath should read "The God of War." His spirit was not broke, could never be broke.

243

At the right moment Gen. Forrest turnd to Morton and says "Okay, Morton, let them have it." With the big guns thunderin, he turnd to us and screamed "Charge boys, charge." We raced best we could down the icy hillside toward the enemy. Our gallent boys on foot, tryin to keep up with us, let out the rebel yell as they run toward the yankees. We was starvin, ragged scarecrows low on amunition but high on courage, and the suprized yankee cavalrymen had fear in there faces and turnd and fled. They become a flyin mass of confusion. Men gettin throwd from horses, pushin there way rearward as gunfire and explosions cut through there ranks. It was a proud moment for us as that fine yankee cavalry rode away in reckless retreat.

For the next sevral days the withdrawl south through Tennessee continude. The men was lowly, for they knowd they was abandonin there homeland for good. Severe storms made the goin unbarable, and many left trails of blood behind as they trudged through the snow. Some fell by the way side, never to move again.

Yet Gen. Forrest would not alow us in the rear-gard to be dishearted. Evry day he was cheerful, full of energy, spoke encouragment and give what-for to the enemy when ever posable. At least once a day the general set us in a position for a ambush or suprize attack, and only this boldness give the Army of Tennessee a chance to escape south. The yankees was confused, careful, scared to advance. They never knowd when they would be set upon by us crazed rebels. How come we didnt know we was a defeated mob? Why would we keep fightin against such a well-equip superior force?

Christmas Day 1864 is one I wont soon forget. The day was bitter, a few boys froze to death on the roadside. Gen. Forrest let the army cross over Sugar Creek, then held back the rear-gard. He made us build brestworks of froze logs and fence rails. My fingers was so cold I could hardly pull on the timbers, my gauntlets stiff as bords. Yet we toild on, makin our position stronger. Early morning of Dec. 26 a heavy fog rold in and hid us from the aproachin yankee cavalry. We lay very still behind our brestworks, some men froze in place I reckon, only our steamy breaths movin at all. The enemy come ridin up in force, and when they was all in close range we opend up a deadly fire that left many blue horsemen on the ground. My numb hands had a good bit of trouble cockin my pistol and pullin the trigger, and reloadin was imposable. Our attack was a complete suprize, and the yanks galluped off in disorder, leavin the dead and injurd behind.

This bought Gen. Hoods army more time to limp toward the Tennessee River. The men sufferd great, as the whole countryside was stripped clean and barren of any sustenence, and many stumbled along for three or more days without nary a bite of food. And the horses fared even worse. The froze ground could not yield one blade of grass or witherd corn stock, and the big beasts one by one fell dead from hunger, overwork and lameness. Just after we pulled out from Sugar Creek, Markbrights faithfull mare Molly pulled her leg from a mudhole and lost a hoof. She was already painful thin and limpin bad, but with the lost hoof she fell on her side. Markbrights heart was broke as he neeld by the beast that carryed him many a mile and over numerous battlefields. He knowd what had to be done but hesatated.

"You want I should take care of her John?" ask I.

"No" he snaps, "I have to do it." With that he drawd his pistol, placed the barrel up against her temple and pulled the trigger. He stood up, pulled off her saddle and gear, and started walkin. But Gen. Forrest give Markbright one of the sevral dozen horses we captured from the yankees at Sugar Creek, so he did not have to stay on foot for long.

Finaly on Dec. 27 a pontoon bridge was put together acrost the Tennessee and the army, or what was left of it, limped over. Yet these men owe there lives and freedom to Gen. Forrest. It was him who directed this long escape from Nashville. Through the worst conditions the forlorn army got back to the southland, along with a long train of ambulences with the wounded, the wagons carryin the desperatly needed supplys, the few guns we still had, the prisners we gatherd, and even the hogs and cattle. And it was Gen. Forrest who directed evry movment of the army, suggestin which roads to take, how the artilery and wagons should best be moved, where and how the enemy should be confronted. He was never at a loss or over-burdend by the severe hardship. He give orders on the smallest evry-day detales, and it was him who saved the army. I have rode with Gen. Forrest for over three years now, and I never seen him rise to greater strength then that retreat.

When at last we was safe here in Corinth, the general seen how our boys in the cavalry was completly wore out. So he gatherd us together and made a speech, something he dont do often. Standin on the steps of the courthouse, he spoke most elequent for maybe ten minutes, remindin us of our great victorys at Okolona, Ft. Pillow, Harrisburg, Brices Crossroads, Johnsonville and many others. He said these victorys was a "imparishable monument" of our prowess and they will "inshrine your names in the hearts of our countrymen and live in history." He tole us "our course has been marked by the graves of patriotic heros" who have fell by our side but added "this course has been more plainly marked by the blood of the invader." And finaly he said that we can now rest a while, regroup, recover, but prepare to "buckle on our armer," for he will be ready to lead us again "to the defense of the common cause."

I beleve we all left the gatherin feelin stronger, with our purpose renewd. But now Lizzie, I am bone-tired and have a nasty cough. Many boys is sickly and weak, and most the horses is unfit for service. Even old Buster is painful thin. We all need the time to rest and regain our strength. Please pass all news on to Ma and Pa, and give my precius Mary a hug for her daddy. Till next time I am as always,

Your loving husband,
Henry

P.S.

Just got the news! You will receve this letter very soon cause Gen. Forrest has orderd a twenty day furlow to all men from north Mississippi and West Tennessee! This time there will be no ambush. Markbright, Bobby and me will be leavin in two days to ride the hunderd miles to Memphis – hope Buster can make haste. The general wants us to bring back evry man and mount not yet in the service. Yippee! I am comin home.

Chapter 15

February 22, 1865 through April 8, 1865

Feb. 22, 1865
Verona, Miss.

Dearest Elizabeth,

We been regroupin here ever since I got back four weeks ago. I find it amazin that evry man who rode off on New Years Day to there homes, returnd twenty days later as orderd. Not one man deserted. We all tole the same story too – complete exaustion after gardin the retreat of the army all the way from Nashville to the Tennessee. Horses broke down, evry man overcome with fatige. Then we got word that we was to be furlowd for twenty days, and evry mothers son was so full a energy they couldnt wait to get in the saddle again, and most was gettin fifty, sixty miles a day outa the horses on the way home, so as to not lose even one hour of that precius time.

And what a time it was. I will never forget the look on your face as Bobby and me come in the door. It was the happyest moment of my life. And little Mary – if she disrememberd me it didnt take long to get reaquainted. With her settin in my lap and her little arms round my neck, I now know what heavens like. Now she knows for sure she got a real daddy.

And when we got to the farm and suprized Ma and Pa – well with her leanin over a steamin pot of stew it was like I never left home at all. Pa, I must say, looks older and care worn to me.

Workin the farm is harder on him I think. When I return for good God willing, I will help him out when ever I can, and I know they love havin Mary runnin bout the place. See how easy she climb to the loft? Maybe when I get back we should move back to the farm, I think they need the company there. This is somthing we must decide later on.

Even our future seem secure. As you know I seen Mr. Gallaway in town, and he is makin preperations to start another newspaper in Memphis. He knows I was a pressman before the war, and he asured me there will be a job for me when the war is over. He says "Maybe I can make a reporter of you Henry, bein how evry time I look up you are writin a long letter home." He says he carryed more mail for me then any other soldier. He has been a great friend in camp to me these past years. Its him who gets me paper and ink and envelopes most often, and Mrs. Gallaway is like a mother to all the boys. Her and Mrs. Forrest spent many a long hour together in our numerous camp sites whenever posable, both stickin close to there husband and doin all they can for us ("there boys" as they say).

I mention before that evry man who left on furlow return as ordered, but I must admit that few was able to bring back new recrutes or fresh mounts. Markbright, as you know yourself, got hisself a fine roan, and your father give Bobby "Highlander" in exchange for poor wore-out Rocky. But most boys was like me, rode back to camp on the same hoof-sore beasts they rode out on. Good old Buster, seems to just keep going.

Gen. Forrest sent a squad a men out, led by Col. Jesse Forrest, roundin up deserters and drifters. You know how dangerus the countryside is with rovin bands of deserters, absentees and stragglers who are nothin more then plunderers, horse thiefs and robbers. The general hates this low class of skulkers more then he hates the yankees, and he would like to personly shoot evry one he can catch. So far Col. Jesse and his men musta brung in sevral hunderd of these lawless run-aways, and Gen. Forrest will see to it that strict disiplin and obediance will reform these caracters. God knows we need evry avalable man. The scouts report a massive union cavalry, maybe 15,000 well-mounted men, amassin on the north bank of the Tennessee near Gravelly Springs, Ala. The scouts say these men is led by a young major general, James Wilson, and that they carry the new Spenser repeatin carbine, a gun they lode on Sunday and keep shootin till Friday. We aint got but 3,000 men here on sore-back mounts, and sure no one here got a fancy rifle. The word is that when the rivers go down Gen. Wilson will lead his great cavalry on a march through Alabama, destroyin our farms and industry like Shermans army did through Georgia late last year. The remnant of the Army of Tennessee has pretty much drifted away, so its up to Old Bedford and us to stop the yankees again.

But for right now the rains keep fallin. Evry creek is sweld over its banks, and most the boys is cold and bord. We want to see some action against the enemy. Maybe the past month Gen. Forrest and his staff is makin plans on how to defete the yankee invaders, just like he done to Sturgis, Sooy Smith and Abel Streight, but the avrage recrute is just spendin time waitin. I got a chance lately to read the Bible some – funny how I recall so much of it from our Sunday school. Markbright and me spend a good deal of time playin checkers, and it seems a whole crop of checker bords has sprung up acrost the camp, and a big checkers turnament been goin on for a couple weeks. Some boys play chess or back-gamon, others gamble on card games or shootin marbles. There was one rifle shootin contest but Gen. Forrest put a stop to it quick – said it was a waste of amunition. One type of frolic I do not enjoy is cock fightin. Many the men got fightin cocks, and big matches take place often. Durin one of these grusom events a big fight broke out amongst the men involved, and I dont know who was in worst shape – the birds or the men. A strong provost gard finaly broke it up. Theres many other activitys round camp too – some of the boys is barbers and will give you a clip and shave for money or

251

goods. Some of the men is tailers and will mend your clothes for a fee. Others is artists and carve fine statues from wood blocks. I seen one fella who folded paper in to the shape of fancy birds and deer. Theres sevral brass bands formed, and many boys got mouth harps and fiddles. At night you hear all sorts of music from all over the camp. I know I am a soldier, and fightin the enemy is my purpose, but I enjoy the peace and veriety of a winter camp. Markbright and me live in a little log hut we built, with mud stuffed in the chinks. Aint fancy, but pretty comfitable all the same.

But I beleve peace wont last long now. I know Gen. Forrest already sent part of Chalmers division on a march toward Selma. The feelin here is that Selma with its iron works, arsenels and navy yard will be the target of the union invasion. When that time comes, we will again defend our country with our lives and honor. But I feel, and most the others beleve too, this wont be no hit-or-miss slipshod raid by the yankees. This will be a determind and destructive invasion. I must admit Lizzie, as I rode back through Tennessee in the freezin snowstorms with Hoods crushed army, I felt in my heart our cause was lost, and now it is a matter of time.

But that is not for me to ponder – I am here to follow orders and serve my country. Till I write again, I am

Your loving husband,
Henry

March 30, 1865
Scottsville, Ala.

Dear Elizabeth,

If I have not wrote you for a goodly while it is cause I aint had the time or opertunity of late. Though we have not actuly engaged the enemy since we left Verona early this month, we see the sines of his destruction all over. Burnt homes, destroyd goverment bildings, ruind factorys.

We gone over a hunderd miles since leavin Verona, but the trekin is slow cause evry creek and river is overflowd its banks. Most bridges on the Sipsey was washed away and the one we managed to get acrost on was narow and unstedy. Just barely got the wagons over. Yesterday we got acrost the Black Warior near Tuscaloosa, and I seen the young cadet corp from the university there drillin and gettin ready to defend there town from yankee invasion.

And we can use evry man to defend our homeland. I beleve I tole you in my last letter that the yankees is tearin a path of destruction through Alabama with the biggest cavalry unit yet. Close on 15,000 well-mounted and equiped horsemen is slashin a swath through the state, and I feel we will encounter them head-to-head fore long, some wheres near Selma.

All we have to stop them is 3000 rough and ready troopers and of course, Gen. Nathan Bedford Forrest. Last month Old Bedford was promoted to lutenant general, and I would wager he is the only soldier in either army who enlisted as a private and rose to such a lofty rank. And does he ever deserve it. I never seen a man work so hard. He studys maps for hours on end, then goes on long reconasance rides hisself to check the lay of the land. He makes sure his soldiers is seen to in evry way, and personly inspects all the horses. I know he is burdend with many conserns, yet he always finds time to sit and talk with the boys or have a laugh with the artilery men, or share a bite of grub with the teamsters. One group a teamsters is black men, maybe forty of them, and they are slaves of Gen. Forrest. Early in the war he brung these men from his Mississippi plantation and promised them he would free each and evry one if they would serve as teamsters through the war. And cept for sevral who died of fever, and one who got killed by a morter blast, they stuck it out. These black fellas stay to therselvs pretty much off in a corner of the camp, but I talked with them on sevral ocasions. Though shy fellas with no formal learnin, for the most there kindly and helpful men, and a good many is smarter then they look. More then a few has the goal of earnin there freedom and then plan to buy the freedom of there wife and children. Many of these nigras has made money over the years doin special services for the soldiers. One, Mark by name, can do damn near anything with leather and does a goodly bisness fixin saddles and gear for the men. I once payed him a new pair of socks for mendin the girth belt on my saddle. Held good ever since. One thing these nigra teamsters got in common is there very high regards for Gen. Forrest. They look on him not just as master, but as a kind of god, and I beleve they would do anything he ask of them. He always treats them like men, not beasts of burden, and sees they got food, clothes and shelter too.

I beleve I tole you how Gen. Forrest hates deserters and absentees so much. He considers them worse then just thiefs and plunderers, but cowerds and traiters as well. He got Col. Jesse Forrest and his squad out daily roundin up these men, and many is brung back at the point of a gun and in irons. Many of these men, not really the pick of the litter to start with, is afeard this next incounter with the enemy may end up like the fights in Franklin and Nashville and is tryin to skedadle before it comes.

Last week Gen. Forrest got so angerd when more then a few men did not answer morning role call, he orderd that the next deserter captured would be shot before evryone, as a example. Sure nough, next day two men was caught tryin to get acrost the Sipsey bridge. They was marched back to camp but no one here knowd who they was. They both admit to bein in the service, but what regiment they would not say. They said they was discharged from the service and headin home to Kentucky. I could almost beleve there reasons for bein discharged. One fella named Joe says he was too old to serve anymore, and I swear by the looks of his white hair and rinkled face he got to be over sixty. The other fella who said his name was Sam, says he was turnd loose to go home cause he was below the official age to serve. I promise you Lizzie, this was a clean-cheek kid of 14 maybe. I felt truly sorry for them two, as they was plain scared for there lifes. I also felt sick at my heart knowin that the Confederacy now turnd to men so old and boys so young to fight for its cause. Who would be left at home? What have we come to?

Anyway, these two fellas was tryed before a court martial, and though they plead with tears for there lifes, they was found guilty of desertion. Gen. Jackson declared that since these two admit to bein soldiers but neither one had no furlow, pass, or oficial papers showin what command they belong to or why they was quittin the army, there considerd deserters and will be executed next morning at sunrise.

Next day we was orderd to attend the event and formed a big arc round the two poor souls who was marched by drum beat to the site of the execution. I was amazed and to be truthful Lizzie, I was ashamed how many men volunteerd quick for the firin squad. I must admit I would have great difficulty carryin out that detale even if I was orderd to it. But orders wasnt needed, more then enough men step forward.

There they stood, a old gray-haird man and a fresh-face boy with there hands tied behind there backs. There they stood, the risin sun in there eyes – the last sunrise they was ever to witness. I was hopin in my heart, and I reckon many others was too, that Gen. Forrest would come ridin through the crowd at the last second and halt the execution, as he done another time so long ago.

But today it was not to be. Gen. Forrest is plum fed up with deserters leavin there ranks and makin other men, loyal and true men, carry on the fight. And he can be hard as flint. So Gen. Jackson gives the command "ready" and twenty rifles went up. Then "aim" was shouted and the gunmen sighted down there barrels. Joe, the old man, stood ramrod-strait starin direct in the faces of the squad, but the boy Sam drop to his knees sobbin, head down and veerd to the right. "Fire" shouts Gen. Jackson and the thunder of rifle fire echo through the cool morning silence.

There bodys was carried to the main road and layed on the ground under a tree. A big sine was painted and naild to the tree and it read "Shot for Desertion." This was to be a warnin and reminder to any one who might consider runnin off.

Well Lizzie, thats it for now and I may have to carry this letter with me a while, as I dont know how or where to post it. I hope it some how makes it to you should something bad happen in the near future. Tomorow we ride ever closer to the yankee hord, and I feel the time to face the bull is near at hand. No matter what happens, know that my soul will always be near you and Mary, forever. With all my love, I am

Your loving husband,
Henry

April 8, 1865
Cahaba, Ala.

Dear Elizabeth,

On bended knees I offer a prayer of gratatude to the mercifull Lord above who seen fit to spare my life. I survived a series of the most savage fights and hand to hand combat I experianced this entire war. The cost of these battles is high and the gains very little. I am most gratefull that me and Bobby fought in and survived this great battle, but I regret most deep that my friend John Markbright receved a serius wound and is probly dead. I pray for his soul. I feel now the enemy got control of the heartland on all fronts, and there is little we can do now. I know from persnal experiance that we are no match in manpower, mounts or fire arms to the northern cavalry that cut its way through Alabama.

The bitter contest comenced late in the day of March 31. At that time Gen. Forrest had his command broke up. Gen. Chalmers on one rout, Gen. Jackson and his brigade on another, while Roddy and Armstrong was spred apart too, but all commands under orders to meet at Selma (where the main union thrust would likely be). So on the last day of March Gen. Forrest was ridin south with but his escort of 75 men and a couple hunderd Kentucky boys under Col. Crossland.

Just as we crost Six Mile Creek below Montivallo our path intersected the very road the yankee hord was travelin on its march southward toward Selma. Here at last we come upon the very middle of there long colum, and in usual fashon the general orderd us to draw our six-shooters and "give them hell." Here we was, less then 300 men, preparin to charge on a enemy colum strechin miles long.

But when the general yells "charge boys, charge" our little pack bolted out screamin and hollerin with pistols flarin right in to the flank of the yankee horsemen. This sudden and unexpected attack burst upon there peacful progres, and so bold and spirited was the charge the yankees fled in mass confusion. We kept up the bulge for but a short time, for the yankee stampede lasted only long enough for the experianced yankee officers to stem the disorder and draw up the men in line of battle. Course, Gen. Forrest knowd we was outnumberd many times over, so he drawd us off after roundin up as many yankee prisners as posable. We circled back east and rode hard for sevral hours till we was out ahead of the yankee colums. We found a most pleasant camp site somewheres near Randolph, Ala. where the horses could graze and a gentle stream flowd near by. Gen. Forrest alowd no fires that night in fear the enemy might come upon us. As I layed on my blanket, which is now more holes then cloth, I stared up to the heavens and I beleve that was the most clear sky I ever seen, and maybe a million stars shinin as bright as can be. I tole old Markbright we was lucky to be alive on such a night as that.

Next morning we rode off still headin south toward Selma, and durin the day we was joind by Roddys Alabama boys and a part of Gen. Armstrongs brigade. I could tell by the comments he made that Gen. Forrest was consernd and angry that the rest of his command, those under Gens. Chalmers and Jackson, was havin trouble meetin up with us, mostly cause of bad roads and high water, I reckon.

In the afternoon of April 1 we crost the swift Bolgers Creek, near a place called Ebenezer Church, though in truth I never did see no church and in fact there was scarcely a soul to be seen anywheres.

The general had us dismount and throw up rails and logs to fortify the high grassy plain we was on. He knowd the yankees was comin on swift and chose a good spot for defense. Even with Roddy and Armstrongs men we had but 1500 or so ready to fight, and we knowd this federal colum was marchin with 6000 or more men.

Sure nough, shortly fore sundown we could hear the clomp clomp clomp of the yankees horse hoofs poundin the earth. On they come by the thousands, us neelin behind our low brestworks spred out sevral hunderd yards in either direction. All our men was dismounted cept Gen. Forrest, the escort and Crosslands 200 Kentucky boys. To us the general says "I want you on horseback in case we need to make a charge." I glance over at Markbright, who cleard his throat quiet.

When the head of the yankee colum got within range our whole line opend fire on them. We had two field guns positiond and these too opend fire. The yankees scatterd in disorder, more then a few horses now riderless, but soon got thereselvs situated to return fire. Thats when all hell broke loose.

Of a sudden bout 400 screamin yankees burst forth from there line swingin there sabers and spurrin there horses in wild headlong attack on our position. Gen. Forrest never once to my recolection receved such a charge while hidin behind brestworks. Soon as he seen them yankees wavin sabers, he orderd us to ride out and meet them head-to-head. "Boys" he says, "keep your sabers at your side, but draw both pistols and wait till there upon us, then start firin."

One moment later Gen. Forrest shouts "charge, charge!" and burst out front toward the on-rushin yankees. We was right with him and thus comence the most savage hand-to-hand fight I was ever involved in. The two cavalrys actuly crashed right in to each other. Horses smashed into horses, nockin men out of the saddle. Clouds of dust was kicked up and there was no semblence of order as small groups of men met in mortal combat.

The yankees, many more then we got, swung and slashed with sabers while our boys was firin pistols. The fightin was so close takin stedy aim was dificult. I had no time to think, just reacted by instinct. At that moment I can truly say I was not fightin for a cause, a principle or a country, I was only fightin to save my life. I fired at any movin thing blue that come within a sabers reach of me. I know not many minutes went by before both my pistols was empty. I just fired one shot after another, with what results I truly cant say.

In the midst of the madness I did catch a glimpse of Gen. Forrest. There was a crowd of enemy horsemen all round him. I guess evry yankee officer wanted to boast the fact he killed the great Gen. Forrest. One man hacked the generals left hand and his pistol fell to the ground while another, a young yankee captain, give a violant slash to the generals arm below the shoulder. It seem at that dire moment even the God of War hisself was bout to face mortality. Just then Phil Dodd, a private in our escort, rode near the general and shot dead two of the yankees houndin him. This instent give Gen. Forrest just enough time to pull his other pistol and shoot in rapid order three more yankees swarmin near him.

By this time I was hackin away with my saber, strikin blows against any one who come near. At times like this I must be out of my mind in rage and exitement, as I can not remember all that happens. I do remember hearin recall blowd on the bugles, and the two sides pull apart from one another while a mass of bleedin men layed on the field of battle. Gen. Forrest hisself was coverd evry inch in blood from many slashes on his arms, face and body.

259

Bobby got a nasty tear from the left ear to the jaw, and was holdin a cloth tight to his face, all soaked with blood. Capt. Boone, who commands the escort when Gen. Forrest is away, took a saber thrust through his ribs and was led away in a wagon. Many of our boys was wounded, but I could see the yankees gatherin up lots of dead bodys.

Bein outnumberd so bad, Gen. Forrest (who stayed in command in spite many wounds) pulled us back after dark but we rode and fought without cease for the next twenty miles. As we struggled along unfamilier roads in the black of night, there was constant gunfire from the pursuin yanks. We finaly pulled up for a few hours rest near Plantersville, where we camped over night. Doc Cowan and the medics was busy men stichin cuts and dressin wounds. I stopped by to see Gen. Forrest who was sendin out messages by curier and makin plans for the morning.

"Sorry to interupt General" says I, "just wonderd how you was feelin. I seen you take a nasty cut."

"Aint got time to be hurt now lutenent" says he, "but I can tell you one thing — if that boy, the yankee captain, gave me the point of his saber insted of the edge, I wouldnt be here now talkin bout it."

"Thank God for that" says I, "he payed for that mistake. Well good night General — try and get some rest."

We was up fore dawn next day April 2, a Sunday. We knowd the yankees would be close on our heels so we rode hard for a couple hours till we come upon our objective — Selma. This city of ironworks and arsenals was to be our last stand against the enemy. Still Gen. Chalmers and Gen. Jackson did not have there troopers here to meet us, and Gen. Forrest was ragin mad. He knowd the crisis hour was almost here, but yet he got only a handful of men to hold the defenses against a yankee hord many times as large. The fortifacations formed a broad arc round the outskerts of the town. This was mainly trenches and brestworks, and was desined for a much larger garison then what we got with

260

us. By the time the general got us where he wanted, there was a good eight to ten feet tween each man. The general was so desprate for manpower, he searched the deserted streets of Selma for any man still on two feet. He shouted "evry man must go into the works or be throwd in the river." It was a rag-tag group of militia Gen. Forrest musterd from the town. Old men, young boys, cripples and cowerds was all gave a rifle and placed some wheres in the line. I did not have a good feelin bout this.

In the afternoon we could hear a noise like a stampede of bison. It was the massive yankee cavalry movin down the road to Selma. They soon drove our pickets back to the defense works, and we could see small partys of scouts on reconasance, sizin up our position and strength.

I could see through the clearin many men on horseback and battle flags spred far and wide. There was a powerful lot of them. The time of attack was now at hand. It felt odd to me, hidin behind logs waitin for the enemy to unleesh the attack on us, and I says so to Markbright. For all these years it was us, Gen. Nathan Bedford Forrests unstopable cavalry that unleesh the wild attack on a cringin garison. Now the situation was reversed.

Just fore sundown it come. The sound of distent bugles blow charge, followd in a moment by thousands of horsemen racin direct at us. There battle flags whipped back and forth by the force of there charge, a risin cloud of dust kicked up behind them. The deep screams of waves of rampagin troopers and the thunder of there artilery was enough to un-nerve even the stoutest veteren.

Artilery shells explode on all sides of me, deafenin to hear, and I tryed stuffin bits of cloth in my ears to muffle the blasts. The yankees rushed on in good formation keepin there lines tight, and attacked with vigor. When they come within rifle range we let them have it. Up and down our whole line, men fixed a yankee in there rifle sight and pulled the trigger. Us veterens of many a battle could load and fire twict, maybe three times in a minute.

And this took a toll as yankees was nocked from the saddles in all directions.

This yankee cavalry, unlike many we faced durin the war, was led smart by experianced officers who knowd when and how to draw the troopers off, shift direction and focus the attack. Still our resistence was good and we held them off with heavy loss for a goodly time.

I was loadin and firin my rifle so fast the barrel got red hot and I burnt my fingers bad when I was dumb enough to grasp it one time. You cant keep track of time durin such confusion, but I spect we held them off for pert near a hour. I did know my amunition was bout gone, and I carryed a hunderd rounds with me. The yankees was poundin at the flanks mostly, tryin to buckle them in, but with Armstrongs boys on the right and Roddys on the left, they held firm.

Then the enemy regrouped for another asault, this time mostly at our center. It was here the local militia and citizen soldiers was holdin on. The yankees next charge hit the middle of our defenses hard, men bein hit and our thin line gettin weaker still. And then, as if they couldnt stand this terror no more, the whole center of our line fell back in panic. Gen. Forrest tryed to stem the confusion by shiftin groups here and there, but it was hopeless. Yankee troopers swept through the line, and the order was spred for us to try and regain our horses and save ourselvs.

Men was runnin in all directions to escape. Hunderds was captured. The men of the escort stuck close together and did make it to our horses. Just as we got mounted a large body of yankees come from the woods near by. In the midst of the darkness they fell upon us, slashin with there sabers. The clash of steel and the crack of pistol shots filled the night air. One yankee horseman made a savage attack on Gen. Forrest, who dodged the swingin saber and thrust his own clear through the yankees body till it stuck out the back of his uniform. That trooper fell dead to the ground. We was breakin loose from the enemy when I seen one slash at

Markbright near by. Markbright tryed to parry the blow, but it slashed his face just above the brow. Even in the darkness I seen the white underside of his scalp as it peeled clean off his head. Markbright fell to the ground, layed on his back with his whole scalp hangin loose and blood evrywhere. I beleve I musta been in shock for a moment and I realize now how lucky I was not to be killed myself that instent as I stared at my best friends body.

Then the scream of "Henry" broke upon my senses. "Come on Henry" screamed your brother Bobby, "you cant do nothing for him now." I snapped to, swung Buster round toward the open road and spurred him on. As hard as it was for me to realize it, there was nothin I could do for Markbright. As we raced along strange roads in the blackness of night, I could see the glare from the city of Selma as goverment bildings and foundrys was already set ablaze.

All night we rode, and along the way was rejoined by small groups of our boys. Twict we was set upon by yankee squads and fought our way through. We rode in the dark till the sun come up, and outside Plantersville was finaly joined by Chalmers brigade and parts of Jacksons, who was slowed up all along there march by sweld rivers and yankee ambushes.

Here we set now, camped out in the old town of Cahaba, slowly regroupin after the confusion and disaster at Selma. I am plum tuckerd out, I hurt inside and out and need to recover in mind and body. The yankee hords continue to slash and burn acrost this state, and Gen. Forrest is man enough to know that any pursute on our part is useless and a waste of life.

I must rest now, will probly retane this letter in my posesion as postin it seems unlikly. I again thank God for sparin my life, as He did Bobbys too, and I pray for the soul of John Markbright. Till I may see you again, I am

Your loving husband,
Henry

Chapter 16

April 26, 1865 through May 10, 1865

April 26, 1865
Gainesville, Ala.

Dearest Elizabeth,

Much has happend since last I wrote sevral weeks ago, and mostly of a good nature. I tole you of our fight to save Selma and our narow escape from that city. Our men, who run helter-skelter away from Selma, slowly regrouped here in Gainesville and actuly a goodly number (over 1000) has showd up.

Selma was the last incounter of a violant nature we had with the enemy, and I do beleve now that might just be our last fight. We hear rumers, storys that Richmond has fell and Robert E. Lee surenderd his grand army. And we herd of the death of Abe Lincoln — even to most of us that seems a sensless act. If all this be true, the war is just bout over, and to continue fightin would be a waste of life. In fact the rumers was flyin round so much that yesterday Gen. Forrest gatherd us together and made this statment: "Men, these storys that been runnin through camp should not control our actions or influance feelings, sentiment or conduct." He asured us that the Confederacy was still alive, the goverment in control, the troops in the field. "At this time above all others" he says, "it is the duty of evry man to stand firm at his post and true to his colors." And he says a few days more would determen the truth or falsity of all the reports now cerculatin round the camps.

Elizabeth, I for one am not afraid to say right now I hope the hostilitys is over, that the two sides can now join forces again, and peace and prosparity be restord to our troubled land. Any man who calls my feelins cowerdly is a damn scoundrel and may find hisself in another fight. I know I am a brave soldier. I served my country and fought loyal for its rightous cause for almost four years. I faced death, injury and hardship evry day. I got a mangled knee that will hinder and pain me till my dyin day. May God forgive me, but I have deliverd many a enemy soul to His side – but always, I will say, in a life-or-death struggle where I had no choice but to kill or be killed. But now the will of God speaks, and the superior forces and industry of the enemy has finaly took its tole, and the south can no longer hold out. I for one am ready to return home to my love ones and begin life anew.

This means that my last remembrence of battle will be of poor Markbright bein slashed to the ground and of Gen. Forrest runnin his saber clear through the body of a yankee trooper. The other day I was talkin with Maj. Strange, the generals adjutent who been with us since day one. He writes up all the official reports for the general. "Well" he says to me "if there aint no more fightin, Gen. Forrest ended up a yankee ahead."

"What do you mean by that?" asks I.

"Did you see Gen. Forrest plunge his saber through that yankee when racin from Selma?"

"I seen it" says I, "what of it?"

"That was the 30th yankee Gen. Forrest killed in hand-to-hand combat. I kept track you know. And durin the course of these four years the general got 29 horses shot out from under him. Thats a fact. So I tole him the other day he ended up a yankee ahead."

Thats quite a thing, aint it Lizzie, how one man could survive so much close fightin. I aint sayin luck played a part, for I never seen a stronger, quicker, more ferocous man in a fight then Gen. Forrest. But how did he live through so much when so many others was killed? Injurd severe at least four times he always come

266

back stronger and more ready to fight. Did He make him like other men?

It pains me bad when I think of so many lost lifes. Men I knowd from my youth like Mark Turner and Jeff Treach. The loss of your brother Johnny Parker I will carry in my heart forever. Boys who was at my side when death took them — Mickey Spillner, Jake Brown and Oliver Heath. It seem so long ago Capt. May and Dr. Van Wick was took, and we still mourn the loss of Col. Jeffrey Forrest and Col. Dawson, Capt. Freeman and men of the escort like Sgt. Kelly and Capt. Merriwether. I could go on and list a hunderd names of men I served with and who can never know what life will be like when the war is over.

But I have not tole you the good news yet. A while back Gen. Forrest and the yankee commander Gen. James Wilson called a truce and met face-to-face. There was many prisners on both sides and many wounded men in ragged clothes and poor condition to be discused. There was sevral days of meetings, and co-operation and trust was the order of the day. It all ended with a prisner exchange and official lists of all who been captured or killed. Maj. Strange come up to my tent next day and showd me a paper which read "Capt. John Markbright, escort company, captured but not exchanged due to head wound. Transported north for recovery." Aint that grand, I said to Maj. Strange.

So many times I thought of Markbright and how much I missed his plesant company. He always said things to cheer me up, make me laugh, get me through rough times. The thought of his death left me lonely and depresed. So this was great and suprizin news indeed. The saber slash was not fatal, the yankees captured him, and now he is recoverin in one of there hospitals. And in truth, he is no dout better off there then in one of our hospitals, where medical supplys and help is so limited.

Speakin of them prisners, I was in charge of a squad watchin over the captured yankees we manage to drag away with us from Bolgers Creek and Selma. Since we had no fence or inclosure, we just spred round the lot of them in a wide circle. The yankees was mostly young fellas like us, and many seem to me to be just as tired of the fightin as me.

One lad near me was handin out pieces of hard candy from a bag he carried in his uniform. He looks at me and says "Want a piece of candy, Johnny?"

"Sure" I says, and he tossed me one.

"Is your name really Johnny" he asks.

"No" says I, "its Wylie, Lt. Henry Wylie. And who might you be?"

"Rob Rash, private."

"Where you from, Pvt. Rash?"

"New York – Niagra Falls New York," and he mentiond his regiment.

"Niagra Falls" says I, "I herd of that place. Is the waterfalls there somthing special?"

"You bet" he says with spirit, "if you aint never seen them your really missin a grand sight. You aint never been to New York state?"

"Never been further north then Paducah Kentucky" says I.

"Well Lt. Wylie, I recomend you bord a train and visit Niagra Falls. You wont be disapointed."

"Oh sure" says I, "ride a train right through enemy teritory. Be captured in ten minutes" says I.

"Wont be enemy teritory for long" says he.

And for the first time I thought how nice it would be havin our whole country back and all this hate behind us.

"Reckon your right there, Pvt. Rob Rash. I do beleve I may do the very thing you sugest" says I, feelin brighter inside.

"If you do, Lt. Henry Wylie, why not stop in and say hello."

And so it was. Next day the prisners was exchanged and I said goodby and good luck to my enemy friend. He said he would look forward to seein me. How would Mary enjoy seein them big waterfalls?

I hope this war is over soon. It makes me mad when so many of the younger men say they will never surender to the yankee mongrels and will fight on no matter what happens to the goverment. In fact there is a good deal of serius talk amongst the men, mostly them without wifes and children, of escapin to Texas and formin bands of gerillas to keep the fight goin. The sad thing Lizzie, is that I know these angry men and I know they might very well do what they say, which would keep the killin and hatred goin on for ever and a day. Some one needs to talk sense in to there heads.

But for now we wait. No one here knows for sure what is happenin in Richmond or any wheres else. So till I find out more we will rest and regroup here in Gainesville. Who knows for how long. Till you hear again, I am as always,

Your loving husband,
Henry

May 10, 1865
Gainesville, Ala.

Dear Elizabeth,

This is the most exitin period in my whole life. Nothin but big news on all fronts. I am sure you know since Gen. Lee and Gen. Johnston surenderd there armys, there aint no useful purpose for us to keep fightin. Couple days ago Gen. Taylor informed Gen. Forrest that he surenderd his command and that all hostilitys was now over. I do not take defete any better then anyone else, but I can realize that our cause is lost and for one more man to die for a hopeless cause would be a sin. Much as I regret losin our effort for freedom, I rejoice that this bloody war is over. Not all the boys is in agreement with me, and I will relate more to you in a while.

The second bit of exitin news is that I just got your letter of April 12 informin me of your wonderful condition. I cant express to you how blest I feel that your in a family way again. For you to be pregnent and me to be comin home, and us to be a family again is bout the greatest thing I could hope for. And now its true. Wont Mary be the best big sister any baby ever had? For this happyness I must thank God and Gen. Forrest. God for keepin me alive these four years, and Gen. Forrest for givin me the furlow back in January.

The third piece of exitin news is that I receved word from the father of John Markbright. He tole me that John is alive and recoverin very nice of his head wound in a federal hospital in Chattanooga. He is soon to be released and anxous to get home to Memphis and his family and see his old mess-mate again. Aint that grand news Lizzie?

Now back to the surender. Gen. Forrest made the anouncment on May 6 and it was not well took amongst some of these proud troops. Many of the older fellas who been fightin for these many years is like me — we dont want to give up, we are sorry our cause is lost, will never admit the yankees could whip our command, but we know in our hearts the fight is now over and are down right happy to be goin home to our familys. But there is a large group of young reckless fellas who cant stop there hatin, cant admit to a losin cause, and want to ride to Texas or Mexico and continue the fight. Pap Nichols, a lutenant in Gen. Bells brigade is goin round makin fiery speeches incouragin the boys to keep up the fight from out west. He is whippin the more hostile and easy-persuaded men in to a fury. This loud group was pleadin with Gen. Forrest to lead them on, to gather the many thousands of soldiers scatterd bout the land still ready to fight for the southern cause. I do beleve the general give serius thought to these pleas. "Surender" is one word Gen. Forrest wont abide. He is a fighter, the best of all times, and can not exept defete.

Then come last night. I seen the general settin alone on a stump starin hard at the fire. "Need company General?" I asks walkin up.

"Tell you what Lt. Wylie, lets saddle up and take a ride."

I knowd the general ponders best while on horseback, so I hiched up Buster and he saddled King Phillip and just us two rode from camp. We spoke but little, I commented on the fine night, but the general hardly answerd. It was clear he was in deep thought, and once slapped his knee as if confounded.

Finaly we come to a fork in the road and I asks, "Which way General?"

In a most dishearted voice he says "Either. If one road led to hell and the other to Mexico, I would be indiffrent which to take."

I thought a moment and says "Maybe you dont have to take either of them roads General."

"Wylie" he says lookin hard at me, "what will you do now the wars over?"

"Me, General" I says, "go home to Memphis and start my new job. Mr. Gallaway tole me he would find a place for me on his newspaper, maybe even make me a reporter."

"A reporter?" he says rasin his eyebrows, "that might be just the thing for you Wylie, seein how you was always doin so much writin in camp."

"Maybe I can write a book some day General, bout you and all our fightin durin this war."

"Indeed Wylie, what might you call that book?"

I thought a moment, "How bout, The God of War."

"Thank you Wylie" he says with a modest smile. "I think you will be a fine writer."

I says "thanks General, but what bout you – what will you do now the wars over?"

"You know Henry," here he spoke slow and looked thoughtful, "before this war come I was a very wealthy man. I reckon tween my bisness and my plantations I was worth more then a million dollars. Then the war broke out and I left it all to fight for our country. Many the troops I rased was outfited from my persnal bank acount. Durin these four years I never once applyed for furlow to go home and tend to my bisness conserns. I give up

271

evrything to be a soldier. Now my bisness is gone, the plantations in ruin, no more slaves of course. And I am broke, nothin left. All I got is bein a soldier."

"Sorry to hear that General" I says, "course, most evry man is startin from scrach now."

"What about bein a soldier Wylie, you want to keep on fightin?"

"No sir, General" I says quick, "I love the south and our rightous cause. I fought as brave and hard as I ever could for it and would died gladly for it had God willed it. But now this war is over. It is over. Its time for me to pledge my life to a even more important cause — my family. I got another little one on the way and I will work hard to be the best father, the best husband and best provider I can."

"What about these men wantin to head for Texas or Mexico and keep the fight on — how serius are they Wylie?"

"I think General" says I, "there mostly young men who got there pride stung bad. Yes I think they are serius and would go on fightin cause thats what they was led to do. I think they need as strong a leader in peace now as they had in war — then they can be led to there homes in peace and made in to good citizens too."

"Wylie" he says in a firm voice, "that settles it. Lets go back to camp."

This morning after bugle sounded Gen. Forrest called all the troops together for one last time and made a most eliquent speech. He started by sayin that all the armys of the south is now surenderd and ours is the last one yet in the field. But he says, "that we are beaten is a self-evident fact, and any further resistence on our part would be the hight of folly and rashness." He knows how brave evry man fought, the persnal sacrafices by all, but that the goverment we fought to establish was at a end, and "reason dictates and humanity demands that no more blood be shed." He said our duty now was to lay down our arms and help restore peace, law and order through-out the land. He said the terms of surender is fair and favorable to all, and its our duty "to put aside our feelings of anamosity, hatred and revenge." He said how proud he was to lead us, wished us best for our future welfare and happyness, and tole us when we return home "a manly, straitforward course of conduct will secure the respect even of our former enemys." And he concluded by sayin "I have never on the field of battle sent you where I was unwillin to go myself, nor would I now advise you to a course which I felt myself unwillin to persue. You have been good soldiers, now you can be good citizens. Obey the laws, preserve your honor, and the goverment to which you surenderd can afford to be and will be magnanamus."

A rousin cheer went up. Men was huggin each other, slappin backs, claspin hands and whoopin it up. I aint herd no more talk of carryin the fight on. I know your brother Bobby was one of them talkin more fightin, but now he is anxous to go home as me.

And now Lizzie, its just a matter of packin up old Buster and sayin my last goodbys. It is a sorowfull and joyous moment. I am no longer 2nd Lutenent Henry Wylie, Gen. Forrests escort, I am just plain Henry Wylie, husband and father.

This is one letter I know will be deliverd prompt. Praise the Lord there wont be no "till next time." But of course, I am as always,

Your loving husband,
Henry

Afterword

Chapter 1

The letter of Oct. 3, 1861 typically describes the formation of a battalion at the start of the war. Capt. Charles May did organize a group of Memphis boys on horseback as Co. C of the "Forrest Rangers" (Wyeth, p. 24). The other names Wylie mentions are fictitious, but it was common for any particular company to be composed of boys who had grown up together.

The letter of Oct. 20, 1861 describes the election of officers, both at the company and regimental levels. The company officers (except Capt. May) are fictitious, while the regimental officers mentioned did indeed serve as Forrest's first officer corps. Major David C. Kelley was a keen observer and scholarly gentleman who became very intimate with Forrest, and much recorded history of Forrest and his exploits came from Kelley (Wyeth, p. 23).

The raiding of the transport and firing by the Conestoga described in the Nov. 22, 1861 letter occurred as reported (Henry, p. 42) with some elaboration by this author.

The sniping of Dr. Van Wick reported in the post script of the Nov. 25, 1861 letter actually occurred, and Wyeth (p. 27) speculates that the sniper probably thought he was aiming at the commanding officer, as Van Wick was in full dress uniform. Wyeth states that if the assassin had hit Forrest instead, "it would have been to the cause of the Union the most valuable piece of metal fired" during the war.

The Matlock fiasco described by Wylie in the letter of Dec. 25, 1861 did happen though the details remain somewhat sketchy (see Hurst, p. 16). Hoot Evers is fiction, but that Forrest disdained vulgarities is fact (Wyeth, p. 558).

The fight at Sacramento in the letter of Dec. 30, 1861 is described simply but accurately. The physical changes in Forrest described by Wylie — the flushed face, piercing voice, extreme violence of action — were marveled at by the men who fought with him. A contemporary account of this startling battlefield transformation, taken from the manuscript of Major Kelley, appears in Jordan and Pryor, p. 53.

Chapter 2

In the letter of Feb. 6, 1862, Wylie's encounter with Hoot Evers is fictitious, and only serves the purpose of getting Wylie into Forrest's remarkable (and real) escort company. Since the high command removed Forrest's command from him three separate times, the only way to keep Wylie close by Forrest was to have him in the escort.

The letters of Feb. 19 and Feb. 20, 1862 describe the fight for Ft. Donelson. The sudden change to miserable weather, the death of Capt. May, the wounding of Jeffrey Forrest, the attempted breakout, the gathering of battlefield articles, and the daring escape of Forrest's command are reported by Wylie as they actually occurred. (For a more detailed analysis of the battle near Donelson and precise regimental numbers involved and surrendered, see the *Official Records*, Serial No. 7, pages 287-416.)

The situation in Nashville described in the letter of Feb. 26, 1862 was derived from an anonymous eyewitness who wrote an almost contemporaneous pamphlet entitled, "The Great Panic." Forrest's clubbing the ringleader on the head is reported by Wyeth (p. 59). Wylie's quick conversation with the fleeing thief is fictional.

Chapter 3

The content of the letter of March 19, 1862 is by-and-large fictional, though Forrest did indeed have his younger brothers William, Jesse, and Jeffrey serving in his command, and son William was his aide throughout the war.

In the letter of April 9, 1862 Wylie describes the first day's fighting at Shiloh. In his usual simplified fashion, the action Wylie depicts is basically historically accurate, though as R.S. Henry testifies, the actual story of Forrest's men at Shiloh is difficult to decipher from a maze of varying, indefinite and conflicting reports. We owe most of our information to Major Gilbert Rambaut, Forrest's Chief Commissary, who wrote a paper, "Forrest at Shiloh," and read it before the Confederate Historical Association of Memphis in 1896 (Henry, p. 480). The story of the runaway artillery horse came from that source.

The second day of fighting at Shiloh is described by Wylie in the letter of April 10, 1862, and as in almost all the battlefield reports, Wylie does not go heavily into tactics, but does accurately report most of the action and numbers involved. The rather famous episode at the "fallen timbers," where Forrest out-distances his troops, gets surrounded by the enemy, and is shot at point-blank range, has been verified by a number of eyewitness accounts, including Gen. William Sherman, who includes it in his *Memoirs*, Vol. 1, p. 243. However, the particular detail of Forrest's snatching a Union soldier up to his horse and using him as a human shield was recorded in the first Forrest biography, that of Jordan and Pryor (pp. 146-148), and not by either Wyeth or Henry. As Hurst speculates (p. 93), could a man with so serious a spinal wound that his right leg was numb be able to drag a soldier onto a horse's back and hold him steady while galloping away? It seems hard to fathom, but how else to explain Forrest's escape from the midst of a regiment of hostile soldiers? When dealing with N.B. Forrest, nothing can be discounted.

In the letter of May 7, 1862 Wylie accurately describes the situation after Shiloh, but does elaborate a bit on the extraction of the ball from Forrest's back. Dr. Cowan, the surgeon who did the operation and served throughout the war with Forrest, was the first cousin of Mary Ann Montgomery Forrest, the general's wife (Henry, p. 481).

That Forrest was sent by Gen. Beauregard to Chattanooga to take command of a new brigade is fact, but much of the information in the letter of June 30, 1862 – the arrival of the Parkers, Wylie's conversation with young William and Gen. Forrest – is fiction.

Chapter 4

The capture of Murfreesboro was accurately detailed by Wylie in the letters of July 16 and 17, 1862, (read Wyeth, pp. 69-80). The ominous disappearance of the jail-burning captured Yankee, reported (and embellished) by Wylie, was recorded in a written statement by Capt. William Richardson after the war (Wyeth, pp. 76-78). In this action, as in all action, Wylie's personal involvement – separating prisoners, carrying surrender terms, etc. – is fictional.

The letter of Aug. 14, 1862 actually (if succinctly) describes the hectic first raid through Middle Tennessee.

The letter of Oct. 2, 1862 accurately describes the command joining Bragg's army and proceeding into Kentucky, only to have Bragg turn Forrest's brigade over to Wheeler (Wyeth, pp. 87-88).

The four regiments and commanders composing the "new" brigade described by Wylie in the letter of Nov. 6, 1862 is factual (Wyeth, p. 90), and Forrest's cool reception of his to-be-superb artillerist John Morton was recorded by Morton in his memoirs, *The Artillery of Nathan Bedford Forrest's Cavalry*, pp. 45-46. The story of Lester Marks and the pie-eating bear is fiction.

Chapter 5

The letters of Dec. 25, 1862 and Jan. 2, 1863 describe simplistically but basically accurately Forrest's raid into West Tennessee. See Wyeth (pp. 89-125) for a more detailed account. Matthew C. Gallaway was not only senior editor of the *Memphis Avalanche*, but also Memphis postmaster and an important personage of the Tennessee Democratic Party (Hurst, pp. 71-72). He frequently rode with Forrest and when Memphis fell into Union hands, he became Forrest's assistant adjutant general. The failure at Parker's Crossroads is examined in detail by Henry (pp. 116-119). The death of Maybelle and Wylie's rescue by Forrest are fictional.

The letter of Jan. 23, 1863 relating the chance encounter with a group of Union cavalrymen is fictional, though not an unlikely circumstance. Morton's story describing Forrest's inexperience with artillery is factual and derived from the written statement of Lt. Edwin Douglas (Wyeth, p. 119).

Wylie's report of the debacle at Dover in the letter of Feb. 6, 1863 is accurate, though the finding of the locket and his personal interview with Forrest are fictitious. The locket presented the opportunity for Wylie to be privy to the very real confrontation between Forrest and Wheeler. Maj. Charles Anderson was in fact there when Forrest rebuked Wheeler, and recorded his observations (Wyeth, p. 131).

Chapter 6

In the letter of March 7, 1863 Wylie plainly describes the battle at Thompson's Station (see the *Official Records*, Serial No. 34, pp. 81-144). The death of Capt. Montgomery Little is fact, and the story of the ever-faithful Roderick was first documented by Jordan and Pryor (pp. 234-235).

Lt. John Markbright is introduced in the letter of March 8, 1863, and though a Markbright did serve in Forrest's escort, his character throughout is fictional, as is his and Wylie's conversation with Forrest in that letter.

The decisive victory at Brentwood in the letter of April 12, 1863 is accurately retold by Wylie, though he and Markbright did not carry the surrender message, rather Maj. Anderson did, and Forrest's words and suggestion of using a shirt for the white flag are fact (Wyeth, p. 150). Wylie describes the action at Franklin as one man involved would have seen it, and the death of Capt. Freeman and Forrest's tearful reaction are taken from the eyewitness report of Lt. E.H. Douglas (Wyeth, p. 163).

The letter of May 4, 1863 is the first part of the exciting pursuit and eventual capture of Col. Abel Streight and his mule brigade. In his usual custom of reporting basic essentials, Wylie reports most of the action including William Forrest's serious thigh injury (from which he recovered) and Forrest's furious reaction to the lost cannons (Wyeth, p. 179).

The Abel Streight episode continues in the letter of May 5, 1863. Forrest's tirade against the unreliable scout (Wyeth, p. 185) and the Emma Sanson story are duly reported by Wylie. The whole account of Emma Sanson was documented in a letter written by Mrs. Emma Sanson Johnson to Dr. Wyeth (Wyeth, pp. 188-190). Wyeth was so impressed by the courage of the young lady that he dedicated his Forrest biography to her.

Chapter 7

The letter of June 16, 1863 details the lamentable Wills Gould episode. The conversation among Gould, Markbright and Wylie is fictitious, and the actual assault is somewhat embellished by Wylie. There are many varying accounts of the incident, the most reliable perhaps being that of eyewitness Frank A. Smith in his letter to the

Nashville Banner in April, 1911. The tearful deathbed scene described by Wyeth (p. 202) has not been verified by anyone else. Hurst deals thoroughly with the topic (pp. 127-130).

Wylie reports various action in the letter of July 10, 1863 including the factual death of Col. Starnes. The two episodes of the obliging Union soldier warning Forrest of the signal flag, and the abusive, fist-shaking woman are actual reports (Wyeth, p. 203 and p. 213).

The letters of Aug. 19 and Sept. 12, 1863 carry the action along as Bragg's army moves closer to Chickamauga. Forrest was hit in the back at Tunnel Hill and Maj. Charles Anderson wrote later that that was the only time he ever saw Forrest drink whiskey (Wyeth, p. 218).

The letter of Oct. 4, 1863 is the first of three by Wylie concerning the battle at Chickamauga and his injury. The soldiers Wylie mentions as being killed, Edwin Close, Henry Eller, Corp. Boyd, Sgt. O'Leary, are fictitious, though Forrest's prize horse, Highlander, recently given to him by the grateful people of Rome, Ga., was mortally wounded (Wyeth, p. 226). Forrest's restraint from shooting the runaway coward was reported by Maj. Anderson (Wyeth, p. 226). The battlefield compliment by the taciturn Gen. D.H. Hill was witnessed and recorded in the manuscript of Maj. Anderson (Wyeth, p. 229).

The letters of Oct. 6 and 7, 1863 detailing Wylie's injury and treatment are fictitious though researched for authenticity. Good eyewitness accounts of the workings in field hospitals can be read in H.S. Commager's *The Blue and the Grey*, pp. 788-792. Dr. Cowan's intervention, of course, is fiction.

Chapter 8

In the letter of Nov. 1, 1863 Wylie's hospital description is fiction, though Markbright's story of Forrest stemming the flow of blood of his injured horse by inserting his finger in the wound is taken from the eyewitness account of Gen. Frank C. Armstrong (Wyeth, p. 235). The remarkable finger-jabbing encounter between Forrest and Bragg was reported by letter from Dr. Cowan to Dr. Wyeth (Henry, p. 199).

The "face the bull" story in the letter of Nov. 20, 1863 is fiction, as is the recruitment of Truman Slack in the letter of Dec. 13, 1863, though the method of rounding up new recruits is accurate.

The letter of Jan. 3, 1864 details the moving south of Forrest's new corps, and the cornstalk-crashing charge by the escort was recorded by an officer present (but unnamed) (Wyeth, pp. 261-262). The scene with Forrest diving in to rescue the capsized mule team, and then throwing the obnoxious, unhelpful private off the bank is an actual occurrence recorded in a memorandum by Pvt. Mack Watson of Forrest's escort (Henry, p. 209).

Wylie's conversation with Forrest in the letter of Jan. 31, 1864 is mostly fiction, though Forrest's comment that he "can't see a pen but what thinkin of a snake" is a quotation (Wyeth, p. 513), and Wylie's claim that Forrest has "a gifted way with words" is substantiated by Maj. Anderson (Wyeth, p. 374).

Chapter 9

Wylie describes the near-execution of deserters in the letter of Feb. 19, 1864. This episode was witnessed by R.R. Hancock, and duly recorded as part of *Hancock's Diary* (pp. 309-310).

In the long letter of Feb. 27, 1864 Wylie details with good historical accuracy the fight and chase with Gen. Sooy Smith's command. As usual, Wylie's description of battlefield tactics is simplified (read the *Official Records*, Serial No. 57, pp. 252-356 for more exact details), but numbers and places, times and names are true (Wyeth, pp. 267-298). Gen. James Chalmers recorded in a letter sent to Wyeth (pp. 278-280) the scene where Forrest manhandled the demoralized trooper. The death of Jeffrey Forrest and the emotional battlefield scene of Forrest's cradling his dead brother was first recorded by Jordan and Pryor (pp. 395-396).

The conversation between Forrest and Wylie in the letter of March 14, 1864 is fictitious, though the biographical information on Forrest is factual, as is the high esteem in which he held his youngest brother Jeffrey (Wyeth, pp. 3-11 and p. 289).

Chapter 10

In the letter of April 9, 1864 Wylie briefly describes the ride into West Tennessee. The deprivation of the area and Col. Duckworth's capture of Union City are described in more detail by R.S. Henry (pp. 238-247).

Wylie's letters of April 15 and 17, 1864 describe the storming of Fort Pillow and its aftermath. What is fact and what is fiction? The whole truth concerning the circumstances of Fort Pillow has never been ascertained. That Forrest was injured in a horse fall and was just an observer at the time of attack is fact. Wylie's account of the actual storming is basically factual. But what of the killings after surrender, or the atrocities as described by Markbright? Much is still shrouded in doubt and controversy. Wyeth's account works hard to defend Forrest (pp. 299-341) as does the account of Jordan and Pryor. R.S. Henry is more objective in his book (pp. 248-268) as is the more up-to-date Hurst (pp. 165-181). Good objective accounts of the Fort Pillow affair appear in Albert Castel, "Fort Pillow Massacre: A Fresh Examination of the Evidence," *Civil War History*, March, 1958;

and John Cimprich and Robert C. Mainfort, "Fort Pillow Revisited," *Civil War History*, Dec., 1982.

Chapter 11

The story of Bobby and Willie "requisitioning" a horse in the letter of May 15, 1864 is fictional, though suggested by the actual account written by Pvt. John Hubbard in his *Notes of a Private* and reprinted by H.S. Commager (pp. 478-479).

The letter of June 9, 1864 describes the days before Brice's Crossroads. (Read R.S. Henry, pp. 269-285 for more thorough details). Forrest's describing his plan for victory was actually made to and recorded by Col. Edward Rucker (Wyeth, pp. 350).

In the letter of June 13, 1864 Wylie describes the spectacular defeat of Gen. Sam Sturgis at Brice's Crossroads. More detailed accounts of the battle can be read in William Witherspoon's *Tishomingo Creek*, John Morton's *The Artillery of N.B. Forrest's Cavalry* (pp. 164-178), and Edwin Bearss' *Forrest at Brice's Cross Roads*.

Chapter 12

In the letter of June 27, 1864 Forrest's words to Morton were recorded in Morton's diary (Wyeth, p. 364), and Forrest's falling asleep on horseback was factual (Wyeth, p. 369) though slightly embellished by Wylie.

The reconnaissance and encounter with Union pickets described by Wylie in the letter of July 17, 1864 was actual and recalled by Lt. Sam Donelson in a letter to Wyeth (pp. 384-385). Forrest's questioning the wisdom of the attack near Harrisburg ("There position is too strong...") was recorded in an unpublished manuscript by eyewitness Maj. Charles Anderson (Henry, p. 317).

A good detailed account of the debacle at Harrisburg, including the wounding of Forrest, is in Wyeth (pp. 388-401). The death of John Parker, of course, is fiction.

The horse race scene in the letter of Aug. 17, 1864, embellished somewhat by Wylie, was actually reported by Capt. J. Harvey Mathes in his book *Bedford Forrest* (p. 364).

The surprise raid on Memphis described by Wylie in the letter of Aug. 24, 1864 is essentially accurate, including the bridge-building feat (first recorded by participant Capt. James Dinkins in his *Personal Recollections*, pp. 179-180), the three-prong offensive and results, and Forrest's encounter with Col. Starr (Wyeth, pp. 412-418).

Chapter 13

The personal information about Wylie in the letter of Sept. 15, 1864 is fictional, of course. That Forrest received a new uniform from Gen Washburn is recorded by Wyeth (p. 415), and the anecdote of Forrest knocking out the annoying sutler Lewis was recorded in a memorandum by eyewitness Pvt. J.P. Young (Henry, p. 350), though Wylie adds to the story.

In the long letter of Oct. 10, 1864 Wylie faithfully records in as much detail as possible the successful raid into Middle Tennessee. He is basically true to the facts. The slightly embellished episode involving Capt. Andrew McGregor was recorded by John Morton in *The Artillery of N.B. Forrest's Cavalry* (pp. 239-240), and the anecdote of Forrest knocking the cocky officer overboard was written in a letter to Wyeth (pp. 446-447) by eyewitness Z.T. Bundy.

The story of the ambush of Wylie and his friends en route to Memphis, told in the letter of Oct. 21, 1864, is fiction, though the proliferation of deserters and bushwhackers throughout the countryside makes the story not unlikely.

Chapter 14

The letter of Nov. 18, 1864 describes the Johnsonville expedition. Wylie's facts are basically sound, though there is some controversy as to who was the intrepid person who paddled across the Tennessee. Jordan and Pryor claim it was Capt. Gracey (as does Wyeth), though Morton and Hancock claim it was Pvt. Claib West, while Dinkins says it was Pvt. Dick Clinton (Henry, p. 254). The gunboats Venus and Undine were commandeered by Forrest and skippered by Gracey and Col. Dawson. (Capt. Frank Gracey, incidentally, had been a steamboat pilot on the Cumberland River before this war [Henry, p. 374]). The shelling of Johnsonville is told in detail in the *Official Records*, Serial No. 77 (pp. 861-875). So complete was the destruction that Gen. William T. Sherman wrote to Gen. U.S. Grant on Nov. 6, 1864, "That devil Forrest was down about Johnsonville, making havoc among the gunboats and transports" (Wyeth, p. 465).

The battle of Franklin is depicted simply but factually by Wylie in the letter of Dec. 2, 1864. That Forrest warned Hood against the attack was witnessed by Col. Kelley who quoted Forrest's protest in a letter to Wyeth (p. 480). The incident where Forrest and his party bumped into a squad of Union men is factual, though Maj. Strange was the man who deflected the shot away from Forrest. This event was recorded in the manuscript of eyewitness Lt. G.L. Cowan (Wyeth, p. 474).

The fight at Murfreesboro and the woeful retreat from Nashville are in the Dec. 30, 1864 letter. The scene with the enraged Forrest trying to rally the retreating southern soldiers and shooting one coward down were eyewitnessed by Pvt. W.A. Calloway, who wrote to Wyeth of this episode (p. 488). For a thorough account of the battle of Nashville read Thomas R. Hay's *Hood's Tennessee Campaign*. That Forrest and his rear-guard remained inexorable was appreciated even by Union Gen. George

Thomas who wrote in his official report, "Hood's army had become a disheartened and disorganized rabble of half-armed and barefooted men, who sought every opportunity to fall out by the wayside and desert their cause, to put an end to their suffering. The rear-guard, however, was undaunted and firm, and did its work bravely to the last" (Wyeth, p. 502). For Forrest's complete speech to his men in Corinth, read Wyeth (pp. 508-509).

Chapter 15

Wylie describes his furlough and camp life in the letter of Feb. 22, 1865. He speaks truth when he says Mrs. Forrest and Mrs. Gallaway stayed in camp whenever possible (Henry, p. 367), and that Forrest despised deserters is evident in a statement he circulated in camp, in part saying, "They (runaways) are in many instances nothing more or less than roving bands of deserters, absentees, stragglers, horse-thieves and robbers, whose acts of lawlessness and crime demand a remedy, which I shall not hesitate to apply, even to extermination" (Henry, p. 420).

In the letter of March 30, 1865 Wylie talks of Forrest's bargain with his slaves who became teamsters and their regard for him (Henry, p. 26). Wylie also writes of the execution of the old and young deserters, and although the account is perhaps dramatized, it is factual (Wyeth, p. 521).

Wylie describes with good historical accuracy the final fight at Selma in the letter of April 8, 1865. The injuries to Bobby Parker and John Markbright are fictitious, but that Forrest did receive a severe gash in the arm delivered by Capt. J.D. Taylor is true. That Forrest then killed the young officer and later remarked he would have been killed himself had the young man given him the point instead of the edge of his saber was made to and recorded by Gen. James Wilson himself (Henry, p. 431). Pvt. Phil Dodd coming to Forrest's rescue is recorded in the manuscript of Lt. George Cowan

(Wylie, p. 532). That Forrest recruited every male still breathing in Selma to fight is recorded by Jordan and Pryor (p. 672).

Chapter 16

In the letter of April 26, 1865 Wylie reveals his feelings about the war, and he meets his enemy friend, Rob Rash – these, of course, are fiction. Forrest's excerpted speech to his men is actual, and the entire speech can be read in Wyeth (p. 540). That Forrest killed 30 of the enemy in combat and had 29 horses shot from under him is stated by Wyeth (p. 536) and generally accepted as fact by most biographers. Wyeth (pp. 600-601) lists each horse killed or wounded and the site and date of the event. He is not so detailed, however, with the soldiers killed by Forrest. Gen. Wilson did in fact meet Forrest several times, under cordial conditions, to discuss prisoners, the wounded, and the like (*Official Records*, Serial No. 104, p. 271).

In the final letter, that of May 10, 1865, Wylie factually writes of the unrest and discontent of the younger soldiers who want to continue the fight, and how Lt. Nichols is inciting them with fiery oratory (Henry, pp. 437-438). The side-by-side ride and heart-to-heart talk that Forrest and Wylie shared actually occurred, though Forrest and the ever-faithful Maj. Charles Anderson were the participants (Henry, p. 437). Forrest's farewell speech can be read in its entirety in Wyeth (pp. 542-543).